Netta Muskett was born in Sevenoaks,
Kent College, Folkstone. She had a vari
first teaching mathematics before worki
owner of the 'News of the World', as well as serving as a volunteer during both world wars – firstly driving an ambulance and then teaching handicrafts in British and American hospitals.

It is, however, for the exciting and imaginative nature of her writing that she is most remembered. She wrote of the times she experienced, along with the changing attitudes towards sex, women and romance, and sold millions of copies worldwide. Her last novel 'Cloudbreak' was first published posthumously after her death in 1963.

Many of her works were regarded by some librarians at the time of publication as risqué, but nonetheless proved to be hugely popular with the public, especially followers of the romance genre.

Netta co-founded the Romantic Novelists' Association and served as Vice-President. The 'Netta Muskett' award, now renamed the 'RNA New Writers Scheme', was created in her honour to recognise outstanding new writers.

BY THE SAME AUTHOR
HOUSE OF STRATUS

- After Rain
- Alley Cat
- Blue Haze
- Brocade
- Candle In The Sun
- Cast The Spear
- The Clency Tradition
- Cloudbreak
- Crown Of Willow
- The Crown Of Willow
- A Daughter For Julia
- The Durrants
- The Fettered Past
- Fire Of Spring
- Flame Of The Forest
- The Flickering Lamp
- Flowers From The Rock
- From This Day Forward
- Gilded Hoop
- Give Back Yesterday
- Golden Harvest
- The High Fence
- House Of Many Windows
- House Of Straw
- Jade Spider
- Jennifer
- Light From One Star
- Living With Adam
- The Long Road
- Love And Deborah
- Love In Amber
- Middle Mist
- A Mirror For Dreams
- Misadventure
- No May In October
- No Yesterdays
- Nor Any Dawn
- Open Window
- The Other Woman
- Painted Heaven
- The Patchwork Quilt
- Philipa
- Quiet Island
- Red Dust
- The Rock Pine
- Safari For Seven
- Safe Harbour
- Scarlet Heels
- Shadow Market
- Shallow Cup
- Silver Gilt
- Tamarisk
- Third Title Unknown
- This Lovely Thing
- Through Many Waters
- Time For Play
- Today Is Ours
- The Touchstone
- The Weir House
- The White Dove
- Wide And Dark
- Wings In The Dust
- Winters Day
- The Wire Blind

TAMARISK

Netta Muskett

This edition published in 2014 by House of Stratus, an imprint of
Stratus Books Ltd, Lisandra House, Fore St., Looe,
Cornwall, PL13 1AD, UK.

www.houseofstratus.com

Typeset by House of Stratus.

A catalogue record for this book is available from the British Library and the Library of Congress.

ISBN 07551 4311 6
EAN 978 07551 4311 5

Chapter One

The buzzer sounded, shattering the afternoon peace of the typists' room and making two of the three girls look up with frowns of annoyance.

The third went on with her work, wrinkled her brows over her Pitman-cum-Wilson shorthand outlines.

'Old Spilliken,' said one of the others laconically, and returned to the task of imparting a gory brilliance to her claw-like nails.

'It isn't my turn, anyway,' remarked the one who was voraciously devouring the last chapters of a novel, her senses busy with second-hand emotions. 'You go, Jane, and soothe the savage beast. Tell him we're busy.'

The third girl looked up, faintly protesting. In her heart she knew she would go. She always did.

'I haven't nearly finished,' she said, looking through the pages of her notebook. 'Mr. Purnell wants these by four-thirty.'

The manicurist laughed and looked across at the novel-reader.

'You can deal with Pansy, darling, can't you?' she asked, and received a self-conscious smirk in reply.

'Probably,' she conceded. 'You go, Jane, there's a lamb. I can't stand old Spillie's dictation. He's so damn' precise and old- fashioned.'

'You mean you can't sit on his knee,' said Miss Wright maliciously.

'Who'd want to anyway?' laughed Miss Gilbert. 'Snakes! There he is again. Better buck up, Jane, hadn't you? I'll settle Pansy for you.'

The girl they called Jane rose with a worried look, passing her fingers across her forehead in an ineffectual attempt at tidying her wispy ends of straight brown hair and leaving a streak of violet ink from fingers which had just handled a new typewriter ribbon. For the rest, she was small and insignificant, and everything about her needed care, her complexion, her cheap, shabby shoes, her badly mended stockings, her well-worn and ill-chosen office frock.

'I do wish one of you would go,' she ventured helplessly. 'It's sure to be some legal document to take down, and I simply can't read them back.'

The other two exchanged glances but made no attempt to move and she began to gather up notebook and pencils, dropping the latter in picking up the former, and knocking her elbow against her desk in bending to retrieve them.

The buzzer sounded a third time, imperatively, and she made a dash for the door.

'Good old Jane,' laughed Miss Wright in tolerant contempt, and, in her confusion, the girl bumped into the filing cabinet and then against the door as she hurried out.

'Extraordinary that anyone so plain can be so damn' clumsy as well,' observed Miss Gilbert serenely.

'Poor old Jane. What a life she must lead! How the devil does she live at all? She always looks like nothing on earth in her awful clothes.'

'She might be made to look presentable with a perm and a make-up and one decent garment, but she'd always be a darn fool, anyway. What on earth did she take up an office job for? She's no damn' good. Wonder old Spilliken doesn't sack her.'

'Perhaps he's got a soft spot for her,' grinned Miss Wright, applying a second coat of blood-red varnish to her thumbnails and regarding the result appreciatively. 'She wouldn't be any more good at any other job. Fancy her as a waitress, for instance!' And they both laughed at the picture the words conjured up. 'Poor old Jane. Must feel pretty putrid to be like that and to *look* it!' – with a mental picture of herself as she spoke, artificially perfect in her dress, her colouring, her grooming, her elaborate attention to detail which had had the effect of turning a quite undistinguished face and figure into something at least noticeable.

Meanwhile the subject of their careless thoughts blundered along the corridor, knocked at a door marked 'Mr. Harrow. PRIVATE', and slid inside.

The senior partner looked at her over his glasses and frowned. He was a tubby little man in the fifties, red-laced and almost bald, and the aptness of his nickname, after a popular feature in an evening paper, was undeniable.

'Will I do, Mr. Harrow?' asked the girl apologetically, as she caught the frown.

'Er—what are the others doing?'

'They're busy, Mr. Harrow,' she said, colouring a little. She could not even tell a lie convincingly.

He grunted.

'I know their sort of business at this time of day,' he said. 'Well, sit down—sit down,' and she slipped hastily into the chair at the side of his desk.

'Can you do a long job and do it decently?' he asked her, peering at her again over his glasses uncertainly.

'I'll try, Mr. Harrow,' she said, but her heart sank. She felt it so unlikely that she would succeed.

'Take these leases and go through them. Put them in order of date first, of course, and then make a comparison of them under these headings. Take the headings down.'

She took them down in shorthand, using every spare moment to scribble in the longhand of unfamiliar or difficult words, terrified lest she should have to ask him to repeat anything. He became aware of her terror and broke in on his dictation.

'What's the matter with you, Miss Wilson? You seem—like a scared rabbit,' the simile leaping to his mind and tongue to surprise even himself.

She flushed and bit her lip.

'I'm afraid of not doing it well,' she murmured.

'Rubbish! How long have you been with us?'

'A year, Mr. Harrow.'

'And how old are you?'

'Twenty-two, Mr. Harrow.'

'H'm. Well, you ought to be able to do a job like this if you're going to be of any use to us,' he said, with an attempt at curtness which somehow did not ring quite true, although to the girl's ears he seemed curt enough. 'Get on with it. What was the last heading?'

'Er—er—title, date of title,' she stammered.

'Date of first title,' he corrected. 'Go on. Next heading: particulars of tithe, if any.'

It was nearly five when he had finished his dictation, and she tried not to feel appalled at the quantity of it as she rose.

'In a hurry?' he asked.

'Oh no, Mr. Harrow,' she said fervently. How dare she be in a hurry? And, besides, what reason had she ever for hurrying away from Harrow and Purnell's?

'Good! See that you get paid for the extra time. How soon can you get it done? Seven? Eight?'

She had been going to say 'nine', but, with a gulp, nodded the eight.

'I'll send someone back to the office for it about eight then. Get yourself something to eat, of course.'

He watched her go. Queer little person. Oddly negative in effect. She was just 'not' anything. The only positive thing about her was a certain wistfulness, the look of a lost mongrel in her brown eyes. Come to think of it, her eyes were very much like those of a dog he used to have, a nondescript, utterly lovable dog whose death he had mourned the more because that short life of perfect love had been laid down for him in the end. Paddy had spent his whole strength in dragging the heavy form of his master out of a burning room and though he could easily have saved himself, he had refused to go, and the firemen who had at last rescued Harrow came too late to save the dog. Harrow had wept unashamedly over that charred body which had held limitless and selfless love. Odd that he should have been reminded of Paddy by little Miss Wilson.

He packed the flat leather case, without which he felt incomplete, went down to his waiting car, opened the evening paper which he had known he would find on the seat, and forthwith forgot her.

Crouched in her corner with its one green-shaded light, she worked feverishly, struggling to make her memory serve her where her shorthand failed, wondering wearily as the hours slipped by why on earth the law could not abandon its wheresoevers and heretofores, its hereditaments and messuages. She had never gathered any clear conception of the meaning of messuage, and could not rid her mind of the feeling that it was something vaguely indecent.

She jumped up with a start as she suddenly became aware of the stocky uniformed figure of Mr. Harrow's chauffeur looming within the circle of light about her.

'Oh! Oh—you—you've come for these, Mr.—er?' she said confusedly.

'Bennett's the name, miss,' he said gravely.

Oh yes. I know. I—they're not quite ready,' she said, in distress. 'Mr. Harrow said eight.'

'It's nine now, miss,' he said, and she verified it in amazement. She had paused for nothing, not even the cup of coffee and the bath bun she had promised herself, and yet she had not finished.

'Can you wait?' she asked.

'Yes, miss,' he said stolidly, and sat down at the other side of the room. She envied him, fleetingly, his assumption of perfect ease and repose. She never at any time or in any circumstances felt as much at ease as he seemed.

In half an hour she had finished and was gathering up the mass of papers. There was no time to go through them. She would have to trust to the luck which, so far, had consistently failed her in her short life.

'Here they are,' she said.

'Mr. Harrow wants you to bring them yourself, miss, in case there's anything wrong,' he said.

She sighed,

'Oh dear! I know there will be,' she said despondently.

'Well, the governor isn't the sort to be hard if there is, miss,' said the chauffeur, in a fatherly fashion. She looked very small and tired and childish with her untidy hair and smudgy face.

She stared at him.

'Not the sort?' she asked incredulously, a vision of the quick, irritable man invading her mind not for the first time that evening. It had gone with her until she had grown too tired to think.

Bennett smiled and helped her to close and lock her desk.

'That's only put on, that way of his when he seems to snap your head off,' he said. 'You should see him at home. Well, you will, won't you? You go and get ready, miss. I'll put things straight here.'

She thanked him and went into the adjoining cloakroom, which was usually sacred to the Misses Wright and Gilbert save for Miss Wilson's fleeting visits to hang up or take down her coat and hat. She seldom looked in the glass, and the casual glance she gave at herself when she had dragged on a serviceable felt hat failed to reveal to her indifferent gaze even the violet streaks across her forehead.

Bennett glanced at her and said nothing, but he tucked her into the luxurious car with added care when they reached the street. Poor kid!

She dozed all the way to Hampstead, and was rubbing the sleep out of her eyes when they pulled up before an imposing house of the type known to house agents as a 'commodious residence'.

'The young lady with the papers,' said Bennett, handing her over in the softly lit, softly carpeted hall to the butler.

'This way, miss,' she was instructed, and found herself in a big, book-lined room facing a Mr. Harrow unfamiliar in an old-fashioned smoking-jacket of brown frogged velvet, a Mr. Harrow who was smiling at her in a quite friendly fashion, a Mr. Harrow who for some odd reason no longer looked like Mr. Spilliken.

'I'm afraid it's been a long job, Miss Wilson. You must be very tired. Put a comfortable chair near the fire, Gough, and bring some sherry or something. Perhaps you would prefer coffee, though?'

She caught her breath sharply, realising for the first time how hungry and cold she was. Strong, steaming coffee! Something of her thoughts must have shown in her face, for Harrow looked at her with a sudden interest and apprehension.

'You've had something during the evening, haven't you?' he asked.

'I—I wasn't hungry, so I didn't bother,' she admitted nervously, though one could not feel as nervous of this comfortable old gentleman as one did of Spilliken in the office.

He made a clucking sound.

'God bless my soul! All that time and nothing since that terrible stuff Greta Garbo serves up for tea! Coffee at once, Gough, please, and ask Mrs. Gough for sandwiches, substantial ones—chicken or something.'

She had begun to giggle helplessly, in the first place at his unaccustomed and surprising little joke, later because she was a little hysterical with exhaustion. Encouraged, Harrow sat back in his chair on the other side of the hearth and smiled at her.

'I remember I asked her once if she could give me a second cup, and she replied that she was sorry but there wasn't a drain left, I always suspected where that tea came from!' – and he chuckled at his little joke before he adjusted his glasses and began to look through the papers she had brought him.

She watched him anxiously. In the ordinary way her work was never very good, however hard she tried. Tonight it must be even worse than usual, she knew, and there was a sick feeling in her stomach as she searched his face for corroboration. It expressed nothing, however. As a matter of fact he was not giving his attention to the typed schedules. He kept remembering his dog Paddy again.

Gough wheeled in a little table set with silver and delicate china, and the fragrance of the coffee made her feel almost faint.

'Shall I pour it out, miss?' he said.

'Please.'

'White or black?'

'White, please,' she said shyly, and though she felt she could have attacked the food like a savage, she ate daintily and slowly, fortunately unaware of Mr. Harrow's furtive interest. The girl was obviously a lady, he reflected, though her manner of speech was rather careful with the habit of years.

He began to talk to her as she ate, putting her at her ease.

I can't remember you coming to us. A year ago, I think you said. Who engaged you? Mr. Purnell?'

'No, Mr. Harrow. You did,' she said shyly.

'Did I? Well, I've forgotten, but probably I did,' and he reflected that the junior partner would be unlikely to select this brand of typist. It was the junior partner who had engaged the Misses Wright and Gilbert. 'Where were you before that?'

She flushed a little.

'I haven't been a typist before,' she said.

'Ah, I seem to remember now. You've got a rather unusual name, haven't you? Jante, or something like that, isn't it?'

'Janine,' she said shortly, a note of contempt in her voice.

He smiled.

'What's the matter with it? It's rather pretty. How did you come by it? A family name or merely a flight of imagination on the part of doting parents?'

An odd look flashed across her face, a look compounded of bitterness and derision.

'I haven't any doting parents,' she said. 'As far as I know, I never had any. I'm the product of a doorstep and an orphanage.'

He looked a little embarrassed.

'I'm sorry. That was clumsy of me, wasn't it?'

'Oh, I don't mind, really. After all, what does it matter how one starts?'

'That's quite right,' he said heartily, 'Quite right. Personally, I started in a comfortable home and have always been thankful for it, though I don't take credit for it myself as a good many people seem to do. Tell me about yourself. You don't mind?'

'No. There isn't much to tell, though. I was left on the steps of the orphanage with a bottle of milk beside me and a piece of paper on which "Janine" was scribbled.'

The bitterness was in her voice again, and he realised how the thing had eaten like a canker at her heart for probably the whole of her short life.

'I'm glad about the bottle of milk,' he said.

Janine's brown eyes stared at him questioningly.

'Whoever put you there must have cared,' he said. 'Otherwise why the milk? It was probably all the poor thing could do for you. It might have cost her her last penny.'

'I hadn't thought of that,' she said slowly.

'She gave you a name, too. You weren't just "it" to her. How old were you?'

'Two months.'

'You see? If she hadn't cared at all, it would have been two weeks rather than two months. And already you were a person to her. You were Janine.'

'I suppose so. Still, she left me, I shall never be able to understand that, or forgive it. To leave one's baby!' And her voice, a soft and attractive voice he was discovering, gave a special value to that word 'baby'.

'You'd be too fond of one to leave it?'

'Why, of course!' And she broke off and flushed, realising what an odd conversation and situation was developing. This was Mr. Harrow, after all, and she the most insignificant of his employees.

He smiled, let his thoughts drift for a moment, and then went to the big table in the middle of the room and settled himself down with the schedules. Janine could just see his profile, and with sinking spirits she watched his mouth purse familiarly and a frown gather on his brow whilst his fingers drummed now and then on the shining mahogany.

'I'm afraid I haven't done it very well,' she ventured at last.

He made an unintelligible sound and flicked another of the sheets aside. What a fool he had been to give her the job! If the other two girls really had been too busy, he could have sent it out to the bureau round the corner where they often did work of a private nature for the firm, He ought to have realised how incompetent she was. Those other two, in spite of their beastly red lips and painted nails and ridiculous eyebrows, could at least do their job reasonably well. If they didn't he wouldn't keep them, Purnell or no Purnell. He wondered why on earth he had kept this little Wilson girl so long. A year! Good Lord!

Suddenly a familiar feeling assailed him, a dull ache which always preceded the sharp pain which the specialist warned him would recur more frequently if he persisted in keeping on at work instead of taking absolute rest for a year. The papers dropped from his hand and he turned in his chair, reaching for the bell which was fastened conveniently under the ledge of the table for just this purpose. His reach fell short of it, and he gave a queer, strangled sound and doubled up in his chair, gasping for breath.

Janine sprang to her feet.

'Mr. Harrow!'

'Bell,' he managed to gasp, but the push was invisible to her, though she caught the word and looked round helplessly.

'Cupboard—two tablets,' he whispered next whilst she hovered about him, torn between the need to stay with him and the urgency of going to fetch help since she could not find the bell.

His eyes led her to a little smoker's cabinet in a corner, and she darted to it, found a bottle, brought it to him, received his confirming nod and tipped out two tablets into her palm. There was no water in sight, and she darted back to her supper-table to pour the now lukewarm milk into her coffee-cup.

'Crush,' he whispered, and she broke the tablets, mixed the powder with the milk and held the cup to his lips, raising his head with her free arm and letting it rest against her whilst he drank.

The drug acted magically, and in a few moments he was able to sit up, his eyes looking more normal and his breath coming easily.

'Thank you, my dear. I must have frightened you,' he said shakily.

The expression he used gave her an odd little feeling of warmth and comfort, though she knew he used it unconsciously, and there was something maternal in the way she offered him her shoulder as a support when he ventured across to his easy chair.

'Shall I fetch someone?' she asked. I can't find the bell. I didn't know what to do.'

'You did excellently. No, there's nothing else to be done. I've had these attacks before. The man in Harley Street warned me months ago. I suppose it will mean giving up eventually,' he said, sinking into the chair and finding a cushion placed exactly to position as he did so.

'Give up the office?' she asked anxiously.

'I suppose so. I'm getting old. Fifty-seven, you know.'

'That isn't very old nowadays,' she said, though to her it sounded an infinity of years.

His beady eyes twinkled.

'You're being polite,' he said, and even managed to laugh when she shook her head. 'Do you think I could have a drink of your coffee?'

'It'll be cold,' she demurred. 'Let me ask for some more.'

'No. If Mrs. Gough gets wind of this she'll hustle me off to bed, and I hate being made to feel in my second childhood. Just half a cup. Your cup will do.'

'You don't mind?'

'I've already used it,' he reminded her with a smile.

'I'm afraid I didn't think of anything but giving you the medicine just then,' she said, and her nervousness returned to her as she fiddled with the coffee-things. She realised, with some surprise, how calm and collected she had been in the small emergency. She had moved neatly and surely, had neither knocked over nor spilt anything as she was certainly doing now.

Her hand shook as she brought him the cup.

'What's the matter? Nervous? Frightened?' he asked her with a smile.

'No. I—I'm always clumsy,' she said. 'They used to call me Jumpy Jane at the orphanage. I've always dropped things and made a mess of what I'm doing.'

He laughed at her rueful face and tone.

'You looked after me very nicely just now, and I didn't notice you dropped anything.'

'No, I didn't, did I?' – and again he laughed at her air of innocent surprise. 'I nearly always do, though. I'm not really much good at anything,' with a sigh.

'Nonsense! That's what you modern young people call an inferiority complex, isn't it?'

'I don't know what that is,' said Janine gravely. 'I suppose I'm not what you call a modern girl at all.'

'No, I don't think you are. Mind you, I rather like this new race that's springing up, with their courage and their sublime indifference to convention, but—well, they take a lot of getting used to' – with a sigh which Janine was able to interpret when she came to know him better.

'I haven't been brought up like most people, I suppose,' she said.

'No. Perhaps that's it. Tell me some more about yourself, about this orphanage. Were you happy there?'

'Happy?' – as if the idea had never occurred to her. 'Oh, well, I suppose so, in a way. They weren't unkind to us or anything, but—well, we were just herded about and kept too busy to get into mischief, and when the work of the day was finished we were too tired to do anything but go to sleep.'

'What was the name of the place?' asked Harrow, wondering if by any chance it figured on his long list of secret charities.

'The Wilson Orphan Asylum,' said Jane bitterly.

'The same name as yours?'

'Oh yes. We were a very large family, we Wilsons! They've altered it now, but at that time everybody who came there without a name was called Wilson. I was unusual in having a Christian name of my own. Matron had a list of names, and they were dealt out in rotation as babies were admitted. When the last on the list had been ticked off, they started again at the beginning. It had its advantages. It was a long list, so by the time they got through it and started again the first Annies and Adas had gone, so there were not many with the same name.'

She spoke calmly, but he caught that undercurrent of bitterness through her whole speech. It sat oddly upon her, he thought, for she seemed a gentle and rather sweet little person by nature.

'You didn't come to us from there?' he asked.

'No. When I was fourteen I left school and went into the kitchen, but I hated it, and I was always in trouble for dropping things and making mistakes over the salt and things. I asked Matron if I couldn't do something else, and then I found out that we were all expected to work out a sort of account they kept for each of us. Some of the girls had friends who paid something towards their keep, and they could leave the Home and take outside jobs when they were sixteen, but all the Wilsons had to stay on and do the work of the Home without wages until the account was squared off. It depended how good your work was how long it took to pay off the debt. Mine would have taken years and years' – mournfully.

'How did you get away, then?' asked Harrow, rather enjoying the recital. As she became more at ease, she became more animated, and he liked to watch the play of her feelings as shown in the brown eyes, the rather wide, mobile mouth, the sensitive nostrils.

'I ran away,' she said, and he laughed. He had a vision of her, frightened, incompetent, purposeless, and he laughed at the sheer audacity of anyone like that scraping up enough courage.

'Tell me about it,' he said.

'There was another girl with me or I shouldn't have dared,' she admitted naively. 'I'd been put back into the kitchen. I'd had charge of some of the little ones, but they said I spoilt them' – regretfully. 'We hated the cook, and it looked as if I should never work out my time, because when we got into trouble and were reported to Matron she put something on the other side of the account, sometimes as much as a pound, and I was always getting reported for breaking things. Anyway, May and I got out one night. She was a Wilson, too. We got out of a window and climbed down the ivy and waited in a tree by the lodge. Matron had visitors, and we knew the gardener would have to open the gates for their car to go through. When he did, we slipped out with the car and ran down the road like mad before he saw us. I hadn't any money, of course, but May had four-and-six. She wouldn't tell me where she got it, but she must have stolen it. Anyway, she paid for a room for us, though I couldn't sleep a wink. I thought they'd be after us every minute. We walked to London the next day, and then in the evening, we—May—well, I wouldn't go with her,' she broke off in confusion, and her tell-tale face and clear child's eyes filled in the gap for Harrow, who nodded understandingly.

'And then?' he asked.

'I was lucky. A lady going along Oxford Street dropped her fur, and I picked it up and ran after her. She gave me half a crown and asked me what I was going to do with it, and when I told her I was going to have something to eat and look for a bed, she took me to her flat and was ever so kind to me. I told her everything, and she laughed about it and said I had more pluck than she had because she was in bondage too, but dare not run away. I didn't understand then, but I did later. I didn't care by then, though. She was kind to me. Nobody had ever treated me like that before. Nobody had ever spoken to me like that. She asked me to stay with her for a little while, and in the end I stayed until—until everything was sold from the flat, even her furs and her jewels, and she—she was found in another house dead. Gas. I—I loved her.' And the girl's voice broke on the words, and her eyes misted with the memory of the only being she had ever had cause to remember with gratitude, the woman who had given her all she could and asked for nothing in return, though Janine would have worked like a slave for her had she been permitted.

'And then you came to me?' Harrow prompted her after a pause.

'Yes. Cora—Mrs. Heseldine—had had me taught shorthand and typewriting, had made me talk properly and behave better. They never bothered about things like table manners or the way we spoke at the Home. They preferred us not to speak at ah really. Cora was lovely about it, so patient and kind. They said all sorts of things about her, but she was an angel from heaven to me, and she kept me—out of things I didn't know about then.'

Harrow nodded again. Her innocence, her essential decency, was so apparent that he realised the truth of what she said.

'She had left me with her luggage in a room at an hotel, and she sent me a letter there before she—died—saying I was to do what I liked with everything she had left. It was only clothes. Everything else had been taken away from her. I didn't quite understand how, but she had given them all up to some man or other and gone off with only her boxes of clothes. I couldn't use many of them, but I kept some and sold the rest and managed to live until I got a job.'

'Was that long?'

She shivered a little.

'Months and months. I was terrified. I scarcely dared to eat anything in case my money gave out altogether. I had only a few shillings left when I came to see you in answer to your advertisement.'

He tried to recall that interview, but it was very vague in his memory. He remembered that she had been dressed in very good, black – probably a suit of the abandoned Cora's – and that she had seemed quiet and ladylike after the procession of highly coloured, self-assured young ladies whom, in Purnell's absence, he had been obliged to interview. He began to realise how this girl had snared him, quite unconsciously, into engaging her by her big wistful brown eyes and her air of helplessness and dependence. He never had been able to resist a crying child or a lost dog or a hungry kitten!

'I see,' he murmured, but he was referring rather to that vague memory than to the present story.

'If you only knew how passionately grateful I was to you!' said Janine, 'I'd have licked your boots if you'd wanted me to when you said you would give me a trial.'

He laughed.

'I don't know what Gough would have had to say to that when I got home,' he said. 'The polish on my boots is one of his life's efforts. What would you have done if I had turned you down?'

'I don't know. I was sick with trying to find the answer to that question by then. You see, I hadn't learned shorthand very well, and my fingers are clumsy with the typewriter. There wasn't anything else I could even pretend I could do. I'd rather have died than be a kitchen-maid again, and I wasn't even a good kitchen-maid. Cora thought at first I could learn to do her hair and her nails and so on, but I could never do her hair without burning it, and I used to make her fingers bleed, though I'd have given my own blood for her willingly.'

He looked at the hands lying in her lap. They were small hands with slim, delicate fingers and well-shaped nails treated in cavalier fashion and owing little to art. Nice little hands, he thought, but his eyes strayed almost unconsciously to the sheaf of papers which those same hands had so inadequately covered with typescript.

She caught the glance and her hands moved restlessly again.

'Is the work I did alright?' she asked him nervously.

Somewhat to his surprise, he found himself nodding amiably and murmuring something about 'do quite well—only wanted a sort of draft—something to go on with', though he knew quite well that the schedules were useless and that an hour or two ago he would have said so without mincing matters. She had confused the headings, and his own knowledge of the subject matter was enough to show him, at a casual inspection, that her facts and figures were inaccurate.

'Anyway, you must be very tired, and I am keeping you here talking. Would you ring the bell? Just at the right of the table, under the edge. See it? I'll send you home in the car, and meantime perhaps you would like to go upstairs and tidy up. The housekeeper will take you. Oh, Gough,' as the butler entered, 'ask Bennett to bring the car round again. Miss Wilson will give him the address. And ask Mrs. Gough to look after her and see that she has everything she wants in the meantime. You go with Gough, Miss Wilson.'

She was handed over to a motherly woman with keen, bright eyes and taken up to an amazing bathroom such as she would never have associated with anyone like Mr. Harrow. It was of black-and-white marble, with a ceiling of what looked like silver, and a sunken bath of transparent jade-green. All the fittings gleamed like silver, and she gave a gasp of amazement when Mrs. Gough opened a wall cabinet, drew down a plate-glass flap and revealed a completely fitted dressing table, innumerable pots and bottles and jars providing everything the most fastidious professional beauty could require for her toilet.

The woman caught the gasp and smiled.

'It belonged to Mr. Harrow's daughter. Miss Felicity, you know,' she said, as if Janine knew all about his private life.

'I didn't know he had a daughter,' she said shyly. 'I don't think I even realised he was married.'

'He's a widower. His wife died more than twenty years ago, before we came to him. I've almost brought up Miss Felicity, if you could say she could be brought up by anyone but herself,' said the woman composedly, though Janine caught a faint note of regret and concern.

'Where is she now then?' – beginning to repair, with ashamed concern, the damage done by the violet ink hours ago.

'We don't really know. She and Mr. Harrow never hit it off, though she's his only child. She's been at school most of her life and only home for the holidays, and when she left school and came here for good there was always trouble. He's settled down and too old for a young girl, and she's—well, she's very up-to-date and different, if you know what I mean. Always bright she was, laughing and smoking and drinking all over the house, and the place always filled with young men doing the same, and Mr. Harrow thought she ought to be more like what girls were like when he was young – cooking and sewing instead of always dancing and having cocktail parties and things like that.'

'So she—ran away too?' asked Janine, and Mrs. Gough did not remark, even if she noticed, that final word.

'When she came into her mother's money, at twenty-one, she just went off. She writes to him now and then and lets him know where she is, but she's never been back, though he keeps her room always ready and even has a regular order with the shop that used to make her clothes in case she ever comes back unexpectedly. I'll show you. And Janine, who had made her modest toilet without disturbing the powders and creams offered her, followed the woman across the landing and into a room which made her gasp anew.

It was a vivid room, ultra-modern in its red and black lacquer, its tubular steel, its oddly shaped dressing-table of many mirrors, its carpet of dead black and walls of some curious, shining grey paint. Janine had never seen anything like it, and it both excited and shocked her. It reminded her of Miss Wright and her black and white and red sleekness, and yet here she felt was the real thing of which Miss Wright's was only the imitation.

Mrs. Gough opened a black door with scarlet glass handle, and inside the cupboard were dresses on hangers, hats, shoes, piles of silk lingerie, delicate and lovely in the soft light which glowed automatically with the opening of the door.

'But if she never comes, who wears them?' asked Janine wonderingly.

Mrs. Gough gave a snort.

'Nobody,' she said. 'Sheer, wicked waste it is, though it's more than I'd dare do to say it to him' – with a nod of her head in the direction of the landing and staircase. 'Every six months they come from the shop, take away these things, and put new ones there. He never sees them. All he does is to give me a cheque for the bill when it comes in. Every six months regularly that happens.'

'How long ago?' asked Janine, struggling to adjust her mind to this bewildering conception of a Mr. Harrow who, at the office, quibbled if the office boy wasted the envelopes or the typists asked for new typewriter ribbons too often.

'Close on four years now. She's nearly twenty-five.'

Janine's eyes were very soft.

'It's rather pathetic, isn't it?' she said dreamily, and the extraordinary inconsistence of a deity who could give so much where it was not wanted, and deny everything where it was so passionately desired, caught at her thoughts rebelliously.

'It is that,' agreed the woman. 'I don't think any of us realised how fond of her he must have been. She didn't herself, or she'd come back and see him now and then. Perhaps she will—when it's too late,' she added darkly.

'You mean Mr. Harrow's really ill?' asked Janine.

'We think he is, though he won't admit it and he won't take any rest. He's been ordered a sea trip, but he won't go alone, and he doesn't make many friends, and there's no one he'd want to have with him, cooped up on a ship.'

Janine left the exotic room regretfully, not because of the weird attraction of the place itself but rather because of the visions conjured up in that busy, oddly furnished mind of hers where dreams and facts, fancies and realities jostled one another to make a queer pattern for themselves.

Mr. Harrow himself came to the door with her, and took her hand in his, patting it with the other in a fatherly fashion. He realised that he was sorry to see her go. She had brought something fresh and new into his unvarying habit of life. She was young, and she was feminine, and surprisingly to him, she had not numbed and stultified him as other young moderns had a habit of doing.

'Goodbye, my dear. Don't hurry to the office in the morning if you fancy staying in bed an extra hour,' he said.

Her eyes widened. He was a martinet for time, and woebetide that clerk or typist who tried to sidle in ten minutes late in the mornings! He himself was always there, summer and winter, sunshine or snow or fog, on the stroke of nine.

'Oh, I shan't do that, Mr Harrow,' she said in confusion, her hand still lying between his.

'Well, you'll see. Good night, my dear—Janine' – with an odd look of appreciation of his own daring, almost as if he were twenty-seven instead of fifty-seven, and still in the era when Christian names were private and privileged property.

She smiled shyly, and not until the car was sliding away down the quiet street did she realise that her fingers were clutching a pound note!

Chapter Two

'Morning, Bennett, everything in order?'

'Everything in order, sir.'

Richard Harrow had asked the same question and received the same answer at the same time every working day for thirty years, though in those days Bennett had been his father's factotum, and his job at that particular moment had been to see that father and son went out with hats and coats suitably brushed and with each his particular newspaper under his arm, to catch the 8.10 train. Now Bennett was officially termed the chauffeur, though, like Gough, he performed many other duties, and instead of the walk to the station, Harrow had only to cross the pavement to the car.

But actually Bennett was making a mistake this morning, and Harrow, contemplating the proof that everything was not in order, wondered whether it *were* a mistake or not. It was barely possible that Bennett, the sly dog, knew that shabby little glove was tucked into the back of the seat in such a way as to peep out when Harrow's considerable weight depressed the cushions.

He spread the glove out on his knee, ignoring for the moment his copy of *The Times*, ironed in the old-fashioned way and put ready to his hand. It was a very small glove, and certainly a very shabby one. At best it had been a shoddy, cheap affair, and the owner had not improved the shape by the badly made darns in the fingertips. He pushed his little finger into the thumb of the glove and regarded a darn, conjuring up instantly the picture of Janine not even half filling his easy-chair and saying in that innocently naive way of hers that she was 'not much good at anything'. She certainly was not much good at darning; and he remembered ruefully that he would have to find means of putting off an important client until such time as the bureau could make correct schedules in place of the blotched affairs Janine had presented him with.

Janine. How extraordinary that he should have thought of her like that! Until last evening he had scarcely known that her name was Janine, and now he was thinking of her by that name.

He tucked the glove into his pocket to give her later, and called himself a doddering old fool as he turned his attention to *The Times* and studied the Stock Exchange prices. He found with regret and some dismay that he could not read the tiny figures as easily as he could even a month ago. Peering at them through his glasses, he found his thoughts wandering, and in the end he put the paper down and closed his eyes. He supposed he would have to give in, take that long rest, probably even the sea trip. Perhaps Barrett would go with him if he paid all expenses – or Charlie Nates – or perhaps it would be better just to go with Bennett, after all. No, hang it, Bennett, for all their long association, could never forget they were master and man, though often Harrow felt he would have been glad to forget it. He began to realise how lonely he was. He had always been a solitary soul, from early nursery days when he had had to play by himself for lack of brother or sister, but lately he had begun to feel the need of companionship – lately – since Felicity had gone, perhaps.

Felicity.

No one, least of all Felicity herself, had any conception how often she was in his thoughts. Repressed by the inhibitions of long years, widowed after only eighteen months of extraordinary and incredible companionship, he had not found it possible to break through the crust of reserve, and Felicity had come and gone, holiday after holiday, and known no more of the man who idolised her than had the least of his employees, had known less than his servants. She had no idea of the effort he had made to adjust himself to her ideas on life when she came home for good and in the whirlwind of her comings and goings, her incessant changes of mind and plan and raiment, her friends of both sexes who were as inconsequent and volatile, the staid, ageing man was hopelessly lost. In his bewildered attempts to understand her she read disapproval, secretly aware that she often merited it. Her resultant attempts to justify herself reacted on him as defiance. He grew irritable at his own lack of comprehension, and she, taking it as censure to herself, drew further from him, entertained her friends elsewhere, rushing in and out of the house for an odd meal or so, to change her clothes, to sleep possibly, though he could never be quite sure that modern youth had not succeeded in doing without sleep altogether.

He remonstrated for the sake of her health and because of his own longing to share some part of her life, but again she misunderstood, and at last, mistress of her own considerable fortune, she had left him and gone her own way, flinging him now and again a careless letter or a picture postcard from remote parts of the world, serenely unaware of how he treasured those unconsidered scraps of paper. She would have been amazed and touched had she known of that room he kept for her, of the wardrobe full of clothes, but he was no more able in his letters to express himself or reveal himself than he had been in their personal contact.

Leaning back and gazing out of the window with eyes which saw nothing, he knew himself to be yearning for her, for his own and only kin. Only they two of his blood in the world as far as he knew, and here was he, in London, old and sick and alone, and she … Where was she when he had had that last card? New York? Melbourne? No, he remembered that it had been a view of some place in New Zealand, though the scribbled words had told him nothing save that she hoped he was well, and had he made a potful out of the last rubber boom? – because she had.

He shook his thoughts up and rearranged them neatly again, folded his paper, adjusted his hat, stepped on to the kerb outside the block in which Harrow and Purnell had their offices, nodded to Bennett and walked up the steps.

Janine was there already. He could hear the sound of a typewriter from the office at the end of the corridor, and as it was still only two minutes past nine he knew that it would be Janine and not one of the others. Indeed, a little scurry behind him led his attention to Miss Gilbert, tired-looking and wearing that slightly dissipated look which he had hated in Felicity, trying to pretend she had been in some minutes, though she still wore her coat and he could see her hat, if that was what she called that silly little bit of wool, crushed in her hand.

He nodded at her and went into his own office. It was Miss Wilson's duty, amongst others, to sort the post and put the letters addressed personally to the partners in their respective offices. He looked through the pile, throwing out one belonging to Purnell which she had mis-sorted.

'Not much good,' she had said, but he remembered it with a smile which surprised him. She was quite right, of course. What would happen to her eventually? He frowned a little at the thought. She seemed so small and helpless, so defenceless, so completely unfitted to shift for herself as these dual-sexed, competent, hard-eyed modern girls seemed so eminently fitted to do. If he had to go away for six months, which was the least the specialist had advised, he could not imagine Purnell keeping her on. For one thing, she was not decorative enough for that enterprising young man, and for another (and here he felt he could not justifiably interfere), she was not competent. He could not imagine how she had hung on for twelve months with the sort of work she did, but perhaps even Purnell drew the line at kicking a weakly puppy that got in his way. If Janine looked at him with those brown doggy eyes of hers, he could not imagine anyone casting her adrift.

And yet, of course, everyone was not as ridiculously sentimental as he, Harrow, knew himself to be at heart.

What would happen to that poor child?

He thrust the thought aside and began to open his letters, and had soon forgotten her. Miss Wright came when he rang, and as he had a great many letters of importance, he was relieved that it was she and not Miss Wilson.

When he had finished his dictation and Miss Wright rose to go he detained her with a hesitating question.

'Er—what sort of work does Miss Wilson do? I mean—what work does Mr. Purnell give her?'

The girl reflected a moment. She and her colleague had a certain contempt for their inefficient assistant, but she was kindly at heart and would not for the world do the girl a bad turn.

'Oh, she does—copying mostly, and stock letters, rents owing and things like that,' she said at last,

'I see. You get a lot of those? Enough to keep her busy on them, I mean?'

Either she or Miss Gilbert could have polished off the whole of such work in an hour or so, but she would not say so. 'Oh yes, we get quite a lot of them,' she said brightly, and he nodded.

'I think—er—I think Miss Wilson had better be regarded as—I think those letters, that type of work had better be regarded as Miss Wilson's job and you and Miss Gilbert can do other work. She's not—er—not perhaps very strong, and we don't want to be hard on her,' he said.

Miss Wright stared. This from Spilliken? Had she heard aright? It was evidently true that he was failing, though she had thought it was his body that was weak and not his mind!

She detailed the conversation to Miss Gilbert in a whisper which, unfortunately, Janine could not but overhear. She flushed miserably and buried her face in the filing cabinet. So the end was in sight already. She had buoyed herself up with the thought that Mr. Harrow's kindness last night, especially after the bad work she had done, would be a sort of protection to her for the future, but evidently he had only been sorry for her and come to the conclusion that she was not strong and must be humoured. She who had never known a day's illness in her life, for all her slight body and look of fragility when she was tired!

She did not see him at all that day, for in the afternoon he went to the Harley Street man again, receiving corroboration of his fears that he was definitely worse.

'Man, I simply can't leave my business for at least another month,' he averred.

The physician shrugged his shoulders and tucked the substantial cheque in the drawer of his desk.

'Alright. You know my opinion. If you must stay out the month take it very, very quietly and attend only to such matters as you feel are imperative. That's all I can say, and, frankly, Mr. Harrow, you're only wasting your time and money in coming to me if you won't take the only advice I can give you. You may have years of useful life if you conserve your strength now. If you don't …' and the shrug of his shoulders was significant.

Harrow walked out into the pale October sunshine and felt that, even considering everything, he wanted to go on living a while longer. His mind ran forward into the work of the next few weeks. There were several important cases coming off, cases in which he was both personally and financially interested. Purnell was a divorce specialist, and the senior partner devoted his closest attention to probate. For years he had been anticipating this case of Hibbert *v* Consam, and he was not going to be done out of it now that it was certainly coming off.

Automatically and without realising it, he made his way slowly back to the office, and just as he entered the main hall, deserted for the moment by even the porter, Janine almost ran into him, drawing back within a foot of him with a murmured apology.

He raised his hat and found himself seeking an excuse to detain her. 'You're leaving on time for once, I see.'

'Oh no. I'm coming back,' she said in a shocked voice, for she still had some copying to do and the weight of Mr. Harrow's pound note still lay on her conscience. She did not feel she had earned it by that work she had done for him, though he had, with extreme delicacy of mind, taken pains to keep from her the knowledge that he had sent the work to the bureau.

'Why? Not finished yet?'

'I've get that agreement with Lawson to finish.'

'No hurry for it, is there? He's not coming in to sign it until Friday.'

'I—I feel I ought to do it,' she said uncomfortably. 'I—I'd rather really.'

'Alright, if you must, but come and have a cup of tea with me first. I've missed Miss Gilbert's confection, and I know from experience what you can do in the way of fasting.'

Dazed, she found herself walking along the street with him, following him to a table in the teashop, listening whilst he gave the order for tea and toast and 'the kind of cakes that young ladies like'. The waitress, who evidently knew him, laughed.

'We don't eat cakes nowadays, you know,' she said.

"Afraid of putting on weight?' he asked.

'Sure,' with a self-conscious twist of her own trim little figure.

'Well, I don't think you need feel afraid of that, Janine,' he said, glancing from her to the shy girl opposite him. 'Bring something you would like if you hadn't to think about weight,' and the girl smiled and tripped away.

He had called her Janine purposely now, in the daytime, almost in office hours, and she realised it, and flushed.

'I rather like your name, you know,' he told her. 'You don't mind if an old man uses it now and then, when we are alone?'

She felt abashed and confused at the suggestion of intimacy, but she laughed a little.

'Of course not. I think I rather like you to. No one calls me that, you know. In the office they call me Jane. They did mostly at the Home, too. I suppose I look more like a Jane than anything as fanciful as Janine.'

Over their tea they grew almost intimate, and her shyness fled as she realised the amazing truth that hers was nothing to his! Actually he was more afraid of her than she of him! The knowledge, incredible though it was, warmed her to sympathy. She knew so well what an agony shyness could be, though, of course, it was absurd that an old gentleman should be nervous of his typist.

He spoke to her of other lands, his mind still occupied with the train of thought started by the specialist, and her eyes glowed at his descriptions, inadequate though he knew them to be and couched in his incurably legal phraseology. Listening to him, one always expected to hear 'soever' attached to his words. His speech was terse and to the point, however, once his nervousness had disappeared, and Janine's quick imagination was able to fill in the colours and details of the sketchy word pictures he gave her.

'You would love the Canary Islands,' he said. 'I think best of all you would like the colours of the flowers and the bird songs. I remember once standing quite alone in some gardens in Tenerife on an autumn evening and hearing the birds in the trees. I can't describe it, but it was music, perfect, natural, a song of pure joy of living. Wonderful!'

'I am trying to imagine it. I love birds – not in cages, though. It breaks my heart to see them shut up behind bars. If ever God created anything for freedom, it was the birds. He gave them wings, and we, tied to earth by a pair of feet, dare to shut them in in little cages! It makes me boil! Matron used to keep canaries, and I went downstairs in the middle of the night once and let them out. I got a thrashing for it the next day, but what I really minded was the news that the other birds would only kill them or they would starve to death without their usual food. Please go on. Tell me some more.'

He smiled and spoke of the flowers.

'Geraniums grow like weeds by the side of the road, and when cultivated make hedges of colour, though, if I remember rightly, the flowers there have no scent. Everything seems to go to making a riot of colour – every shade of red and pink and purple you can imagine, pelargonium, bougainvillaea, hibiscus. The trees are beautiful, too. Mimosa and pepper and tamarisk.'

'What is tamarisk like? It sounds nice.'

'If it's left alone, it grows into a very delicate, feathery tree with fragile pinky flowers, but if something more than a merely decorative effect is aimed at, the shrubs have to be pruned constantly, and eventually they make a very strong, protective hedge – without flowers, of course.'

'I'd rather let the poor things grow naturally and have their flowers,' said Janine dreamily.

He looked at her curiously. 'You know, you're an odd little person,' he observed, and she came back to earth with a start and a little laugh.

'Because I should want the flowers? It isn't only that. I feel the same as I do about the birds when I see a big brave hedge being cut into shape after it's taken all the trouble to throw up long spikes and perhaps flowers.'

'My dear, you're a sentimentalist, and there's no more room nowadays for sentiment than for spiky hedges with flowers on them!' He laughed, but there was a curious gentleness in his voice. 'If you've finished, shall we go now? I shall have to call in at the office.'

He persuaded her not to work any longer that evening, surprising himself as much as her, but when they stood at the corner of the street to say good night he detained her for a moment.

'That has been very kind of you,' he said, with a return to his stilted manner, a sure sign of nervousness with him, as she soon began to recognise.

'Oh no, Mr. Harrow! I've loved it,' said Janine fervently.

'What are you going to do with yourself now?'

'Nothing. I never do. I read a lot, and I have to do the work of my room in the evenings.'

He tried to place her as dissociated from her typewriter and pencil, but failed. 'But you go out sometimes? Theatres? Pictures? Dinner now and then?'

She shook her head. 'Can't afford such luxuries,' she laughed, but there was nothing bitter or resentful about the simple statement. She merely stated a fact.

'Why not come and have dinner with me one evening?' he asked on some extraordinary impulse. He and impulse were the veriest strangers.

She stared at him.

'Do you—really mean that, Mr Harrow?'

'Why yes, of course, of course,' he said, already regretting the suggestion.

'I'd like it very much if—if you wouldn't find it too dull,' she said shyly.

'Nonsense! Shall we say tomorrow evening?'

Might just as well get it over now that he had been such a fool as to make it inevitable.

'Yes, please.'

'I'll send the car for you. Better than going straight from the office. We could have dinner at seven and go to a theatre. Would you like that?'

Her eyes shone. Paddy's eyes, he thought almost irritably.

'I can't tell you how much,' she said earnestly. Then, at a sudden thought, I—I haven't an evening dress,' she stammered.

'Never mind. People don't dress nowadays,' he told her gruffly, irritated afresh. He was old-fashioned enough to prefer to sit in the stalls in immaculate 'tails' with his womenfolk suitably arrayed. 'I'll tell Bennett to be at your house at quarter to seven then. I shan't be at the office tomorrow myself. Good night,' and he raised his hat and walked away with that brisk step which the doctor had told him he must slow down.

Janine waited for the Highgate bus with a fast-beating heart. Extraordinary to relate, she had reached the age of twenty-two without ever being invited to an evening out. Cora Heseldine had protected her fiercely from the temptations of the life she herself led, treating her as the child she really was at heart, and, for reasons which will appear later, since she had been at Harrow and Purnell's she was too intent on saving every penny ever to spend money on amusement or unnecessary food. She had no friends nor was she of the type to attract casual invitations.

And now she was invited out to dinner and a theatre by no less a person than her employer!

All the next day she was self-conscious, remembering exultantly that she had risen to the ranks of the Misses Wright and Gilbert, that she 'had a date' as well as they, though she would have died rather than let them know it was with old Spilliken.

Miss Gilbert commented on her unusual animation.

'What's the matter with you, Jane? Lost sixpence and found a shilling?' she enquired with careless interest.

'No. I—I'm going out tonight,' she said, unable any longer to keep the whole thing to herself. 'I'm going out to dinner and to a theatre.'

'Good egg! Time you had a bit of fun, kid. Who with? Boyfriend?' – not in the least expecting an affirmative.

Janine hesitated, coloured hotly and then nodded defiantly.

'I've known him a long time,' she said, as if in preparation for the probable conclusion that this was a mere 'pick-up'.

'Well, see to it that you don't have to walk home,' laughed the other girl good- humouredly, as she went out of the room.

Janine scurried off at five o'clock just as the other two did every night, pausing at the chemist's at the corner to buy herself a very small box of face powder, her first venture in make-up, but when she reached her tiny room at the back of the cheap boarding-house she felt anxiously that it would add very little to her appearance to powder her nose, since she had no choice but to wear the navy blue silk dress which she had kept from Cora's wardrobe and altered not very successfully to her smaller figure.

Her landlady, Mrs. Mote, scenting something in the air, hovered about on the staircase whilst her 'top back' dressed, and Janine went out to her at last in desperation.

'Can I do anything to make this look better, more fashionable Mrs. Mote?' she asked, turning herself about to show the badly bunched silk frock.

'Going out, dear?' asked that worthy, looking her over. It had not escaped her lynx eyes that her young lodger had been brought home two evenings previously by a chauffeur in an expensive car, and she remembered that she had her 'first floor front' empty and badly in need of a tenant. Her mind was of the type to connect Janine, the expensive car and the better rooms.

Janine nodded happily. Not even the navy silk could damp her spirits entirely. 'I haven't got another frock,' she said, after another twist and pause before Mrs. Mote's appraising eyes.

'The belt at the waist wants to go higher, and the neck's untidy,' she decided at last. 'Wait and I'll get a pin or two,' and she waddled into her own quarters and returned with some pins and a piece of lace.

'I'll lend you this collar,' she said, and though the girl felt an instinctive recoil at the thought of wearing anything that had been in contact with the landlady's stout, not too clean person, she had to agree that the lace was an improvement.

She thanked the woman fervently when the alterations were complete, for Mrs. Mote had been a good dressmaker before she became too lazy, and her fingers had retained much of their cunning.

Somebody called up the stairs.

'Mrs. Mote! Car for Miss Wilson at the door!' And Janine felt hot and uncomfortable at having her affairs blazoned through the house. She knew that every curtain would quiver and every door be a little ajar whilst she took her departure, and she pulled on her only hat resentfully.

Mrs. Mote swayed down the stairs in front of her and insisted on opening the front door, taking the opportunity of having a good look at Bennett and the gleaming car.

'Nice gentleman, dear?' she asked, with a would-be friendly smile, as Janine sidled past her in the narrow hall.

'Yes, thank you,' she said hurriedly, her face aflame. She was innocent but by no means ignorant, and she was well aware of the construction Mrs. Mote was putting on the affair.

Bennett greeted her with a discreet smile and tucked her into the car, drawing the sable rug about her as carefully as if she were a duchess, and she sank back luxuriously to enjoy the ride and to forget, if she could, Mrs. Mote and the quivering curtains and wagging tongues at 18 Lavender Street, from which the perfume of lavender had long fled.

Gough offered her the same discreet smile and handed her over to Mrs. Gough, but in spite of her landlady's pins and lace, she felt very shabby and out of sympathy with Harrow's beautiful, dignified home.

They dined at one end of a huge mahogany table in a room which overpowered her and made her tongue-tied, though Harrow used his best endeavours to entertain her and set her at her ease, but when they reached the theatre and the seats not too near the front of the stalls sheer excitement loosed her tongue and made her more animated.

He had chosen a musical show, one of the light, frothy affairs whose story is the thinnest possible chain on which to hang sparkling baubles of colour and music and laughter, and though he was as a rule bored by such an entertainment, tonight he found a new enjoyment through Janine's unaccustomed eyes. She loved every moment of it, laughed at the smallest jokes, grew stiff and wistful in the sentimental moments and sank back in her seat with a sigh of pure joy when the Curtain fell for an interval.

It amused him to treat her as he would have liked to be allowed to treat Felicity. He plied her with ices and lemonade and bought her an enormous box of chocolates topped with a pink satin bow, pointed out to her various well-known people in the boxes, entertained her with little stories about them to which he added a touch of dry but not malicious humour.

Janine grew amazingly at her ease with him and forgot the ugly blue dress, and hair which she had wished passionately she had had waved for the occasion, the hands which looked uncared for beside the pale, manicured fingers of the girl next to her.

After the show, he took her somewhere for coffee in preference to the cocktail which she shyly refused, and they got into his car again before midnight.

'Where do you live, my dear?' he asked her. 'We can take you home first.'

'Well, it's really Kentish Town, though Mrs. Mote likes to call it Highgate,' laughed Janine, and he gave Bennett the order and settled back in his seat.

'I've loved it so,' she said, with a little sigh of enjoyment.

'I've enjoyed your pleasure,' he said. 'How is it that you have as little as you say?'

She hesitated. 'I—I can't afford it,' she said at last.

He frowned. 'Surely we pay you enough for some sort of pleasure? How much do you have?'

'Oh, I have a good salary, really!' she said hastily. 'I have two pounds a week.'

It did not sound very much to him out of the office environment, but he had always considered that they paid good wages compared with other firms, and he retained just enough common sense not to be drawn into a discussion of her salary in the circumstances.

'Can't you get an occasional evening out on that?' he asked. 'Oh, I could, I know,' she said. 'Only I—I'm paying off a debt, you see.'

He was surprised.

'A debt?'

'Well, that's how I think of it. To the orphanage, you know. I still hadn't squared my account with them when I ran away.'

'But surely to heaven they don't expect to go on draining you all this time? Isn't the place supported by charity or something?'

'Well, it's supposed to be. It was always rubbed into us that we were living on charity, anyway,' said Janine bitterly.

'Then how can you owe them for your time there?'

'I don't suppose I do, legally,' with a little smile at her choice of words to a solicitor. 'It's only in myself I feel I want to pay them, for my own self-respect. I want to feel—independent of them, not so much a charity child.'

He felt that it was rather pathetic. She was so essentially of the type that should depend rather than stand alone, and yet here she was struggling gallantly along under a load of self-imposed debt whose repayment was both unnecessary and quixotic, though something of the sturdy quality within him sympathised with her. 'You poor child,' he said. 'How much is this debt?'

'Still a terrible amount. A hundred and seven pounds four and sixpence.'

'Good heavens! What a fiendish system! How and when do you propose to pay so much?'

She gave a little helpless gesture with her hands.

'I don't know. It seems as if I shall have it with me for ever at the rate I'm going on, I pay seven shillings a week for my room, and my fares and food cost me twelve-and-six however carefully I work it out. That's—how much? Nineteen-and-six. Then there's my insurance stamp, and I pay three pence a week to a sick club and a shilling for gas. In the winter I have to have oil for the lamp. It's cheaper than the coal Mrs. Mote sells us. You see, that doesn't leave very much to send to the Home, though I do my own washing and go to bed early these dark evenings so as to save the light.'

He listened to her with mixed feelings, the paramount one being of pity. She had spoken simply and with no intention of making an effect or of evoking his sympathy. It was merely a statement of the way she lived, and he realised that she was accepting it without any particular resentment, though to him, secure in his comfortable life, these details of her quixotic straggle were appalling. He resisted the first impulse to offer to pay off her debt, to increase her salary out of all proportion, to do something – anything – to make life more pleasant for her. He thought of Felicity and of the luxuries with which her every hour had been made one of infinite leisure when she was this girl's age. He thought again of offering her the money, but he knew intuitively that he would offend her and humble her rather pathetic pride.

He said nothing, and she sat quietly at his side, wondering a little uncomfortably if she had presumed too much on his kindness. After all, he was Mr. Harrow, the senior partner of the firm. She supposed that when Mr. Purnell took one of the other two girls out, as she knew he did, they talked to him quite naturally and freely, but she and Mr. Harrow were different.

He held her hand closely in his when the car stopped before 18 Lavender Street, and his beady little eyes were kind.

Thank you, my dear,' he said simply.

'It is I to thank you, Mr. Harrow,' she said shyly.

'No. Age always owes a debt to youth for such of its bright hours as it can spare. I've been very happy this evening, and I hope you have, and that you will come again another time,' he said, in his deliberate, stilted fashion.

'I shall love to,' she said sincerely, and he watched her from the car until the door had closed behind her.

She was uncomfortably aware of Mrs. Mote's heavy breathing on the stairs above her, but she went steadily and quickly up to the flight which led to her room before they actually met. Mrs. Mote beamed on her in what was supposed to be a motherly manner, though to Janine the smile had the elements of devilry. 'Had a nice time, dear!' she asked, blocking the way,

'Lovely, thank you,' said Janine stiffly.

'Your friend bring you home in his car?'

'Yes' – knowing quite well that Mrs, Mote had missed nothing. 'Pity your room's up here where you can't exactly entertain a gentleman,' said the landlady reflectively. 'Not that I should mind, but—'

'I shouldn't dream of doing such a thing, Mrs. Mote,' said Janine, a little indignantly,

'Well, times change, you know, and it doesn't do to be narrow-minded, but—well, there's the first-floor rooms empty. If you like to bring your friend into the sitting-room there whilst it's empty, *I* shan't mind, and I shan't charge you anything, dear.'

The girl could read her mind perfectly, and her lip curled.

'I don't want to, thank you,' she said, very distinctly. 'May I come up? I'm rather tired.'

The woman heaved her bulk out of the way, still smiling in spite of the rebuff. She knew far better than Janine the temptations which probably lay ahead of her, but to her mind a girl was the more valuable for being hard to get, and if this one chose to keep her man dangling, well, so much the better for Mrs. Mote in the end. She could judge to a nicety what that sort of affair might be worth to her.

Janine shut herself in her tiny room and felt resentful that the woman with her filthy mind had managed to rub the bloom of her beautiful evening. Mr. Harrow had been so kind to her, so considerate and courteous in his manner, treating her as if she were of his own world, a woman to be respected and cherished. Mrs. Mote, with her unspoken comments, had spoiled something of that memory and set her thoughts along channels which alone they would not have found.

Was the landlady right? Did Mr. Harrow mean anything other than kindness to a lonely girl? She knew how Miss Wright and Miss Gilbert would look at it. More than once she had heard them recount, to a point, their experiences with 'old This' or 'old That', and it seemed that though they might give their favours in return for an evening's pleasure with a young man, they expected more than that if they lent their charms to an old one. Janine never let herself speculate as to just how far those favours went, though sometimes they made it fairly obvious. How beastly, how utterly *beastly*, if Mr. Harrow were like the men they went out with!

She wrenched her mind away from the thought, remembering his delicacy, his tact, his gentleness, so oddly at variance with the brusqueness of his manner in the office and his reputation for irritability and meanness. If ever anyone had a dual personality, she felt that Mr. Harrow had, and she went to sleep at length with the determination that she would keep this affair strictly to herself so that the evil minds of other people should not despoil it.

Chapter Three

The evening with Mr. Harrow was followed by others, and Janine, for once rebellious against the silent demands of the Wilson Home on her earnings, boldly spent on a new frock the money she had saved for the next month's remittance.

He noted it with pleasure.

'You look quite festive tonight,' he said. 'You ought to have something lighter and brighter than brown, though. You're young enough to wear all the colours of the rainbow.'

She laughed. They were sitting in their favourite corner of a restaurant become pleasantly familiar to her, and she was bright with the consciousness of that new frock, brown and high-necked though it was. She had yearned to buy an evening gown, but her remaining prudence had bidden her choose something she could wear more often.

'As this will have to last me years and years, I am less likely to get tired of brown than I should of all colours of the rainbow,' she said.

Their friendship had grown rapidly during the few weeks past, and she had lost that early fear of his real meaning. His manner had never changed, save to become more fatherly, and though often he would have liked to buy her things, he had contented himself with chocolates and flowers.

'I should like to see you in something really young and gay, though,' he told her. 'I wonder—'

'You're not going to offer to buy me a dress, are you?' she put in hastily, and he smiled at the swift fear.

'No, I daren't do that,' he assured her. 'Mrs. Gough told me that she had shown you my daughter's room and that you therefore know what an old fool she has for a father. What I wondered was – whether, if some night I want you to dress particularly smartly, you would – borrow one of those frocks. They'll never be worn otherwise, I know.'

She caught the wistful note of regret in his voice, and it checked the impulse to refuse outright.

'I don't expect they'd fit me,' she said. 'In her photographs she looks much taller than I am.'

'She is, but Mrs. Gough is quite clever and could no doubt alter something for you. It would give me—such great pleasure, my dear.'

It was not in Janine to resist any appeal, and her brown eyes looked at him with doggy affection.

'Well—if the occasion does arise …' she conceded, hoping that it would not.

But he made one during the following week, calling her into his office.

'I want you to do me a favour, Janine. Will you?'

'But of course I will!' she said eagerly.

'Then—have dinner at my house tomorrow evening and help me to entertain two friends of mine—oh, only old fogies like myself,' as he caught her swift dismay.

'I might be so stupid about it,' she said. 'I'm always so horribly shy with strangers, especially men.'

'Do you think I've not achieved *any* expert knowledge of you, my dear?' he asked, with a quizzical smile. 'Do me this favour, will you?'

'Well, you don't leave me any choice when you put it like that,' she said reluctantly.

'And—you'll wear one of Felicity's dresses? Please?'

'Are you sure you want me to?'

'Absolutely'

'Well, if I come, I shall have to have the right sort of frock, shan't I? And I simply can't afford to buy one,' she said, with obvious hesitation.

'Suppose you come over this evening and consult with Mrs. Gough on the matter? There may not be anything you like, in which case …'

'In which case it's *off,*' said Janine, so definitely that he gave in.

She called at the Hampstead house with some return of the shyness she had felt when she had entered it for the first time as his guest, but the servants put her at ease by their respectful acceptance of her as their master's honoured guest, though she had no idea that Harrow had issued explicit instructions to that effect. He himself was not in, but she went to Felicity's room with Mrs. Gough and found several frocks already laid out on the bed.

'You must think this a very strange procedure, Mrs. Gough,' she said uncomfortably, wishing she had not agreed to the thing but the housekeeper appeared to accept it as a quite ordinary situation.

'I think it's a very sensible one, miss,' she said. 'I always have thought it a cruel waste of money these things never being worn. This is the one master thought might do,' and she picked up a frock of some filmy rose-coloured material as fine and soft as cobweb.

Janine caught her breath. She had never been so close to a frock like that. She had seen them fleetingly through shop windows, but she was sensible enough not to torment herself with a detailed inspection of something she could never attain. And now she was being asked, begged, to wear one!

'Oh, if only I could, just once!' she whispered, fascinated, and Mrs. Gough helped her off with her well-worn navy blue office dress and slid over her head the rose frock with its lining of clinging, shimmering silk.

'It'll be too long, but I've thought of that and know what I can do,' Mrs. Gough was saying. 'This last piece can come right off the skirt like this'—tucking it up—'and the shoulder-straps can be shortened' – busy with pins.

Clearly it could be made to fit, and Janine realised with pride and surprise that her arms and shoulders looked quite well in their unaccustomed setting.

'I shall have to have my hair waved,' she said reflectively, and experienced a certain heady sense of abandonment at the thought of spending a whole half-crown on a mere luxury!

She did not regret, it when she saw the effect of the remodelled pink frock the next evening, nor did she grudge the wild extravagance of a pair of satin evening shoes, for those in Felicity Harrow's cupboard were useless.

Harrow was alone when at last she went down to join him in the library, which he used as a sitting-room, leaving the other rooms closed now that his daughter had gone, taking her trail of visitors with her. His face was a study in conflicting emotions when Janine came across the sombre, book-lined room to him, radiant and sweet in her rose-pink frock, her hair waved about her head in neat ripples, instead of the straggling mass to which he was accustomed. Mrs. Gough had suggested face creams and powder instead of the mere dusting to which she had lately been addicted, and excitement had given colour to her cheeks. She looked almost pretty, Harrow thought in surprise. She looked something better than pretty, was his second thought. She had the indefinable charm of youth and eagerness about her – that charm which no art in the world can provide.

He took her hand and held it between his own after that first uncertain moment of surprise.

'You look charming, my dear,' he said, and his sincerity made the little compliment perfect.

'Will they be frightfully learned or anything, your friends?' she asked.

'They're the simplest men in the world and they'll be at your feet at first glance,' he told her with a smile, and before she had time to glow nervous they were announced.

She did not know until afterwards that one of them was an eminent philosopher and the other one of the world's historians. To her they were just simple, kindly men, anxious to please and be pleased, talking of things she could understand, or explaining in simple language anything which might have gone over her head.

Harrow had introduced her as 'Miss Janine Wilson, who is being good enough to act as my hostess tonight,' and there was not the slightest suggestion on their part that there was anything unusual in the situation. Harrow called her 'Janine' and 'my dear', just as if they were alone, and the two guests were charmed with her simplicity and gentle dignity.

'Did I do alright?' was her first breathless question, when they had taken a somewhat ceremonious departure.

'You did excellently well, my dear,' Harrow assured her, 'Do you really want to go or will you stay and drink a nightcap with me? I have whisky, but Gough will find you something more ladylike.'

He had educated her tastes in wine a little during the past weeks, but tonight she had had her first experience of champagne, and she was feeling a little uncertain of herself.

'I daren't drink anything else,' she told him. 'I ought not to have had that champagne really. I feel—funny a little.'

He teased her with his laughter and made her have a special liqueur which Gough brought in, assuring her that it would make her better instead of worse.

'Are you quite sure it won't make me drunk?' she asked him.

He laughed at her again and then became strangely serious.

'Do you think I would harm one hair of your head, my dear?' he asked her, and she stood hesitating for a moment and then lifted the little glass to her lips with a smile.

He took it from her when she had finished and put his hands on her shoulders, looking at her with that new gravity. It frightened her a little. She felt that something was going to happen, and she wanted everything to remain the same.

'You've made me very happy tonight. Janine,' he said.

'Have I? I'm glad. It's never been my turn before,' she said shyly.

'You could make me happier, my dear, if you would. I am a very lonely man, Janine and quickly growing an old one. I have felt lately that I am throwing away the last precious sands of life. For years I have lived on the hope that my daughter would return, but I am beginning to realise at last that she—won't, I wonder if you understand at all what I am trying to say to you?'

She shook her head. She could not speak. All sorts of fantastic ideas jostled one another in a mind which was not even as clear as usual. The champagne had been sweet and heady, and through the subtle warmth of it she tried ineffectually to keep a cool hold on herself.

'You see—I find it difficult to put it into words,' went on Harrow as she did not answer. This sort of conversation is not quite in my line,' with an attempt at lightness. 'I – my dear, it seems I can't have Felicity, but is it at all possible that I could have – you?'

Her head began to swim. Hazy conjectures formed themselves into a jumble of thought. What did he mean? What was he asking of her? What a fool she had been to drink that stuff after the champagne! Vague memories of highly spiced novelettes once read voraciously raced through her mind. Was he thinking of the sort of thing which used to be represented by a row of dots?

'Have—me?' she echoed at last, uncertainly.

'It is asking a lot, I know, but I wouldn't let you regret it. I am a rich man, and Felicity has her own fortune and needs nothing from me. I shan't ask anything of you in return that an old man has no right to ask of youth. All I want is to have someone belonging to me, to companion me, perhaps even to care for me a very little. You're not afraid of that, Janine?'

Still she could not discover his meaning, in what capacity did he want her if, as he said, he would ask so little of her? As companion? Daughter? The natural conclusion was as mistress, but he had almost implied he did not want her that way.

'I won't press you tonight, my dear. That wouldn't be fair. I shan't be at the office tomorrow, but will you come and dine here quietly with me, just the two of us, and talk things over?'

Gough entered the room whilst she was still struggling to find a reply, and she was thankful for the reprieve.

'Bennett wants to know if you need the car again, sir,' asked the butler.

'Of course,' said Harrow, rather sharply, 'in five minutes, tell him.'

'I must go now,' said Janine, a little uncomfortably. 'Oh! This frock!'

'Please take it, Janine. It would hurt me for you to refuse. You've never let me give you anything at all.'

She felt she could not refuse, and just then the matter of a frock seemed so unimportant.

"Thank you,' she said quietly. 'It is very kind of you.'

'I want to be kinder, Janine. You'll realise and remember that, until tomorrow evening?'

'Yes.'

'And we shall still be friends, whatever happens?'

'Yes.'

And they parted like that, both uncertain and uncomfortable, with eyes averted.

Janine lay awake and worried. What did he mean? And whatever he meant, what was she to do?

She reviewed her past and her uncertain, clouded future. Harrow had told her enough to make her realise that his years of work were over. He would have to retire within the next few months, possibly within the next few weeks, if he were to find any measure of health again. What would become of her then if she refused his suggestion now? She had no delusions about herself. She was a round peg in a square hole as far as a business career was concerned. She had worked and worried to the very limit of her capacity at Harrow and Purnell's, and yet she knew that her work was unsatisfactory and that she was kept on more out of pity than anything. No one except a man like Richard Harrow would tolerate her in these days of hard efficiency, and once he had retired from active participation in the business Mr. Purnell would not hesitate to get rid of her. She was wretchedly aware that he would be able to justify himself in so doing.

And what then? If she refused whatever it was Mr. Harrow was asking, she could not possibly turn to him for help of any sort, even to get her another job. She could never go to him for anything at all, in spite of what he had said about their friendship continuing. She was fiercely honest in her thoughts of him. She would not take where she refused to give.

There would be nothing but domestic service for her, and that of the cheapest kind, where people would put up with her clumsy ways and her incompetence because she was cheap. She had had long enough experience at the Home to know exactly the kind of work which would fall to her share – scrubbing and washing and brass-cleaning and floor-polishing, all the hard tasks about which she could not make a mess or do damage.

Harrow would have laughed her out of her 'inferiority complex', as she called it, but he was not there, and in the long hours of the night, when everything seems at its worst in one's mind, the future loomed before her like a nightmare.

And if she did whatever it was he wanted? Became his mistress, which seemed the most likely requirement? She supposed confusedly that he would take rooms for her, perhaps a flat, and live there with her for as long as he wanted to do so, giving her an income, clothes, jewellery perhaps. She had gathered such ideas from many sources. Girls in the Home had openly talked of that sort of success as being their one aim once they were free. Marriage to them meant only more of the hated housework and the perpetual care of babies. They had had their fill of housework and babies at the orphanage.

She shivered. Innate was the desire to keep herself clean in body and mind. She had always been fastidiously clean in her person, her habits and had a sense of moral rectitude, apparently her heritage, oddly enough. She had never hoped for love and marriage. She was aware of her lack of physical beauty, and she could see nothing else in herself which might commend her to the affectionate desire of any man. She was a very humble little person, which made Richard Harrow's interest all the more amazing to her.

He would be good to her. She was sure of that. And she would no longer be in debt to the Home, no longer screwing and saving to repay it. She would be comfortable, probably in luxury, and she would not have been feminine if the thought of lovely clothes made no appeal. She had had her first taste of it that evening when she wore the rose frock.

In the morning, after a broken, fitful sleep, she was still no nearer a decision, and her work that day was even more unsatisfactory. Mr. Purnell made biting comments on it when she brought him the copying, which was all she had been given to do, and she turned away with her eyes filled with tears and despair in her heart. What was the good of trying? Why not give it up now as well as later?

She looked so pale and tired when Gough showed her into the library that evening that Harrow hurried to her in concern.

'Aren't you well, child?' he asked, and when she insisted that she was, he made her drink a glass of wine to put a little colour into her cheeks.

She was so tired and dispirited that his care of her was like heaven.

He did not refer to the subject nearest to their minds until they had finished dinner and were back in the library, and then he stood and faced her, his bald head shiny in the firelight, his red face heavy with gravity.

'Have you thought of what I asked you last night, dear? But of course you have. And you have decided?'

'I—I—'

She could not frame the words which suddenly she had decided to say. She meant to ask him if she might come to him as a daughter, to do everything in her power for him, serve him in any way they could devise. But the words would not come, and he helped her out gently.

'You'll do as I ask, my dear? I want it so much, and I would never let you regret it. It is—for so short a time, though I don't want you to come to me only out of pity.'

'Oh, Mr. Harrow, do you really want it—so much?' she whispered.

'I didn't know how much until after you had gone last night, and I wondered if I had said enough – or too much.'

She was silent, closing her eyes against the tears which so foolishly threatened them. If only she were a modern girl, to meet this thing with the assurance, the jauntiness, which she felt either Miss Wright or Miss Gilbert could have done!

'You will, Janine?' as she stood without answering.

And suddenly she nodded her head and smiled through the tears, groping half-unconsciously for his hand. He was such a dear, and she would give all her life to making up to him for what he was going to do for her, she told herself hysterically.

He lifted her hand to his lips, and at that moment the butler came in, saw them standing like that, and was about to withdraw with a little cough when Harrow called him back.

'Gough, don't go. I want you to drink a toast. Call Mrs. Gough, and bring four glasses and a bottle of that '08 champagne.' And whilst he was gone, Janine stood silent and wondering, scarcely hearing what he said. Did one call in one's household, then, to celebrate the bargain she was making?

The Goughs came back smiling, and Harrow filled the four glasses with the priceless liquid and lifted his own.

'To the second Mrs. Harrow,' he said, and drank with his eyes on the bewildered Janine. 'May she live long and live happily, and may all her dreams come true. Janine, to you, my dear!'

The servants drank with him, and Janine was too confused to see that their glances towards her were friendly and pleased. They had long expected their master to take another wife, and they were relieved that he should choose a young and inexperienced one, rather than one of his own age who would naturally want to relieve a housekeeper of her job. It seemed that Janine herself was the last one to become aware of Richard Harrow's intentions and to her they were a complete amazement.

His wife! Mrs. Harrow! Mistress of this grand house! To marry the senior partner! Mrs. Spilliken! And at that thought she began to giggle helplessly, hysterically, hating herself and yet unable to stop.

Harrow made a sign to the servants, who slipped away quietly and Janine found his arm about her.

'My dear, I have been thoughtless. It has been too upsetting to you. I ought to have waited. Forgive me.'

She leant against him, glad of the support of his arm, spent with the unexpected emotional storm.

'You meant that?' she asked him shakily, at last. 'Your wife? I—I didn't understand.'

'Good heavens, you didn't think I was like that, my dear, did you?' he asked, aghast. 'Haven't you any knowledge of me at all, even now?'

'I'm sorry,' she said. 'It—it's all too—surprising that you should want me like that. I'm not the sort of person anyone like you should marry, Mr. Harrow.'

'You're exactly the sort of person,' he said, with a heartening smile. 'I quite realise that I am not at all the sort *you* ought to marry, though. Youth ought to consort with youth. I know that. It is pure selfishness on my part to marry you, Janine. Only – it isn't for long, and I can give you all the things you are missing and still leave you plenty of your life for love. You seem so extra-ordinarily … innocent that I feel you can afford to wait a few years,' with a smile at her serious, troubled face.

She disclaimed the need or the desire for love.

'I'm not likely to find that even if I do have time,' she said. 'I'm not made that way. I can't imagine why you want to marry me.'

'Perhaps I am a vampire, feeding on your youth and vitality,' he said, half jesting, half in earnest. 'Anyway, I'm not going to let you take back your word even if you want to. Doesn't that prove that I'm a vampire?'

'I don't want to take it back.' she said gravely, 'It's only that I feel you're getting the worst of the bargain.'

'Let me be the judge of that, won't you? In a few minutes I'm going to send you home. You're too tired to go out as I had planned. We'll go another time. During those few minutes, can you make up your mind to marry me in a week hence?'

She gasped.

'A *week!*'

'Why not, if it's going to be done at all? I'm going to tell you the absolute truth, Janine. We'll always do that, won't we? Even if you come to hate me, tell me so rather than let me just grope for the truth.'

'I couldn't ever hate you,' she said, in her earnest fashion. 'How could I when you are so good to me?'

'You've got to live with me if you marry me,' he said grimly. 'That's a very suitable ground for the growth of hatred, as you should know from being employed in a solicitor's office. Still, we'll start as others do, believing everything will be gold and not just tin gilded over. I want it to be gold in actual fact. We're not lovers, Janine, in the ordinary sense, but I care for you very deeply and I believe I can make you happy – but let's be absolutely honest with each other. Agreed?'

She nodded. There was a lump in her throat stopping her speech just then.

'Alright. I'm going to make a start. I'm a sick man, my dear. The man I see in Harley Street is hustling me off on a sea trip straight away. That's why I want you to marry me next week and come with me. We'll go south into the sunshine. Madeira and the Canaries. Further south still if we want to. You'll like that?'

She felt she must be dreaming and she could only nod her head speechlessly again. Of course presently she would wake up and find herself in the hard little bed in Mrs. Mote's top back, with no kind Mr. Harrow, no wedding, no Mansion at Hampstead and no holiday in Madeira. Whilst the dream lasted, though, it was lovely, and she dare not move lest she wake herself.

'You mustn't be foolish about things, dear,' he was saying now. 'You'll want things – clothes and so on. Go to Estelle Moreau in – where is it? I'll look up the address and send it to you. I'll ring her up as well and tell her to see that you get the right things—'

But she realised now that she was awake and stopped him in distress.

'Please don't make me do that, Mr. Harrow. Please! I should feel ... dreadful about it, letting you buy me things.'

'Don't be ridiculous, my child. In a week you'll be my wife, and the law compels me to provide for you then!'

'Don't make me now, though,' she begged him, knowing she was being foolish and yet persisting.

'But you must have things for a sea trip, evening dresses and things,' he said, with a worried frown.

'Let me buy them myself then, please. I—I know I shall have to let you pay for most of it, but give me just a little, for the things I simply must have.'

'Well, I'm not going to start a quarrel already, though I think you're being rather silly about it. How much shall I give you if you won't go to this woman for your things?'

'I don't know,' she said unhappily.

He went to his desk and took out a bundle of notes, counted them carelessly and pushed them into her hand.

'I couldn't possibly take all this, Mr. Harrow!' she said, appalled, trying to thrust them back at him.

'Oh, take it, my dear, and do what you like with it,' he insisted, and she dare not risk his rising anger and tucked the bundle into her bag unhappily.

'Better give notice at the office tomorrow,' he told her. 'There's no need to talk yet. Just hand in your written notice without giving a reason. You need not finish out the week, of course, but go in tomorrow to give proper notice. I shan't come in.'

She overslept the next morning, worn out with hours of thought and worry and regret. How could she have been persuaded to do this mad thing? She remembered the dreams she used to have before she realised that she was not likely to attract a husband, dim and lovely dreams which she had laid aside in lavender but never forgotten. Where were they now? What had she done to them by promising to marry an old man for his money? That was what she had done, of course, and when she slept at last her sleep was troubled with fantastic dreams in which Harrow was by turn a devil, a hobgoblin and an old, old man weighed down by his moneybags over which she struggled in vain to climb.

Miss Wright and Miss Gilbert exchanged meaning glances when she hurried past their desks, and when she had flung off her hat and coat and taken her seat before her own machine she realised that they were talking 'at' her in a friendly, interested fashion which held no malice.

'Comes of late hours, of course,' said Miss Gilbert.

'And wealthy admirers,' said Miss Wright.

'No longer young, but none the less valuable,' added the other.

'You know what they say – an old fiddle plays the sweetest music. Doesn't it, Jane?'

She lifted a flaming face to them. Obviously they knew, but how on earth had it got about already? Surely Mr. Harrow, after telling her not to talk, had not given out the news himself?

'How should I know?' she asked.

The two girls laughed.

'Who better? You've been listening to that music lately, or so they say,' said Miss Wright.

'I don't see that my concerns are of any interest to anyone else,' said Janine hotly.

'Heavens, the child is really upset! Sorry, Jane, my sweet, but if you don't want the world to know, you shouldn't go and sit with him in Rymer's, you really shouldn't!'

She could find nothing to say to that. So they had been seen. Well, it wasn't her fault if they knew, and she was thankful she had been told she need not come to the office after today.

'I'm leaving this week,' she said suddenly.

The two girls gasped.

'Jane! You aren't!'

'I'm going with Mr. Harrow to Madeira,' she said defiantly.

There was a moment's silence. Then Miss Gilbert whistled, and Miss Wright leaned forward and spoke in an altered tone.

'Jane, you're only a kid. Do you really know what you're doing? It is worth it for a good time and furs and pearls and things? He's so old. It won't even be fun.'

'He'll be good to me,' she said quiveringly. I'm … fond of him. He's nice.'

'Yes, but—my dear! What when you come back? What will you do then? Everybody says he won't be able to come back to the office again, and you'll never get another job after that. Don't be a fool, Jane.'

She stared at the speaker, not understanding.

'But I shan't want another job,' she said, puzzled.

'Of course you will. You're such an innocent, trustful kid. They're always going to provide for you for life and all that, but girls don't fall for that sort of thing nowadays, not girls like Gwen and me. He wouldn't have tried it on us. Get what you can out of him, but for the love of Mike don't be such a fool as to chuck up your job and go away with him.'

Suddenly she understood, and rose to her feet, hot and indignant.

'I'm going to marry Mr. Harrow,' she said very distinctly, and walked out of the room, holding in her hand the letter of notice which she had already typed.

Chapter Four

In an ultra-modern room, startling in its bizarre colouring and strangely shaped furniture, a girl lay on a couch smoking from a long, scarlet holder, and a man stood uneasily by the window, which was never closed and through which drifted the intermittent sounds of life in the riverside town on which already the pall of winter had fallen.

The girl was golden and lovely. To the man who watched her moodily from the other side of the room she was perfect. Her hair was of that rare, warm gold of sun ripe corn, and she wore it waved loosely about the delicate oval of a face which an artist might have conceived in a waking dream of beauty. Her deep blue eyes under their accentuated, narrow lines of eyebrow were stormy just now, and one foot in its gilt sandal tapped restlessly on the multi-coloured brocade of the couch covering.

For the millionth time, you're a fool, Terry,' she was saying.

For the million and oneth time, my dear, I know it,' he replied moodily.

She sprang up and came across to him, her mood changing, her arms going round his neck, the loose sleeves of her frock falling open to show their rounded beauty.

'Darling, if you love me, you simply couldn't possibly contemplate leaving me,' she said.

He held her arms with his hands, his fingers tightening until she told herself, subconsciously, that tomorrow there would be bruises on them. Tonight that was too small a thing to matter. What did matter was that Terry was leaving her, or would leave her if he could.

'My sweet, it's because I do love you that I have the strength and the sense to leave you,' he told her unsteadily. 'And if I did as you ask, if I stayed and let myself marry you and live on you, we should both of us lose the very thing we're trying to keep – our mutual love and respect.'

'Respect! *Respect!* My God, what a lukewarm mixture of emotion! I don't want you to respect me, Terry. I want you to love me, to hold me and take me and keep me – never to let me go,' and she wound her arms more closely about him as if she would force his will to hers.

His face grew more white and strained, and the two lines which had recently begun to etch themselves from his nostrils to his firm mouth seemed to dig more deeply into his skin. His eyes, eyes of that mixture of blue and green and brown that goes to make up hazel, narrowed, and his fingers loosed a little of their grip. He was so determined that she should not win what she wanted, but the effort to resist her was almost killing him. She was so lovely, so desirable, and he had loved her for so long, waited for her so hopefully, until hope had been ground down and crushed and beaten.

'Darling, you make it so hard for me,' he told her in a low voice.

She wrenched herself free, her eyes blazing again, though they had been so soft a moment since.

'It's you who make it hard for yourself, you and your wretched god-forsaken pride!' she stormed.

'Would you really have me without it?' he asked her with a weary little smile. 'Have we got to go over it all again, my dear? We've thrashed it out so many times, and I came here tonight to—to have a few last hours with you before I go, not to wrangle and fight with you and go over the thing again. It's done, dearest. It's quite final. I'm taking this job on, as far as Madeira, anyway, and if I'm lucky enough to get what I want out of Ferrida, it will mean only six months, a year at the outside, before I can ask you to come out to me, if you will.'

'Terry, I've waited for you for two solid years, and I'm telling you right now that I'm not waiting any longer. Either you give up this fool scheme of working your way out to Madeira and taking up some potty job for a dago, or you go for good as far as I am concerned,' she said, and her voice was as cool and decided as her actions as she fitted a fresh cigarette into the scarlet holder, lit it from a tiny lamp which burnt constantly on the tiny gold lacquered table, and set it between lips grown hard and cold.

'Do you mean that?' he asked quietly.

'Yes.'

'That if I go, I must never come back?'

'Not to me, anyway. Please be quite clear what you are doing. Terry, before you do it. You know me, or you ought to by now. When I am determined on a course of action I go straight for it and let nothing – *nothing* – stand in my way.'

'Not even ... love?'

'My dear Terry, we're moderns, you and I. We don't go into declines, or fade away, or something like that when we can't get the jungle mate we want. We just take stock sensibly of what's left, and pick again.'

'Meaning that it would actually not hurt you at all if I were to go and never come back?'

'Well, it would hurt for a time, but I shouldn't let it get me down. For instance, if you go off to Madeira tomorrow, I shall at once book a world tour, or a geographical expedition to study the bird life of the North Pole, or join a mission to the Booia-Booia Islands and teach them to knit pullovers or something. When I am quite cured, and could hear the name of Terry Forder without batting an eyelid or losing a heartbeat, I shall come back. That's all. Simple, you see!'

He came and stood beside the couch on which she had flung herself again.

'I wonder if you are really like that or only pretending to be?' he asked.

'I'm like it.' Then she sprang up and leant against him, her head on his shoulder, the fingers of one hand threading themselves in between his.

'Darling, don't make me have to be like it,' she said. 'Stay with me, Terry. Stay now – tonight. Mrs. Tuck thinks we have gone over the border long ago, so she won't be at all scandalised to find you here in the morning, and you can marry me any old time. I shan't worry once I've got you.'

'I wouldn't do that to you. You know that,' he said stiffly.

She rubbed her cheek against his.

'So virtuous, my sweet?' she said.

He crushed her for an instant in his arms and let her go so suddenly that she fell back on the couch and lay there looking up at him, half afraid, half exultant, seeing the side of him she had so often tried to rouse in vain.

'Do you think I'm virtuous? I'm not. I'm just like other men. I've as much knowledge and experience as most men – but I'm not taking you unless I've married you. I love you. You're more than the sun and the moon and the stars to me. You're more than my life.'

'And yet you won't give up your own way to get me, Terry,' she broke in softly.

'It's more than my own way you're asking me to give up, Joy. It's everything that makes a man – self-respect and decency and tradition.'

'You can still keep your self-respect as my husband.'

'Perhaps, but not as your … gigolo, my sweet.'

She recognised the utter inflexibility that set that tone in his voice, and she turned her head away from him and traced with a careful finger the pattern on the couch cover.

'Alright. You'd better go, hadn't you?' she said, in a cool little voice.

He stood with his hands clenching and unclenching at his sides, his eyes taking in every last detail of her – the way her silky hair folded itself at the back of her head, the little baby tendrils carefully cultivated by her ears, the smooth satin of her skin, her nose small and fine, her lips pencilled with bizarre crimson.

That one look he took to cherish. Then without another word he left her, and she did not even know he had gone until the silence of the room, its chill feeling of emptiness, struck her and she turned to find herself alone.

She rose to her feet and stood quite still for a moment, her lips a little indrawn, her eyes closing as if in sudden, intolerable pain. Then she went across the room steadily and turned on the radio, fiddling with the knobs until the medley of screeches resolved themselves into the strains of a dance band.

'And that … is that,' she said aloud, slowly and thoughtfully. 'Definitely.'

And Terry Forder was finding his way blindly through the well-known, narrow streets with their smell of the river and their background of dark and silent boat-houses.

He was seeing them probably for the last time, but there was no consciousness in his mind of anything save that he had seen Joy for the last time – Joy who for more than two years had filled his waking thoughts and idled through his dreams, thrilling him when he was away from her, intoxicating him in every minute of every hour spent with her.

And there had been so many hours. That was just it. She had filled more than his thoughts. She had filled his actual time, days and weeks and months, and so he had pictured her filling the years ahead. Life without her was unthinkable, and as he found his way to the dimly lit station to wait for one of the dawdling, infrequent trains he groaned in spirit.

Almost he could have turned back, taken her in his arms, promised her anything so that he could keep her there. She had asked him to stay there that night. She might have been in his arms now, intimately as she had never been, and in the morning have been so wholly his that nothing could ever part them. Fool to have left her!

He paced the platform, forcing his feet to stay upon it and not take him back to her. Tomorrow, he knew, he would regret bitterly the chains which, if he went back, would bind him for ever. Was he so weak that he would sell his birth right of self- honour for the sake of possessing a woman, even if she be Joy?

He wrenched his thoughts away from her and began to think of the future. Two years ago he had been in a promising position, a partner in a firm of launch-builders. That was how it came about that Joy had taken a flat near the river, the idea being that they would share it when they were married.

Then, twelve months ago, the firm had gone bankrupt. Terry had lost all his small capital through the imprudence and wild speculation of his partners, but even greater than that blow was the knowledge that he had to share with them a certain amount of mud which was flung, and justly flung, at the firm.

Fiercely proud of his integrity, he had had to bear the blow as best he could, and the first rift with Joy had been his utter refusal to let her do as she suggested and bolster up the firm's credit with her considerable means. They weathered that storm, however, only to find another breaking about them, for as the weeks turned into months Terry realised that, at twenty-eight, he stood very little chance of getting a job without influence or money and without any knowledge save of a moribund trade.

Joy did what she could in the way of recommendations to her friends, pleas on his behalf, letters of introduction. No one seemed to want him in any capacity, and at last, down to bedrock, he had had to face the fact that he and Joy must part, for a time at any rate. In vain she stormed, pleaded, promised, threatened. He refused utterly to marry her until he was at least earning his own living. He would not be a parasite on anyone, he told her, least of all on a woman.

And ten days ago had come an invitation from Pedro Ferrida, a friend of Varsity days, to join him in a wine-making business which he had inherited in Madeira and which he intended to turn into a paying concern. Ferrida had believed Terry to possess some small capital, but that had been swallowed up in the smash, and he had written frankly to the Spaniard saying he was working his way out to Madeira in any case and hoped he could be allowed to invest his brains and muscle in the business in lieu of hard cash.

To Joy's fury and disgust, he had refused to take from her even the cost of his ticket, and had got a job as a cabin steward on a ship which called at Madeira. Through it all, be had never seriously believed that Joy would throw him over. She seemed a part of his life and he had believed himself as indissolubly a part of hers.

Yet here he was, treading the familiar unlovely platform for the last time –having said goodbye to her for the last time – hearing still her declaration that if he went this time he would never be allowed to come back.

The train came in and he took his weary, hopeless thoughts with him to the cheap hotel in which he had been living, spending his last ten pounds on the outfit which the shipping company had demanded. He hoped to sell it again when he reached Madeira, but he had drawn the line at buying a second-hand outfit, as a kindly fellow-steward had advised him to do.

He looked at the white coats and aprons, but tonight they gave him none of the amusement he had had previously out of them. Was he a fool or a hero? Was anything in this world or the next worth losing Joy for?

He packed his clothes moodily, denying himself the luxury of taking even a snapshot of Joy with him. If he must cut her out of his life, he must do the job cleanly and thoroughly. So into the fire went everything connected with her – letters, photographs, silly little souvenirs potent to wound. Then he went to bed and slept, waking the next morning to the realisation that for a week, at least, he was T. Forder, cabin steward on board S.S. *Venturer.*

That was a week before Janine Wilson was married to Richard Harrow.

Chapter Five

Janine stood on the deck and watched her husband fussily giving orders as to the disposal of their luggage. Seasoned travellers were not always good travellers she had already discovered, and she had seen with surprise how much the train journey from London to Liverpool had upset him. In vain she had told him more than once that Bennett had actually seen the pieces of their luggage put into the van. He had to go the whole length of the train, through swaying, rocking carriages, across gangways which frightened her by moving as she trod on them, merely in order to find the luggage van and personally satisfy himself that his own wardrobe trunk, his dressing-bag, the bundle of rugs and Janine's one suitcase were on the train.

They lunched later, and the meal was a nightmare to Janine because he had been nervous and moody and she was not accustomed to eating and drinking when everything swayed and swung all the time.

Whilst they had waited to go on board, he slipped a hand through her arm.

'Sorry, Janine,' he said in a low voice, and her face cleared as if by magic. She pressed his hand against her side and held it there, feeling oddly comforted in being asked for comfort. If only she could do something for him, she would not feel so badly about having married him.

And now they were actually on board the big white ship, and her feet in their new shoes trod the deck and her hand in its new gold band held the rail. She was married. She was Mrs. Richard Harrow. That tubby, fussy little man along there was her husband. Janine

Wilson had gone for ever. She had a name of her own. She was Janine Harrow.

A deck steward passed her, paused and came back.

'Anything I can do for you, miss?' he asked. 'Have you found your cabin?'

'No, not yet. My—Mr, Harrow is seeing about the luggage,' indicating the spot on the lower deck which still held that fidgety little figure.

'No need at all for that, miss,' said the deck steward indulgently. 'If the gentleman will just find his own cabin, the stewards will see that everything gets there safely. What is your number?'

'I don't know. I haven't the tickets,' she said helplessly.

'I'll go and find out for you, miss. Name?'

'Wii—no, Harrow,' she corrected herself hastily,

'Two cabins?'

'I—I don't know,' said Janine again, and the steward looked at her curiously. Surely she did not imagine that on-board ship one had to share a cabin with one's parent of the other sex?

He looked at her quite differently when he returned after an illuminating interview with the irascible old gentleman on the lower deck.

'This way, madam,' he said to Janine, and she wondered if she only fancied the look of something like contempt he gave her when he left her with the steward who escorted her to her cabin.

Harrow had engaged a suite on the most expensive deck, with two bedrooms, sitting-room and bathroom all adjoining, and here she was left, feeling lost and forlorn, until her husband came to her, hot and tired.

'That sailor who came to me said the stewards would have done all that,' she told him anxiously.

'That wasn't a sailor. That was a deck steward,' he told her testily. 'Anyway, I prefer to see to things myself.'

'I'm afraid it's made you very tired though,' she ventured. Mrs. Gough told me particularly that you ought not to be allowed to get tired.'

He dropped into a chair with a sigh of relief.

'Bother that woman! I'm not a child now. I'm a married man!' – with a smile and a sudden return to the old kindly way she loved. 'I've made your first journey with me trying, my dear, but I'll make up for it when I've got over this. I think I'll lie down and rest for a bit. I'll have some food sent in to me here, but you go down to dinner and enjoy yourself.'

'Oh, Mr. Harrow. I couldn't!' she said in alarm.

'Janine, you really must not call me that,' he reminded her with a smile.

'Well—Richard, then,' with a nervous little laugh. She felt she would never use his name without a feeling that she was being impertinent to her employer. 'Please let me have dinner here with you. I couldn't go down amongst all those strange people. I should be terrified.'

'Nonsense! It will do you good. You're a married lady now, you know. There are only four at a table. You'll be quite alright. Will you let me be alone now for an hour, my dear? I shall take a dose of that new medicine and get a sleep.'

She wandered back to her own cabin and found her stewardess there waiting to know if there was anything she wanted.

'They don't dress the first night as a rule, madam,' she was told. 'I've brought hot water for you, though, and dinner will be at half past six tonight instead of seven. Can I do anything else for you?'

'No, thank you. My—Mr. Harrow is having something in his cabin. I suppose I couldn't do the same, just for tonight?'

The woman smiled sympathetically. She judged Janine to be on her honeymoon, from her new suitcase, her obviously new clothes and her difficulty in mentioning her husband. So far she had not seen Harrow.

'I should go down if I were you, madam. The steward will see to your husband, but it's much jollier and brighter to go down to the dining saloon the first night and get to know people.'

So down at last she went, still in the cheap little grey suit in which she had been married, though she had unpacked and hung in the wardrobe the few plain, inexpensive dresses, which were all she had been able to persuade herself to buy with Harrow's money.

One glance at the crowded saloon made her shiver. Few of the women were in evening dress, but everyone seemed well and expensively clad in their travelling-dresses, or in dark afternoon gowns, with furs slung round their shoulders, and a general air of well-being and assurance about them. She felt like a little grey field-mouse strayed into an aviary as she went shyly to the place allotted to her and returned the noncommittal greetings of the two already at the table, a middle-aged couple who soon became engrossed in their food and in the occupants of the neighbouring table, whom they had apparently met on a previous cruise.

Janine chose at random and swallowed with difficulty, leaving the table as soon as she dared and going back to their staterooms, only to find that Harrow had gone to bed, leaving a message for her that she was to enjoy herself and that he would feel alright by the morning.

She went back to the deck, almost deserted whilst people were unpacking in their cabins, and walked about feeling utterly forlorn. This was her wedding night!

A man strolling by gave her a friendly smile, and she froze him instantly, not realising that on board a cruising ship the passengers consider themselves in need of no formal introduction. He shrugged his shoulders and thereafter avoided her though later she regretted her hasty refusal of his overture. He was one of those invaluable members of a cruising party who could and would do anything – organising sports, finding the right people for the various jobs, playing deck tennis or completing a hand of bridge or whist, entertaining a select few with ribald songs at the piano, holding wool for old ladies or holding hands with young ones in the quiet of the after-dinner decks.

No one else attempted to speak to her that evening, though several glanced at her curiously, noting her dull little grey suit and serviceable but scarcely suitable shoes, catching perhaps a surprising glimpse of the magnificent diamond solitaire which Harrow had that morning placed on her finger above her wedding ring and which she thought she ought to wear rather than leave in the cabin. It frightened and troubled her with its size and value. It would be just her luck to lose it, she thought unhappily.

She went to bed before nine, but the noise on the deck, the band and dancing, the passing to and fro, kept her awake, but at last the ship was quiet and she was surprised to wake up and find it morning.

She hesitated when she was dressed, feeling that she ought to go and see how her husband was and yet embarrassed at the thought of going to his room. In the end, she sent a message by the stewardess, regretting her decision as soon as she saw the curious expression on the woman's face. She flushed and drew back, realising that it was a look bordering on contempt. She must know by now, of course, that her bridegroom was elderly and in failing health and, from the fact that he could engage the most expensive suite on the ship, undoubtedly wealthy.

The woman returned with the message that Mr. Harrow had passed a fair night, and would be glad if Mrs. Harrow would call and see him when she had breakfasted.

Breakfast was more or less a repetition of dinner as far as her companions were concerned. They appeared to know many of the officers and some of the passengers, and Janine, pale, shy and aloof, found herself isolated amongst what was almost a family party, with comings and goings between the tables, friendly calls across the room, exchange of recollections, discussions on the itinerary and so on.

One of the officers who had been called to the table as he came to breakfast turned in a friendly fashion to the pale, quiet girl and tried to interest her in the daily tote on the ship's run, but Janine, bound still by the habit of a lifetime of poverty, shook her head when invited to put her shilling with the rest.

'I don't gamble,' she said, and her very nervousness made her seem chilling and prudish.

'A very mild gamble, Mrs. Harrow,' said the woman at the table, Mrs. Marsh.

'I'd—rather not,' persisted Janine in a further access of shyness, and the young officer shrugged his shoulders and turned away.

As soon as she could, she left the table and went to see her husband, knocking uncertainly at the door, and entering with a rising colour. He was still in bed, an unfamiliar figure in his striped pyjamas, his few ends of greyish hair standing out round his cars.

'How are you, Richard?' she asked shyly.

He held out his hand to her, and she went to him and hid her own in his.

'I am feeling a bit better this morning, my dear, but the doc. thinks I had better stay here for today, anyway. The journey in the train must have upset me a bit. I shall be alright long before we reach Madeira, though. Too bad for you, isn't it? A lonely bride, my Janine.'

'I don't mind so long as you get better,' she said gently, wishing she did not hate the feel of his rather clammy hand on hers. 'What is there I can do for you?'

'Very little, my dear, except go out and about and enjoy yourself. I expect there are dozens of nice young men on board, and you won't find me the jealous old husband if you dance with them and enjoy yourself, you know.'

'I'd rather stay here with you Richard,' she said wistfully.

'I shouldn't dream of it, my dear.'

Suddenly she laid her cheek down on his hand. He wanted to give so much, to ask nothing. She felt abased because she had not wanted him to hold her hand.

'You're so good to me, Richard, Let me do something for you – anything, please!'

'But what is there to do?' with a smiling glance round the neat little room which the steward had already placed in perfect order.

'There aren't even any letters to answer, because, thank heaven, there isn't any post.'

'I could read to you,' she suggested desperately, wanting both to do something for him and to be provided with an excuse for not going alone on deck again.

He humoured her, though secretly he wanted to be left alone.

'That would be charming of you. I was reading Emerson's essay on demonology. That little green book on the shelf. I don't know that his ideas are particularly modern, but I'm not particularly modern myself, and I enjoy his choice of words.'

She found the book and its marker and began to read, but the subject and its treatment were beyond her understanding, and she could not do as she tried to do when reading to herself, rereading a passage or a sentence as many as a dozen times until she thought she had grasped the meaning. Hence her reading was disjointed, sometimes wrongly phrased, revealing her want of comprehension as she floundered along.

He stopped her at last, with a kindly hand on her arm.

'Thank you, my dear. Perhaps I could sleep a little now, and you ought to be out in the fresh air.'

She closed the book.

'I don't read well enough, do I?' she asked wistfully.

'Well, it was a dull subject for you, wasn't it? Next time we must choose something brighter. Look in again later, won't you? Then yon can tell me what you have been doing.'

She left him and wandered away, humiliated by her lack of success with the only thing he had required of her. Everybody seemed to have something to do and someone with whom to do it. The weather was still cold, and people were either playing vigorous games or sitting in their steamer chairs muffled in fur coats and rugs. Janine did not know even how to secure a chair and she caught sight of the deck steward who had helped her the day before.

He came to her.

'Shall I get you a chair, madam? I am afraid all the best places on the deck have gone, but I could get a chair in further along.'

'By myself, please,' she said shrinkingly, and he established her in an unfrequented part of the promenade deck, gave her a cushion, tucked her firmly in with a rug, found her a magazine and left her.

As she watched the people passing and re-passing, she longed with all her soul to be of them instead of merely with them. They must have been strangers for the most part yesterday, just as she was a stranger, and yet they all seemed to know one another now. She listened to the gay chatter and badinage, marvelling how they thought of the things to say, trying to make up things like them in case she ever had a chance to say them. She watched the tactics of a pretty girl who was endeavouring to annex for herself the best-looking man on board, and before the luncheon bugle sounded they were strolling round the deck with his arm thrust through hers, her pretty face glowing and vivacious.

How did they do it? Janine had no conception how they even began.

An odd-looking little man, middle-aged, with very bad teeth, came and took an empty chair next to hers, gave her a casual glance and felt in his pocket for pipe and pouch.

Don't mind if I smoke pipe, miss?' he asked her with a strong Lancashire accent, and she gave him a frigid negative, though she had made up her mind to practise talking some of those frothy nothings on the first person who spoke to her.

The little man made no attempt to say any more, but when his pipe was alight he got up and strolled away, and a little later Janine saw him in deep conversation with a girl who was evidently pleased with whatever fish she could catch. Well, she, Janine, would have been pleased, too, by the end of that morning, and she was resolved that she would spend the rest of the time until Harrow was about in her own cabin or in their little sitting-room.

She peeped at him after lunch, but he was asleep, and she stayed in the sitting-room until she heard him move and then went in to him.

For an hour or so they talked, and then he made her go and dress for dinner.

'Put on one of your new evening dresses, my dear, and let me see you in it,' and she had to do so, though she had toyed with the idea of going to bed with a headache.

She had brought only one evening dress, a cheap little affair of black satin which did not suit her.

'I like you better in the pink one,' was his comment, and she realised that she had made a mistake again. The girl in the shop had tried to dissuade her from having black, saying it made her look older and sallow, but she had insisted, feeling that she would be inconspicuous in black,

'I shall be up tomorrow, dear, I hope,' he said. 'You'd better not come in again as I have a sleeping draught to take and may go off straight away.'

'Shall I give it to you?' asked Janine, and she did so, spilling some of it as she carried it to him.

'Oh, I'm so sorry!' she said.

'Never mind. The ship's rolling a bit tonight. That was only one dose, though, so perhaps on the way down you had better see if the doctor is in his surgery and ask him to send me up a little more.'

The doctor was surprised when he saw her and she told him who she was, and again she saw, or fancied she saw, that same look of veiled scorn in his eyes. Of course they all thought she had married him for his money – and it was true! That was the horrible part of it. She *had* married him for that, and that only.

'Do you know much of the history of your husband's illness, Mrs. Harrow? I understand you have not been married long.'

'No, I—I don't really know how ill he is. Is it serious?' she asked.

He looked at her gravely. In other circumstances he might have hesitated at telling a bride the actual facts, but he felt that this was a case when he could be blunt. Obviously the girl had married him for what she could get out of him, and no doubt she could feel she was getting an even better deal than she had anticipated when she realised how ill Harrow was.

'I am afraid it is. He ought to have given up his work months ago, of course. Now it is probably too late.'

'Too late!' she echoed, with blanching face and wide eyes. 'You don't mean he—he isn't going to get better?'

He shrugged his shoulders.

'Well, no one can answer a question like that, of course, but his own doctor sent me a record of his case, and I am inclined to agree with his opinion that there is very little we can do. I am afraid this is rather a … shock to you, Mrs. Harrow,' regretting a little that he had taken it for granted she would be relieved. She certainly seemed quite upset about it.

'Yes, it is,' she said. 'You see, we—we were only married yesterday. Does Mr. Harrow know?'

'I don't think so. Anyway, we may be mistaken, and certainly a sea trip with its perfect rest has been known to work miracles.'

'Is there anything I can do for him?' asked Janine shakily.

'Very little, except keep him cheerful, talk to him, read to him, play games with him if he likes, cards and so on. I wouldn't play chess or draughts or anything to tax his mind too much.'

'He doesn't want any actual nursing, you mean?'

'Oh no. If he does, we have a nurse on board, you know, so don't worry about that.'

She went down to dinner, but could not eat anything, and soon afterwards the ship struck rough weather, and she had no choice but to go down to her cabin, where she was terribly sick. The stewardess looked after her, and during the evening the doctor looked in after he had been to see his patient in the next room.

'This is what's happened to the plans for cheering up my husband,' she said to him with an uncertain smile.

'Never mind. He's sleeping peacefully. You'll be alright again tomorrow. I'll send you some tablets.'

But the next day she felt even worse. The ship was in the Bay of Biscay by now, and though the stewardess told her cheerfully that the Bay was never as bad as it was reputed to be, Janine became steadily worse. Harrow came in to see her during the day, but she could not even speak to him, and all he could do for her was to leave her. He had done himself no good by leaving his bed, and his temperature began to soar again.

On the Monday Janine saw a nurse going through the sitting-room and called to her.

'Is it my husband? Is he worse?' she asked.

'Well, he isn't really a great deal worse, but the doctor thought that whilst the ship is rolling like this, someone ought to be with him, especially as you are *hors de combat*!' – with a smile at her haggard, greenish face.

'I ought to be with him,' she whispered. 'It's my job, isn't it?' The nurse gave her a reassuring smile.

'I shouldn't worry about that if I were you. We shall be out of the rough weather tomorrow or the next day, and then you'll be able to take over your own job,' and she bustled away.

Certainly the next day brought calmer seas, and Janine was able to join the white-faced, staggering procession on their way to their first meal for some days.

Harrow was sleeping, and though she had gone twice to his cabin door, the nurse cautioned her and seemed as if she wanted her not to go in, so she had wandered off again disconsolately. She idled away the rest of the day, reading in her corner of the deck, and as no one spoke to her or took any notice of her, she spent the hours quite alone and was thankful when she could reasonably go to bed.

Harrow was awake, and called to her when he heard her in her cabin. She went in, alarmed to see how white and ill he looked. His round face was growing almost thin, and he looked an old man now.

'I've called two or three times, but the nurse thought I had better not disturb you,' she said gently. 'How do you feel now?'

'Better tonight now that the sea's calmer,' he assured her with a smile. 'I have been so distressed at knowing you were under the weather and not being able to do anything for you, my dear. You aren't likely to have another turn of it, though, if that's any consolation.'

'Oh, I'm alright now. I felt such an idiot, specially when I ought to have been in here looking after you.'

The stiff skirts of the nurse rustled behind her.

'Not too long, Mrs. Harrow,' she said pleasantly, but with the voice of authority.

'Nurse is a regular martinet, Janine,' he said.

Janine seized the opportunity of a whispered word to him whilst the nurse was emptying his hot-water bottle in the bathroom.

'Can't you get rid of her and let me nurse you now, Richard?' she begged him.

He was touched and grateful, but he shook his head.

'I'm not going to keep you cooped up in here, my dear,' he said. 'Besides, it's her job, and it isn't nearly as much work to her as it would be to you.'

The nurse came back and stood by the bed, obviously waiting for Janine to go.

'My wife wants to give you the sack and do the job herself, Nurse,' he said. 'I've told her to enjoy herself instead.'

'Do let me, just for a little while,' said Janine pleadingly. 'Does someone have to stop up with him tonight?'

'One of the stewardesses offered so that I could sleep at night,' was the grudging reply.

The nurse had her own ideas about this helpless-looking girl her patient had for some extraordinary reason married.

'Please let me do it. I can, really, if you'll tell me what there is to do,' begged Janine.

'Well, there's really nothing to do, except see that Mr. Harrow is comfortable and take his temperature if he wakes round about midnight. He can have a dose of this white medicine then as well but he need not be awakened for it.'

'I can do that,' said Janine.

'You understand how to take a temperature?'

'Well, you could show me,' said Janine, and when the nurse explained the reading of a clinical thermometer, she dare not say she could not see the little column of mercury, but nodded her head and promised herself a 'good look at the thing' when they were alone.

'If it is above a hundred and one, no matter how little above it, the doctor wants to be told immediately. This bell has been made to connect directly with his cabin, and if you ring it, he will come at once.'

Janine swallowed and nodded, and presently she was alone with her husband.

He lay with closed eyes, his hand in hers, but presently he opened his eyes to look at her.

'I haven't given you much of a deal, my dear, have I?' he asked.

'Don't think about me, Richard. I only want you to get well quickly.'

'I shan't do that … very quickly, Janine. It's my own fault. I ought to have given in months ago. But if I had, I might have missed knowing you—really knowing you, that is. Isn't it odd to think that we have been in the same office for a year, and yet I never realised it until that night you came to Hampstead with those schedules?'

'Very badly done,' put in Janine ruefully.

He held her hand against his cheek.

'What does it matter? Your hands are much more useful to me than when they tapped a typewriter for me.'

'They haven't been so far,' she told him.

'Look what they're doing for me now! We're going to have a wonderful time when I can get about again, child. The doctor won't swear to me that I can go ashore at Madeira, but I think he means to patch me up by then. We are due there on Sunday.'

'You won't be walking about by then,' she said.

'Well, we're only putting in there for a few hours and calling again on the way back, so if I can't take you ashore on Sunday, I shall surely be able to do so on the return journey. Ever since I first talked to you about Madeira – do you remember? – I have looked forward to showing it to you – the flowers and the birds – and the trees.'

'I remember. Pepper trees, mimosa, and tamarisk, and geraniums growing in the hedges,' said Janine.

'We'll see it together, darling,' he said.

She flushed at the endearment. No one had ever called her love names. The word sounded oddly on the pale lips of an old man when her dreams had made her hear it from young and virile lips.

'You mustn't talk any more, Richard, or your temperature will go up, and I know I shall never be able to read that funny little thing. I couldn't see what she called the column, though it must have been there.'

He smiled and turned his head more comfortably on the pillow.

'Turn off the bed-light, dear, and put on the other. Nurse has rigged up a screen so that it won't be in my eyes, and you can sit in the armchair and read. When I wake, I shall love to see you there. Good night.'

His eyes seemed to ask her something his lips dare not say, and, nerving herself to the task, she bent and kissed his cheek.

'Good night, Richard,' she said gently.

'That was nice of you, Janine. Good night, my dear. God bless you.'

She adjusted the lights and settled herself in the comfortable chair to read, but she was too comfortable, and she found herself dozing, so she changed chairs and sat in a high-backed wooden one, trying to keep her thoughts on the light novel she had found in the reading-room. Now and then she glanced at her husband, who seemed to be sleeping, and as the clock ticked the night away she prayed that he would not wake so that she would not have to take his temperature.

Her prayers were unanswered, for just after midnight he stirred, opened his eyes and spoke in a queer, unfamiliar tone.

It's very close. Open the window wider.'

She came to him and looked down at him anxiously.

" Are you sure you won't be cold?' she asked.

'Open the window,' he said again, and she pushed the porthole glass wider.

Midnight. She would simply have to take his temperature. She drew the thermometer from its case with shaking hands and slipped it in his mouth as she had seen the nurse do. His lips would not close round it, though she begged him to make them do so, and in the end she had to hold the glass tube under his tongue whilst she guessed the necessary seconds.

When she had taken it from him, she held it near the light, peered at it this way and that, screwed her eyes up, twisted her head in all directions, but no silver column could she see.

She laid it down, measured out the white medicine and gave it to Harrow, who seemed very hot but inclined to sleep again, and after another futile effort with the thermometer, she put it back in its case as a bad job. After all, he was asleep again, and the nurse had said his temperature need not be taken if he did not wake. No one would know that she had had to take it.

She settled herself in the hard chair again, but gradually her head dropped, and at last she rested her arms on the table, laid her head on them and slept.

She awakened with a start to find the cabin full of people. The doctor was bending over the bed, and the nurse stood beside him holding a tray on which were a basin and some instruments. Another man was at the end of the bed working something like a pump, which made a hissing noise as his hand moved up and down. All three were in dressing-gowns, and all the lights were turned on, proving to her startled senses that it was still night.

'What is it?' she asked, starting up and joining the group at the bed.

The nurse put her finger to her lips, and the man at the pump said, 'Don't talk, please,' in a quick, authoritative tone.

The doctor raised his head at last and dropped into a basin something he had been using.

'Alright,' he said briefly, and the pump was silent.

The three gave sighs of relief, and the nurse put the tray down on the table and said something to a steward who had been standing by the door. He nodded and went away quickly.

'Better go and dress now, Nurse,' said the doctor. 'Thorn and I will stay here whilst you do so.'

'Sure you can manage? I'll tell Mrs. Watson to keep within call.'

'Don't be too long. And bring another cylinder from the surgery in case,' said the doctor.

None of them took the slightest notice of Janine, and, after a moment's miserable hesitation, she followed the nurse out on to the deck.

'Do tell me what happened, Nurse. Can't you see I must know?' she asked urgently.

The nurse paused for a moment, her face and voice polite but ice-cold.

'Your husband nearly died half an hour ago,' she said. 'Why didn't you ring for the doctor as I told you?'

'I didn't know he was worse,' said Janine, white-lipped.

'Then how is it that the thermometer registered nearly a hundred and five when you took his temperature?' asked the girl.

Janine shivered.

'I—I couldn't read it,' she whispered.

"Well, it's a good thing I happened to wake and came along to see if you wanted anything. I found you asleep and your husband obviously very ill. When I looked at the thermometer to see if it was alright before using it, I found it at 104.7 and rang for the doctor. He inserted a tube and gave him oxygen.'

'I—' began Janine miserably, but the nurse cut her short.

'I can't stop and talk now. I've got to dress and go back,' she said curtly.

'But what can I do?' asked Janine.

'Keep out of the way,' said the nurse cruelly, and the poor little bride crept to her cabin and cried herself sick again.

All next day she found her different efforts at seeing Harrow frustrated. It was clear that everyone concerned intended to keep her out, and some sort of warped tale must have gone round the passengers, for when she ventured on deck, or into the dining saloon, curious and hostile eyes followed her.

At the end of the day she discovered what they thought they knew. She was standing in a shadowy part of the lower deck, feeling forlorn and wretched, and a man and woman came to stand near her and lean over the rail, watching the phosphorescent water. They were oblivious of the fact that they had an eavesdropper, and Janine was in such a position that she could not have moved away without passing them closely.

'Seen the happy bride tonight?' asked the girl.

'Saw her at dinner,' said the man.

'How she can eat anything at all is more than I can understand. I'd be sick with shame if I were in her shoes. That poor old man! Their stewardess, Mrs. Watson, is mine as well, and she says Mr. Marrow is a dear old chap, so kind and so nice to everyone, and dotes on that little beast.'

'You know, Betty, she might not have meant to do it,' ventured the man, obviously uncomfortable in the conversation.

'Bunk! Why else should she have married him at all, if not to get rid of him at the first opportunity? All very nice and clever. Marries him, gets him to bring her on a cruise, though Mrs. Watson says the doctor says he ought never to have started in his state of health. Of course he's worse, and she practically forces the nurse to let her stop up the night with him, and then lets him almost die and never calls for help, though there is a bell right to the doctor's cabin and the steward within call all night.'

'Still, it might have been unintentional, you know. She's been sea-sick, and she was probably feeling played out. You did yourself you know, Bet.'

'I know I did. But I didn't insist on playing nurse the next night to an old man who was nearly dying, did I?'

'Oh, never mind. The poor kid's got enough to put up with, I expect, without us running her down behind her back. Come and dance. They're playing "Katinka".'

Janine stood rooted to the spot, every pulse in her body throbbing with exquisite agony. That was what they thought, then! That she had brought her husband here, a sick man, and hoped that he would die, tried to make him die! How vile of them … how utterly vile!

She watched the water gleaming in the ribbon of moonlight, and wished she had the courage to jump and end it all, but she knew with a sick appreciation of herself that she would never have the courage to do that. People talked of suicides as cowards, but she knew now they weren't.

Someone came near her, paused for a moment, and then spoke to her. It was one of the stewards. He had recognised her and wondered if she were about to do that very thing she had longed to do. After all, everyone knew about her, he imagined, and she must feel pretty cheap, but he wasn't going to have the cruise spoilt for the rest of the passengers by anybody jumping overboard, though that was probably the best place for her.

'Evening's getting chilly now, madam,' he ventured. 'It isn't wise to stay on deck without a coat, or something warm on.'

She turned to him, grateful for the sound of a human voice to break her miserable thoughts.

'Does it matter?' she asked him bitterly.

'Well, most people think so,' he told her with a smile, and as he evidently had no intention of leaving until she moved, she thanked him wearily and went to her cabin.

In the rest of the suite was perfect silence. Out of consideration for the sick man, who was too ill to be moved to the ship's hospital, the orchestra was playing for dancing on another deck, and there was scarcely a sound to disturb the quiet of the night save the soft plop of the water against the ship. She bent to listen at the door, and heard the faint chink of a medicine bottle as it was set down on the table.

'Richard,' she whispered. 'Richard!' But she dare not let her voice be heard in that room where, once more and so terribly, she had proved how useless she was, even to the man to whom she owed so much.

My dear, I'd give my life for you,' she whispered brokenly, in a passion of gratitude and remorse.

But Richard Harrow lay in the blessed calm of sleep and did not even know she was there.

Chapter Six

Not until the morning of the day when they were scheduled to reach Madeira was Janine allowed to see her husband again, and it was a very chastened and remorseful girl who stood looking at the mere ghost of the man she had married.

He held out his hand to her with his customary kindly smile, a smile specially reserved for her.

'Hullo, dear stranger,' he said in a weak voice.

'Are you feeling better, Richard dear?' she asked fearfully. To her horrified gaze he looked as if he were dying.

'A lot, my dear, thanks to all the kind people to whom I have been such a bother,' with a smile at the nurse who hovered near, obviously not intending to leave husband and wife alone. 'How are things with you? Making the best of your unsatisfactory honeymoon? I'm afraid it's dull for you, dear, unless you're busy making nice friends. Are you?'

She shook her head. If only the nurse would go away, she felt she could say so much to him, tell him of her contrition, of her passionate desire that he should get well. Beneath that hard, chilling gaze she could say nothing but the merest banalities.

'I don't want to make friends,' she said in a low voice. 'I have been too anxious about you.'

'That's nonsense, my dear. There's no reason why you shouldn't get what enjoyment you can. I am in the best of hands and there is nothing at all you can do for me. I hoped so much to be able to take you ashore myself at Madeira, but it seems it can't be, and we must make the best of it. I want you to go ashore, though, dear—yes, I insist!' as she made a gesture of dissent. 'There may not be another opportunity as we may not call there on the way back after all. I understand we have lost a day somewhere, and it will have to be made up and the majority of the passengers will probably prefer not to lose a day in the Canaries. You're please to go, dear. Get someone to take you in my place.'

'I don't know anyone, Richard. Honestly, I should be miserable. Do let me stay here with you,' she begged.

'No, dear. Humour me in this. If you don't know anyone to take you, go to Cook's office. There's sure to be one on board, isn't there, Nurse?'

'Oh yes, Mr. Harrow. They'll fix up everything for Mrs. Harrow if she goes along there,' and she gave Janine concise directions as to the position of the office.

'You see, dear? I am disappointed at not being able to take you, so the least you can do is to give me the pleasure of seeing it through your eyes afterwards. Have you got any money?'

'Oh yes, really,' said Janine unhappily.

'Not enough probably. You'll want to buy things – tablecloths and things. Give me my wallet out of the top drawer, dear. Oh, thank you, Nurse.'

He took out a bundle of notes and pushed them into Janine's hand, letting the wallet drop back on the bed with a little gesture of weariness. Instantly the nurse was at his side with a warning glance to Janine.

'Better go now, Mrs. Harrow,' she whispered. 'He is not very strong yet, you know,' and as he lay with his eyes closed and no sign of consciousness, she slipped miserably away.

Land was already in sight, and she joined the excited passengers who were leaning over the side with field-glasses, or eyes shaded from the sunshine, watching the great mass of rock grow gradually clearer, the rows of white houses taking form, the harbour coming into view.

The somnolence of the last few days had given way to activity on board. Officers were at their appointed posts, and sailors, their blue overalls exchanged once again for uniform, hurried to and fro. The anchor was dropped and the yellow quarantine flag run up, and everyone watched eagerly for the fussy little tugs chugging out from the harbour, bearing officialdom to the ship.

Rowing-boats came across the clear, blue-green water, some of them filled with vendors of embroideries, laces, baskets and leatherwork, which they proceeded to display to the people on the decks above them, shouting out prices, offering to bargain, dexterously flinging cords up to the ship and following them with baskets containing the wares they had offered for sale.

Other boats had two, sometimes three, half-naked boys in them, and these kept up a continuous cry of 'Small boy dive! Very small boy dive!' and invited the passengers to throw down sixpences which they retrieved neatly from the translucent water.

Janine, fascinated and drawn out of herself for a moment, opened her purse, and looked for sixpence. Not finding one, she threw down a shilling, and her laughter when a boy leaped into the water like a fish and brought up the coin in his teeth was stilled as she heard behind her, quite distinctly, 'Plenty more where that came from, I suppose!' said in a mocking, contemptuous tone.

She went white and turned away, meeting the second officer as she did so.

'Better take a light coat if you're going ashore,' he warned her.

'I don't think I am,' she said, stammering as she always did when a stranger spoke to her.

'Oh, I should. They'll look after your husband alright, you know, and we're sailing again at six. So it will only be for a few hours.'

So they all knew who she was! They had probably all heard the vile things that were being said about her.

'I don't think I want to go alone,' she repeated dully.

'You'll get a guide on shore. I should go, if only for the sake of saying you've been to Madeira,' and he passed on to more congenial company.

The formalities were completed by now, and a gangway had been lowered near to where she stood so that the passengers could get down to the launch which was to ply between the ship and the shore all day. She tried to turn back towards the cabins, but somehow or other she got swept into the crowd of people all eager to land and make the most of the few hours ashore. She struggled against the stream, but in the end she was rushed down the steps with the rest and found herself being handed into the launch.

'I didn't really want to go ashore,' she told the steward breathlessly, but he only smiled and gave his hand to the next comer.

Once ashore, she was bewildered and frightened, for suddenly everyone else from the launch seemed to have vanished, leaving her surrounded by a crowd of men, dark-haired, bold-eyed, strange-looking and, to her inexperienced eyes, terrifying. She looked wildly round, clutching her bag closely to her, firmly convinced that she was in the midst of a band of desperadoes who would stop at nothing.

She could not understand what they said, though now and then she caught a familiar word – 'Good guide, leddy – all same as Cook's – ver' sheep – bullock *carro* to mountain?'

Then came others, displaying their wares with what seemed to her threatening insistence, and she thought wildly of opening her bag and giving them all she had so that they would go away, but she remembered the wad of notes Richard had just given her and felt that that was too desperate a remedy even for this predicament.

Suddenly, when she felt actually faint and sick with fear, the crowd parted and a wholesome English voice told them roundly to go away, finishing up with a few unfamiliar words which had a magic effect.

She looked, and through the lane he had made came striding a young man, tall, bronzed, good-looking, with that open-air look of a muscular, clean-living Englishman, his eyes of brownish grey smiling at her.

'Unholy crowd when you're alone,' he said, as he reached her. 'Are you alone by the way?' for now that he was face to face with her she seemed oddly small and helpless. The women tourists who chose to be alone for their shore-going were usually of the hard-bitten, capable type.

'Yes. I've just come off the *Carina*, out there,' said Janine shakily.

'Lost your party?' he asked cheerfully.

'No. Not exactly. I—I am alone, really. You see, my husband is on board ill, and he wanted me to come ashore, but—but I didn't really want to, and when all those men came round me I was terrified,' she finished with a nervous laugh.

The would-be guides drew near again hopefully, but the newcomer waved them off.

'Zimborra!' he told them, or that was what it sounded like to Janine, and they shrugged their shoulders and drifted away.

'That was a magic word,' she said shakily, hoping he would not go and leave her to them again, for she felt it would be quite beyond her to make them go, even if she said 'Zimborra!' to them.

'About the only native word I know, but you wouldn't believe how useful it is.'

'Do you live here?' she asked, for he looked so much at home.

'Not exactly, though I'm hoping to. I came out here to see a man about a job, but he's gone to Lisbon and I've had to cool my heels for a week. Oh, to hell with these merchants! Do you want to buy anything? Tray-cloths, silk undies, baskets, postcards? No? Zimborra all of you – zimborra – go away! Here, we'd better get out of this if we hope to get rid of them,' and he slid a hand beneath her elbow and marched her along the quay and up the steep cobbled street which led to the market square.

Janine was enraptured, breathless, excited. Conscious in every nerve of his hand on her arm, of his presence and his possessiveness, she let herself be led by him, looking about her with curiosity and interest, it was her first glimpse of a foreign land, and she was thrilled at everything she saw.

In the square, cobbled as were all the streets, a strange mixture of vehicles jostled one another or stood at the side of the road, indifferent to their neighbours. Luxurious, high-powered cars looked out of place beside the romantic-looking bullock *carros* with their wicker carriages, their awnings and curtains of gaily striped canvas, the patient oxen yoked to a central pole and gazing moony-eyed and aloof at the passers-by. The drivers, lounging against the sides of their beasts or sprawled in the carriages waiting for custom, wore a picturesque mixture of garments, but in one respect all were alike. All of them wore little white straw boaters with pale-blue ribbon bands on them.

Terry had meant to abandon her there, but something checked him, and he stood irresolute, looking down at her, wondering again how anything so helpless and untravelled could have got itself cast up alone in Madeira.

Janine looked up and caught his speculative gaze.

'You've been most terribly kind to me,' she said, and there was a decided suggestion of panic in her voice as she glanced to right and left as if fearing heaven knew what. Of course he would go now, this stranger who had been so unbelievably kind to her. What else could she expect? Dare she ask him to take her back to the quay, and put her safely on the launch again?

'What are you going to do with yourself now?' he asked.

'I—I don't know,' she said, hesitating before committing herself. These few minutes of his cheerful companionship, his acceptance of her without suspicion or distrust or curiosity, had grown out of all proportion to their true value in comparison with the treatment she had had meted out to her on board, where everyone seemed to know who she was and to despise and distrust and dislike her.

Suddenly be made up his mind. He and adventure were old friends, and this odd, shy little girl offered a quite fresh experience.

'Let's see Madeira together,' he said. 'Like to?' And before she could gather her scattered wits, he had signed to a bullock-driver and handed her into the little wicker carriage. 'I'm not kidnapping you, you know, and you've only to say one word to be safely set down again but – mightn't it be fun?'

Much more experienced women had found that smile of Terry Forder's irresistible, and Janine's heart missed a beat and then raced on.

'I—I haven't been having much fun lately,' she said suddenly, the words coming with a rush.

'What? And you on a cruise? We shall certainly have to do something about that.' He laughed, and she found herself laughing with him, her spirits rising, something bubbling up inside her in a most unusual fashion. 'Did you venture to land by yourself like that in search of fun, by the way?' he asked her. She did not look at all that type, he told himself, but then one never knows.

She shook her head.

'I didn't really mean to land at all, though Richard – that's my husband – wanted me to. He's ill. I sort of got rushed down the steps and into the launch before I knew what was happening, and the next thing I knew I was on the quay with all that crowd of dreadful, wild-looking men round me. I was terrified!'

He laughed.

'You looked it. That was why I came to the rescue, though I am not by way of being a Galahad or whatever was the name of the gentleman who made a hobby of dashing to the rescue of damsels in distress. What would you have done if I hadn't turned up?'

'I can't imagine. Given them all the money I had with me and jumped into the sea, I expect!' with a laugh which still held traces of her nervousness.

'Idiot! Well, seeing that I've saved both your money and your life, the least I can do is to preserve them for you for a few hours. Do you mind if I say something extremely personal?'

'Of course not.'

'Then – are you really married? Have you really got a sick husband on board?'

'Really,' she said, colouring and looking away.

'How long have you been married?'

'Only a week,' she admitted, wishing he would end an inquisition she found embarrassing.

'A bride of a week and a sick husband! We shall have to see what we can do about it,' he laughed, embarrassing her the more.

He was amused and intrigued by her confusion. He had thought the age of that kind of modesty gone for ever. Where on earth had she germinated?

'It isn't Richard's fault,' she said soberly. 'He's really very ill. That's why we came on the cruise, but he would make me come ashore today.'

He saw that she was getting a little sad, and he hastened to change the tone.

'Sensible Richard. And you're going to enjoy it? Enjoying it now?'

She hesitated, feeling a little heartless at the very idea of enjoyment whilst Richard lay so ill in his cabin. Then she succumbed to his infectious smile.

'I am – terribly,' she said, and gave a little sigh of delight in the novelty of her surroundings, in the unusual mode of progress, the bullocks ambling forward effortlessly, the light carriage slithering over the cobbles on steel runners which proved their superiority to the wheels of cars made by moderns for modern roads but not for Madeira's streets of polished pebbles.

Terry watched her animated face, trying to analyse its odd, elusive charm. She was totally unlike any previous conception of feminine attractiveness, and yet he knew that the attraction was there.

'What's all this about having no fun on the cruise?' he asked her, conscious of her unusual capacity for enjoyment.

Her face changed and she frowned a little.

'Oh … nothing,' she said.

'Why not tell me? I am quite safe, and – we are so unlikely to meet again.'

But she shook her head, though he knew she wanted to confide in him.

'I … don't think I will,' she said soberly.

'But you'd like to?'

'Mm. I'm not going to though. I don't want to think about anything hateful just now.'

'But surely that's rather a strong word, isn't it?' he asked with a smile.

'No. I've had a perfectly beastly time on board. I—'

'Yes?'

She shook her head.

'No. Just let's enjoy everything whilst it lasts,' and in her 'everything' she included this personal young man so oddly and bewilderingly become her companion, shot into her kin from nowhere, to return there when this day was over. Already she had to force herself not to think of that. Terry's voice, his smile, his eyes with their extraordinary long lashes, were getting into her blood.

'Atta girl! What do we do now? Go up the mountain?'

Her eyes shone.

'Could we really do that?'

'Why not? We can come down on a toboggan.'

'Now I know you're only teasing,' she said regretfully.

'But I'm not. You'll see. I think it would amuse you, and it strikes me very forcibly that you need amusing, sister. No, on second thoughts, I am not sure that I want to be – brother,' and she felt her eyes drawn to his as if by force and held there during an infinitesimal, endless moment. 'Tell me your name, won't you ?'

'Janine.'

'And I am Terry. We don't want any other names, do we? Ships that pass in the night. But what is this terrible thing you were going to tell me? You were going to tell me, weren't you?' She shook her head.

'I don't want to tell you it now. I don't want to do anything but just enjoy … all this,' and the wave of her hand included the narrow, cobbled streets and, beyond them, towering up above them, the mountain with its wooded slopes, its giant palms, its glowing colours where flowers rioted and where all the seasons, as she knew them, seemed to have joined forces.

'Do I come into that comprehensive term?' he asked.

'Why – yes, I suppose so,' she admitted shyly. 'You know – I can't imagine how I come to be driving with you like this. If you knew me, you would realise what an extraordinary thing it is for me to be doing.'

'But you like it, don't you – Janine?'

She laughed, and there was an odd little note of happiness and youth bubbling up in her laughter. She realised with a shock of excitement that it had never been there before.

'I think I do – Terry,' she said.

'How did you get your odd, nice little name?'

She told him, quite simply, what she knew of her origin, and for the first time she could invest the story with a spice of humour which did not relieve it of all its pathos.

'How much more exciting a beginning than the common or garden gooseberry bush variety,' he remarked. 'And how pleasant to have reached your advanced age and have no acquisitive or inquisitive relations to interfere with one's freedom.'

'I hadn't thought of that,' said Janine.

'But you have acquired a husband.'

'Yes.'

Somehow Richard and the ship and the passengers, the doctor and the nurse and that stuffy little room, seemed to have receded into a dim and distant background for all this colour and beauty and laughter. She considered this for a moment, and he studied her profile. She was not pretty; she was execrably dressed; she was not smart in her sayings or thoughts. In spite of being a married woman, she was obviously inexperienced and unsophisticated, In short she was none of the things which had always constituted charm for him in women. Where, then, lay that vague allure?

The driver popped his head round with a sudden question.

'You like market? Yes? I wait.'

Terry nodded, and helped Janine out.

'Fruit market,' he explained, putting a hand beneath her elbow and guiding her under the narrow archway into the great covered hall where fruit and flowers filled the air with their fragrance.

'I shouldn't buy anything yet,' he warned as she paused before a great pile of luscious-looking grapes. 'You'll only have to cart it about with you, and they almost give the things away when the ship is due to leave. What time do you sail, by the way? Not tonight?'

'Yes, at six,' she said regretfully, though an hour or two ago she had wished miserably that they were not stopping at all.

'Pity. You would have loved night-time in Madeira,' he said softly. 'There's no magic like it – the stars, and the utter blue of the sky which is never really black, the velvety softness of the breeze, and the scent of the mimosa.'

She drew a sharp breath, and he turned aside to a stall where they were selling great branches of the yellow-balled fragrance, bought an armful and gave it to her.

'We can take it with us and leave it when you're tired of it,' he said, and she buried her face in the perfumed mass, leaving little patches of gold on her skin.

'I should love to see the night here,' she said, half to herself, half to him, and he glanced at her sharply, wondering whether, after all he had not underestimated her as a woman of experience.

But her face was sweetly innocent, and he wandered on with her through the market, resisting the blandishments of merchants with his casual 'Zimborra', which made her laugh and imitate him.

They reached their bullock-cart again and went on up the steep streets, changing later into the funicular, or mountain railway, which was like a lift, except that behind it puffed a steam-engine, which blew out poisonous clouds of smoke, mercifully drifting behind them instead of before them.

He pointed out to her the unfamiliar trees and flowers as they wound their way slowly upwards, cog by cog, through the cutting in the mountainside.

'That feathery stuff is pepper. It looks much more romantic than the powder we sneeze over in the restaurants, doesn't it? And that is sago, which I remember I used to loathe when I was a kid. Lower down you can see a field of sugar-cane. See?' –and he pulled her forward so that she could see where the lighter green of the sugar showed against the darker foliage of the bananas.

'That is tamarisk,' he said later, and she looked with interest at the delicate feathery fronds with their pink-and-white flower-tips.

'Richard says they make hedges of that,' she told him. 'The poor thing has to be pruned and never allowed to flower. It seems hard lines on it when it can be so lovely to look at.'

'I expect it is much more useful as a hedge, though.'

She sighed.

'I suppose so. I suppose everything and everyone ought to be useful rather than merely ornamental, or so Richard says.'

He laughed.

'What a queer kid you are! What made you say that so regretfully, as if you really minded what they do to the tamarisk?'

'I don't know. I suppose it's because I'm neither useful nor ornamental, but I don't think it'll make me any more useful to keep pruning me!'

'That sounds morbid and self-pitying.'

'Oh, I didn't mean it that way, really. Only—oh, I'm such an idiot at doing anything. I always make a mess of things. I – that was what I was going to tell you just now, and then I didn't.'

'Well, if you want to, why not?' he asked, smiling.

'Yes, why not? You don't know me, and we shall never meet again, so it won't matter whether you remember or forget, will it?'

'Perhaps not.'

'You see – I told you my husband had been taken ill. There is a nurse on board, and the other night I felt I was so useless, leaving him to other people all the time, and I offered to sit up with him and they let me. I had to take his temperature, 'but I simply couldn't read the thing, and I didn't know it was so high, and – I went to sleep. Wasn't it awful?'

He smiled at her distressed face.

'Why, if you were tired? I don't suppose you're the first nurse to drop asleep on night duty.'

'No, but, don't you see? He had a perfectly terrific temperature, and I didn't know, and I nearly let him die, and—and—people said on the ship, all of them, that—that I wanted him to die and leave me his money!'

He realised, now that it was out, that the thing had been corroding her mind, growing out of all proportion to its value, and he could feel the trembling of her body in the arm which touched his.

'You poor kid!' he said softly, and suddenly, dreadfully, she began to cry.

He was horribly embarrassed, and glad that at least they had the compartment to themselves, and that the other people in the train were well to the front of it. He slid an arm about her and drew her close to him, comforting her as if she had been a child, and in a moment she sat up, dried her eyes fiercely, and turned on him a tremulous smile.

'Whatever must you think of me?' she asked.

'That you've been very foolish to brood on what you probably only fancied in the first place. Why on earth should they suppose you want your husband out of the way when you have only just married him?'

She could not tell him the truth. Somehow, it seemed horrible and unnatural that she should have married an old man now that she was with Terry, young and vigorous and virile. She knew instinctively that he would think it wrong of her, avaricious and grasping. In a way it had been that. She could never hope to make anyone realise how desperate she had been, how hopeless, how tired of the struggle, nor how tempting had been Richard's kindness and the comfort he gave her.

'Are you in love with him?' he asked her when she did not answer,

'I—I am very fond of him and grateful to him,' she said in a low voice. 'I wouldn't hurt him for the world, and I don't want him to die—I don't!'

'Ssh! Ssh!' he soothed her, his arm still about her, and the train slowed down and came to a stop with a jolt.

'Are we at the top?' she asked in surprise.

'Not quite. There is an hotel here and some beautiful gardens and a water garden which people usually like to see. You can go up to it in a hammock. It will amuse you, I think. Shall we go? We can have lunch at the hotel and go to the top afterwards.'

She hesitated.

'I—I don't like to—to cost you so much,' she said at last, but he laughed and helped her from the train.

'Because I have told you I'm out of work? At the moment I'm passing rich, and it is amazing on how little one can exist in this place. Here!' and he signalled to two swarthy men who carried a striped hammock between them, and transferred Janine to laughing as she clutched at the sides and swayed to and fro.

She was set down outside a little church set on the side of the mountain, and they were instantly surrounded by children dressed in picturesque rags, little dark-skinned, brown-eyed, black-haired mites whose eyes asked mutely but more eloquently even than their tongues and their outstretched hands.

'Zimborra!' Terry told them, but Janine opened her purse and scattered loose coins amongst them, laughing as they dived and scrambled and squealed on the ground.

'They'll come swarming from near and far if you once do that,' he warned her.

'It costs so little to make them happy,' she said, and searched in her bag for more until he drew her inside the church forcibly and forbade the children to follow them.

'Do you realise that our beautiful peace and privacy will be gone for the day if you go on like that?' he asked her.

'I didn't know that was what we came up here for,' she said demurely, and was forthwith amazed at herself. Could it possibly be she, Janine Wilson, talking like this to a strange young man on a mountainside in a foreign land? Again in her thoughts she had slipped away from that unreal marriage of hers, and Richard Harrow might be a denizen of another planet for all that he counted just then in her scheme of things.

Terry's eyes flickered curiously in a way with which she was to become familiar. It gave them an impish light, speculative, enquiring, oddly tender. He was realising, with a quickening sense of adventure, that he was attracted and intrigued, and it was a long time since any woman had done that to him. For so long his mind had been concerned only with Joy that no other woman had really existed. Now he had had to school himself to strangle at birth every memory of Joy it had left his mind strangely empty.

'I'm beginning to wonder what we did come up here for,' he said at last, and his eyes held hers for a second and smiled as she refused any longer to look at him. So she was interested too. It might be amusing.

They moved softly up the aisle of the little stone church. There were a few silent worshippers, here and there candles burnt, and before the dim altar swung a red lamp like a jewel. The perfume of incense drifted about them. Unconsciously Janine drew more closely to him and they stood looking at a garish, much decorated statue of the Virgin, an impossible Baby in the crook of her arm. Janine looked at the face of the Mother, sad and sweet and young, with a yearning tenderness which not even the crude plaster nor the garish robes could deny her.

Neither spoke until they were outside the church, walking about in the sunshine, the brief spell of an age-old, possibly outworn creed broken and yet lingering with them.

'I should like to be a Catholic,' said Janine suddenly.

'Why?'

'It looks comforting.'

'Do you need comfort?'

'Don't all women, in their hearts? It seems so easy, too, just to believe all the priests say and have no responsibility yourself.'

'Could you believe all they say?' he asked her curiously.

In common with most of his generation, he took little interest in religion, dismissing it, if ever it entered his thoughts, as something for the elderly, a phase of a passing generation.

She shook her head.

'About the water becoming wine, and bread becoming flesh, do you mean? No.'

'About other things too. They believe in the virgin birth, don't they? Could you? But of course you couldn't. You're too intelligent, and you're a married woman.'

She coloured. She had never in her life had occasion to discuss such a thing with a man, and the very word 'virgin' filled her with confusion. She had always worked too hard and played too little to make friends with people, or it would have been impossible for her, in this age of frankness, to blush at the mention of virginity.

'Perhaps not,' she agreed vaguely. 'It is the religion itself, taking one's burdens and responsibilities and—well—running one's life for one.'

'A religion for the spineless,' was his comment.

'Perhaps that's why it attracts me.'

'Suggesting that you are spineless?'

She sighed.

'I think I must be. I never seem capable of making up my own mind, and I always feel I want someone to lean on, though heaven knows I've never had anyone.'

He laughed and slid a hand closely within her arm.

'That's an irresistible suggestion,' he said. 'And now what about finding that hotel and lunch? You've had enough of churches and incense and altar lamps. Hell! Tourists!' as their solitude was suddenly invaded by a crowd of sightseers, probably from the *Carina*, laughing and talking and exclaiming about everything.

He drew her into a run, and together they raced along a little path between the trees, never pausing nor turning until, breathless and laughing, they found themselves too far to hear the voices, too deeply hidden amongst the trees for discovery.

Janine stood with the laughter dying from her face, her head raised, her eyes closed, drinking in the utter beauty of a silence broken by nothing but the stirring of the leaves and, high above them, the song of unseen birds. The scent of the mimosa was all about them, heady and sweet, and a shaft of sunlight striking through the trees turned the little balls into a million golden lamps.

'I shall remember this all my life,' she said softly, and into her memory of that moment was woven inextricably the consciousness of Terry's presence, of his hand within her arm, of the peaty, tobacco-scented tweed of his coat. In every pulse of her body she was aware of him, and yet she kept the awareness hidden from her conscious thoughts, something to give her amazement, wonder, joy, perhaps, a little regret when this moment had passed with the others into memory.

She was no longer just Janine, frightened, shy, bewildered at life, muddling through, making endless mistakes. She was a part of this beauty and perfection and stillness.

Instinctively she turned to meet his eyes, and they smiled. Of such moments is memory made.

'And God saw everything that He had made, and behold, it was very good,' he said softly, and even as he spoke, down the hidden path came the sound of little hurrying steps, and a short, fat man came smiling and gesticulating as he parted the bushes.

'And the next day He got up early, and made a man!' added Terry in a low voice. 'I always did think early rising a mistake.'

Janine giggled, the exalted mood passing and leaving her a happy, breathless, wide-eyed child again, intoxicated with her first taste of life.

'Monsieur and Madame want something, yes?' asked the intruder ingratiatingly, and between the bushes which his fat little form parted they saw the white terrace of the hotel.

'Lunch, I think,' Terry told the man, and they walked sedately behind him and into the hotel.

The huge, stone-pillared dining-room had deep windows to the floor, and from their table near one of them they could look out over the mountainside and down into the bay which, from this height, looked like a painted picture of a pool with toy boats on its surface.

'There's your ship,' said Terry, pointing out to her the white vessel anchored a little way out, its masts gay with bunting. It all looked unreal and impossible to Janine, but then the whole adventure was so extraordinary that she could no longer expect anything to seem familiar.

They ordered from the menu, Terry advising, but when he asked her what she would drink, she shook her head.

'I never know what to say when I am asked that,' she said. 'I know I should choose quite the wrong thing.'

'Thank heaven for that! There are times when a man likes to feel superior to a mere rib, you know, and girls know everything nowadays. Have you ever drunk the beer they sell in this part of the world?'

'Beer?' asked Janine incredulously.

He laughed at her face.

'Call it *biere*, if you like. It doesn't sound so low. It's very light and very cold, and it knocks wine off the board when you're thirsty.'

'Alright,' she said recklessly. 'Let's drink beer!'

'Biere?' he reproved her, and ordered it when the first course, an amazing array of hors-d'oeuvres, arrived.

He told her what the various dishes were, but she could not decide whether to believe him or not, so fantastic were some of his explanations. She let him help her to all of them, and felt when she had finished that she could not possibly eat anything else.

She did, though, and went steadily through the gayest, happiest meal of her life, with odd dishes washed down with quantities of the amber ice-cold beer with its refreshing bitter taste. She, who could never find anything to say, who was being terrified into a state of collapse by the gaiety of her cruise companions, found herself chatting to him thoughtlessly, with rising spirits and quickening sense of humour and delight.

Terry Forder knew quite a lot about women. In his twenty-eight years he had known many of them, with varying stages of knowledge and intimacy, and he could usually sum them up at a first meeting with a fair appreciation of their possibilities and availability. With this girl he had been definitely out of his reckoning, and the discovery piqued his interest. He amused himself by making her talk, finding a range of subjects on which she had never known before she had any opinion, surprised to find that from the rather jumbled contents of her mind came little gems of thought and feeling and originality. She was not overlaid and dulled by the sort of life lived by most other women he had known. She was fresh and unspoiled. He could not reconcile his thoughts of her with the knowledge that she was a married woman, however.

Listening to her, watching the swift play of emotion on her face and in her dark and really lovely eyes, he tried to fit in the rest of the jigsaw puzzle she presented to him, failing utterly to visualise this husband to whom she referred now and again without enthusiasm.

What sort of man was he? Young? Virile? Eager? He must love her, presumably, for she admitted ingenuously that she had brought nothing but herself to the marriage. But quite certainly she was not in love with him, and she had already made the rather sinister suggestion that he could have been married for his money.

He frowned at the thought, finding it hard to reconcile his mind to that aspect of her. She seemed so innocent, so unworldly, still cherishing dreams. Surely she could not be merely mercenary? And yet she had married a rich man whom she did not love.

He watched her mouth, that tell-tale feature. It looked soft and yielding and desirable. He imagined himself kissing it. He had never kissed any girl save Joy since the first day he had met her and been enchanted by her. Well, why should he not kiss this girl of a day's amusement? She was married, experienced, and must know what she was courting in being alone with him on the mountain like this for long hours at a stretch.

They finished their meal, and she left the table almost regretfully. One more milestone of this stolen journey passed. He caught her look and interpreted it rightly.

'Pity you've got to join the ship again so early,' he said.

She gave him a startled glance as he read her thoughts.

'I should like to see how you react to the mimosas in the moonlight and starlight of a Madeira night,' he went on banteringly, and yet with a note of seriousness beneath the lightness which set her pulses throbbing strangely.

'They might go to my head,' she said uncertainly.

'That's why I'm wishing you were to be here for just one night,' he said. 'You are so careful about yourself and your emotions, so nervous lest you be spendthrift with them. It would amuse me to see you grappling with the unearthly magic of a southern night.'

'That's all you think of, isn't it? Just amusing yourself,' she said with a touch of scorn.

'No. I'm thinking of amusing you too, Janine.'

'I am not at all sure I should be amused,' she told him, and marvelled that this self-possessed, unfrightened girl should be herself, thrilling to the adventure of the day.

They were in the gardens of the hotel now, out of sight of the windows, and again his hand went through her arm possessively, and he leaned down so that his darker head was very close to hers.

'You would, Janine. I swear it. I'd teach you – many things you've never learned.'

She was afraid and yet thrilled, and in her heart she had the protective knowledge that when night came to Madeira she would be safely on board the *Carina* with Richard again.

'I don't think I want to learn them,' she said in a low voice.

'No? Do you know, Janine, I can't realise that you're married. You seem so curiously virginal to be a wife and to know all sorts of things nice little girls ought not to know, which are quite alright for nice little wives.'

She kept very still and did not answer him. Again came that feeling of shame in her elderly husband. Of course Terry thought her married to a man like himself, mated as in her dreams she had been. She felt she would die of shame were he to know the truth, that she was actually not a proper wife at all.

As she did not answer, he spoke again.

'Are you happily married, Janine?' he asked curiously.

'Utterly,' she said with unnecessary emphasis.

'He's good to you?'

'He's an angel to me,' fervently, and her conscience was stricken as she realised how completely she had forgotten him, lying sick and in pain whilst she ran and laughed and talked with this stranger.

He felt her withdrawal from him and let his hand slip from her arm. He could bide his time. He knew so well how to play a woman, when to give her a run and when to jerk her back.

'There's an amusing water-garden here you might like to see here,' he told her, and she followed him down a narrow winding path and out into a garden cut in the hillside with a little rock pool with tiny boats at anchor, and a frail bridge spanning it.

They went across the bridge, and from somewhere came the ubiquitous little man who had found them in their retreat.

'Monsieur and Madame would like to see cave?' he invited, and they passed under a damp, mossy arch into a tiny fern-covered cave, with the water trickling down the walls. The next moment Janine gave a little cry and clutched his arm, for a curtain of water had been drawn across the entrance by a million tiny jets, and they were utterly cut off from the outside world in their cold green cavern.

Terry laughed and flung an arm about her, held her against him for a moment and looked down at her half frightened, half fascinated eyes.

'Afraid?' he asked her in a whisper, though no one could possibly have heard them through the curtain of rainbow-hued water.

'No, I—I'm not afraid,' she whispered back, but at that moment the attendant turned the water off and peered in at them, laughing at his ruse.

He caught Terry's eye and winked.

'Too queek, yes?' he asked and, when Terry laughed and nodded, he beckoned them to a little tower which stood a few feet further up the mountainside.

'Up in ze tower you see, yes?'

But Janine would have none of it and ran back to the hotel, flushed and laughing.

'Might as well go on up the mountain,' he said when he rejoined her. 'Feel equal to walking a bit? We are more than halfway up, and the mountain path is worth the struggle.'

She glanced at her watch, an expensive trifle in platinum and diamonds which Richard had given her.

'Are you sure we've time?' she asked. 'It's three o'clock and I have to be on board by half past five.'

'Heaps of time,' he told her airily, and sighing with contentment, she went with him to where the rough little track led upwards.

Chapter Seven

After that dawdling, unforgettable climb up the mountain slope they came out on the sparsely wooded top where, beside the inevitable hotel, was nothing save an enormous statue of the Virgin, her crown a ring of stars which he told her at night dominated the island, for they lit the stars at dusk.

Terry translated for her the simple inscription to those fallen in battle.

'Do you remember the war?' she asked him.

'Quite well. It made an enormous upheaval in our lives. My father and brothers were in the Army.'

'Did you lose anyone?'

'One brother, a flying officer. Crashed in France. The other one lost a leg. He's in Australia now, doing well, I believe. I never hear of him. Odd, isn't it, how a family can break up and lose sight of one another after all the inseparable intimacies of childhood? Of course they were a good deal older than I. There is a sister in between, Vanna. She's married and living in Ireland. I scarcely ever see her, and they're as poor as church mice, so they wouldn't thank me for turning up on them without a job! There was no suggestion of complaining or hard luck in his voice. It was merely a statement of fact, and Janine appreciated it. Timid herself, she loved courage and thought the more highly of people who possessed it because she felt herself incapable of ever achieving it.

'And your parents?' she asked.

'My mother died two years ago. My father … was the sort of war casualty they don't put up statues to and don't pay pensions for. He came home to be demobbed and returned to his French lady love, and we've never heard of him since Mum died. I haven't any grouse against him. They never got on very well but he always sent her enough to live on and came to see her when she was ill. He was with her when she died, and we had an uncanny sort of feeling that, in spite of everything, each held an unassailable position in the heart of the other. Queer thing, isn't it? Marriage, even the most unhappy variety, does seem to link two people in a bond that nothing can really break. Perhaps it isn't marriage that does it, though. It's rather the first experience of mating, when two people come together rationally and intentionally. I don't mean the silly, unconsidered satisfaction of a moment's temptation, which is merely the prerogative of the beast.'

He enjoyed testing her out with such a speech, which he knew gave her a sense of shock and yet which she tried manfully to survive.

'Don't you agree?' he pursued, when she said nothing.

'I—suppose so. I don't know much about it.'

He stared at her with a puzzled frown.

'You're a most inexplicable person, Janine,' he said, and filed that impression with the rest for future consideration. What a thousand pities that down there, in the blue bay, a boat waited inexorably to bear her away from him with her limitless possibilities unexplored.

They wandered round to the back of the statue and discovered a small shrine built as a memorial to the dead, and guarded by a woman with a bunch of keys and the usual upturned palm. For Terry's shilling she opened the rest of the little building, revealing to their amused and surprised gaze a set of rooms, half furnished, complete with dressing-room and toilet, into which she led them without consideration for Janine's scandalised blushes.

Terry joked with her in his smattering of Portuguese, and from her expression the girl decided that it would be better not to ask for a translation. The woman looked from one to the other of them, winked prodigiously, and said something which made him roar with laughter and slide another shilling into her hand.

'She suggests that we let the ship go without us and move in,' he explained to Janine as they walked away.

'Was that what you laughed at?' she asked suspiciously.

'No, my dear, but I couldn't possibly sully your young and innocent ears with what I think she said. After all, my knowledge of the language is so slight that it may have been my mind rather than what she said.' And his eyes teased her as he slid his hand within her arm again and they resumed a pose which had become quite surprisingly familiar to them.

'What's the time by the way?' he asked, 'I haven't got my watch on.'

She looked at her wrist.

'Quarter to five,' she said regretfully.

'Good Lord! Did we take all that time coming up? Sorry our day is almost gone, Janine!'

He drew her arm a little closer to him as he spoke, and she felt the warmth of his body through the thin sports shirt he wore. He had long ago cast his coat, and carried it with hers on his free arm. Up in the mountain as they were, they still felt warm and comfortable.

'Terribly sorry,' she said in a low voice, and he recognised even a hint of passion there.

He still promised himself that kiss, and looked round. Not here on the mountain top, with the threat of tourists all about them, with that incredible Virgin overshadowing them, with the eyes of the old hag with the keys probably not too far from them.

He drew her away from the little plateau of the shrine.

'Let's start to make our way down. Actually we're going in a toboggan, which is the greatest fun, but if we walk through here we can pick up a man at the first turn.'

Into the woods they went again and, though at this altitude the vegetation was more sparse, Terry frowned. He was an artist in the ways of love and flirtation, and he liked his setting to be perfect. With some women this might be romantic enough. With a girl like this, he knew he would need at least the appearance of isolation or he would merely scare her.

They found a fallen log and sat down, Janine drinking in the peace and stillness, registering every moment on her mind for memory, resolutely refusing to think that only one short hour remained. Terry spent the moments looking at her, following the soft line from temple to chin, the rather deep setting of her eyes, the rounded, not very determined chin, the lips with their uncertain promise, the white V revealed by the modestly cut blouse, the curve of the breast only just hinted at.

She would look a darling in a bathing costume, one of those new and very daring affairs which girls wore so blatantly now, a triangle drawn across their breasts and the smallest possible trunks below it and nothing else at all.

'Do you swim, Janine?'

She looked surprised. To her it was rather a far cry from the top of the mountain to the sea, and she had no means of following the course by which he had arrived at this question.

'I can't, but I love the water,' she said. 'I want to learn to swim.'

'I was thinking what a chuck you'd look undressed,' he said calmly.

'Terry!' she cried, adding to her confusion by using his name aloud.

'Janine!' he mocked her. 'I meant in a bathing costume, of course, one of those amusing little things without backs.'

'What an extraordinary thing to say! – Especially up here,' she said.

'When you are your age and I am mine, that sort of speculation is never extraordinary,' he said. 'Don't you realise, and can't you be honest enough to admit, that the primitive instinct is still the prime factor in life? That for all the talk of the highbrows, the clergy and the hermaphrodite self-appointed custodians of our morals, sex is still the most important interest in our lives? After all, the impulse to procreation is the one thing common to all life, and the only absolute essential to the continuation of the scheme of things.'

She edged away from him, repelled and yet fascinated.

'I—don't think I like to—to talk about those things,' she said primly.

He set a hand beneath her chin and tilted up her face, looking down into her eyes with teasing laughter in his own.

Janine, you're that exquisite survival of a bygone age, a prude,' he told her. 'I believe that if you heard anyone call you a thoroughly respectable woman, you wouldn't feel outraged.'

'Well, why should I?' she asked, puzzled, and he roared with laughter.

'I could fall in love with anyone as unsophisticated as you,' he said. 'What would you do or say about it if I did? No, I amend that. What would you *do* about it? To hell with what you'd *say* about it!'

'I think we'd better be going,' said Janine quickly. 'How long does it take to get down on these toboggan affairs?'

'Heaps of time yet,' he said, pulling her down beside him again as she attempted to get up. 'Why worry about time when we both want it to stand still?'

'I don't know that I do,' she said, but the voice she had meant to make cool and collected quivered absurdly, and when she rose to her feet and smoothed out the creases in her linen skirt, her hands trembled.

He got up with a sigh. After all, perhaps it would be better if he denied himself that kiss. Such an adventure with many women would be completely rounded off with a kiss and goodbye, but he was aware of the exciting quality of her awareness, and he was coming to the conclusion that that kiss, if he achieved it, would leave the incident incomplete.

He remembered the moment in the woods below the hotel garden, her rapt face, her voice, the intensity with which she had felt the beauty of that silence cleft by the song of the birds. There had been passion in her, a depth of emotion which he felt instinctively was as yet untapped. He amused himself by imagining the probable effect of unleashing that passion. The picture stirred his senses.

He shook them free of it. In an hour, less than an hour, she would be gone and that queer, disturbing element with her. He would never see her again, never even know her name. There could be no episode to follow the prelude of that kiss. He would let her go, but he repressed a sigh for the possibilities within her which some other man would one day awaken if that surprising husband of hers had not by then managed to do so.

They made their way silently between the trees and out to the ubiquitous cobbles with which the mountain track was paved. A toboggan came gliding by, two girls seated in it, laughing and shouting. Terry made a sign to one of the white-coated attendants, who pulled on his rope and brought the sledge to rest.

'Any more coming up?' he asked.

The man understood the tone and gesture, if not the words, and nodded and laughed with a flash of white teeth.

'I blow for heem,' he said, emitted a shrill blast with two fingers to his lips, and set his sledge in motion again. 'He come pronto,' he assured them.

And a few minutes later Janine was seated in another of the wicker sledges, which was like a small garden couch with runners in place of legs, the back and seat comfortably cushioned. Terry folded his long legs beside hers and they were off, one man at the back pushing them and another pulling on a rope in front.

'You'll be glad of the cushions as we go down,' Terry assured her with a laugh.

'You lak heem queek?' asked one of the men.

'I like most things queek,' agreed Terry with a laugh, and as the toboggan gathered momentum both men stood at the back, guiding with an out flung foot now and then whilst the sledge rushed downwards over cobbles worn smooth and shiny by years of such treatment.

Janine shrieked. It was a spontaneous shriek of pure delight, and Terry flung an arm about her and held her close. She was soft and small within his arm, and when they came to the next hairpin bend and took it at terrific speed, the sledge swaying first on one runner and then on the other, she threw her arms round his neck and hung on for dear life, laughing and shrieking like a child.

'Pong, pong!' called the men, using a cry which was evidently peculiar to their trade, and Janine and Terry took up the cry.

'Pong, pong!' they yelled as they reached each hair-raising turn in the road, the sledge heeling over and then righting itself as by a miracle when it seemed inevitable that it should turn right over and fling them down the precipitous side of the mountain, for the path was merely cut narrowly into the face of the slope.

'Not frightened, are you?' Terry asked her after one such breathless moment.

Her shining eyes answered him before her 'I love it!' reached him, and his arm closed more tightly about her.

'You're a queer kid, aren't you? You were terrified of the merchants on the quay, and more than a little frightened of me, and yet you aren't afraid of this!'

They were proceeding at the moment along a more gentle stretch, and could talk.

'It isn't things I'm afraid of,' she said. 'I suppose it's people,' but she became aware of her position and sat up, detaching herself with a certain spurious primness, though at the next bend she was in his arms again, clutching and laughing.

'Heaven send another corner soon!' laughed Terry, and got ready to grab her.

They arrived at the spot where, during what seemed another existence, they had been left by the bullock *carro*, and Janine began to tuck in the loose ends of her hair and generally straighten herself out. He was amazed at the change in her now that she was flushed and laughing, a little ashamed of her daring, not quite as neat as she had been, much younger and more alive.

'I suppose we haven't time to go and get tea somewhere before your boat sails, have we?' he asked her. 'What is the time? It takes about quarter of an hour to get to the quay from here by bullock-cart, or five minutes by car.'

She pulled back her cuff, looked at her watch, and then looked again in incredulous dismay and held it to her ear.

'Stopped!' she said. 'It still says quarter to five.'

In any other circumstances, her dismay, her bated breath would have been comical. As it was, he realised that he could only look on it as tragic – at the moment, anyway.

'We'll go in here and ask the time,' he said, turning into a bazaar at the corner.

She waited outside, feeling slightly sick. They must have been hours and hours up the mountain. Whatever could she have been thinking about to let this happen? What would Richard think or say? Would the ship wait? She had no idea what they did nor even whether they troubled to find out if all the passengers were aboard.

Terry came out with a comical expression on his face.

'It's half past six,' he said.

Janine blanched.

'No! Is it really? 'Whatever shall I do? Do you think the ship will have waited? They might not even have missed me.'

'Your husband would know that you were not on board, surely?'

'No, he wouldn't. He is in his cabin, in bed, not allowed to get up at all. How would he know? Oh, do let's hurry! Can we get a car?'

But of course there was none to be seen, and they ran down the steep street waving aside the offers of the bullock-cart drivers.

'There's an empty car!' cried Terry. 'Come on!' and he grabbed her hand and ran with her to the bottom of the street, waving to the car as they ran.

'The quay, quickly,' he said. 'To catch the *Carina.*'

'*Carina,* she have gone,' said the man nonchalantly, but they bundled into the car, and it tore away at top speed, scattering children and animals in every direction, though for once Janine neither saw their danger nor cared.

They paid the driver and dashed up the quay, hoping against hope that he was wrong, but the place where the *Carina* had berthed was empty, and, straining their eyes, they saw her white against the skyline.

Janine and Terry turned simultaneously to regard each other in stupefaction.

Marooned!

He was the first to recover his speech.

'I'm most frightfully sorry,' he said.

'It was my fault not noticing my watch had stopped, I might have *known* it was later than that. What on earth shall I do?'

'Where are they putting in next? Grand Canary?'

'Yes. Las Palmas. But they may not call here again.'

'They will. It may cost your husband something, but I don't suppose he'll mind that.'

'Oh no, of course not. But he'll think it was so careless of me. He may think I did it on purpose, but I really didn't, did I?' she asked in distress.

He smiled.

'Of course you didn't. Neither did I. It's just one of those unlucky things that have to happen sometimes. I suppose it is, isn't it?'

'Is what? Unlucky? Why, of course it is! And whatever will all the people on the ship think of me? How could I have done such a mad thing?'

He saw she was really distressed, and took the matter in hand in his capable way.

'No good worrying what other people think. Let's go and do the only possible thing – enquire at Government Building, I expect we can wireless Las Palmas.'

Janine was comforted a little at the prospect of any sort of action, and they found a charming and most interesting cosmopolitan at Government Building who was paternally reassuring and who quite obviously mistook the situation.

'Missed the *Carina*? Oh, the little lady has? And her husband is on board? Well, well, many a worse thing might happen, eh?' with a look at them which only just missed being a wink.

Janine coloured hotly and looked very self-conscious and uncomfortable.

'My husband is ill and will be very worried,' she said.

'I have no doubt he will – no doubt at all,' said their genial friend with another beam. 'Well, we must see what we can do, but you will have to stay in Madeira tonight anyway. If you will write down the name of your husband, the name of the ship and the next port of call – Las Palmas, didn't you say? – I have no doubt we can wireless either Grand Canary or the ship herself, and everything will be alright.'

'Oh, do you think so?' asked Janine, and wrote down the particulars he wanted with shaky fingers.

Terry watched her.

Harrow ... Queer. Still, it perhaps wasn't such a common name, and he had little more curiosity.

'And what shall I say to Monsieur Husband?'

'Oh—that I am alright, that I missed the ship and—oh, ask him what I am to do,' she said hurriedly. 'If you could get a message to him tonight he would be so relieved. He'll worry about me, you see.'

'Oh, but assuredly, assuredly! I shall see what can be done, and you come back—let me see—about nine o'clock. You have money?'

'Oh yes,' said Janine thankfully.

'Ah, that is good. Well, run along now and I will—what you say—get busy,' and he fluttered his chubby hands at them and vanished into an inner room.

Janine and Terry went out into the street again, finding it quiet and somnolent now that the British ship was no longer in the harbour.

'Let's go and get a drink or something and make plans,' said Terry. 'You'll have to get a room. You'd better go to Reid's.'

'Is that where you are staying?' she asked anxiously.

'Good Lord, no! The finances of an out-of-worker don't run to Reid's. I'm putting up at a little pub at the back of the town.'

'Can't I get a room there?' she asked, unconsciously pressing more closely to him.

She could not bear the thought of being cast adrift again, even for a few hours.

He made a grimace.

'Hell, no! You'd hate it. You'll be alright at Reid's. It's the season now and there'll be mostly English people there. We can go round now and have a cocktail and you can take stock of the place.'

And this they did, Janine feeling uncomfortable and miserably out of her element amongst the smartly dressed crowd making the most of what remained of the soft warm evening. Many of the women were already dressed for dinner, their gowns marvels of colour and sheen and line, but there were some of the younger set still in beach suits, or with gaily patterned wraps over scanty bathing kit.

'Jolly here, isn't it?' asked Terry from the other side of the little table with its brilliant orange umbrella.

Janine thought swiftly how well he fitted into this environment, how much at ease he was. He belonged here amongst these people. It was she who was an outsider, awkward and ill at ease.

'I feel—uncomfortable here,' she admitted, wishing they could be alone again, regretting the gay comradeship which seemed to have vanished as if it had never been. Even Terry in these surroundings seemed remote and a stranger.

'Uncomfortable? What on earth for?' he asked her in surprise.

'Well, I—I don't belong to people like these. I don't do any of the things they do in the way they do them. I don't even talk like them!' she burst out.

'Well, what of it? I think for the most part they talk execrably, but why worry? You don't have to be like them to enjoy the things they do.'

'But I don't think I enjoy them. I feel ... out of place.'

'What you're suffering from, my dear child, is an inferiority complex, a delusion that these bright young things and pseudo-bright old things are superior to you, that you'd like to be like them, but that that and they are out of your reach. Rubbish! Footle! Rot! They are in no way superior to you, and, in fact, you could give them a lot of points and still win.'

She had to laugh at that.

'Well, that's not true, anyway!' she said.

'Don't contradict me. I'm telling you things for your good. You could give them a point in manners. They have none. Look, for instance, at that amazing young thing in orange silk, eating and drinking and blowing smoke and probably chocolate eclair over her cavalier, all at the same time. Would you eat and drink at the same time? Of course you wouldn't. Neither would you envelop me in a blue haze of smoke with cream spots in it, would you? Not even if I were as old as the hairless monstrosity who is presumably paying for the privilege of seeing nearly all of the orange charmer.'

Janine felt herself grow hot. The man in question was probably not as old as Richard, and certainly not as bald or as fat.

'It makes me sick to see anything as young as that girl selling her charms, as they are called, for an old man to gloat over. I'd almost rather see that bedizened old woman in the far corner, in blue and white spots, buying an embryo like the youth sitting with her. There's something revolting in all of it, though. Youth to youth and age to age. It's more suitable and it possesses the charm of dignity, though that is almost a lost art now. And that's another point where you score. You've got dignity – poise.'

'I have? But I'm nearly always scared of everyone,' said Janine.

'You are, but you needn't be. You haven't been scared of me, have you?'

'No, but you're—different,' she said,

'My sweet, if I had a job, or any prospect of one, I'd be staying here and strutting it with the best of them. Would you be scared, for instance, of that sporty youth in the black-and-white trunks over there, the one with the red, upstanding hair?'

Janine looked.

'Frightfully,' she admitted.

'Rot! If I had complete control of you for, say, a fortnight, I'd have him eating out of your hand.'

'What would complete control consist of?' she ventured to ask.

'You won't be offended?'

'N—no,' wondering what was to come.

'Well, first of all, I'd dress you. Oh, I said dress, not undress – though that might come into it as well, all in the sacred cause of education – yours, of course, not mine.'

'The things you say, Terry!'

'The things you've got to learn, my darling child!' he mocked her.

'Why—*got* to?' she asked him a thought wistfully.

'No, I take that back. You're terribly sweet as you are, and in one way I wouldn't like you to be changed at all, or to learn anything you don't yet know. But we were discussing and considering your reactions to such a crowd as this, and that inferiority complex of yours. In order to get rid of that, you've got to learn things.'

'Teach them to me, Terry.'

He reflected that she could have no idea how attractive she was, how provocative, as she leaned forward under the orange umbrella with that half wistful, half daring look on her face and in her really marvellous dark eyes.

'I might teach you a lot more than you really want to know, my child,' he said a little unsteadily, and both of them were glad that at that moment the cocktails came and gave her occupation.

Afterwards they went down to the bathing-beach. There was a special terrace for sun-bathing, but by this time of the day even the hardiest and most resolute had ceased to expose their limbs to sea and sun, and they went up again and walked in the glorious grounds amidst which the hotel was set.

'Well? Resigned yet?' he asked her with a smile.

'What to? Staying in this hotel?'

'That, and – staying in Madeira at all. Remember that was what I wanted you to do? To watch your reactions to a southern moon and stars, though, as a matter of fact, there ain't going to be no moon. Shall we go and book you a room?'

'No. I'd be terrified, really.'

'What, of those?' as a pair of very precious youths passed them, calling each other 'darling' in ladylike voices.

Beside them, Terry looked very masculine, and Janine laughed.

'Not of those, but of the women. They sort of *look* at you, and you wish the earth would open. Besides, I haven't got any clothes.'

'Well, those are obtainable, even in Madeira, you know.'

'Not the sort of clothes people wear at this hotel,' she said.

'Perhaps you're right. We mustn't forget we've got to get things of some sort for you, must we? And Casanova at Government Building has got to be interviewed, too, at nine o'clock. He may even produce your husband, brought here by special 'plane!'

Janine's expression made him double up.

'You looked as if you believed it possible!'

'Well, I should be glad if it were,' she said vehemently – too vehemently.

'Liar!' he said softly, and tucked his hand through her arm.

'Let's walk about and see if we can light on an hotel which you might feel would meet with your approval. We can have all the old crows staying there lined up for your inspection so that you can see whether any of them is likely to put the fear of Mammon in you, my poor linnet,' he mocked her.

'Why on earth "linnet"?'

'Oh, I don't know. You're small and brown, and, by the way, you ought never, never, never to wear just that shade of brown, you know.'

'Does this begin the first lesson?'

'If you like.'

'I do. I never know what to buy, nor what I look best in. I've never really thought much about it. When you've worn uniform, day and night, summer and winter, for eighteen years, you lose the instinct for clothes, you know.'

The poor kid! She was not asking for sympathy, though, so he wisely did not offer it.

'I dare say it gets hidden, but not really lost. No woman worth the name could exist without the instinct for clothes, unless she is so infernally highbrow that clothes become no more than a covering, in which case she has probably something which is better covered! But *you* lose it – never! You should wear – let me see – browns, yes, so long as they are rich and warm browns, never that drab sort of colour. You don't mind?'

She shook her head.

'I'm feminine enough to enjoy being the subject of discussion,' she told him, and again felt amazement at herself for the ease with which she said such things to him. 'I really dislike this costume myself, but I thought it would be serviceable for the cruise.'

'It's smarter to call it a suit,' he commented, 'and unless you really *must*, don't wear things which are merely serviceable, not at your age and with your figure. You should wear very trim, belted things for the right occasions, and those slinky, tightly fitted satins which need so exactly the right type of figure.'

'I'd never dare to wear those,' said Janine, her thoughts flying to just such gowns on women on the ship.

'You're just the sort who could and should. I'd love to help you buy your frocks, Janine – and everything else as well,' with a sideways mischievous look at her.

'Well, you're not likely to get an opportunity,' she told him. 'No? What about a nightie for tonight, anyway? You can get delicious ones in the shops.'

'I can choose that myself,' she said severely.

'Don't be selfish, with only one night to share.'

'I never said we were going to share it.'

'I never dared to hope you would,' he retorted. 'But what about this hotel business? We shall have to have you fixed up somehow before we face Casanova again.'

Eventually they settled on one of the smaller hotels a little way up the side of the mountain on which Funchal was built. It was, like nearly all the buildings on the island, picturesque both in design and construction, and the balcony of the room which Janine was shown was of the carved Spanish type, overlooking a square, formal garden set in Spanish style in the centre of the house with the three wings bounding it, the fourth side being a highly ornamental wrought-iron gateway to the street.

Janine loved its peace and its perfect cleanliness. Terry went with her to the balcony and stood beside her, looking down on the little garden with its air of stately withdrawal from the turmoil of life. Flowering trees in tubs glowed against the white walls, and in a marble basin a tiny fountain sprayed its myriad jewelled drops amongst ferns and mosses.

'I love it here,' site said softly, as if even her voice would break the enchantment.

'It suits you somehow,' said Terry, realising it suddenly. 'You ought to have a long silk gown and a mantilla. You don't belong to this restless, vulgar age at all.'

She turned on him laughing eyes.

'Are you trying to make excuses for my dullness?' she asked him.

'You aren't dull, and you don't need excuses, and if Casanova doesn't do something about what he calls Monsieur Husband I might easily fall in love with you,' he said. 'Especially if you go on standing on your balcony, with your little white room behind you and your little white soul at my mercy.'

'You're laughing at me, Terry!'

'Heaven forgive me, I'm laughing at myself!' he told her, and she could not decide whether there were any earnestness or not beneath his mockery.

The fat señora came panting out to them, not at all scandalised at finding him there, though she would have been horrified and ashamed had one of her own daughters received a man on the balcony of her bedroom. The English and American visitors had long ago taught her to be surprised at nothing, and so long as they paid, which certainly they always did, what did it matter? They were heathens, anyway.

'You would like dinner, madame? And monsieur? I serve it here, yes?'

'Oh, could we?' asked Janine, clasping her hands in instant delight. Then she opened wide eyes on Terry, who laughed softly and nodded.

'Oh, definitely,' he said, and the fat señora laughed, and Terry laughed, and, finally, Janine laughed.

The señora had already been told the tale of the missed boat, but as her English was uncertain and limited to the things usually demanded of her, it was doubtful whether she understood the situation, save that for the moment madame had no luggage but would pay in advance.

'We will sally forth and buy the necessities of life meantime. I suppose you do classify a nightie amongst those?' he asked.

'Definitely,' said Janine, and they laughed at her use of one of his catchwords.

He took her to one of the silk shops, an odd place to London-bred Janine, and made her buy a cobwebby affair in apricot ninon, a gay satin kimono and a pair of mules, and then took counsel of a taxi-driver as to where a chemist might be found.

'I take you,' he promised them, and to Terry's infinite delight and Janine's utter confusion, he not only put them down before a furtive little shop with drawn shutters, but led them in, held swift converse with the wizened little man behind the counter, and produced for them triumphantly a mysterious box at whose contents she could only hotly guess.

Terry, almost speechless, explained again, and at length there were produced hairbrush and comb, toothbrush and soap.

Back they went to dinner, and the peace of the little balcony restored Janine's balance after the experience at the druggist's. The meal was perfectly cooked and served, a buxom, dark-eyed girl taking the place of the fat señora, who was doubtless below at the cooking-pots, and her eyes rested on first one and then the other of the guests with something like longing in them. So free these English were! Such extraordinary things they could do! Such things they must know!

In the room within were two beds, ancient carved affairs with wooden pillars and embroidered linen curtains. Terry had observed, though Janine had not, that both beds had now been made up with clean linen, and when they came in from dinner the apricot nightie had been decorously laid out on one pillow whilst the other, with the sheet turned back from it, was tenantless.

He looked at her speculatively as they passed through her room on their way down to the street and Government Building. What were her real thoughts and feelings about all this? He wished he knew. Was she a heaven-born opiate to his longing for the absent Joy, or was she really the prude she seemed?

Anyway, he would kiss her tonight and find out for sure. Not for many more hours should that rite be delayed.

Casanova had gone, but a dark-skinned young clerk awaited them with much less English at his command. From him they gathered that a wireless message had been sent to the *Carina* that Mrs. Harrow was in Madeira and safe, and instructions had been promised for the next day.

They came out again with lightened minds if not consciences. At least the absent husband had been relieved of immediate anxiety, and Janine resolved for once to take what the gods offered and forget the morrow.

'I feel really dreadfully grubby and creased in this,' she said, eyeing the brown linen distastefully.

'One can buy frocks of a sort, though I don't know where to go. Shall we explore?' and they set off, arm in arm, towards the square and the shops again.

They were lucky, for Janine's eyes spied a shop in a side street which promised success, and she bought a simple little thing of some soft blue silk, embroidered in tiny flowers. She would probably not have worn it at home, but when she slipped behind a screen, tried it on, and returned to Terry for inspection, he would not hear of her taking it off again, and, with the linen suit in a parcel under his arm, they set off again.

'It's rather a little-girl affair, isn't it?' she asked doubtfully.

'Well, you are a little girl, aren't you? Or aren't you?' he added speculatively. 'I almost wish I knew, though the uncertainty is rather deliciously aphrodisiac in effect.'

'What does that mean?' she demanded.

'I might possibly tell you – later on,' he promised her. 'Come in here. I'm going to buy you a shawl. Please, Janine, let me!' He made her choose a white one, exquisitely embroidered, and wrapped her in it, though she half wanted a thing of glowing colour, rose and gold and blue. It seemed to stand for so many dreams of her life, so many things that she had never had, but she let him buy her at last the white one.

'For most girls the coloured one, but the white one for you, my sweet,' he said, and though she had grown used to his promiscuous terms of endearment and recognised them as merely part of modem conversation, she liked the memory of them and wrapped them about her mind as his shawl caressed her body.

'And now what?' he asked. 'Shall we dance somewhere?'

'I dance terribly badly,' said Janine regretfully.

'Nonsense! With a figure like yours? I'll show you,' and he turned to the shopkeeper. 'Somewhere where we can dance, without having to change?' he asked, using the mixture of English and Portuguese which had so far proved successful.

The man directed him volubly, and they set off laughing. 'We'll call at your hotel and leave the parcel,' said Terry. The husband of the señora was at the door, and received the parcel amiably enough, managing to convey to them that the door would be open at any time for them and offering, with large smile and spreading hands, all the hotel and its contents.

They found the cafe to which they had been directed, a queer dark little place at the end of a dimly lit passage, with a stage at one end, a collection of tables set round the room, and a cleared space in the middle. Evidently it was not a place discovered by the tourists or the English population, for those tables which were occupied showed a collection of dark-skinned Portuguese men with a mere sprinkling of women of the lower classes.

Terry hesitated, glancing at Janine, but she walked serenely ahead, looking about her with interest, quite oblivious to the fact that she was causing a mild sensation.

'Isn't it queer and foreign?' she turned to ask him, and he nodded and selected a table not too near the platform. He wondered how he had missed this place, for he had spent many weeks in Madeira at different times, and he felt a little nervous on Janine's behalf of the type of entertainment likely to be provided.

He ordered coffee and a light, sweet wine and prepared to meet developments.

They came, discreetly enough, in the guise of two over-ripe dancers who performed on the stage to the accompaniment of some weird rhythm produced by a trio of niggers on a piano and two saxophones. Two other turns followed a banjo solo, and then a song sung by two men which brought the house down. Terry thought it as well they did not understand it, for at its conclusion the customers who had girls with them became rather more amorous. Two couples got up to dance on the cleared space.

'Like to dance, Janine?'

'I've told you I dance terribly badly,' she said doubtfully.

'Not with me,' and he held out his hand to her and drew her amongst the dancers, multiplying now.

The trio played a queer, haunting, lilting tune in no known rhythm, but their feet seemed to follow it unconsciously once they had begun to dance.

'Don't strain yourself away from me,' Terry told her. 'It's perfectly respectable to dance, and I can't guide you if you won't let me hold you properly.'

For a second she resisted, fluttering, and then, at the pressure of his arm about her, she suddenly relaxed and let him draw her closely. No man had ever held her like that before, and she was conscious in *every* fibre of her being of his nearness, of the warmth of his body against hers, of the rapid beating of her own heart. He let his cheek rest against hers. The lights were dim, and in any case what did it matter? No one took any notice of them, and though at first they had seemed the only people of their own class there, several others had drifted in and were dancing much as they were, close-held, and in dreamy abandonment to the haunting rhythm.

Janine took no conscious or considered steps. Held in Terry's arms, her body swayed with his and her feet obeyed his unerringly without effort. When the music stopped, she clung to him for a second, mind and body adjusting themselves to independent action again. Then she laughed, and her voice broke in an odd way, and she sounded breathless.

'That was … wonderful,' she said.

'And yet you dance – what was it – terribly badly?'

'You made me dance like that.'

'What a confession for modern womanhood!' he teased her, and they sat down again, whilst a troupe of girl dancers took the stage and began to perform weird and wonderful gyrations, contorting their bodies and twisting their limbs in a way that made Janine feel slightly sick. After them came a girl and a man, whose appearance was the signal for a round of applause.

They began to dance, the music little more at first than a monotonous tapping and droning. Gradually the noise increased, the saxophones wailed, and the dancers began to weave a pattern with their dancing, twisting like snakes and posturing, the girl with her body flung back from the flips, twirling this way and that, whilst the man circled about her, nearer and ever nearer, until, with a crash from the pianos and a discordant shriek from the saxophones, he caught her, their two bodies fused and whirled and the curtain came down amidst rapturous applause.

Terry, a little uncomfortable at an exhibition which had not been meaningless for him, glanced at Janine, but she was sitting quite unmoved, sipping her wine. At the next table, a fat old man drew his chair nearer to a girl who had joined him, passed his hand over her neck and her throat, and tried to draw her to him. She repulsed him with a shrill vehemence, but the next minute they had risen and could be seen making their way behind the curtains which shrouded a door at the side of the stage.

The band struck up a popular foxtrot, and Terry drew her to her feet, hoping she had not seen.

'I shall do this badly,' she warned him.

'Not if you leave it to me,' and he gathered her closely to him again, finding her pliant and unresisting this time.

He turned so that his lips rested for an instant on her hair.

'You're sweet,' he whispered uncertainly, and he felt her tremble in his arms.

'I don't want any more of this, do you?' he asked her when the dance was over. 'Let's get out into the fresh air,' and he wrapped her in her white shawl and slipped her bag into his pocket.

Outside was a night of stars, but no moon.

'Let's get away from the streets and the houses, Janine. I wanted to show you a southern night, but didn't dream I should ever have the chance.'

She was past caring where they went or what happened now. The feel of his arms was still about her, and her body thrilled at his nearness. So long as she might go with him, she would have gone anywhere just then.

They climbed the steep, cobbled streets, pausing by the side of one of the ravines which split the island and looking down at the fitful gleam of the wafer below. The croaking of a thousand bullfrogs tore the peace of the night, and yet in some way they made a fitting accompaniment to the turmoil of their emotions.

Up they went, Terry's arm about her to guide her step, the street into which they turned being so steep now that it consisted of a series of rounded humps, set like steps, the houses on either side almost meeting.

Everywhere was silence and darkness, and soon they came out above the houses and stood on the lonely hillside, looking down on the lights and their ghostly reflection in the dark water. Above them were the stars set in a sky which, even at night, was blue rather than black, and about them was the scent of a thousand flowers.

Janine stirred, and his arm held her more closely.

'It's too—much to bear,' she whispered, and he saw to his amazement that her eyes were wet.

'Why, Janine!'

She blinked and, smiled through the tears.

'I'm such an idiot,' she said. 'I'm always like that when I see anything really beautiful, I suppose it's because I was starved of beauty as a child. Believe me, there isn't much of it in an orphan asylum!'

'Your husband's a rich man, isn't he?' asked Terry unexpectedly.

'Yes. What made you ask that?'

'Only that he can give you all the beauty you want now, can't he?' and there was that note of bitterness in his voice again.

He thought of Joy, of all the beauty with which she managed to surround her life, beauty without which she would wilt and fade and cease to be Joy at all. It was as necessary to her as sunshine to the earth, and since it seemed he would never be able to give it to her and could only share hers at her expense, she was to be denied to him forever.

'You say that as if you—you were envious,' said Janine.

'I am—a little. It must be wonderful to have the power to give the beauty of life to—someone you love,' he said in a low voice.

Janine's heart leapt and for a moment she felt almost dizzy. Did he mean that? His arm was about her as he spoke, her head rested on his shoulder, and he said – that! Someone you love!

'Is there someone you love, Terry?' she dared to ask.

'Yes, and can never have,' he said shortly, and they were silent again.

So he did mean that incredible thing! To him, as to her, this strange day had meant upheaval. In those few hours her virgin heart had both budded and flowered, had opened to the sunshine and the warmth. It never occurred to her to interpret his words and his tone as meaning anything other than that he, too, had found the miracle of love. Why should it be more incredible that he should have found it than she?

She turned her face a little towards him. It lay like a white flower against the darkness of his coat, a white flower just flushed with colour. Her eyes sought and found his.

'Terry!'

He bent his head and kissed her. She was a sweet little thing, and obviously invited his kisses. He was startled and amazed, however, at the passion of her lips, of the arms flung round his neck, of the slim little body pressed against his in abandonment to her emotions. Not for a moment had he imagined her capable of such feelings, and he flung aside the memory of Joy and promised himself to take what the gods had so miraculously provided as a narcotic.

'You sweet kid,' he said.

'I adore you!' whispered Janine, and stood there in his close embrace, forgetful of past and future, content with the miracle of the present.

'Let's go down, shall we?' he asked her, and, regretfully, as if already she were laying her dreams away in lavender, she let him guide her steps down the rough path of the hillside and through the cobbled streets again.

The wrought-iron gates were closed and locked when they reached them, but they had been shown the little door which would be open, and Terry followed her into the dim, quiet passage from which ran the staircase to the upper rooms.

She lifted her face to his, and he had an odd impression of her as she stood there, wrapped in the white shawl, the faintly coloured light from a window of blue glass shining down on her. It took the colour from her cheeks and made them as white as marble, but it turned the shawl to a curious chalky blue. His thoughts searched for and found instantly what they sought – the blue-robed Madonna in the church on the hillside. There was that same youth and gentleness and purity about her, that same incongruous look of trust and innocence which the artist had caught in a moment of religious fervour.

Terry did an amazing thing. He bent and kissed her lips and left her.

Chapter Eight

Terry Forder walked back to his own lodgings half amused, half annoyed with himself.

He had come down from the hillside firmly intending to stay with her that night, satisfied from her manner and conduct that she intended him to do so. After all, though she gave the appearance of shrinking, innocent virginity, she was married and knew exactly what his thoughts must have been when they kissed like that. She had been passionately emotional about it, and when he recalled the way she had pressed her body against his and let her lips and arms cling to him, he was tempted to go back and follow out his original programme.

Then he decided against it. To be perfect, the thing should have gone on without a break, the completion of a well-spent day. By leaving her, they had missed the moment. He could imagine her cool and collected by now, her conscience inconveniently awake and her body inconveniently sleepy. She had had time to review the rapid course of the day's events, and, if he summed up her type rightly, would have decided in a panic that it had been too rapid altogether.

Never mind. The *Carina* was not likely to alter her cruising programme so drastically as to return three days too soon to Madeira for a late passenger. The most likely thing was that Janine would be wirelessed to stay in the island and the ship would make sufficient detour to call in for her on the homeward journey in three days' time.

It must not be supposed that Terry Forder was in any sense the villain of one-time fiction. He was no different from any other young man with time and opportunity and a healthy body. Given the first and second, the third was seldom unwilling, and it seemed that the first and second were to be his within the next few days even if, on some quixotic impulse, he had let tonight go by.

In the morning he called for Janine and found that she was up and had breakfasted early and alone, to the fat señora's secret surprise.

She met him shyly, with eyes suddenly grown wiser and more beautiful, with a smile born of the night's thoughts and the long vigil which had preceded a dream-haunted sleep. Odd that he had not realised yesterday, even on the hillside, that she had the makings of beauty, an elusive, pixie-like beauty all her own.

She came to his arms like a homing-bird and gave him her lips.

'Darling!' she said happily, and he held her closely.

She was going to be fun if she could make him feel like that at ten o'clock in the morning, thought Terry.

'Slept ?' he asked her.

'Mm. A little. I didn't want to though.'

'Why not?'

'Too happy. I wanted to think.'

'Silly child!'

'What are we going to do today?'

Already she had linked herself with him, and the thought gave her a little thrill of satisfaction. For almost the first time in her life a man figured in her plans.

'Well, I'm afraid the first thing is to go and see Casanova, isn't it?' he asked reluctantly.

It might be as well, he reflected, for heaven knew how and where they would put in the day if it had begun at such a temperature!

She sighed, and her bright face clouded over. She had forced herself to forget the ship, Richard, her marriage, everything in the world but this marvellous thing that had come into her life.

She was in love – and she had to go and get a wireless message from old Spilliken! She checked her thoughts remorsefully. She mustn't think of him like that, ever.

She wore the blue silk dress, and this morning needed no other warmth.

'Don't put on a hat,' said Terry.

'I shall get so untidy.'

'Why don't you have your hair permed?' he asked, touching it and tucking in the stray ends without any idea of the thrill his fingers gave her.

'I don't know. I've never been able to afford it, and somehow it didn't occur to me,' she said.

'Let's go and get it done this morning somewhere. There's a place at the back of the town, or I dare say we could get it done at Reid's.'

She loved the way he took possession of her, and sighed in pure satisfaction as he tucked a hand within her arm and led the way out. She wished he had kissed her again, but decided there would be other opportunities.

Casanova was in evidence this morning and full of smiles, the quality of which Terry appreciated more than did Janine.

'Any news?' asked Terry,

'Alas yes. I have here a wireless from the captain of the *Carina* for madame. A Dutch boat calls in here this afternoon and leaves again at four, and we are asked to arrange that madame travel on her to Tenerife, where she may be reunited with her husband.'

He gave them a comically commiserating glance, and they turned to look at each other in dismay, their house of cards fallen about them.

Terry was the first to recover himself, and he hastened to gloss over the impression they must have conveyed in that first moment.

'That is splendid,' he said. 'Is a ticket necessary or anything? What does one do? Will the boat put in here, or use launches?'

The official became impersonal again, gave them all necessary information, shook their hands and repeated his instruction to Janine to be on board the Dutch boat at half past three at the latest.

'Yes, of course,' she said, and they were out in the sunshine again, feeling at a complete loss.

'Well,' said Terry with a cheerfulness he did not feel, 'it's not eleven yet. We've still got more than four hours. What shall we do? Let's go and bathe and lie in the sun, shall we?'

Janine wanted passionately to be alone with him without realising all that that might convey. Terry realised it only too well, and was determined that, since matters had resolved themselves this way, he would take no more chances. Janine should return to her husband as she came, as far as he was concerned. He tried to feel suitably virtuous, but only succeeded in feeling he had been an ass the night before.

They bought her a swim-suit, scant and orange and backless, and she wore it, feeling nude but exhilarated, whilst they bathed at Reid's private beach and lay in the sun afterwards, browning and dozing and saying little. Janine was too acutely aware of the passage of time really to enjoy it, and she felt resentful at the suspicion that Terry, stretched out beside her, was conscious of little save the luxurious warmth.

No one took any notice of them, and she wriggled a little more closely to him so that he became more aware of her, turned on his side with a lazy smile, and flung an arm across her shoulders.

'Lovely, isn't it?' he murmured.

'Glorious, but—'

'But what, my sweet?'

'So short a time, Terry. I may never see you again,' she said in a very small voice.

'Perhaps it would be better if we hadn't met, Janine.'

She sat up at that.

'Oh, no—no! It's been lovelier than anything I've ever, ever had,' she said.

He smiled lazily and pulled her down again, wriggled himself into a more comfortable position with his arm about her, and closed his eyes again. He was trying to remain oblivious of her slim, supple body so very near his own.

'Don't think about it too much or too often when you're gone, darling,' he said.

'I wish—'

He put a lean, sunburnt hand over her mouth and checked the words.

'No, dear. We can't change things,' he said gently.

'I've been such a fool, Terry. I might have waited – for you,' she whispered.

'But you'd never have come to Madeira then, would you? So we should never have met at all.'

'Are you going to stay out here, Terry?'

'I shan't be able to afford it. I shall try to work my way back on one of the cruise ships – yours perhaps!'

'Work? What as?' she asked him, puzzled.

'I came out here as a cabin steward,' he told her calmly.

'No! Terry!' Then she giggled. 'Rather fun,' she commented, and he warmed to her unexpectedly. He had imagined that she would be shocked, disdainful, superior, as Joy had been.

He made her laugh with some of his experiences, told with a discernment and an appreciation of human frailties which recalled types on the *Carina*.

She had an idea, wondering why it had not struck her before.

'Terry! Come to Tenerife with me and see Richard. He may be able to get you a job.'

He made a grimace.

'As your cabin steward?' he asked with a mischievous grin.

'Of course not, silly!' she giggled, though the very thought of him going in and out of her room gave her an odd feeling. 'What I mean is – you see, he knows lots of people, has an interest in a good many things. He could take you to England with us and see people about you.

She was quite unconscious of the fact that her mind was placing her husband as a sort of kindly parent or uncle to both of them. Terry, who had no vision of elderly, kindly Mr. Harrow, did not share her view.

'Many thanks, my sweet, but quite definitely not,' he said lightly.

'Why not?'

'Do you seriously imagine I want to be beholden to anyone, especially your Richard, for my ticket home? What do you take me for?'

His voice was quiet and smooth, but she detected the steel beneath it, and flushed. She was blundering again.

'That's being rather silly, I think,' she said uncomfortably.

'Well, that's the way I'm made, I am afraid,' he said lightly. 'If I get home later on (and I shan't try until I've definitely decided I shan't get the work I want out here), I *might* bring myself to look you up and perhaps get an introduction from your husband to some pal of his, I say I *might*, if I am desperate, but – not otherwise. I still have my rag of pride, you know, sweet.'

'If I were a man and Richard were my—my father or something you'd do it, Terry,' she objected.

'Ah, but then you're not a man, praise the high gods!' he laughed, and pulled her a little more closely to him and kissed her.

She lay silently after that, her impulses hammering, her whole body one surge of desire for him though she did not know it. She only knew that never in her life before had she felt like this, and that she both liked and feared it.

Presently, feeling the need to get back to a normal plane, she spoke again.

'What sort of work do you do, Terry, I mean, what sort of job do you want?'

He laughed.

'The two questions ask for very different answers,' he said. Let's tackle the second one first. Actually I wanted to be a doctor. I started to study for it. The man under whom I worked for anatomy and surgery was enthusiastic about me and I trod the clouds, seeing myself a Harley Street surgeon, a saviour of the world and what not. Then my mother died. That was over two years ago now. It meant I had to chuck everything up, though I was in my third year, and earn a living. I had three hundred an uncle had left me. I was saving that towards a practice eventually. In any case, it wasn't any good using it for finishing my course. I invested it in a launch works owned by some friends of mine and worked damned hard to make the thing go. Well, it was the money that went. I was cleaned out, and I was twenty-seven and—well—that was pretty bad. I snatched at anything I could get. I sold things on commission and sometimes made the magnificent sum of three pounds a week, but more often I made nothing at all. I did a month at a petrol station, which was messy though not too bad, but when the wet weather started and business slackened off I had to go. I was a porter at a summer holiday camp, which was fun, but darned hard work. Then—a girl I know got me a paid job with a charity organisation, but I was always falling out with the silly women who ran it. They had absolutely criminal methods and an utter lack of discrimination between the really needy and the spongers. It was after that that I decided to work my way out here and try to pick up one of the old and more promising threads again. It broke off, with my usual luck, so here I am! And you ask me what I can do! Lady, nothing and everything,' he wound up with a laugh.

'Then come to Tenerife, and talk to Richard,' she urged.

'Never on your life! In the first place, I should have to borrow the passage money there!'

'I can lend it to you,' she said eagerly.

It was so ravishingly new to her to be able to play Lady Bountiful after having been so hard up all her life.

He gave her a squeeze which robbed her of breath.

'Thanks, my sweet, but nothing doing. I don't sponge on women – or their husbands.'

'At least give me some address to which I can write if I know of anything,' she urged him.

'Perhaps. And now, though this is heavenly, we've still got to have lunch and see you on board. Go and dress, though you look such a chuck in that swim-suit. I knew you would. You're built on the right lines for that shape – small and compact and all in proportion. Pocket Venus!'

Janine flushed and laughed and felt agonizingly conscious of herself and of the look in his lazy, laughing eyes. Without comment, she ran away from him, to rejoin him later in her blue silk again, and the wide-brimmed hat which the strong sun made necessary.

They had a rather difficult lunch in the hotel. Janine had no idea what she ate or drank, or even what she said. Over her hung the thought of parting from him, of the end of her brief, delightful playtime. For these few hours she had been someone she had never known existed – not Janine Wilson, nor Janine Harrow, not even Janine at all. When he was not looking at her, she observed him intently, impressing on her memory every least thing about him – the extraordinary long lashes which fringed his eyes, his lean sunburnt face, the way his hair grew in crisp waves, strong and wiry and, after his bathe, not to be controlled. She watched his hands. They were rather large hands, the knuckles slightly prominent, and at the wrists began the strong little hairs which ran up his arms.

In repose, his face was almost stern, but when he smiled, the joy of living was in his eyes and his mouth with its strong even teeth.

Suddenly she put down her fork and interlaced her fingers in her lap, struggling with the thought which had come to her, the wonderful, terrifying thought. She had fallen in love with him.

He looked up and smiled at her.

'Don't you like it!' he asked. 'It *is* rather a weird mixture, isn't it? Let's ask for something else,' and he signed to the waiter in that easy way of his which betokened the born master of men, wherever the Fates had actually placed him. He was of the type which gets willing and efficient service without demand or bribery.

But the substitute dish was just as meaningless to her, though she ate it, her eyes every now and then meeting his with something startled in their depths.

When the meal was finished there was little time left, and they could see from where they sat that the Dutch boat was in and her quarantine flag hauled down.

'We may as well go aboard,' said Terry. 'We shall be much more on our own there than on land now. The passengers will swarm ashore even if they have only an hour or so.'

She was glad of his help with the formalities when they finally got on board, and at last they were alone in the tiny cabin which was all that could be found for her. At least she had it to herself.

Terry closed the door and took her in his arms.

'Let's say goodbye here,' he whispered, and she clung to him.

'I've been so happy, Terry,' she said shakily.

'So have I, Janine.'

'Oh, Terry, have you? Have you really?' and she leant away from him to look in wonder at him.

'Of course I have. You're the dearest little pal. If only it hadn't been so short.'

'Perhaps it's as well,' she said in a very low voice.

It was his turn to look searchingly at her.

'I wonder what exactly you mean by that? We've still got an hour, you know, and we're quite alone here,' he said unsteadily.

She *was* very sweet and seductive, and why not take the goods the gods seemed about to provide?

'It isn't right,' she said soberly, but he drew her down on the narrow bunk bed and found her lips.

She let herself sink into his embrace, passion possessing her, her mouth warm and eager and clinging against his.

'I love you so!' she said incoherently, but he did not even try to hear what she said.

Suddenly she felt his hand close over her breast, and realised, with a shock, that it was her bare flesh which he touched. In an agony of oddly mixed delight and shame, she started away from him, pulling the silk of her frock about her and holding it across her breasts with both hands, her cheeks very pale, her eyes wide and startled.

'No—not that! Terry, we mustn't,' she said, her voice trembling.

He bent his head and kissed the hands which guarded her modestly, laughing a little.

'Why mustn't we? Our bodies are our own, my sweet, and surely we can do what we like with them? If I want to hold you and kiss you, and you want me to do it, who is there to stop us?'

'You forget I am married,' said Janine shakily.

He put an arm round her and drew her to him again, letting her hands still lie on her breast. He set her head back against his shoulder and looked deeply into her eyes, finding there fear and joy, triumph and shame, wonder, bewilderment, possibly love – but no knowledge.

'It's so hard to believe that, Janine,' he said.

'It's true, Terry.'

'Why did you marry him? Do you love him?'

'I—oh, it isn't fair to ask me that! He's been so good to me. I owe him so much!' She cried in distress.

Her whole world turned upside down, and she seemed so very recently to have adjusted herself after the last upheaval.

'Gratitude and payment of a debt is a very poor basis for marriage, you know, my sweet,' he said soberly.

'I know. I ought not to have done it,' she said in a low voice.

Then, 'Oh, Terry, kiss me just once and go. I want you to go.'

He held her and looked down again into her eyes. She was so defenceless, so entirely at his mercy. If he insisted, he believed he could take her – and regret it ever after, as if he had injured a child or an animal wantonly.

He kissed her, and then, on an impulse, took a card from his pocket and put it down on the bed beside her.

'That will find me if ever you—want to find me, Janine,' he said quietly, rose to his feet and stood looking down at her for a moment.

'I envy your husband,' he said. 'He doesn't know his job, though.'

She looked up at him with her questioning eyes.

'Why do you say that?'

'Because a man who knew his job would never let his wife go wandering around spare with the look that is in your eyes, my dear.'

'I don't understand,' she said, frowning a little.

'I know you don't. That's why I say he doesn't know his job. If he did, you couldn't *have* that look about you after a week or two of marriage.'

She still looked at him in perplexity, and he bent to take her up in his arms again, lifted her clean off her feet, kissed her until she felt spent and breathless and set her down again.

'I think I'd better go,' he said, and went without another word or look, closing the door behind him and leaving her standing there bewildered, confused, uncertain.

'I'm such a fool,' she said quiveringly, and flung herself down on her bed to cry her heart out.

A kindly Dutch stewardess brought tea to her later, and persuaded her to go to the dining-saloon for dinner, though she felt shrinkingly self-conscious again amidst the fresh crowd of strangers, most of whom stared at her and seemed to know her story and to have formed their own various, but not too varied, opinion of it.

She slipped away to bed thankfully, and awoke to find the ship at anchor, with the rugged outline of Tenerife stretching before her, and the usual array of little boats, of 'small boys' diving for sixpences, of insistent vendors of merchandise trying to strike their bargains and even boarding the ship whenever they could find an entrance not too vigilantly guarded.

Janine dressed and hurried on deck, and almost the first person she saw was one of the stewards of the *Carina* searching for her.

He saw her and saluted her with a smile.

'Sent to take you off, Mrs. Harrow,' he said. 'I have seen the purser and settled everything up, so if you'll get any luggage you have we can get aboard the *Carina*. She is lying over there,' and Janine followed the direction of his hand and saw the gleaming white and blue funnels a short distance off.

She felt oddly relieved when, ten minutes later, she was being helped up the gangway to the familiar deck again. She had thought she would hate this going back, away from enchantment and Terry and her brief dream of romance, but that essential need of her nature for security welcomed the place where she would be taken in charge again, left without the need for choice of action.

She hurried to their stateroom and to Richard's side, flinging off her hat as she came and throwing down the little parcel of her purchases in Madeira.

'Oh, Richard, I'm so sorry!' she said contritely, and the next moment bit her lips to keep back the involuntary cry that rose at sight of him.

Even in those few hours she saw the change in him – or perhaps it was that mentally she contrasted his appearance with the robust health and strength and youth of Terry. Richard looked so fragile and old, almost transparent in his lack of colour, and the hands which took and held hers seemed to have lost their grip and to fumble at her fingers.

'It's alright so long as I have you back safely,' he said, and even his voice seemed changed – or was it because the lazy, laughing, virile tones of Terry's voice still rang in her ears?

She dropped on her knees beside the bed and put her lips to his hand.

'My dear, you aren't worse, are you?' she asked, filled with remorse, ashamed of her gladness that he had not asked for the lips which remembered other kisses.

'I don't think so. I've been worried about you, of course, but now that you're back I shall soon get well again. Ah, is that you, Doc?' as a tap at the door preceded the entrance of the doctor's white-clad figure. 'Here's the truant back, at her post again, and looking none the worse for her adventure.'

Janine rose to her feet, and as she did so she caught the expression in the doctor's eyes. Why should he look at her like that?

She watched him in silence as he touched and prodded the sick man with gentle but enquiring fingers, producing every now and then a muted 'Ah—h!' of protest. Then he covered him up again and turned to Janine, who had stood by all the time without a movement.

'Well you've brought him the sort of medicine that will do him the most good, Mrs. Harrow,' he said cheerfully. 'Yourself! Not going ashore again just yet, I take it?' with a sly grin at her and at his patient, who joined feebly in the joke.

'No,' said Janine rather breathlessly.

'Ah well, after such an adventure, you'll probably find enough to amuse you on the ship for an hour or two. We leave at six this evening, anyway. Care to come for a turn on deck, Mrs. Harrow? I think your husband likes to be left alone for half an hour or so after I have put the thumbscrews on him, don't you, Mr. Harrow?' The sick man smiled and nodded, but did not try to speak. His eyes followed Janine's slim form wistfully as she turned, after a moment's hesitation, and went out of the cabin.

Once on the deck, with the door closed behind him, the doctor abandoned his air of cheerfulness and looked earnestly at her. 'Oh, Doctor, he looks very ill!' she said anxiously.

'I am afraid he is, Mrs. Harrow,' said the doctor gravely. 'Very ill indeed.'

'He ought not to have come! I didn't know,' she said,

'Of course you didn't. Neither did he, I think, or he would not have married you. He is so anxious and worried about you that I have had to bolster him up with even more lies than is usual in these cases, but I doubt whether he believes any of them.'

'With—lies? You mean ...? asked Janine, startled and wide-eyed.

'Mrs. Harrow, you're young and, I think, sensible. Can you bear to have the truth?'

'Oh, yes—yes! I'd much rather know!'

'Then I had better tell you. I am afraid your husband is beyond human aid, even if we could get him ashore at once, which we can't,' he said gravely.

Janine caught her breath in an agonised gasp and turned to grip the rail with both hands, the doctor coming to stand beside her, his professional eye upon her. He had long ago summed up the probable facts of this marriage, and he wondered whether that stop-over in Madeira had really been as unintentional as it seemed. He gave her credit for some human feeling, however, and he decided she was taking this revelation in the only decent way, whatever the circumstances of her marriage to Harrow.

'Does he know?' she asked at last in a low voice.

'I think so.'

'How—long do you think.'

'Probably another few weeks. Naturally I shall do my best to keep him alive till we are home again. It would be a disaster for—anything like that to happen on a cruise, apart from other considerations. You'll have to help me, Mrs. Harrow, though. No more missing of boats, you know!'

She flushed painfully.

'I didn't mean to,' she said, 'but I shan't go ashore again, not anywhere.'

'I think you would be wise and kind if you stayed on the ship now,' he said, and as someone paused beside them to speak to him, he excused himself to her and left her, her hands still gripping the rail till the knuckles showed white against the tan.

Richard dying! Dear kind Richard, who had shown her more human kindness and gentleness than anyone in her life before or since. Richard who had given her so much and asked nothing!

Dying! ...

And a few hours ago she had been in another man's arms, kissing him, telling him she loved him!

Passionately she thrust from her thoughts the image of Terry, of his arms and his lips, of the hand which for one exquisite, frightening moment had cupped her breast. Henceforth she would think only of Richard – Richard who needed her and to whom she belonged.

She crossed the deck again swiftly, and from her own cabin crept to the door of his. He lay with closed eyes, quite still, and for a moment her heart almost stopped. He looked dead already. But he opened his eyes as if aware of her, and he smiled.

'You, my dear?'

'Yes, Richard,' and she slipped into the room and down at his side again, her cheek pillowed on his hand.

For a little while they remained like that. Then he spoke again.

'I think the doc. must have told you, my dear.'

She turned her face and pressed her lips against his hand in mute, passionate revolt, and he laid his other hand on her hair, ruffling it gently.

'If I had known, I wouldn't have married you, Janine. Forgive me,' he said softly.

'Oh, Richard, don't! Don't! I don't want you to die!'

He smiled.

'It's almost worth it to have lived to hear you say those words just as you said them, my darling. Perhaps, after all, I need not be sorry I married you. I haven't done you any harm, dear – not any harm at all. Now that I know this has got to happen, I am utterly thankful that you are still … just as I married you. I haven't robbed any other man of you, and I haven't robbed you, my Janine.'

'I want to be yours, Richard! I want to belong to you!' she cried wildly, passionately moved by her pity for him and scarcely aware of what she said. It was as if, in that moment, she flung a challenge aloud to that other man who could not hear her.

Harrow only smiled gently and went on stroking her hair.

'That's impossible now, my dear, and I am glad of it. It's enough for me to have your sweet companionship, and to know that I have been able, in marrying you, to put you forever beyond the need to worry. I saw to all that before we left England. My lawyer will explain everything to you. I don't want to waste time now talking about it.

Let's forget all that and make the most of the days that are left, shall we?'

She lifted her face and smiled at him through tears.

'Oh, Richard, I'll do anything in the world for you! You know that, don't you?' she cried.

Chapter Nine

Richard Harrow was still living when the ship put in at Liverpool and the ambulance, ordered by wireless, drew up close to the gangway to receive the stretcher with its motionless burden,

Janine's white, distraught face, her obvious reluctance to leave her husband for a second, her entire devotion to him during that tragic journey homeward, had fired the sympathy of the passengers who had been only too ready to condemn her, especially after the small scandal of her stay-over in Madeira. The doctor had had something to do with it in his quiet way, too, and during those days, Janine found nothing but kindness and sympathy when she met any of her fellow-travellers. She took her meals alone in the sitting-room of the suite, but as long as Harrow was able, he insisted on her spending certain hours on deck. Later, the doctor took the duty on himself, and first one and then another of the passengers would join her and talk pleasantly to her, receiving in return her shy answers and her nervous, grateful looks.

Even the nurse had relaxed a little, and since she knew now that no human power could keep Richard Harrow alive, she made no demur when Janine begged to be allowed to take regular hours of duty.

During those days he came to know a great deal more of the girl he had married, to appreciate the sweetness which underlay her nervous fear of life. In a secret passion of repentance for her interlude with Terry Forder at Madeira, Janine responded to his least physical demands on her, ready with her kisses, her tender clasp of his hand, whenever he seemed to need her.

On the last evening on board she had stayed with him during the hour she usually spent on deck, and he had not insisted on her going. He talked, for almost the first time, of her future without him.

'Felicity has plenty of money of her own,' he said. 'Still, she is foolish and extravagant, and I want you to set aside a sum of five thousand pounds which she can have if ever she comes to you in need. Otherwise it is yours along with all the rest of it. I have left you with no burdensome-conditions, my darling.'

'You trust me so, Richard,' she said, humbled and touched.

'Why not? Do you think I don't know your utter honesty?'

And she thought of Terry – Terry, whose memory would not go, against the thoughts of whom she fought constantly, winning the fight until those small hours between midnight and dawn when he would not always be denied.

'You think too well of me, Richard,' she whispered, and laid her cheek against his so that he might not see her tell-tale eyes.

He smiled and stroked her hair.

'I may not live long enough to arrange that five thousand, but you'll remember it and put the money by in something very secure, won't you? Get Tanner to advise you. You can trust him. You can't do better than rely on him for everything in the way of money. You'll be a rich woman, Janine, so I want you to be careful that no one, no man, makes you unhappy because of it. You take Tanner's advice, my dear. And I should like you to keep on the Goughs, if you care to. They are decent people and will look after you as well as they have looked after me.'

And then, later, he had spoken to her of marriage.

'Some day you'll love someone, some man of your own age. Oh you will, my darling! I want you to ... you need love and children. I want you to be happy and to have all you want in the world.'

And again, fiercely, she had crushed down the memory of Terry.

All she wanted in the world! Love and ... children. Terry's children, with his kinky hair, his eyes which could mock you and yet the next moment be so kind, his laughter, that quick way he had of throwing out his chin—his lips ...

No, she must not think of him—would not!

And now they were carrying Richard down the gangway, carefully, slowly, after all the other passengers had left the ship, many of them going out of their way to come and bid goodbye to the tragic little bride, not knowing what to say and yet finding kind things which lay warm against Janine's heart, so hungry she was for kindness, so starved of it until Richard had come into her life.

One of the ship's officers went with her to the Customs House, saw her through without trouble, and took her back to the ambulance which had waited for her. A special coach had been reserved on the London train, and soon it seemed that all the sea and the strange lands and the life of the ship was a dream. The peaceful English scenery slipped by, and swiftly they were in London again, with another ambulance, but with kindly faced, anxious, inexpressibly shocked Gough in attendance this time.

As in a dream, they were at home in the Hampstead house, its master in the merciful oblivion of a morphia injection, its new, timid young mistress wondering how she was ever going to feel she belonged to this great silent padded house, where even one's breathing seemed too audible to be dignified.

Mrs. Gough came in and out, and it seemed to Janine's confused senses that there were at least a dozen white-capped maids where there had once been only the housekeeper. There was a stiffly starched nurse, too, to relieve Richard's wife of her labour of love, and when she ventured to his door she was informed politely but unmistakably that Mr. Harrow was sleeping.

As soon as she could, she went up to her own room – the room that had been Felicity's, and which she entered dubiously when Mrs. Gough had first escorted her to it.

'The master wishes it, madam,' said the woman gently. 'He sent a long message through the wireless, though it came by telegraph boy, and in it was that I was to get Miss Felicity's room ready for you.'

And so her first night in her husband's home was spent in that room which had held some of his most cherished memories. Everything was luxurious to the point of extravagance. For the first time in her life Janine slept between silk sheets, the pillows cased in the same pale lavender and lavender-scented. The bed was a miracle of hygienic softness, giving to her form when she turned and making her feel she was sleeping on a warmed and scented cloud.

Yet she was restless. She had thought that, with the return to England, she would forget Terry, or at least be able to think of him as dispassionately and remotely as of everything else connected with the cruise. Instead of that, she found him obsessing her mind. On the ship, she had been able to slip from her own bed and satisfy herself that Richard was sleeping quietly, drawing comfort and relief to herself in the act. Here she would have to face that starched, efficient-looking nurse, and she could not summon up the courage to do so, so she lay awake, restless and trying not to think of and long for the forbidden fruit of Terry's arms.

In the morning it was obvious that only by a miracle had life been kept in Richard Harrow's body for so long.

Janine sat beside him all the morning, waiting for him to awake again from the morphia-induced slumber which the doctor said pityingly would not be his last.

Towards two o'clock he stirred and opened his eyes. Janine bent over him and caught the whispered word 'Felicity'. It was the first time he had asked for his daughter, and Janine's repeated offers to write to her had met with steady refusal from him.

'I sent for her first thing this morning,' she said composedly. 'I sent a telegram.'

He smiled, nodded his head and closed his eyes again.

'I want to see you with her,' he said, speaking with difficulty, and obviously gathering his thoughts together with an effort. 'I want you to be friends, my—two best beloveds,' and he opened his eyes again to let them rest on her with such tender longing and love that Janine could scarcely bear it.

Throughout the afternoon they expected Felicity, but by tea-time she had neither come nor sent a message, and it was apparent that the dying man could bear his pain very little longer. The doctor offered him an injection, but he shook his head.

'The last,' he said with difficulty. 'I shall—sleep and—not see—my daughter,' and the hours dragged on painfully, almost as intolerably for the watchers as for the suffering man himself.

'Stay with me—tonight—Janine,' he said at last, though on the previous night he had insisted on her getting her rest. 'If—Felicity—comes, you will be here. Just you. Nobody else.'

The doctor spoke to Janine before he went.

'If he asks for morphia, he must have it,' he said. 'I can't think how he has gone through the day as he has without it. He must have been in agony – sheer diabolical agony.'

'He's so afraid he might miss seeing his daughter. He knows it will—be the end if he has any more,' said Janine pitifully. 'Oh, why, why, why doesn't she come?'

The strain of the day had been terrific. Hour after hour the dying man had striven to bear the agony, the sweat streaming down his face at each spasm of pain, his eyes almost starting from their sockets, his hands, those feeble, nerveless hands, tearing the sheets as the paroxysms shook him. And all the time, if only Felicity had come, he could have been spared it. He need not have suffered one hundredth part of that anguish. Only his will and his passionate desire to see his daughter again kept him from the merciful drug which would bring him death.

Janine had telegraphed again, more urgently, but with the same negative result, and now she had given it up and was filled with an intense and bitter resentment against the girl. The post office authorities, appealed to, had assured her that the wires had been delivered, and surely if she were away, some message would have been sent either to her or to the sick man.

That night was unforgettable.

Alone in the big gloomy bedroom, with one shaded light near the bed, with the dying man partly unconscious though still aware of pain, she sat hour after hour, a book of prayers in her hand which she tried fitfully to read but on which she could not concentrate.

Tomorrow at this time she would be alone again. Richard's goodness, his kindness, his tender thought and love for her, would be gone. The thought was almost intolerable, and when it caught and held her she would cross to the bed and slip down on the floor and lay her cheek against the thin, transparent hand. Usually he moved it to let her know he was aware of her, and she would put her lips to it for a moment.

Just after midnight he stirred and opened his eyes, and she saw stark anguish in them. His whole body seemed to shrink with the pain, and she hastened to his side.

'Richard?' she asked in passionate pity.

Feebly he made a movement and pushed the sleeve up his arm a little way.

'Now,' he whispered. 'No more. I cannot—wait.'

She knew what to do. She had seen the nurse do it, and though her fingers trembled, she took the syringe from its bowl, inserted the needle, drew back the plunger until the tiny glass tube was full of a dark liquid, and went steadily to the bed again.

He smiled at her, though the sweat ran down his face and into his eyes, and all her life Janine remembered that smile.

'Thank you—for—yourself,' he managed to whisper, and she bent to kiss his lips.

For a moment he remained still and silent. Then, very gently, he released himself and held out his arm.

'Now, dear,' he whispered, and she pushed the needle into his arm, withdrew it, and stood watching the potent drug take effect.

Peace superimposed itself on the pain and for a few moments he seemed almost to rally. Then he smiled at her again, dreamily, and closed his eyes.

Once more he opened them and tried to speak.

Janine bent to catch the words.

'Tell—Felicity—'

But no other word came.

She went on her knees beside the bed and prayed mechanically, using the childish prayers she had been taught at the Home. They had no meaning for her, but in some odd way they brought her peace.

Towards the morning the nurse came, rustling stiffly, rubber-shod, energetic, slightly disapproving still of the way in which she had been relieved of her job overnight. Janine rose from her knees, stiff and aching and cold, and went to meet her.

'He is dead,' she said in an odd, quiet voice.

The woman rustled swiftly across to the bed, felt pulse and heart with professional hands, lifted the eyelids, and then turned back to Janine.

'When did this happen? I ought to have been told. He is cold already.'

Janine, unexpectedly, was calm and controlled, and the nurse treated her not at all as an ordinary wife newly widowed. She took it for granted that there was nothing but money involved in this marriage on the wife's part, whatever the old fool of a man might have felt.

'What concern is it of yours?' asked Janine steadily. 'He is my husband,' and something in tone and manner arrested the further criticism of the nurse, who stared at her a little abashed and then rang the bell for help.

Janine went away to her room, too numbed as yet to feel anything, and when Mrs. Gough appeared, it was the older woman who clung to the younger for comfort.

'If only Miss Felicity had come,' moaned the housekeeper. 'Cruel it was of her, right down cruel. Her own father, too.'

Janine's face hardened. She would never forgive Felicity for the agony of those hours when Richard Harrow had endured hell to see again the daughter who had not even thought it worth her while to send a message.

'Her name is never to be mentioned in this house again, Mrs. Gough,' she said stonily. 'What she has done is unforgivable. Please tell Gough and the servants that, as far as this house and everything in it is concerned, Felicity Harrow is dead.'

'Surely she'll come to the funeral,' said Mrs. Gough tearfully, aghast at this new version of her late master's young wife.'

'She will not be admitted to the house if she does,' said Janine. 'Please tell Gough.'

But when, three days later, Richard Harrow's tortured body was burnt to ashes according to his own wishes, there was no sign of his daughter, nor did she send any message.

Janine, small and pathetic and yet oddly advanced in dignity and poise, repeated her instructions to the butler and his wife together.

'Miss Felicity is as if she had never been. I forbid anyone ever to mention her name again in this house,' and she gave orders that everything that had belonged to the girl, even the furniture and the silk bed sheets, the rugs and hangings, should go out of the house.

Nothing remained, and Janine herself flung into the fire the large studio portrait which had always stood on Harrow's table in the library.

She looked at the pictured loveliness for a moment, and her face grew hard.

'I'll never forgive you as long as I live,' she said. 'You're dead, Felicity Harrow—dead—dead—dead!' and she poked viciously at the burning pasteboard, stabbing it again and again with a fierceness that amazed herself.

Then she flung herself down and wept out her heart for the one human being in the world who had loved her.

Chapter Ten

Terry Forder rang the bell of the big Hampstead house rather uncertainly.

He wondered why he had come. Only a couple of hours ago he had decided that on no account would he do so, yet here he was, and when the dignified butler ushered him in he realised that he was to be treated as an honoured guest and not the mere suppliant for favours that he felt.

It was a year since he had seen Janine, a fortnight since he had had her first and only letter.

> *Dear Terry [she had written], I wish you would come and see me. I have been going to write to you before, but things have been rather difficult in many ways, and I thought it best to let a year go by. I shall be at home most afternoons this week and shall hope very much to see you.*
>
> *Your sincere friend,*
> *Janine Harrow.*

That letter had set him thinking. It sounded like her, direct and rather immature, but there was a hint of a new assurance about it. Why had she thought it best to let a year go by? He had been back in England a little over three months, and he had more than half expected to find a letter from her awaiting him when he came home. He was amused to find his pride a little piqued at the discovery that she had apparently forgotten her earnest desire to interest her husband in him – or perhaps the husband had refused to be interested! Might even have been jealous! That was possibly why she said, now that she had written, that she had thought it best to let a year go by.

And, not in the appointed week but very soon after, he had come to her call.

The year had not been financially a success, and the final three months of it had reduced him to desperation, so that he had decided at last to pocket his poor remnant of pride and go, cap in hand, to the husband of that odd, shy, emotional little girl of the Madeira adventure.

Janine came to him on swift feet, and at first glance she seemed to him utterly different. For one thing, she looked much more than a year older in the sombre black she still wore. For another, she had acquired a certain poise, a repose of manner, which made her fit into this dignified house in a way he would not have believed possible.

It was only when she came close to him, looked and smiled at him, spoke to him and held his hand in her slim, nervous fingers, that he realised she was just as he had remembered her.

'My dear!' he said, in that easy way of his with women, and, to his embarrassment, her fingers twined themselves round his with a sort of desperate eagerness.

'Terry, how *nice* of you to come!'

The very adjective she used, school-girlish and old-fashioned, helped to put her back in the dim niche she had occupied in his memory. The eyes of his mind peered into the dimness in the effort to bring her into the light, and he was surprised to find how well he really had remembered her now that he was with her again.

'Janine, how *nice* of you to ask me!' he mocked her, and they both laughed, and the tension was eased.

'Let's sit down and talk,' she said, and he noted that she chose a low couch rather than a single chair.

He smiled and settled himself beside her, preferring that she should set the pace, but quite prepared to keep up with her. He thought she looked thin and pale, that deep black did not suit her, but there was that odd, elusive attractiveness about her which had brought them very near indiscretion on a night of southern stars.

'What do we talk about? You?' he asked. 'You're thinner and too pale, and you look …'

'Well?' she asked rather diffidently, as he hesitated and looked at her with speculative eyes, as if unable to decide whether to utter his thoughts.

'Am I to be allowed to say it?'

'Why not?'

'Then ... as if you had been left too long to get cold,' he said.

He felt annoyed with himself directly he had said it. He had come without the least intention of carrying on a flirtation with her. He hoped to get a job, or at least an introduction to some possible employers. Certainly he was going the wrong way about it to start flirting with Richard Harrow's wife within the first five minutes!

Janine flashed, and his memory of her became still more vivid. He had forgotten that she, alone amongst all his feminine acquaintances, had either retained or learned the almost obsolete art of blushing.

'I—I have been rather lonely,' she said in a low voice.

He told himself he must walk warily. Young wives who felt lonely might be the greatest fun to vigorous young bachelors, but on the other hand, this was Richard Harrow's wife.

He pressed her fingers perfunctorily, wondering how to bring the subject round to his own needs.

'Why is that? Husband too much the busy city man?' he asked her lightly.

Her eyes widened in the childish way they had, and her mouth drooped.

'Don't you know?' she asked. 'Richard died a year ago, just after we came home.'

He felt and looked profoundly uncomfortable. The situation had rapidly changed, and he had no time to adjust himself to it with any nicety. His look and tone expressed conventional sympathy.

'I'm so terribly sorry. I had no idea. You must have thought me unfeeling.'

'No. I didn't realise you didn't know, though there is really no reason why you should. Have you been home long?'

'Three months. I got work of a kind in Lisbon, but foreigners are no more welcome there than anywhere else, and I came home in July to see if my Suck had changed.'

'And has it?'

'Unfortunately, no,' he said, with the grin she remembered so well.

It warmed and excited her. It had taken so much courage to write to him and ask him to come, and she had suffered horrible pangs when the days had gone by without bringing him. The relief of his presence, of his remembered friendliness, was wonderful after those anxious days.

'I wish Richard could have done something for you,' she said. 'I couldn't even ask him. He was too ill.'

'What was it? An accident?'

He still pictured her husband as a man of their own generation, and certainly he had never associated him with thoughts of death.

'Cancer,' said Janine, and even now her voice shook with the memory of that agony she had had to witness.

'Poor chap. How old was he?'

'He was—a lot older than I.' said Janine, wishing she had not to answer that question. 'He was—over sixty.'

'Good Lord!'

The ejaculation was spontaneous. He had had a shock. It had never occurred to him to associate her with anything like that.

'I was fond of him. He was so good to me,' said Janine, in defence of herself after that almost tacit reproach.

'No doubt,' said Terry dryly. 'So that's why you've felt lonely? No baby or anything?'

'No. I haven't anybody at all now.'

'And he had no relations either?'

'No, none at all,' said Janine, and he wondered a little at the hard finality of her tone, though it was not of sufficient importance to be dwelt on.

Rigidly throughout the year of her widowhood her edict had been obeyed, and never had the name of Felicity Harrow been spoken in her hearing. It was only when directly questioned like this that Janine even remembered her now.

Her utter loneliness caught at his imagination. She was so definitely not the type to be alone. Physically and mentally she needed sympathy and love and care. She appealed to the masculinity of the male. Her type, like her blushes, was almost extinct.

'You poor kid,' he said, and somehow, amazingly, she was in his arms, her face buried against his shoulder, her soft hair tickling his lips.

He looked out over the top of her head and wondered what to do next. The obvious thing was to kiss and make love to her, and yet he felt that the obvious thing would be a mistake. They had reached this stage too quickly for it to be merely at amusing affair of the moment. It revealed too poignant memories on her part, and he felt that it behoved him to be careful, especially as she was extremely attractive in her almost obsolete femininity.

She sat up, unkissed, and pushed the hair out of her eyes.

'You shouldn't have done that,' she said, and he smiled and forbore to tell her that it was she who had 'done that' rather than he.

'Why? Did you mind?' he asked her.

She hesitated.

'That isn't a fair question. I ought to have minded,' she said in that prim little way he remembered.

'Still determined to keep all the windows shut and the blinds drawn in case the sunshine gets in?' he asked her teasingly. Then, as she did not answer, 'Well, you asked me to come, Janine. What for? Obviously not to make love to you!'

'Terry! As if I should do such a thing!' And then she wondered, confused, whether that was not in essence the very thing for which she had asked him to come.

She had wanted to see him again. In the lonely year when she had conscientiously mourned Richard Harrow, her thoughts would not always be controlled, and her very isolation had magnified the importance of the episode in Madeira with Terry Forder until she had come to feel that nothing else mattered but seeing him again, assuring herself that he had been real and not a mere dream. She had endowed him with qualities he had never hoped to possess, made him her prince of romance, hung about him that radiant fairy web, of dreams through which he had long since ceased to bear the outlines of Terry Forder.

A little of this he realised, but it is certain that had he been more aware of it he would have gone from her as quickly as he could and never ventured near her again. He knew enough of women not to underrate their strength and a man's weakness. Only the very young and inexperienced or the very old and hard-bitten boast of their immunity from sex-allure, and Terry was neither.

'Well, whatever the reason, I'm here. So now what?' he asked her lightly.

'I—wanted to know if you were—alright, if I could do anything,' she said hesitatingly. 'You see, I had promised you that Richard would do something for you, and I didn't want you to think I had forgotten.'

He patted her hand which lay confidingly on his arm.

'Sweet of you, my dear, but I don't stand in need of your help, you see,' he said.

He had a moment's horrified fear that she meant to offer him a fiver or something like that!

She wrinkled her brow.

'But you said just now that you hadn't any luck. Doesn't that mean that you haven't a job?'

'In a way, yes, I suppose it does. I'm trying to sell cars at the moment, but of course no one buys cars at this time of year, and all the business likely to be done for some time was done at the Motor Show last month. Still, I daresay I shall survive until the spring, when people begin to be car-conscious again.'

'Well, I—I want a car, Terry,' said Janine.

He laughed and slipped an arm round her and gave her a little squeeze.

'Darling, what a good thing for you it isn't coal-barges or submarines I'm selling! You're too adorably transparent for words, you know.'

'But I do really want a car, Terry, a—a Talbot, I think,' picking at random on a make which she believed to be expensive.

'I should have a Bugatti Sports as well,' he suggested gravely. 'And a couple of Rolls are always handy if one has an extra suitcase or two.'

'You're teasing me.'

'No!' and they both laughed, youthfully, absurdly.

'Do you know, I haven't laughed, *really* laughed, since we came down the mountain at Madeira on that toboggan,' said Janine.

'What a waste of a year! And you've got the loveliest laugh. We must see what can be done about it. What are you doing tonight? Dine and dance with me somewhere?'

'I'd love to—oh!' with a sudden realisation that he probably could not afford it. 'Have dinner with me here, Terry.'

'Haven't I told you you're amazingly transparent? My dear, I'm not broke yet—and you're giving me an order for four or five cars, or was it six?'

'Seriously, Terry—'

'*Seriously*, my sweet, will you dine and dance with me?'

'Well— alright. I'd love to, if you're sure—'

He slid a finger over her lips, closing them.

'Don't make me feel too humble in my own estimation and yours, Madame Croesus,' he said lightly, but there was an underlying note of irritation in his voice which silenced her half-hearted objections.

'Do I call for you, or meet you?' he asked. 'One of the benefits of my line of business is that I get the use of a car even if I don't sell it. I'll call, shall I? Seven?'

She agreed a little breathlessly and he prepared to take his departure.

'Don't wear black, Janine. Let's be gay.'

'But I haven't anything gay,' she said, distressed.

He glanced at his watch.

'I know. Let's go and get you a frock—oh, you can pay for it yourself!' as he caught the scandalised look on her face. 'Only let me help you choose it. Where do you go for your things?'

'Well, I haven't bothered much lately,' with a deprecatory glance at her plain little black crape frock, which was good its way but quite undistinguished. 'Richard used to want me to go to a place in Hanover Square.'

'Then well go somewhere quite different,' he said decidedly, remembering the unbecoming suit she had worn in Madeira. 'We'll go to a little shop I know, and Mélisande will find you something exactly right. I expect her name is really Rebecca Isaacstein, but who cares? Coming?'

She hesitated and then nodded, her eyes lighting up, her mouth curving in a smile which bore the faintest imprint of the gamine he had once suspected in her. Heavens, but how bored the kid must have been to find such delight in a new frock!

'Shall I order the car?' she asked.

'I've got one outside.'

He took her to a smart little shop, where he was greeted by the black-haired, hook-nosed 'Mélisande' as a long-lost friend.

'Mrs. Harrow wants a really chic evening outfit,' said Tarry. 'What do you suggest? Something she can have for tonight, not black.'

'Oh no! But not black, *certainement!*' said the modiste very decidedly, and she excused herself, tripped away on her very high-heeled shoes, and returned some minutes later to usher in the first of her mannequins, someone small and dainty like Janine, in a creation of scarlet and silver at which the prospective purchaser gasped and protested.

Terry laughed and regarded appreciatively the bare back and tantalising shoulders of the model, but he also shook his head.

'Too sophisticated, Mélisande,' he said.

'Ah, so so! Perhaps, Monsieur. You will see others,' and she clapped her hands to invite the entry of another girl in a gown of silver tissue, low-cut and cunningly devised at the hips: 'Still, Monsieur?'

'I think so. Madame is so very young,' laughed Terry, letting his eyes rest mischievously on Janine's startled, protesting face.

The modiste had a rapid conversation with the first mannequin, and in a few moments the girl returned in a frock of palest shell pink, very young and doll-like, with a fragile lace bodice and tiers of tiny frills from waist to toe.

Terry nodded.

'Exactly right, Mélisande, don't you think?'

'But perfect, Monsieur,' and the two of them studied Janine reflectively: Madame with her head on one side like a bright little bird, Terry with his lazy, half mocking smile which had that oddly exciting effect. 'The hair dressed—so,' and with lightning fingers she gathered up the mannequin's neat, flat waves into a bunch at the back of the head, caught up from a side table a few pins to secure it, snatched something from a drawer and in a second had fastened above the bunched curls a halo of fine silver net, stitched at the edge with something which shimmered in the light. It gave to the rather hard, worldly face of the girl a look of spirituality which, mentally added to Janine's expression, enchanted the conspirators.

'Mélisande, you're a witch!' said Terry. 'It's absolutely and entirely perfect. What do you think about it, Janine?' turning to her suddenly.

She smiled.

'Oh, I do come in on this then?' she asked, and they all laughed, for they had treated her like a doll to be dressed.

'Try it on,' commanded Terry, and she went with Mélisande, excited and thrilled.

The effect was delightful when she returned to show herself, complete with halo and silver slippers. Madame brought a cloak of silver lined with shell pink and possessing an enormous collar of white fur out of which Janine's face rose like a flower.

'My dear, there's absolutely nothing to say,' said Terry, and she held his eyes for a second and caught her breath at the look in them. 'Have you argued about the price with Mélisande? Don't pay her more than half she asks you, the old thief,' with a grin in the direction of the smiling modiste.

'Monsieur, it is what you say calumny!' she cried, in her carefully and artistically broken English which she had found so valuable an asset, but she smiled without rancour, mentioned a sum which took Janine's breath away, and gave orders for the things to be packed.

Janine, back in her uninspired black clothes, wrote out a cheque with trembling fingers. After all, she had spent so little of the money which she still felt was Richard's that old Mr. Tanner had more than once expressed polite surprise.

'I'll never do my hair like that,' she said, when Terry had tucked her and Mélisande's ribboned boxes into the roadster again.

'Right!' and Terry swung the car round a corner, narrowly missing two jay walkers, pulled up at a shop, got out of the car and returned a minute or two later with the calm announcement that a hairdresser would call at Mrs. Harrow's house at six o'clock.

She was bewildered, but thankful to be piloted through some of life's difficulties, though Terry was like a tornado after the precise and gentle propulsion of old Mr. Tanner and the Goughs.

'You—sweep me off my feet, Terry!' she laughed breathlessly.

'I lak heem queek,' grinned Terry, taking a corner on two wheels. ' 'Member, Janine?' with a glance sideways at her.

'Yes—everything, Terry,' she told him with a catch in her voice and a swift rush of colour to her cheeks.

How well she remembered! And all this time she had thought she was forgetting, thought she could send for him and meet him just as a friend, cool, casual, impersonal—Mrs. Harrow!

'I too,' he said, and enjoyed the little flutter of her hands in her lap.

It was like playing on the strings of a sensitive instrument, he thought, a violin—no, a harp, with a mental grin at himself.

'You'll have an accident,' she warned him a little nervously.

'Not with you in the car and the day still comparatively young,' he told her with a smile that made her pulses leap, but he slowed down and finished the journey more decorously.

'Then you'll be ready, and beautiful, at seven?' he asked her when they were outside her house again.

'I'll be *ready,'* she amended, with a little fluttered smile, but when, an hour or two later, she stood before the long mirror and surveyed herself, she wondered joyously whether she need have amended his speech after all .

The hairdresser had done her work well, knowing exactly what effect was desired, and she had brushed and waved and coaxed the soft brown hair and set it into little curls at the back and above the ears, the silver halo gleaming like a fairy crown and making entirely perfect the effect of the pink frock. She looked fragile and delicate and delightfully feminine, and when the hairdresser had gone, leaving her with Mrs. Gough, that good lady wiped a sentimental tear from her eye.

'You look lovely, madam,' she said. 'I wish the dear master could see you now.'

'You don't think it's dreadful of me to be dressed up like this so soon, and going out with Mr. Forder, do you?' Janine asked her anxiously.

'No, madam. I think it's right and as it should be, and what the master would have liked. He told me he didn't want you to stay a widow if you found someone you could care for and be happy with, and you did everything you could for him and were a good and true wife to him to his dying day, which no woman can say more.'

Janine remembered those hours in Madeira, Terry's kisses, his arms about her, his voice saying incredible things to her. She wished she could have blotted that out from her memory. But then, if she could, Terry would not be here now, waiting downstairs for her!

She hung the silver cloak over her arm and kissed Mrs. Gough.

'Dear Mrs, Gough!'

'Bless you, my dear,' said the old woman, laying aside for once her formal manner and mode of address.

Down in the sombre library where Terry waited for her Janine glowed like a jewel, and he caught his breath at sight of her. Beautiful she would never be. He was not sure that she would ever be even pretty. But there was that elusive charm and fragrance about her which needed no beauty of feature to enhance them. She was so essentially young and feminine and – yes, desirable. He admitted it at first sight of her, and something glowed in his eyes and coloured his speech as he took her hand and held it between his own and then, aware of her mute imitation, bent and kissed her lips lightly.

'You're like a fairy princess,' he told her, and she flushed and laughed, intoxicated with the knowledge that she was perfectly dressed and looked as she had never dreamed she could look.

'You like me in it?'

'I adore you—in it!' he said, and their eyes met and held each other's for a magic moment until she looked away, confused and glad.

It was an evening of sheer delight for Janine, and of amused speculation and enjoyment for Terry. She was so naive in her appreciation, so obviously inexperienced, so much like a schoolgirl given an unexpected treat and not quite sure whether the mistress would approve.

It was when he danced with her that he began to realise that the schoolgirl effect was a delusion. He held a woman in his arms, alive and palpitating, aware of him in every fibre of her being, and excitement crept into his veins. On that former occasion there had been a husband in the background, and she was the possessor of that weird relic of the middle ages, a conscience. Now there was no husband in the background, and he had yet to discover how elastic was that conscience when she heard the mating call.

A year was a long time, especially when one was twenty-three.

He held her more closely, the subtle fragrance of her all about him, her body warm and yielding against his, though he could not decide whether she were aware of him as he of her. There was still about her that intangible aloofness, that barrier as thin as mist but as strong as steel which held her back from him. The knowledge piqued him and acted as an aphrodisiac to his senses.

'Happy, Janine?' he asked her.

She pressed her cheek more closely to his and gave a little sigh.

'In heaven,' she whispered.

They danced a little longer and then he drew her towards the open door.

'Let's get a breath of air, shall we?' and, her eyes like stars, fear and yet exultation in her heart, she nodded and went with him.

He wrapped her in her coat, standing for a moment with the edges of the huge fur collar in his hands, drawing it about her.

"You're lovely,' he told her unsteadily. 'Do you realise you've gone to my head?'

'Have I, Terry?' with a little catch in her voice. 'I'm glad.'

'And knowing that you have, you'll still come with me for a breath of air?'

She nodded, only half comprehending his meaning.

'Then—on your own head be it, Mrs. Harrow,' he said, tucked her hand under his arm and took her round to the car, which he had parked in a quiet street adjoining.

'Why did you call me Mrs. Harrow like that?' she asked him curiously, for he had accented the words.

He looked down at her with his odd smile.

'Perhaps I wanted to assure myself that you really had been married, though you look like something very innocent strayed from fairy-land and not for the use of mere mortals.'

She knitted her brows.

'Why have you to remember that I've been married?'

For her own part she would have been glad to forget Richard just then and to remember only that she was young and free and in love and, amazing thought, beloved! She could not doubt that he loved her. She was too inexperienced and ignorant of men to be able to set a fair value to his words and looks and actions. She was too sincere herself to doubt his sincerity, and she accepted as frankly and generously as she gave.

They had reached the car, and before opening the door for her he stopped and looked down at her deliberately.

'I don't know that I should risk taking you out at thus time of night, with you looking like something out of a fairy tale, if you hadn't been,' he said, and she smiled, but did not in the least understand.

'Still want to go?' he asked her.

'Of course. Don't you?'

'You know I do,' he said in a low voice, and as he settled her into the car he bent and kissed her lips fleetingly.

They drove in silence until London lay behind them, and Terry switched on the headlamps to illumine the dark country roads, the trees with their burden of autumn gold interlacing above their heads and making a tunnel through which they swept behind their shaft of white light.

And amidst the stillness Terry drew in under the trees, switched off the engine and the headlamps and sat very quietly beside her. The unearthly silence could almost be felt, and Janine, sensitive always to beauty, drew in her breath with a sigh that was half a sob.

He turned to her and laid a hand on hers.

'Still happy, Janine?'

'Still in heaven, Terry,' and she smiled at him with lips that trembled a little.

'Let's walk under the trees,' he said, and he helped her out, guiding her with a hand in hers until the leafy boughs shut out even the lights of the car.

They seemed alone in the world, and if now and then an owl hooted or a bat flitted above their heads, neither was aware of it. Absorbingly they were aware of each other, though Terry's perceptions were the keener and he was conscious of that awareness, able to analyse and appreciate his feelings as Janine could not do. All she knew was that she was alone with him and in love with him and filled with a wild unreasonable exultation and expectancy of she knew not what.

He let her hand go and reached to unfasten her cloak.

'You won't be cold,' he said softly. 'I won't let you be.'

'Oh, Terry—Terry!' she whispered, and clung to him as she felt him take the cloak from her and hold her in his arms.

She remembered poignantly the moment when his hand had cupped her breast, and knew that she longed for him to touch her again like that. When she felt him push the fragile lace from her shoulder, she shivered a little but made no movement to prevent him.

'I'm going to love you, Janine,' he said unevenly, amazed at his reaction to the warmth and sweetness of her. He might be in his teens again and thrilling to the first contact with the mystery of sex.

'I love you now, Terry,' she whispered, aware and yet oddly unaware of her emotions. She seemed drugged with happiness.

'You're going to let me, Janine?' he asked her insistently, his hand still adventuring.

'I want you to!' she said, scarcely aware of his meaning.

He spread his own coat on the mossy, leaf-strewn ground, made a nest of rose and silver for her with her cloak, and drew her down, 'Janine, you're so sweet. How could a man not love you?'

'Did you before, in Madeira?' she asked him.

'You wouldn't let me,' he reminded her.

She wound her arms round his neck, and again he was amazed and enchanted with the warmth of her passion. She looked so cool and undisturbed at other times.

'I've loved you all the time, Terry, every hour, every minute. I've longed to see you again, to be in your arms again, to kiss you. Is it dreadful of me to be saying things like this to you?'

'Dreadful? It's adorable and natural. We're both young and full of life and—ready for love. Give me your lips, Janine—yourself.'

Just for a second something reasserted itself within her, and she struggled in his hold.

'Terry, it's—wrong,' she said.

He laughed against her lips.

'How can it be when it's natural? If it is, then everything in the world must be wrong – the birds, the animals, the flowers – kiss me, Janine.'

Chapter Eleven

Janine awoke and stretched herself luxuriously, lay for a moment wondering why today was different from any other day she had lived, and remembered with a smile and a little sigh of pure happiness.

She rang the bell beside her bed, and Hetty, the neat, smiling housemaid, came in with her tea and her letters. Only after an effort of months had Janine schooled herself to sleep later in the mornings and to have a tray brought to her room.

Ridiculously, she looked for a letter from Terry, though she had only parted from him – at what hour the night before? One? Two? She had not even troubled to look at the time when at last he had set her down outside the house and held her in his arms for a last kiss which she might take to bed with her for memory, as he whispered.

Memory!

She had no need to keep that one kiss for memory when she could relive, glowingly, with a certain breathless sense of guilt and a sneaking shame, every moment of those enchanted hours with him.

She drank her tea slowly and without appreciation, went as in a dream to the bath Hetty drew for her, and dressed herself carefully, forcing herself to concentrate on her appearance for once, going through her meagre and uneventful wardrobe, regretting that she had not one really attractive frock to wear.

She surveyed the result with dissatisfaction. In the wardrobe hung the frilly pink gown, the gleam of her silver cloak next to it. Would his memory of her in that be sufficient to make him overlook the dull dowdiness of her 'best' black crepe-de-chine, or would he, on first sight of her like this, in broad daylight, in the conventional surroundings of Richard Harrow's house, regret in amazed discontent those hours of enchantment, all the things he had said to her?

But the morning went by and he had not come; the afternoon, and still there was no word from him.

And just as she had finished her solitary tea, served to her in state in the drawing-room, he was announced.

She waited until the door had closed on the impressive figure of Gough. Then, like a homing-bird, she flew into his arms.

'Oh, Terry, I thought you were never coming!' she said.

'Sorry, sweet, but I thought I'd got a chance of a job, and I couldn't miss it, even for the sake of seeing you, could I?'

He thought how different she looked in the uninteresting frock she wore – colourless and without any of that appeal which had made him make rather a fool of himself the night before.

She laughed a little happy laugh and crept more closely into his arms.

'But that sort of thing doesn't matter so much now, does it, darling?'

'What sort of thing, Janine?'

'Well, getting a job. I've got such heaps of money, you see.'

He stiffened and let his arms slide from her, looking down at her with uncomprehending eyes.

'What difference does that make?' he asked.

'All the difference in the world, if you don't want me to do what I would really like, which is to settle something on you, you can't prevent me from – well, sort of employing you, can you? Please don't say anything yet, Terry. I've thought it all out in the night. You see, I am so stupid over business matters and I don't understand anything about stocks and shares. I never could do them at school, and as I never imagined I should have any stocks or shares myself, I never bothered! Since Richard died, Mr. Tanner has seen to everything for me, but you see, you could do that. Then there's Merrow. That's a sort of village place that belonged to Richard, a hobby of his, model farms and sanitation, and all that. I didn't know much about it until it belonged to me, and Mr. Tanner thought I ought to sell it, but somehow I felt Richard would have liked me to keep it. There's ever such a lot to be done there, and Mr. Tanner said only last week that I ought to have an agent or a bailiff or something, though I thought bailiffs were men who came and lived in your house if you owed debts and couldn't pay!'

He could tell, by her rapid speech and its most unusual length, that she was greatly excited, but he was still at a loss to understand her. Was she offering him a job, or what?

'Darling, I'm still at sea. Are you inviting me to become your bailiff, or something like that?'

She laughed.

'Well, it would be only natural for my husband to do that sort of thing for me, wouldn't it?' she asked happily. 'You wouldn't like some other man to do it, would you?'

Terry felt half stunned with the force of the blow, and he let her go and caught automatically at the back of a chair, as if he reeled from a physical shock.

'Your—husband?' he asked stupidly, but Janine did not appear to notice anything. She was blind with her own happiness.

'Darling, it isn't that I *want* you to work or anything,' she said. 'Only I feel that you'd prefer it that way, wouldn't you? You wouldn't feel that you were—well—'

She hesitated for a word, and he supplied it grimly.

'Living on you?'

She nodded.

'It sounds pretty horrible, doesn't it? Not that I should mind the least little bit in the world. All I want is to be yours and to have you for mine, Terry darling, for ever and ever.'

'Janine, dear, it's all wrong,' he said desperately. 'I—I simply couldn't marry you. It wouldn't be fair.'

She smiled gently. This feeling of being able to give so much to the one being in the world was marvellously satisfying. She had never experienced such bliss in her life, and secretly she sent a thought of blessing towards the dead man who had made this moment possible.

'Darling, it wouldn't be fair *not* to, after last night,' she said happily.

She took his reluctance merely as what one would expect from him, having regard to the difference in their positions. She would have hated to think of him jumping at the chance of marrying a rich woman.

'Janine, you don't understand,' he began wretchedly, trying again to extricate himself from this incredible position.

Damn it, a man wasn't expected to marry a very willing widow merely because of what had happened, to their mutual satisfaction, the night before.

She closed his lips with soft fingers.

'Darling, believe me, I do. You see, Terry, I had thought it all out before I—gave myself to you last night. Otherwise, of course, it couldn't have happened. I knew you loved me, though even now I can't believe it. But, of course, if you hadn't loved me, last night couldn't have been, could it?'

'My dear child, that sort of thing does happen,' he said uncomfortably, wondering what on earth he was to say to her without hurting her too abominably. 'People don't always—marry afterwards.'

'I know, Terry – but it couldn't happen to anyone like me, not a first time, like that,' she said simply.

He stared at her, and slowly realisation came, and the conviction that she was telling the truth, though it had not at the time even dimly occurred to him. He had been too much enthralled with her appeal to his emotions to be aware of such a possibility, and her surrender to him had been so absolute. Good heavens!

'Is that—true, Janine? Was last night—the first time?'

She faced him bravely, though her face was scarlet and her eyes shamed even in their triumph.

'You know it was, Terry,' she said in a low voice.

'But—your husband—you are a widow,' he stammered.

'We never—slept together,' she told him, holding on to her waning courage with both hands, but feeling a little sick and wishing this inquest were not necessary. 'He was ill all the time, you see.'

'I—see,' said Terry slowly, and wondered how he could have been such a colossal idiot as not to have realised it before. Of course, that accounted for her extraordinary air of innocence, which he had come to believe must be either a pose or a freak of nature.

Suddenly she dropped down in a chair and buried her face in her hands.

'Oh, Terry, I'm trying not to feel—ashamed, but I do a little bit,' he heard her say.

He stood staring down at her, aware rather of himself than of her. Could he, in honour, get out of this situation without marrying her? And if he could, did he really want to get out of it? The bitter years of failure passed before him in review, the ceaseless, certain downward trend. What lay ahead of him? He was down to his last few pounds, and he had nothing in the world that could be turned into money, least of all his brains, his hands, his youth. There was no place in civilisation for him and thousands like him – millions, probably. There never would be any place. Machinery and its misuse had so driven and cornered manpower that a third of the world's possible workers were doing far more than was just and reasonable, whilst the remaining two-thirds had nothing at all to do.

Joy was lost to him for ever. When they had parted, over a year ago, it seemed they had parted for life. Thoughts of her were still a dull ache in his mind. No woman would ever oust her. And if he could not have the only woman he wanted, why should he not take the one who wanted him? Janine was simple and sweet, easily satisfied, easily hoodwinked. She believed he loved her, and it would be so easy to keep her in that belief. She would be happy – and he would be rid for ever of this carking worry and care, of the feverish search for a mere pittance, earned at jobs he hated whilst heart and brain and body ached for the one job he felt he could have done, and done superlatively well.

He looked down at his hands. They were roughened and stained, the nails badly shaped and broken at the edges. That was from the week's work he had got at the docks. Surgeon's hands! Yes, they still were that, and, with Janine's money at his call, could they not be surgeon's hands in actual fact?

The thoughts raced through his mind so quickly that there seemed scarcely a noticeable pause between her speech and his own, but in that pause his mind was made up.

He crossed to her, lifted up her head and made her meet his eyes. His own were grave, and there was a sort of desperate resolution in his voice, but Janine, absorbed in her own feelings, noticed nothing unexpected about him.

'You love me, don't you, Janine?'

'I adore you, Terry.'

'And you would be happy married to me?'

'It would be—the happiest thing that could ever happen to me,' she said quiveringly.

'And you wouldn't expect—impossible things of me?'

Her eyes widened a little.

'What sort of impossible things, Terry?'

'Well—I am older than you, my dear, not so much in actual years as in experience in life. I'm not so unsophisticated as you, Janine. It's rather hard to put what I want to say into words, but I wonder if you catch a glimmering of what I'm trying to say?'

She smiled.

'I think I do, Terry,' she said gently. 'You mean that you will want a wider life than the sort I shall be content with, don't you? That what will completely satisfy me, just being your wife and sharing a home with you, will only be part of what you want of life?'

He was surprised at her speech, showing as it did a perspicacity which he did not know she possessed. His spirits rose a little. He was not one inclined to suffer fools gladly, and it was a relief to know that she was not such a fool as he had imagined. There were possibilities about her if she could make such a speech as that.

'Yes, that's something of what I was trying to say, dear,' he said.

She rubbed her head against his arm in that friendly kitten way she had.

'I shall love you too much to make many demands on you, Terry darling,' she said. I've been thinking other things, too. Do you remember telling me once that you had always longed to be a doctor, a great surgeon, but that you had had to cut your studies short when your mother died?'

'Yes.'

'Well, when we're married you could go on with that if you liked, couldn't you? Then I should feel that I had given something to humanity as well as taking something from it. I should both take you and give you, Terry.'

He slipped his arms round her, drew her to her feet, and held her within the circle of his arms, looking deep into her eyes, those faithful, trustful, innocent eyes of hers.

'You're very sweet, Janine,' he told her, and his voice was not quite steady.

'It's easy to be sweet when you're as terribly in love as we are, isn't it, Terry?'

He kissed her.

'Darling, I'll never let you regret it for an instant,' he said, and suddenly she was transported back to the first time Richard Harrow had held her in his arms.

He had said something like that! She wished she had not remembered that. Desperately she wanted to receive in the measure that she gave, with no room for thoughts of possible regret.

'Terry, you do love me, don't you?'

'You know I do, darling,' and he forced himself to remember her sweetness, her gentleness, the passion of her abandonment to his love-making of the night before. Surely a man would be hard to please if he could not answer as he had done to a girl with so much to give, a girl so ready to give it?

'As I do, Terry? Heart and soul and body?' she urged him.

And again what could he say but, 'You know I do, Janine.'

She gave a sigh of happiness and relief.

'That makes me feel better about last night,' she said. 'Do you know, for one ghastly moment I thought you were going to be noble and dignified and all that, and refuse to marry me because of my money,' and she gave a little gurgle of amusement. 'What would you have done then?' he asked her.

'I don't know, quite. I think I should have given it all away and then come to you with empty hands and said, "What about it now?" and you couldn't have refused any more, could you?'

'You mean I should have had to make an honest woman of you?' he asked, purposely making his tone light to conceal his real feelings.

She nodded.

'Isn't it horrible to think that people can do—what we did last night, for anything but love?' she asked. 'I joke about your refusing to marry me, but if it could possibly have happened in sober earnest so that I felt you had been treating me like – well *that* sort of woman, you know – I think I should have committed suicide.' She spoke quietly, but with such certainty in her voice that Terry knew the trap had closed firmly upon him. She was capable of going to such lengths. She was of the timid, helpless type which did, in an emergency, commit suicide rather than have to grapple with life.

'Don't talk like that, Janine,' he said sharply. 'It's silly.'

'Is it? I don't know. I suppose that's the way I'm made. You see, after being like that with you, everything is different, and I just shouldn't have wanted to live any more if I had thought you didn't mean it, didn't love me. With me, that means so much more than my body. It means that I gave you all of me – my heart and soul and body for ever and ever.'

He felt the stranglehold of the trap now, and made one last struggle for freedom.

'Dearest, aren't you getting this all out of perspective?' he asked in as matter-of-fact a tone as he could command. 'Aren't you making too much of the mere physical act which is a primitive instinct and common to everything that has life? The animals don't get all het up and tragic about it. They just take life as it comes and are thankful and happy and—natural.'

She shrugged her shoulders.

'Well, that's me, anyway. The girls in the office used to say I was a prude and, I suppose I shall always be one – even after last night. Will you mind having a wife like that, Terry?'

Her sweetness might cloy, would almost certainly cloy, in time, but at the moment there was something irresistibly appealing to him in it. It was restful, easy, comforting after his passage of arms with Joy and the gnawing ache for her over the past year.

His arm tightened about her almost unconsciously, and he felt her instant response to it.

'I wouldn't have you different by so much as an eyelash,' he told her, and she was supremely satisfied.

'We'll be married quite soon, Terry, won't we?' she asked presently. There's really no reason to wait.'

'Janine, you're sure you want to marry me? It isn't just a sort of sop to conscience after last night?'

He knew that he was hoping for some sign of reluctance on her part, but it did not come. She opened wide eyes on him. 'Darling, of course I'm sure! Aren't you?'

'Of course.'

She sighed with relief and snuggled down against his shoulder. 'You gave me such a fright for a second! It's really rather awful to love anyone as much as I love you, Terry. I shall die a thousand deaths every time you are out of my sight, seeing you ran over in the streets, or having an accident in your car. I wish you didn't drive so fast, darling!'

'Look here, my sweet, this won't do. We've got to be ordinary normal people in an ordinary normal world, and if you're going to have an attack of nerves every time I go out you'll be a candidate for the lunatic asylum before long.'

'Alright. I'll keep my thoughts to myself. You see, Terry, I've never had anyone who really belonged to me before, and I just couldn't bear to lose you!'

He resisted.

'Dear, no human being *belongs* to another, and that's where so many husbands and wives come to grief. They try to own each other, body and soul, and it just won't do.'

She kissed him again, but he could see that he might just as well not have voiced his protest. She was just blindly adoring him, and he felt the stranglehold of the trap in which she had him.

'Well, you'll own me, anyway. You do now, don't you? I suppose it is really awful of me, but I simply can't feel any regret or shame about last night now.'

'Why should you?' asked Terry, but he knew that he felt both. He must have been mad not to realise the sort of girl she was and the probable end to such an adventure. He cursed himself for his facile emotions, for the lure of the night and the countryside and this yielding, cloying sweetness of hers. He could not even yet believe that his destiny had been decided for him by that one act of madness.

They sprang apart as, with a tap at the door, Gough entered to satisfy himself about the fires. Janine knew they looked guilty, and she took the matter into her own hands for once.

'You can be the first to congratulate us, Gough,' she said, with a simple dignity which sat well upon her. 'Mr. Forder and I are going to be married.'

'I'm sure I wish you every happiness, madam – and you, Mr. Forder, sir,' said the man in his irreproachable manner. Is it in order for me to tell Mrs. Gough and the servants?'

Janine and Terry looked at each other, and she smiled and turned back to Gough.

'I think so. We don't want it kept a secret, do we, Terry?'

'Er—no dear—of course not,' he murmured, and the butler withdrew in his slow, dignified way.

'I shall always be a bit scared of Gough,' said Terry, covering an awkward moment.

'He's a dear really, and we shall have to keep them on because they've been ages and ages with Richard, and I sort of promised him I would look after them.'

'Janine, are you horribly rich?' asked Terry desperately.

'Well, I seem to have far more money than one ought to have, with so many people in need,' she said. 'That's one of the things I want you to help me with, Terry. Mr. Tanner, Richard's best friend, advises me, but he is getting old and he is so old-fashioned in his ideas.'

'He wants you to save it and you want to spend it?' he asked. He still felt wretchedly self-conscious about the whole affair, and knew that he would have a good many bad hours over it, whichever way he took in the end.

She nodded.

'Something like that. I don't want to spend it on myself, though,' eagerly. 'I'd like to do something for other people, though, people who haven't got enough. I've tried to, but somehow it doesn't happen the way I want,' wrinkling up her nose. 'I always did make a mess of things, you know.'

'What have you made a mess of?' he asked, giving her only half of his attention, the other half occupied with his own reactions to this amazing affair.

'I wanted to do something for the Wilson Home. You know, the place where I was brought up. I didn't want to face Matron though, so I sent a hundred pounds anonymously, with a letter just asking her to use it to give the girls a treat. I suggested an evening out and a little present each. What do you thick she did? I read about it in the local paper. She took them to a symphony concert and gave them all new Bibles and new aprons!'

Terry burst out laughing, both at the picture she painted and her tragic face.

'My hat! What an old crow!'

'I wanted them to go to something really silly and bright, where they'd laugh and forget themselves, and perhaps have a box of chocolates each and some flowers, something that would not keep except in their memories. A symphony concert for a treat! And *Bibles!* I made a mess of that alright, didn't I?'

'I'll say you did,' he agreed.

'So you see how really necessary it is for me to have someone to help me to help other people – Terry – darling,' the final word coming with exquisite, shy tenderness.

His mind had run on ahead down the avenue she had pointed out. Unemployed himself, hopeless to despair, seeing himself flung before he was thirty on the world's scrapheap in company with so much that was fine and valuable and unwanted – what a prospect she held out to him! He did not know the extent of her wealth, but he imagined himself using it to make work, to employ labour, to bring back hope and joy and health to dozens – to hundreds – to thousands perhaps, as his imagination noted.

'We could give people work, Janine,' he said very softly, his eyes looking into the future with its undreamed-of possibilities.

Her face glowed.

'Oh, could we, Terry? How?'

'Just how rich are you, Janine? Do you know?'

'Not really. There were some figures dealing with probate somewhere here, though, if I could find them,' and she went towards the door. 'Come to the library, Terry,' and as he followed her he took appreciative note of the solid comfort of the house, a dignity which breathed of ample means.

They ransacked a drawer in the table that had been Richard Harrow's, and amongst the jumble of papers he found enough to show him that she was indeed a wealthy woman.

He sat on the edge of the table and looked at her thoughtfully, her brow wrinkled in the effort at comprehension of facts and figures at which his quick mind had leaped, her hair a little untidy, her black dress crumpled, her hands grubby from the mass of old papers they had turned over.

Suddenly he leaned down and took her in his arms, holding her so that her face was on a level with his own, looking deeply into her eyes.

'You're terribly sweet,' he said unsteadily, the realisation borne in upon him of her trustfulness, her essential kindness, her unselfishness.

She flushed with pleasure.

'Oh, Terry, I'm not really, but I love you to say so.'

'And you think we shall be happy? You really think so?'

'I know I shall be, and I hope—oh, I do hope, you will be!' she said.

'You're giving everything and I have nothing at all to give. Do you realise that, and what people will say? That I am marrying you for your money?'

Her face clouded over a little.

'Perhaps they will,' she agreed, ignoring the first part of his speech as negligible. 'It's horrid. I know because I've been in that position, only ... Oh, Terry, I've got to be honest with you, whatever happens! You see – when they said things like that about me, they were really true. I was ever so fond of Richard. He was kind and good and considerate in every way. But really I did marry him because I was poor and sick of screwing and scraping and I knew that I could never earn a decent living. I—you don't hate me for telling you the truth like this? You see, I've just got to tell you, haven't I?'

His arm tightened about her.

'Poor kid, who can blame you? Don't I know myself what it is to be down to my last cent and hopeless?'

She sighed with relief and let her head rest against him, utterly content.

'My poor Terry,' she whispered.

'Janine, suppose I were to tell you that that is why I am marrying you?' he asked suddenly.

She raised her head at that and laughed. It was a laugh of pure triumph.

'Ah, but darling, haven't I the memory of last night to give the lie to that? You held me in your arms and told me you loved me. Remember? You said you were mad for me, that you could never rest until I belonged to you utterly. *That* wasn't for my money, was it?' and he had the grace to look away from her loving, exultant child's eyes touched now with a woman's knowledge of her power.

At no time in his life, neither before that moment nor after it did he feel so utterly despicable in his own eyes as he did just then, and he put out a hand and laid it over her eyes lest she see what had leaped into his own.

'I was a beast last night,' he said unsteadily. 'Forgive me, Janine.'

She tore his fingers away and laughed again, laying her own against his lips.

'Forgive you for the loveliest hour of my life? I shall keep it here in my heart forever – until we are both old and grey, and you are on one side of the fireside with your slippers and your pipe, and I on the other side knitting for our youngest grandchild. And you'll look at me, and I'll look at you, and then you'll say, or I'll say, "Do you remember that night when—?" and I shall nod, or you will nod, and we shall smile and not say any more because there won't be any need. We shall both remember, shan't we, my Terry?'

Her love was so sweet, so unhidden, so utterly without pretence or coquetry. He remembered, as he had remembered all along, the casual hard brilliance of Joy, her fear of showing her feelings, the cloak of modernity and scepticism and flippancy with which she had hidden her love. He had so seldom been allowed to see the real woman, even when he held her close within his arms for some swift moment of passion.

Here were so many things he had looked for in vain in Joy – surrender, tenderness, unashamed emotion. And yet they left him longing the more for Joy's glittering hardness. It was as if he thought to touch a diamond and found only a drop of water beneath his fingers.

Yet to a thirsty man, the water was of infinitely more value than the flawless diamond.

He gathered her closely and looked out over her bent head, his eyes seeing visions, his strong young face filled with purpose and resolution.

'I'll make you happy, Janine. I'll never let you regret it,' he swore to her.

It was only when, hours later, in his bedroom in a cheap lodging-house, he went over the events of the day that the feelings of remorse and repugnance returned to him. Whilst in Janine's presence he had been uplifted by her love and happiness, by his own lofty ideals and hopes. Now he saw himself as a self-seeker, as nothing better than that gigolo which Joy would have made of him. What a fool! To refuse to be the beneficiary of the woman be loved, and to become that very same thing for a woman he did not and never could love!

Hour after hour he paced his room, making up his mind a dozen times to write to Janine and say that he had made a mistake, that he did not love her, that that night had been to him only a mad orgy of passion. But a dozen times he saw her brown eyes, like those of a faithful spaniel, and he knew he could not do it.

He slept at last, still undecided, and the first thing he knew was that someone was banging at his door with the information that he was wanted on the telephone downstairs.

He slipped into a dressing-gown and went, sleepy-eyed, down to the hall.

A man's voice spoke to him – elderly, courteous, dignified.

'My name is Tanner. You may have heard Mrs. Harrow speak of me. I have managed her business affairs for her since her husband died, but I shall be only too glad to be relieved of them, as she tells me is to be the case. I wonder if you could come along and see me, Mr. Forder? I think the sooner this thing is settled, the better. You young people seem to be in a hurry, and I can't say I blame you. Youth's fleeting.'

Terry took down the address and agreed to call during the morning.

'So – that's that!' he said to himself as he hung up the receiver and went back to his dressing. 'That most emphatically is that.'

Chapter Twelve

Janine was sitting on the lawn with her lap full of kittens.

It was June, and she had been married to Terry just six months; six, unutterably happy, absorbed months. They had changed her almost beyond recognition. They had matured her, given her poise and a very little self-assurance. Beyond all else, they had given her contentment and peace, and these qualities radiated from her and warmed and coloured with happiness all she did and said.

She was joyous in her happiness, conscious of it, hugging it to her and daring at last to believe in it. At first she had gone so warily, afraid at every step of finding the path not what she had dreamed it would be. She had been so uncertain of herself, so mistrustful of her power to keep Terry's love, so sublimely amazed at herself for having caught even the semblance of it.

Then, with the weeks at Merrow, health-giving, busy, crowded weeks, with the days too short for all the work that must go into them and the nights too short for all the love that swept and thrilled her, gradually had come belief in happiness, and with that belief an unutterable calm and contentment.

The Hampstead house was still theirs. Janine had not felt able to sell Richard's home. But it was kept closed except when she and Terry were detained in town by business or pleasure and called in there for the night. The Goughs lived there as a rule, coming down to Merrow when required, and returning thankfully at the first opportunity.

Janine owned Merrow. It was a village of some considerable size, off the busy main roads and therefore unspoiled and secluded. There were one or two large houses which Harrow had never troubled to acquire. There were the Challoners, the Denbys, the DeCressys, moneyed people with country houses at Merrow. The vicarage belonged to the Challoners and they disposed of the living, the present incumbent, a man in the eighties, taking no part in the village life at all. Possibly he went to the church occasionally on Sundays, but no one seemed to know or care much about his activities. Dr. Arkwright and his pleasant, cheerful wife lived in the only other fair-sized house.

The rest of the place was Janine's – the rows of cottages, the mill, the old paper mill, the saw-yards, the prosperous farms stretching out on every side, the little huddle of cottages which formed the village street, the few isolated houses which seemed to have been dotted about here and there and forgotten. In one of these, at the far end of the street, they lived, she and Terry.

Four Ways had once been a row of cottages, but Harrow's former agent had thrown them into one house, added modern necessities, and left the place to grow picturesque in its own rambling fashion.

Janine had loved it on sight. Its latticed windows had been flung wide to welcome her, and when she had discovered, with Terry's help, that the agent was not worth the princely salary he was being paid she had had no compunction in turning him out and taking possession of Four Ways herself.

She had managed to impress her own personality on it during the few months of her life there. There was nothing bizarre about it, nothing very modern, but everywhere was daintiness, scrupulous cleanliness and neatness, and a restful sense of home.

Beyond seeing that certain improvements were carried out for her comfort, Terry had left the house entirely to her, taking over the task he had set himself, a task for a lifetime to which he brought high hopes and a stout heart.

First of all the village had to be overhauled and put in order, and here he found intense opposition at first. Harrow had bought the place for a hobby, but he had fallen ill soon after and his schemes had never fructified. Janine had discovered an outline of his plans for Merrow, and it was on that they began to work.

Everything possible was done to hinder and discredit their work at first. The villagers were distrustful and intensely conservative. They had grown up in the dark, insanitary, inconvenient little cottages, and Terry fought a hard fight with them before he could persuade them that the creepers, the ivy, the dense masses of roses, which were eating into the bricks, were the cause of much of the disease and ill-health brought about by dampness and lack of light. Men and women reviled the workmen who came to tear down some of the offending growth in order to make good the walls of their homes, and though everything possible was done to preserve the beauty of the little village, Terry had to confess privately that by the time he had made the cottages weatherproof and sanitary Merrow had lost much of its old-world charm.

Mrs. Challoner, the great lady of the village, had driven down in state to Four Ways to remonstrate with him.

'Such a charming old place, so picturesque with its ivy and its roses and its lovely old thatched roofs,' she had wailed to him after the first stilted distrustful exchanges of civilities.

'And its walls crumbling and its ceilings half down and its thatch full of mice,' said Terry steadily.

'Surely you could have patched up the cottages in such a way as to preserve the beauty of the place, though, Mr. Forder,' she had said loftily. 'My friends have always come down here to enjoy the lovely rural surroundings. Now what will they see? Bricks and mortar where there were roses and ivy, hideous red tiles and towny-looking walls.'

'I'm really very sorry, Mrs. Challoner,' said Terry with that enchanting smile of his. 'If you could persuade your friends to get to your house the other way, by Chag End instead of Merrows, I am sure they will see all the crumbling walls and rotting thatch they can possibly desire. I am told that Chag End belongs to Sir Lucien DeCressy.'

'Yes, the old skinflint. Won't even repair the fences between his fields and mine,' said Mrs. Challoner resentfully.

'But surely they're more picturesque broken down than in a conventional straight line?' asked Terry innocently.

'His cattle get through to my parkland,' she said wrathfully.

'Why not, if you are an advocate of mice and rats, and damp and disease and death getting through the broken walls to my wife's tenants?' retorted Terry.

Mrs. Challoner glared at him. Then quite suddenly she laughed.

'Ever since I first came in here and met you and your charming little wife, Mr. Forder, I have been feeling a fool to come. I assure you I have only been keeping my end up because I simply never allow myself to be baulked of a purpose, and my purpose today was to rag you for spoiling Merrow.' 'Sort of came to curse and remained to pray,' murmured Terry, letting his gay eyes flirt with her shamelessly.

'Don't know about praying. Well, it seems I'm outnumbered, outwitted, something or other. I like your house, Mrs. Forder.'

Janine had sat silently observing, thinking how brave Terry was to stand up to this terrible old woman – and here suddenly was the terrible old woman tamed and become a smiling visitor. She took her round Four Ways, and henceforward Mrs. Challoner had used her commanding presence and her caustic tongue in the service of 'those ridiculous children', as she termed the new owners of Merrow.

Forder seized eagerly on the coming of the grid system of electricity to Merrow, and when the great metal giants carne stalking across the fields he made it possible for every villager to light and warm his cottage, for every wife to cook and work by electric current, though it proved a colossal task to introduce labour-saving appliances to these women who had known nothing but hard toil and who would not have known how to occupy the free time offered them.

Here Janine's services were requisitioned, and she worked early and late in her efforts to reconcile the village women to the use of electric kettles, electric irons, vacuum cleaners, washing and ironing machines, refrigerators even.

It had been uphill work, thankless work, for it had cost Janine thousands of pounds, and she had received not even gratitude for it for the most part. Here and there an overworked housewife managed to master a washing-machine and came to tell her what a comfort it was, but Janine was aware that in all probability in a few weeks the expensive machine would be pushed into an outhouse, its owner not proof against the carping criticisms of neighbours who regarded labour-saving notions as 'downright laziness' and not to be countenanced by anyone with a real care for their homes.

She was thinking, half amused, half angry, along these fines when Hetty, the parlour maid, came across the lawn to her.

'Oh, Hetty, not callers,' she said.

'The vicar, madam,' said the girl with a little smile.

Janine stared.

'Snakes! Whatever does he want? The master'll never go to church no matter what I promise,' but she rose to her feet, kissed the kittens before she let them gently roll on the grass, smoothed her frock and went into the house.

She greeted the venerable man with her usual shy courtesy, but as he was deaf and almost blind the interview was not very enjoyable to either of them.

'You wanted to ask me something, Mr. Cade?' she shouted.

'What is that you say? I can't hear very well – but never matter, never matter. What I wanted is a small subscription for the poor. Your predecessor, Mr. Cotter—mm—ah—used to make a small subscription at this time of the yeah—mm—ah—yes.'

Janine looked round helplessly. How could she go into detail with this deaf old man and explain to him that there were now no poor to aid? It had been their first job, hers and Terry's, to see that every able-bodied person of suitable age in the village had work and adequate wages for it. The sick and aged had been provided for out of a special fund, and any unexpected happening was always dealt with when brought to Forder's notice. His aim was not to dispense charity, but to make this little community prosperous by their own efforts. Terry hated Janine to give away money promiscuously. How was she to say all this to Mr. Cade, though?

She approached his ear and shouted down it.

'There aren't any poor,' she shrieked.

'The poor we have always with us,' he said sententiously.

'Not here in Morrow,' she screamed.

He shook his head.

'For the harvest festival,' he said with an amiable smile,

'What's for the harvest festival?' she demanded at the top of her voice.

'Vegetable marrow,' he said. 'This is just a small subscription at this time of the yeah—'

'You said that before,' yelled Janine.

'Er—yes—er—quite so. I might, as you say, have come before, but not knowing you very well, my dear young lady, nor your estimable husband, I scarcely liked to come before—mm—ah— yes.'

'But there aren't any poor now,' she tried to explain.

'Er—well—of course, one should leave it with you, but if I might suggest, perhaps, ten pounds?'

She swallowed hard, looked at him vindictively, taking advantage of the fact that he could not see her, and at length went to her desk and wrote him out a cheque for ten pounds, thrust it into his left hand, shook his right vigorously, and with it drew him towards the door. In the hall she picked up his soft black hat, put it firmly into his hand with his stick, and stood at the hall door until, mumbling, muttering and gesticulating, he passed over the threshold.

She came back to the sitting-room to find Terry in it, rocking with laughter.

'How much did he get out of you?' he asked as she sank down beside him, joining in his laughter.

'Ten pounds,' she admitted.

'Gosh! It was worth it to see the business-like way you got rid of the old blighter. Wish you could come down to the works and get rid of some of my unwelcome visitors like that!'

She paused in her laughter to look at him seriously, struck by a sudden thought.

'You know, Terry, it's queer, isn't it? A year ago I should have died at the very thought of interviewing him, and I certainly could never have got rid of him!'

'You're growing up, darling,' he told her teasingly. 'Don't grow up too fast though. You're so beautifully right as you are.'

She had not lost her trick of blushing, and she coloured now at his praise of her.

'Oh, Terry, am I? That's terribly nice to hear.'

Hetty came in.

'The telephone, sir,' she said and with a, 'Damn! Forgive me, dear,' he was gone, and she sank back in her chair with a little sigh.

To her simple and undemanding soul, Terry as lover and husband was perfect. Her own adoration covered any deficiency his might have, and it never occurred to her to question the shortness of the hours he spent with her nor the unequal division of his interests. It seemed natural and right that his work should come first, should absorb him and constantly distract his thoughts from her. Yet there were times, such as these, when he seemed to be drawing very near to her, that the demands of his work disappointed her.

Once the machinery was set in order for the reconditioning of the cottages, the provision of light and heat and power, the last especially on the farms, and the various schemes for adequate wages and allowances settled, Terry had turned his insatiable energies to providing the extra work needed to keep the villagers employed, to absorb newcomers who must not be turned away, and to provide an outlet for boys leaving school. The old paper mill, which by antiquated methods continued to turn out some of the finest paper procurable, had been subsidised to enable it to install more modern machinery, and this provided work for a number of men, both for the working of the machines and in the increased business which Forder was able to put in their way. It was but a drop in the ocean of work he hoped to provide, however, and he reopened a derelict sawmill, importing from some of the big towns men skilled in delicate veneer work, and sending out a challenge to the builders and decorators, the cabinet-makers and designers of fine furniture, to illustrate the uses of the work turned out. He spent long hours in consultation with some of the great employers of labour, with cabinet ministers whenever they could be persuaded to see him, with thinkers and workers and idealists up and down the country.

'Show me! Teach me!' was his cry to them, and from their experience, their wisdom, their ideals, their follies even, he took much knowledge back to Merrow with him.

On the brow of the hill overlooking the village already the steel carcase of a great factory was rising, and here he intended to experiment with all sorts of discoveries and patents, inviting cooperation and interest from patentees who had failed to find a market, sparing no pains in getting into touch with factories, offices, workshops, finding out some of their needs and setting good brains to work on the provision for them.

Working as he did, early and late, his material the pliable, fascinating medium of human kind, Terry was happier than he had ever imagined himself to be without Joy. He never forgot her. She had woven herself into the fabric of his life and his dreams and stood forever in his memory for all that was enchanting to a man. Yet in his way he loved Janine, though it was a different love. It was like sitting at the fireside after having been lying in the sunshine. It was warmth, but it was flickering, spasmodic, artificial warmth.

He never forgot what he owed to her, though he conscientiously tried not to make that colour his attitude towards her. His reward lay in the knowledge that she was really happy with him, and that by his work he was bringing untold happiness to others. Already hundreds of families had cause to bless him for renewed hope and vigour and health, for the means to earn. His great hope was that the hundreds would be thousands before another year was gone.

His telephone call took him back to his office in the village for an hour, and when he came back he found Janine hot and bothered, a visitor just departing.

'Who was that?' he asked her, dropping into a chair and taking the cup of tea she had poured out for him.

'That dreadful housekeeper person from the DeCressys,' she said. 'Mrs. Hodder, I think her name is.'

'What does she want?'

'Says I must really take away the electric ironing machine we gave Mrs. Platt.'

'What on earth has it got to do with the DeCressys?' asked Forder.

Janine began to speak, and then broke off and giggled.

'It didn't seem nearly so funny when she was here,' she said, 'but it seems Mrs. Platt is making a positive habit of scorching Sir Lucien's pyjamas, and the poor man hasn't a pair with a seat in them!' and Janine collapsed on the sofa and rocked with laughter.

Forder, sharing her mental vision of the portly, purple-faced, fierce-looking Sir Lucien striding about in seatless pyjamas, rocked with her, and when she sat up and wiped her eyes she assured him she felt a lot better.

'Why, it didn't really worry you, did it?' asked Terry, controlling himself.

'At the time, yes. You see, Mrs. Platt does the washing for the DeCressys. The poor soul seems to do the washing for half the county, which is why we gave her the electric machines, if you remember. She is ever so pleased with them and really looks a different woman since she's had them, but you know the DeCressys are furious with us for what we are doing in Merrow, and this Mrs. Hodder says that if we don't take the machines away from Mrs. Platt she'll send the washing from the Grange to somebody else, which will mean a loss of about a pound a week to poor Mrs. Platt.'

'To hell with the DeCressys and their pyjamas! I don't expect Mrs. Platt burned them all at. It's quite possible that that Hodder woman upped with an iron and applied it good and hot to Sir Lucien's seat, knowing that by so doing she would find favour in the eyes of Lady DeCressy. Well, let them take their pyjamas where they like. There'll be six dozen aprons at least from the mill next week, and Mrs. Platt can have those every week.'

She looked tragic.

'Oh, Terry, why didn't I wait? I might have known you'd find a way out! Mrs. Hodder simply insisted, and so I telephoned to the electricity company whilst she was here and told them to go and collect Mrs. Platt's machines.'

'Oh, you idiot, Janine!' he said, half laughing, half annoyed.

He went out of the room and she heard him telephone a message that the instructions re Mrs. Platt's machines were given in error and that the machines were to stay.

'Now write to Mrs. Redder,' he instructed her, and she sat down and wrote to his dictation, a masterly epistle whose substance was, as he said, 'Go to hell,' but whose actual wording was irreproachable.

Janine sighed as she folded the letter and found an envelope.

'Terry, I'm such a fool. It looks as though I shall always go on making a muddle of everything I do,' she said.

He caught the quiver in her voice and was beside her in an instant, his arms about her, his face full of contrition.

'Forgive me, sweet. You're not a fool, and you don't make a muddle of everything. Look how you got rid of old Cade only an hour ago!'

'By paying him ten pounds for the non-existent poor,' she said ruefully.

'Never mind. You're doing splendidly, darling. Don't get morbid. I thought we'd done with that inferiority complex.'

She clasped her arms tightly round his neck.

'Oh, Terry, you're such a *comfort!* Sometimes I really do believe I'm being a bit of use in the world, and I've never dared to believe it before. I've never been of the slightest value to anyone so far, until we came here.'

'You're of the greatest possible use here, Mrs. Forder,' he told her teasingly, but she frowned a little.

'Am I? I wonder. Perhaps it's only that I'm getting comparatively ornamental, and am kidding myself that it's usefulness.'

'What's the matter with you today, Jan? Got the hump? I know. Let's get out the car and buzz up to town for dinner and a theatre, and dance afterwards somewhere. We could stop the night at Hampstead.'

'I'd love to, but I've simply got to get the rest of those invitations out for the garden party you insist on our giving.'

'Alright, darling. Business before pleasure. Want any help?'

'No—only—well, Mrs. Arkwright's been, and she says that if we invite the Challoners, we simply can't have the Denbys, because Mrs. Challoner once had an affair with Mr. Denby, and everybody knows about it except Mrs. Denby, and if they're both here—'

Terry laughed.

'Leave that to me,' he said comfortingly. 'I'll keep my eye on Mrs. Challoner myself, and if I have read the lady aright, she won't be at all averse to keeping her eye on me!'

A wild and foolish spasm of jealousy shot through Janine. What if she ever lost Terry? She was still so unsure of herself, so amazed at having achieved anything so adorable as her husband, that the least thing could set her throbbing with fear.

He caught the look in her eyes. He had come to know her so well that he could read her thoughts unerringly. He smiled and set a hand beneath her chin, tilting up her face.

'Mrs. Forder, I believe you're jealous!' he teased her.

She flushed, but let him go on looking into her eyes.

'Mr. Forder, what if I am?' she asked.

He responded to her mute invitation, letting his lips rest on hers in a way that was meant to be cool and brotherly but which in some unforeseen way developed into one of those clinging, passionate affairs which could by no means be regarded as brotherly. He released himself at last with a shake and a laugh.

'Don't you realise, my sweet, that whilst you can make me feel like that, you won't ever have to be jealous of anyone?'

Her face grew grave and her mouth drooped into a line of sadness.

'Yes?' he asked her, aware of the change in her.

'Terry, you've said that before, but—oh, I know I may be silly and ignorant about it, but it seems such a fragile sort of thing on which to hang our happiness,' she said hesitatingly.

'Is that what you think? My dear, a long time ago, when we were in Madeira and never dreaming that this could happen to us, do you remember something I said to you? That the physical aspect of love is and always has been and always will be the one basic fact on which all creation rests? We superimpose other things – affection, respect, sympathy, our idea of honour and fair play – but the one thing that has the power to hold is what we have, Janine, what you give to me and I give to you.'

She shook her head, her eyes heavy with tears which she felt were ridiculous. She had been so happy. Why on earth should she allow this cloud to appear? It was rather presentiment than anything, and she felt she must fight it for her own sake.

'I can't put it into words, Terry. I just feel it inside me. It's that—I love you so terribly, you see,' she ended with a smile. 'You don't doubt my love for you, darling, do you?'

'No. I—I couldn't live if I did. I never cease to marvel at it, though, because I seem to have nothing to offer you, nothing for which you could possibly care in the way I care for you.'

He felt very tender towards her. He was always conscious of how much more she gave than received of her selfless devotion.

He loved her, but it was a mere shadow of the passion he had known for Joy. The very thought made him remorseful, Janine had given him everything that made his life worthwhile, had poured into his hands the means to make his dreams come true, and asked nothing of him but that he should take what she gave and be happy. Of that other happiness for ever denied him he refused to think. He had gone into this marriage with his eyes open, knowing how much she brought to it and how little he could ever bring. The very least he could do was to give her what he knew meant all her happiness to her. If ever he let her suspect the truth, he would never forgive himself.

He gathered her up in his arms and held her crushed against him, as if by his strength he would force away from her the thing which threatened her peace.

'Never say things like that, Janine. Never think them. I love you. Don't you realize that? We're lovers, my sweet, and always will be. There isn't anything in the world to be afraid of.'

She drank in his words, his tone, loved the close pressure of his arms which in an instant could shut out the rest of the world for her and leave only the two of them in it.

'Sometimes I wish I didn't care so much,' she whispered. 'It—it hurts to care so much. It's a sword in my hand, but the blade is turned towards me.'

'Try not to be self-analytical and introspective, darling. You're happy with me, aren't you?'

'Oh—terribly, beloved.'

'Then don't make bogies for yourself and stick them up in dark corners to frighten yourself with when I'm not here,' he said, laughing her out of her unusual depression. 'About our little jaunt to town. If you don't feel you can go today, what about tomorrow? I've got to go up anyway, and we could have lunch together or perhaps meet for a tea dance and go gay for once. We've both been working too hard and getting a bit stodgy. Like to?'

'Love to,' she said, her mood changing and showing her still the child. 'I've got to go to Hampstead anyway to see what china and silver they've got there. The Goughs could bring it down with them.'

'Well, we'll go tomorrow morning and I'll drop you at Hampstead. If we go in the M.G., Bennett can call for the Goughs and bring them and the luggage down in the Bentley. That do?'

'Beautifully. Darling, I shall get quite a lot of you if you hurry up and finish your business – *and* I've got a new frock from Mélisande's.'

'Good,' he said absently, his thoughts already running ahead to the work to be got through tomorrow.

After dinner he went off with Conrad, the manager of the workshop which for the moment housed some of the schemes which would come to maturity in the giant building on the hilt.

Janine, unresentful, sat alone, knitting a pullover for Terry and listening to a wireless crooner, interpreting all that he whispered or wailed in her ear according to her own thoughts.

'She'll be comin' down the mountain very soon,' sang the crooner.

'He'll be comin' through the village very soon,' sang Janine to herself. 'Knit two, purl sixteen.'

And after that, with the curtains blowing at the open window:

'I pretend that it's the breeze
That's fillin' the sails
That's movin' the ship
That's bringin' ma honey back tu me!'

When it seemed that Terry and Conrad were in for a long sitting she put out the light and went upstairs, pulled back the curtains and threw open the window. From it she could see the lights in his office.

She undressed and went to bed, lying so that she could see the lights across the fields. He was happy there, she knew. That was his life and his passion, and she, Janine, had been able to provide it for him. What greater happiness was possible than that knowledge?

They went up to town the next day in the fast little sports car which had been Janine's first present to him, and he left her at what she felt would always be to her 'Richard's house'. She could never conceivably think of it as home, or even as hers. The few weeks she had spent with Harrow were like some dim dream to her now, though she remembered with passionate gratitude to his memory that it was he who had made all her happiness possible.

The house was shrouded in hollands and Mrs. Gough volubly apologetic.

'Everything gets so bad, madam, with no one using it,' she ended.

'That's alright, Mrs. Gough. I don't feel I could ever bring myself to part with Mr. Harrow's house and I don't know what in the world I should do without you and Mr. Gough.'

She found it difficult even now, to leave off the 'Mr.', though Terry teased her about it.

It was obvious that the Goughs adored her. Not only had she kept them on and retained the house as it was, but she was always so considerate towards them and they admired the way she showed what they called 'proper respect' to the memory of the man to whom she owed so much. She never came to the Hampstead house without bringing flowers, which she placed in the library, spending a little time there in affectionate and grateful memory to him.

'Will you lunch here, madam?' asked Mrs. Gough, when she had brought vases for the great armful of roses from Merrow.

'Oh, possibly a picnic lunch, but don't bother. Mr. Forder may call for me before then, but, if not, I can get something.'

'I'd better stay and see to it, madam,' demurred Mrs. Gough. Janine laughed.

'Bless my soul, I haven't forgotten, if you have, that it isn't long since I had to do everything in the world for myself,' she said.

Her simplicity and utter want of snobbishness were not the least of her endearing qualities to her servants, though there was a certain dignity about her which forbade any undue familiarity.

The two of them worked hard, sorting and packing, with Gough to carry the parcels to the hall, and Janine heaved a sigh of relief when at last the two servants with the boxes and bundles were safely stowed into the Bentley and she was alone.

She wandered about the house, recalling memories of the man whose home this had been, growing tender in her thoughts of him. She touched his books, his chair, his walking-sticks in the hall, with very gentle hands. Since she had been married to Terry she had realised that Harrow had loved her and must have suffered greatly by the enforced denial of the possession of her. It made her especially tender to remember that.

At last she went down to the kitchen and made tea and boiled an egg, deciding that Terry was not able to call for her before lunch. She had her new frock on to celebrate the occasion, so she had fastened round her one of Mrs. Gough's overalls and pinned a duster over her hair. She decided not to tidy up until after she had had her lunch, and when she had filled a tray she carried it up to the library.

Once inside the room, she gave a cry of amazement and nearly dropped the tray.

Seated in Harrow's chair, her legs crossed, a cigarette in a long holder between her lips, her hat flung off to reveal a head of burnished gold, was a girl, looking entirely at home in her surroundings.

'Good morning. Sorry I startled you. Mrs. Harrow in?' she asked calmly.

Janine managed to get the tray to the table and stood staring at her visitor, the truth leaping to her mind.

This was Felicity Harrow. The face whose picture she had seen so many times was not so easily forgotten, and she remembered how fiercely she had stabbed and stabbed at those same features after Richard's funeral.

'Are you—Felicity?' she asked.

'Sure. And who are you?' came the cool question.

'I am Janine.'

The other girl stared incredulously for a moment. Then she flicked the ash off her cigarette with an indescribable gesture and laughed.

'No, are you? I had no idea you were so young. What on earth possessed you?' she asked, her tone displaying interest rather than criticism.

Janine flushed hotly. She had toyed once or twice with the prospect of one day meeting Harrow's daughter and telling her in no uncertain terms just what she thought of her, and now, within the first minute of that meeting, Felicity was turning the tables on her and opening the attack!

'Is it necessary to discuss that?' she asked curtly.

'Good Lord, no! I don't want to discuss it. Why should I? Live and let live's my motto, always,' said Felicity lightly, rising to her feet to fling her cigarette-end out of the window.

'You didn't care to let your father live!' burst out Janine, all the bitterness she had stored up in eighteen months rising in her mind.

The other girl turned a surprised face to her. It was genuine surprise. In fact, Janine was realising to her annoyance that Felicity Harrow was quite different from what she had imagined. But for this barrier of hatred which she had raised between them she might almost have liked her. There was an air of friendliness about her, an absence of restraint, which invited return.

'What do you mean by that? How could I have made any difference?' she asked.

'You could have come to him. Oh, I know it wouldn't have kept him alive. Nothing could do that. But he wanted to see you so much. He—he went through hell at the last rather than have another dose of morphia because he was afraid you might come and he would die under the morphia and miss you. But you never came, and he endured all that agony for nothing.'

Felicity still looked puzzled.

'My dear, how could I come? I never even knew he was ill,' she said, 'I didn't know he was dead until I saw it in the papers weeks afterwards. I went on a world cruise and didn't see an English paper till we reached the Cape.'

'But I sent you two telegrams, and the Post Office said they were delivered,' said Janine doubtfully.

A strange expression passed over Felicity's face, and she whistled softly.

'So – that was it, was it? My dear, you must believe me, and not think me absolutely mad when I tell you that I tore up those telegrams unread. I had—parted from a man I cared for. There were reasons we needn't go into, but I had told him I never wanted to see him or hear from him again and that I should tear up anything he sent me. He used to send me heaps of telegrams at one time. He used the telegraph office much as one uses a postcard, and I was idiotic enough to jump to the conclusion that the wires were from him. I—was a bit afraid of myself. I thought I might weaken if I read what he had to say, and I didn't want to weaken. I was just starting off on a world cruise that very day, and I meant to go and not let him stop me when I felt nothing could come of it. We were both pig-headed and neither of us would give way so what was the good of going on with it? Anyway, I tore up the wires and ran away. Janine, you do believe me, though it sounds mad?'

'Yes, I believe you,' said Janine briefly. The store might have been, as she said, mad, but the candid face and voice bore the unmistakable mark of truth. So all the hatred and bitterness and disgust she had felt, all the agony Richard Harrow had endured, had this simple explanation.

'Of course I would have come,' Felicity went on, and there was distress in her voice. 'Dad and I never got on very well, as I expect you know, but after all he was my father, and I should have whatever it cost. What a fool I was! Was he—upset because I didn't come?'

'It was a great grief to him,' said Janine soberly.

'Poor old Dad. You didn't have much of a time with him, did you? He must have been ill from the first. Didn't he know? The papers said it was cancer.'

'Yes. But he didn't know, or he wouldn't have asked me to marry him I am sure.'

'I don't know so much about that,' said Felicity, fitting a fresh cigarette into her holder. 'I dare say he felt he wanted someone of his own to leave his money to – or perhaps he wanted to leave it to you and couldn't see any way to do it except by marrying you first.'

Janine turned away.

'Please don't!' she said chokingly. 'I was—very fond of him and I hate discussing him in this cold-blooded way.'

'My dear, don't be an idiot. You did a very sensible thing in marrying him, and a very clever thing, if I may mention it. Why waste regrets *now*?'

'I didn't marry him for his money,' said Janine fiercely.

Felicity laughed and struck a match.

'No? Then why the hell did you marry him, my dear?' she asked. 'You needn't play up to me, you know. I'm the most honest and cold-blooded person on earth and I believe in calling a spade a spade. If I were poor, which thank God I'm not, I should whisk around until I found an old man like Dad, well lined, and marry him toot sweet!'

'I think you're beastly,' said poor Janine, aware that she had really done much as Felicity suggested, though she hadn't actually 'whisked around' after Richard Harrow.

'Be yourself, my dear!' laughed Felicity good-humouredly. 'If we're going to be friends (and I'd like us to be), let's at least be honest at the start. I'm not blaming you. I dare say you gave Dad all he asked or expected out of the marriage, so why worry about having got all you asked and expected? It was a fair, square deal. By the way, is that your lunch on the tray? And what the hell's the matter with the house? And don't you keep any servants? Luckily I still have a key of the front door, but I don't see Gough about. Have you sacked him?'

Janine explained briefly that they had gone down to Merrow for a week or two.

'Merrow? Where and what is that?'

Again Janine explained, wishing her visitor would go, and yet aware of that strong attraction she felt for her in spite of everything and of the disapproval she wanted to retain.

'That must have been after my day, then,' said Felicity. 'Never heard of the place, and I suppose it's never heard of me! Anyway, I'm starving, and your boiled egg and tea don't appeal to me. Come out and lunch with me somewhere and let's get acquainted – Step-mamma!' with a laugh in which Janine could not help joining.

She hesitated, clinging feverishly to the memory of her disapproval of this girl because of the way she had treated Harrow, even accepting the explanation of the final act in staying away from his death-bed.

Possibly Felicity sensed something of this.

'Take the plunge!' she urged her gaily. 'You know you're going to like me in the end, and I like you already, so why waste time?'

'I've been grubbing about and I shall have to wash and so on,' said Janine reluctantly.

'I'll wait. Any radio here? No? Well, you didn't really have time to civilise the old dear, did you? Don't be too long,' and she flung herself down in the easy chair again, selecting another cigarette and lighting it carelessly.

Janine spent more than her usual time and care over her appearance, aware of Felicity's perfect finish to the last detail, and feeling, in spite of the becoming clothes she now wore, gauche and unfinished in comparison.

Felicity, left alone, rose from the chair and sauntered to the window, looking out at the formal, well-kept garden which was still reminiscent of Richard Harrow's love of precision. For all her apparent unconcern, she was feeling in this house the loss of her father as she had never imagined she would feel it. Perhaps his kindly, indulgent presence lingered in this room which had been peculiarly his, and the obliterating hand of time had wiped out the remembrance of their constant jarrings, the recriminations, the misunderstandings, the mutual inability to see the point of view of a different generation.

She turned at last, slowly, as if subconsciously she was aware that destiny itself turned with her.

Framed in the doorway was Terry Forder, his eyes wide with a sort of fascinated unbelief, his face pale, his hands gripping the sides of the door.

Chapter Thirteen

'Joy!'

She stood quite still for a moment and then came to him in that light, swinging way she had, her hands outstretched, her eyes alight and deeply blue.

'Terry, my dear! How on earth did you know I was here?'

'I didn't know. How could I? What are you doing here?'

His questions came in short, staccato tones, as if forced from him by something beyond his control, and his eyes were still startled and incredulous.

'Well, you don't sound nearly as pleased to see me as you ought – or as I am to see you! As for what I'm doing here – isn't the boot on the other leg? This is by way of being my home still, I suppose, and I am just about to take my surprising stepmother out to lunch and make her further acquaintance – though why I should have to give an account of myself to you, Terry Forder, I don't know!' she ended with a laugh.

He still looked at her with that stupefied stare, struggling to make his mind assimilate what she said – and still more what she implied.

'Your—stepmother?' he asked.

'Sure. Dad married again. What I didn't know, and what really amuses me very much, is that Janine is quite young! Fancy going gay like that in his old age!'

'Janine? You mean—you can't mean that—that *Janine* married your father?'

'Apparently. I take it you know her as you have come strolling into the house as if you lived here, though at first sight of you I had the extraordinary idea that you had followed *me* here!'

'Joy. Don't—make a joke about it. I—we—Janine—you see, Janine and I are—married.'

There was a deathly silence in the room. Felicity stood staring in front of her with eyes that saw nothing. Terry stood staring at her with eyes that saw only her. Then she laughed, a hard, strained, mocking little laugh, and moved away.

'Life's really funny, isn't it?' she said.

He followed her and stood close to her, longing to touch her but not daring to do so.

'Joy, forgive me.'

'Why should I, my dear Terry? Is there anything to forgive? You're a free agent, just as I am,' she said in that hard, bright tone.

'I wasn't a free agent, Joy. I ought not to have married her. I loved you. I love you now. I ought to have realised that.'

She gave him a slow, merciless smile which cut him.

'So you didn't even have the excuse of this so-called love business? It was purely a financial deal?'

'Was that gibe necessary?' he asked, his face very white, his hands clenched against his sides.

She shrugged her shoulders.

'No – only natural. As I said before, life's funny, isn't it? Here I am, returning like the prodigal son, to find *you* already guzzling the fatted calf! Laugh, Terry! Don't you think it's funny?'

He put a hand on her shoulder, roughly.

'Stop it, Joy!'

'But, my dear man, why? Surely you don't grudge me my capacity for seeing humour in a rather grim joke? You ought to be glad that I can still—laugh.'

In spite of the brave show she made, her voice quivered a little and his grip on her shoulder tightened.

'Joy, don't!'

She set her face into hard lines, and her eyes, meeting his, were like points of blue steel.

'*You* shouldn't be squeamish, my dear Terry. You've shown quite a different sort of courage from anything I suspected of you possessing.'

'What do you mean?' he asked harshly.

'Isn't it obvious? You refused to marry me because you were so high-souled about my money, but you marry my father's widow who must have at least ten times my modest portion!'

'I can explain how it happened, Joy,' he said desperately, wondering miserably, now that he was with her again, how on earth the thing had happened. Gone in a flash were the six months of contentment and happiness he had had with Janine. He could remember only Joy—Joy whom he had loved for years – Joy who could draw him to her with the crooking of her little finger.

She gave that hard little laugh again.

'But why on earth should you trouble? Besides, I'm not a fool that I should need such an explanation. I could wish, though, that you had selected any other woman than my father's wife. It makes it a little awkward for me now that I have, in my innocence and ignorance, made my appearance here.'

'I didn't know, Joy. I had no idea. There was the name of, course, but I didn't dream that Harrow had a daughter. Janine has never so much as mentioned you, and, as you know, I didn't know anything of your circumstances, nor where your home was nor anything.'

'Well, such is fame!' said Felicity flippantly.

'What can we do about it, Joy?' he asked miserably. 'It's a rather impossible position, isn't it?'

'Personally I find it quite amusing. It's so hard to find anything really novel nowadays that the situation intrigues me.'

'You can't stay here, Joy,' he said in sudden alarm that such might be her intention.

'The idea really never occurred to me, though now that yon suggest it, it is worthy of consideration. You see, you are really so well matched, you two, aren't you? You're birds of a feather. She married Dad for his money; you married her for hers.'

'Joy, I—'

'Darling, don't let's argue about that. History would repeat itself far too quickly, for Janine has just been trying to assure me in this very room not half an hour ago that she didn't marry Dad entirely for money, and I reserved my judgment, though really I don't see why she shouldn't have done so. It's up to a girl to sell what she's got in the best market, and Janine made a good deal. With you, it's rather different, isn't it? Anyway, you're both about level now, and I shall be the interested and impartial onlooker to see what you make of it. Dad was too intelligent not to be aware that a girl of Janine's age must be marrying him for his money, but does Janine realise the present situation as clearly?'

'You are quite unnecessarily offensive, Joy, especially as I can't see what it has to do with you—now,' said Terry, trying to match her coldness but succeeding badly. He felt himself to be despicable, and the knowledge that she had the same opinion of him was salt in the wound. A man can bear to be a worm in his own eyes at times, but when he realises that he is that same worm in the eyes of the woman he loves, he finds it intolerable.

'How right you are, my dear! It really hasn't anything to do with me—now, as you say. Give me a cigarette, will you? My case is empty and I don't know where Janine keeps hers. By the way, is it in order for me to call her Janine, or would you prefer me to call her "Mother" and you "Father"?' she asked mockingly, taking a cigarette from the case he held out to her.

'Hadn't you better go, Joy?' he asked.

'What? Turning me out of the house already, Stepfather? Won't Janine think it rude? She is upstairs powdering her nose to come and lunch with me. I invited her before I realised that this contretemps was before me. Won't you find it a bit difficult to explain why I should dash out as soon as you dash in?'

'Janine must never know about—us, Joy,' he said.

'It *would* rather spoil things, wouldn't it? Are you equal to pretending that we have never met, then? Or what does your bright brain suggest?' she asked, picking up her hat and pulling it on at a rakish angle, patting and pushing her hair into position beneath it.

'I don't think such a position would be tenable,' said Terry stiffly, and Felicity laughed again.

Only someone who knew her well and loved her well could have detected the hurt beneath the laughter.

Terry detected it.

'Darling, I'm—oh, it sounds so footling and inadequate to say I'm sorry,' he said in a low voice. 'If I had dreamed you would ever come back into my life, that you really—cared ...'

She turned on him swiftly, the laughter gone.

'You knew I cared. You knew that some day we should have to be together again. It wouldn't have been possible to keep away from each other.'

'You never wrote or gave me any sign, Joy.'

'I knew we might come to our senses apart whilst we never should when we were always together and wrangling. I hoped and believed that some day you would either get a decent job or else see sense. And you've seen it, but not for me!'

'Darling—'

But she put up a hand to stop him.

'Oh, what's the *use*? You're married, and to a woman to whom presumably you owe something. Is she in love with you?'

'Naturally. Why else, with her money, should she marry me?' he asked bitterly.

'Rather a rotter, aren't you, Terry?'

'Yes.'

Her face softened at the unequivocal word of agreement, but she would not let her mind relax.

'Well, what are we going to tell her? Everything or nothing?'

'It would hurt her terribly to be told—everything, Joy,' he said quietly.

'Yes. She's rather sweet, isn't she? In spite of the fact that she married my old man for his money, she *is* rather sweet. Well, we tell her nothing then?'

'I think it's best, Joy.'

'Then don't call me Joy. In any case—it isn't true any more,' and her voice quivered for an instant until he made an involuntary step towards her and she drew back, mistress of herself again. 'Please let's be as sane as we can. To you I am for the moment Miss Harrow, and you are—Mr. Forder. In a moment she will be down. Can you behave as if we are the veriest strangers, just introduced?'

'I suppose so,' he said moodily.

'Well, not even Janine will believe you if you look like that about it. For the love of heaven, Terry, try to make the best of it. You got us into this mess. The least you can do for all of us, including yourself, is to put a decent face on it, and give your wife what she has a right to expect from you. After all, she's bought you and probably paid a good price for you!'

'You're horribly bitter.'

'Well, it's my last chance. Ssh! I think she's coming. Try to look pleasant.'

And when Janine, rather hot and still not quite sure of the rightness of the blue suit, joined them, Felicity was putting the finishing touches to her hat and hair, and Terry was trying, with indifferent success, to look the perfect host.

'Terry! I didn't expect you till tea-time!' exclaimed his wife happily. 'Have you made the acquaintance of—well, I suppose I must say my stepdaughter, though it sounds odd!'

'We've introduced ourselves,' said Felicity serenely. 'Seeing that you hadn't even broken the news to me that you had married again, I think it is rather clever of us, don't you, Mr. Forder?'

'I thought you'd only get a scratch lunch, left to yourself, Janine,' he said, ignoring Felicity and turning in a sort of desperation to his wife. 'Will you come and have something?'

'Well—I was going with Felicity, really. You don't mind my calling you that, do you?' with a charming little air of diffidence.

'Of course not. We couldn't really adopt anything but Christian names at our age, could we? But since Mr. Forder has been so nice and husbandly over your lunch, why should he not take us both, and solve the problem? Will you, Mr. Forder?' with an innocently radiant glance towards him.

'I should be only too delighted,' he murmured, and Janine laughed from one to the other and led the way to the front door.

'Come along then, it's really rather fun, isn't it?'

The other two were understood to agree, and the sense of strain was lost for the time being in the necessity for packing the three of them into the front seat of the two-seater, both the girls having declined Terry's offer of a taxi rather than the car.

Felicity chose the place for luncheon, and during the meal she was gay and mischievous, tormenting Terry with her two-edged remarks, forcing him into the conversation and giving him no quarter.

Janine was perplexed now and then. It worried her to suspect that her husband did not like this new-found stepdaughter of hers, for she herself liked Felicity with increasing warmth, and long before the meal was ended found herself hoping that they could be friends. If Terry really disliked the girl, a genuine friendship would, of course, be impossible, though she could not imagine how anyone, least of all a man, could fail to be attracted by Felicity's loveliness and radiant personality.

After luncheon the question of the afternoon was mooted. Terry had not completed his business, but would have to return to the city for an hour or so; Felicity had 'nothing in the wide world that must be done', and Janine had only to take the keys of the house to the gardener, who was to act as caretaker.

'Let's go to a matinee,' suggested Felicity. 'Mr. Forder can meet us somewhere for tea,' and so it was arranged, though Terry would have been more content to say goodbye to Felicity, if only to give him breathing space. He realised that the last thought in her mind was a definite parting for them. Now that she had adjusted herself to the changed conditions, something Puckish in her nature prompted her to get what mordant pleasure she could out of seeing him suffer. He was the grub on her pin alright!

He gave only half-hearted attention to the matters in hand during the afternoon, and looked and felt tired when he arrived at the rendezvous to wait for the two girls.

Felicity, with mischief in her soul, had persuaded Janine to go with her to the American Club when they left the theatre.

'I simply must have a refresher, and we shall be in loads of time to meet the blessed one,' she said airily when Janine tried to object. 'Always make a man wait for you, my dear. They think they're too important to you if you rush to meet them.'

'Well, Terry is rather important to me,' said Janine, uneasily aware that she might just as well try to turn the tide as to prevent Felicity from doing what she wanted.

'Don't let him suspect it, then, if you want to keep him,' said the other girl, piloting her into the smart little club and insinuating both of them into the line at the bar. 'Two Mae Wests, and don't forget the ice,' she said, flinging at the tired attendant a ravishing smile which acted on him like a tonic, making him positively dash for the right bottles.

Felicity immediately appeared to know nearly everybody in the place and there were cries of 'Felicity Harrow, by all that's amazing!'

'Hullo, Joy! Where've you been?' and she was swallowed up for the moment in a sea of hands and faces, whilst Janine, uncomfortable and embarrassed, sat perched on her high stool and watched her.

A moment later she herself was drawn into the affair.

'Look what I've found!' exclaimed Felicity gaily, and there was a note of warning beneath her gay tone which the others, her familiars, recognised, though it passed Janine by. What had Joy been up to now?

'This *was* my stepmother, but now she's Mrs. Terry Forder. Janine, meet the crowd.'

There was a moment's silence, and then Janine was greeted with an enthusiasm all the more eager because it served to cover up that moment's embarrassment. She was bewildered and not at all comfortable, and she was made to drink quite a lot of queer things which she knew would go to her head. She became aware that some at least of these people must once have known Terry, but she grew rapidly too muddled to be quite clear about anything.

Her one distinct idea was that Terry was waiting for them, and at long last she managed to detach a reluctant and glowing Felicity from the bar and urge her towards the door and the taxi which had been ticking away outside all this time, to Janine's private horror. She would probably never recover from her habit of thrift, and she would not have dreamed of keeping a taxi waiting.

'Terry will be so worried.' she said, but for the life of her she could not remember where and precisely at what time they were going to meet.

Felicity laughed at her and gave the instructions to the driver, ending with a 'Step on it, my lad!' which made him smile and nod.

If I do, I shall 'ave this 'Ore-Belishy man after me,' he told her.

'Well, if you don't, you'll have this lady's husband after you, and he's heavyweight champion for the Paregoric Isles,' Felicity told him as she jumped in beside Janine.

She laughed at Janine's flushed and worried face.

'Heavens, the child's really worrying!' she said.

'Terry will be so anxious.'

'Do him good, my dear. Keep a man on tenterhooks and he'll be too busy with his own pains to look for fresh ones. Sit him down in an easy-chair and he'll soon begin to look for things to grumble at! You'll spoil him, Janine.'

And she was perfectly serene when at length the taxi deposited them at the spot where they had agreed to meet, a spot which Forder had worn smooth with his impatient pacing for over an hour.

Felicity sent Janine to make their peace with him whilst she overpaid the driver radiantly.

'Oh, Terry, I'm so sorry,' began Janine.

'I wondered what the devil had happened,' he said irritably, looking a little keenly at his wife as he observed her flushed face and distended pupils.

'Have you been drinking?' he asked sharply.

Felicity came smoothly to the rescue, her eyes challenging his, her tone one of mockery and derision, as if daring him to criticise what she did or said.

'We were hot and thirsty and went to the American for a cocktail. Where do we go for tea? Isn't there a new band that's a sensation at Kalliope's?'

Terry set his lips grimly. She was determined, then, to spare him nothing. They had danced together at Kalliope's a dozen times, intimately and blissfully.

'Janine's never been there, and I don't think she'd like it,' he said, but they fitted themselves into the two-seater again, Felicity laughing and talking, the other two silent.

Janine stared at Kalliope's in some surprise. Walls and ceiling were painted in broad red and black and gold stripes, and against that background the figures of the attendants, all of them negroes dressed in skin-tight black, showed grotesquely, disappearing entirely against the black stripes to reappear with gold or scarlet outlines a second later. The floor was opal-tinted glass, the colours in it shifting and dissolving into one another as the dancers moved across it.

They had a curious, very bitter tea served in black glass cups with scarlet handles and scarlet spoons, and the tiny cakes tasted of brandy. Janine disliked everything about the place, and when Terry invited her to dance she shrank back: feeling out of her element and decidedly wrongly dressed.

'Dance with Felicity,' she said, and, after a momentary hesitation, he turned to their guest.

'Will you dance?' he asked stiffly, and the next moment she was in his arms, his well-remembered arms, their bodies pressed closely, her cheek against his.

They did not speak. There seemed nothing to say, and yet everything was said in that close pressure, in their consciousness of each other.

'Do you remember, Terry?'

'Every least thing, my darling.'

And silence again whilst their feet obeyed his will without hesitation, neither aware of any choice of movement.

Janine watched them with a curious pain at her heart. It was not envy or jealousy. She was too loyal to Terry, too devoted to him, to question his own loyalty or devotion. It was only that Felicity seemed so exactly right in these surroundings – her dress, the way she wore her clothes, the way she moved and spoke and smiled. She was exactly right for Terry, too – almost as tall as he, if not quite, exquisitely fair against his brownness, so definitely of his own world. She had never been so conscious that he had stepped out of his world to marry her as when she saw him here in these bizarre, ultra-fashionable surroundings and looking as if he belonged to them.

After they sat down he would not dance again, and Janine was rejoiced to see that he was relieved when they were out of the place and standing on the pavement by the car again.

Felicity was going on to the house of some friends and then to her hotel.

'But I'm coming down to this place, Merrow, for Janine's bust-up on the twelfth, though I must admit a garden-party sounds pretty deadly. How about coming up to fetch me, Mr. Forder? I don't possess a car at the moment.'

'I shall be delighted,' said Terry stiffly, feeling now that the magic of the dance had worn off that he never wanted to see Felicity again. It would be better for his peace of mind, the only decent way out now.

'I'll ring you up and let you know. I shall be seeing Janine, anyway, as I'm going to help her choose her frock.'

'May I get you a taxi, or drop you somewhere?' he asked curtly.

'A taxi, I think.'

Then, as she sat inside and made him put his head in to give him the address, 'Little man, you've had a busy day!'

'Where did you take Janine?' he asked suddenly, almost before he had framed the thought.

She looked at him in surprise.

'I told you. The American Club.'

'I don't want her to get that cocktail habit. That's all,' he said.

'Poor Terry! Afraid I shall spoil your lily of the field?' she mocked him, but there was pain beneath her words and pain in his heart.

'Possibly,' he said, and closed the door on her and gave the order to the driver.

Janine received him with a rather diffident smile. The tea and the fresh air had cleared her head, and she was feeling a little ashamed of herself. She had been almost drunk!

'Don't you like Felicity, Terry?' she asked him on the way home.

'My dear, I scarcely know her.'

'Neither do I, but I like her.'

'I don't want you to—to go about with her, Janine,' he said, looking straight ahead. 'I don't think she's particularly good for you. She's—not your style.'

She sighed.

'I almost wish I were *her* style,' she said. 'She's so terribly attractive and smart.'

'I prefer you as you are,' he said shortly, and she hugged the words to her heart and felt their warmth. He preferred her, Janine, plain and ordinary and stupid, to someone like lovely, sparkling Felicity!

'Oh, Terry, I do love you so,' she whispered.

'Then don't be too much with—with Miss Harrow,' he said.

She wrinkled her nose in the way she had when perplexed.

'Darling, you're not quite fair to her. I wasn't before. That's why I would never have anyone mention her. It's why I never even told you Richard had a daughter. I thought she was mean and horrible to him, not coming to him when he was dying, even when I telegraphed twice to her. Now it seems it was all a mistake. She had had an affair with a man and she didn't want to have anything more to do with him, and she thought the two telegrams were from him, so she tore them up without reading them. Then she went round the world to forget him.'

'I see,' said Terry grimly, negotiating a difficult corner. 'And did she?'

'I don't know. She didn't say so, but I expect she did because she seems so gay and happy now, doesn't she?'

'Quite,' he agreed.

'Darling, I wish you liked her, because I do, really. And we shall have to see her. I mean, she'll come to Merrow whenever she wants, or to Hampstead. I've told her I shall always keep a room for her.'

He frowned.

'Is that wise?'

'Isn't it? We can't very well do less, can we? After all, she is Richard's daughter, and—well, Merrow and everything else is really Richard's.'

'Alright, dear. Don't rub it in,' he said, and she was wise enough to sit in silence for the rest of the journey, sensing that something was troubling him out of all proportion to the fact that he had been kept waiting.

When he helped her out of the car he held her for a moment in his arms.

'Darling, forgive me,' he said, and his eyes looked unhappy.

'Terry! Whatever for?' she asked in surprise.

'Oh—I'm just being a fool,' he said, and went to put the car away.

Never until today had he realised what a poor deal he was really giving Janine. He had hoodwinked himself with the belief that their six months of happiness meant that he could give her all she wanted. These few hours with Felicity had sufficed to show him what Janine was missing, the rapture, the passion, the devotion, the completeness of love, which Joy still gave him. He had asked Janine's forgiveness, and in the same moment he had prayed that she might never know what need he had for forgiveness.

During the fortnight that followed he knew that the two girls were meeting, but it was not until the day of the garden-party itself that he and Felicity met again. He knew she was in the house, for he had in the end sent Bennett to fetch her rather than risk the hour of close companionship she had herself suggested.

He could hear them upstairs, laughing and talking, but he would not go up until he knew the room was empty.

She had dressed Janine in bridal white in spite of half-hearted protests – white lace, beautifully cut, edged with dark fur in cunning contrast, and designed to add depth to the dark eyes and accentuate the shadows in her hair. She looked elf-like and fragile and almost beautiful when she stood alone – but Felicity, in tailor-made yellow, unostentatious and severe, dwarfed her and took the colour from her without any intention of so doing.

She had taken an impish delight in making the best of Terry's wife, turning the knife in her wound by some freakish, sadistic impulse. Perhaps she felt that only by making Terry satisfied with the girl he had could she, the girl he could not have, feel safe.

He came across the lawn to her as she stood in the midst of their guests, self-assured, perfectly at her ease, blending with a nice discrimination the rather ill-assorted ingredients of Janine's party. Undoubtedly she was making a success of the affair, and Janine hovered near her, obviously adoring.

Felicity smiled mockingly when for an instant she and Terry stood isolated.

'Am I doing the honours nicely, sir?' she asked him.

'Joy, I want to talk to you. I must.'

She shook her head.

'No.'

'We can't go on like this, strangers after everything we both remember. You're in my blood, Joy.'

'And in your wife's home too, my sweet,' she replied serenely, and she gave no inkling of the fires that raged within her at his voice, his famished eyes, his lips denied to her. 'Oh, Janine! Come here! There, isn't she a pet, Terry? I shall call you that eventually, so you might as well get over the shock at once.'

He looked at his wife but saw only Joy.

'Very nice,' he said, and the first little thrill of apprehension shot through Janine. She was so conscious all the time of Felicity's possession of all the things she herself lacked.

'Go and get her some tea. I'm sure she hasn't had any,' said Felicity.

'What about you?' persisted Forder.

She made a grimace.

'I've already had five and a rather odious little man called Denby is even now bearing down on me to share a sixth with me. Heaven help my waistline!' and she slipped away with a charming smile for the newcomer, as if this were the crux of her day.

Terry did not see her again except from a distance until all the guests had gone and she was with them in their little sitting-room, which they called the morning-room and kept sacred to themselves.

'I'm going to get Janine a highball. She's played out,' she announced, and he followed her to the dining-room in spite of her declaration that she needed no help.

'Are you avoiding me purposely, Joy?' he asked when they were alone. 'You haven't been near me all day, and you'll scarcely speak to me.'

She looked at him coolly over her shoulder as she bent to the door of the cellarette.

'Are you accusing me, or complaining about my behaviour as a guest, or what?' she asked.

'Janine notices things. She—she thinks we dislike each other and keeps worrying me about you. Is it really necessary to make *such* a distinction between my wife and me?'

Felicity laughed.

'That's really rather priceless, all things considered. What exactly do you want me to do, you and she? Flirt with you? Oh fie, sir, as Gladstone said in eighty-two.'

'Well, surely there's a happy medium. For instance, Janine has asked you to stay down here for a few days, but you refused, and she blames me and says I make you feel I don't want you.'

'Nor do you. Or do you, Terry?' with a sudden, disarming softness.

'Every hour of every day—and night, Joy.'

She caught her breath.

'You mustn't say these things, Terry. They aren't—fair.'

'Then will you come and stay, if Janine asks you again? Will you, Joy?'

'I'm only human, Terry, and so are you.'

'Can't you trust me to behave decently to—Janine?'

'I doubt if one can ever be trusted in certain circumstances,' she said in a troubled voice.

'I swear to you—'

She put cool fingers on his lips.

'I wouldn't, if I were you, Terry. What about that highball? Is this the bottle you want?'

Janine had her drink and, when Terry had darkened the room, she dozed on the couch. The other two stole out and left her, reeling guilty and yet caught up in the net of their own emotions.

'Let's go down the orchard. There's a stream there and a crazy old boat,' said Terry, and they went there hand in hand through the long grass, under the gnarled old apple trees with their promise of a heavy crop, and down to a willow-hung, lazily, flowing stream and the blunt-nosed, flat-bottomed dinghy which drifted at its moorings.

Terry flung in an armful of cushions from a little shed on the bank, found a paddle, established Felicity at the far end and pushed off.

'We can't get very far because it narrows and gets very shallow, but I've had this part cleared and deepened for Janine. She likes to come here in the afternoons with her book or her needlework, and she can't drift far even if she goes to sleep. The boat would ground.'

Felicity watched him as she had watched him dozens of times, manipulating the paddle skilfully, the muscles rippling and flexing beneath the thin silk of his shirt.

'You're fond of Janine, aren't you, Terry?' she asked suddenly.

'How could one be otherwise?'

'And yet you're in love with me?'

'Again, how could one be otherwise?' and he flung her a look which answered a question she had asked herself more than once since their strange reunion of a week ago. She did not know whether it was answered to her satisfaction or not. Sure all her life previously of what she wanted and how to set about getting it, she felt that she was no longer sure of anything – not even of what she wanted.

Terry ran the boat in under a willow and made it fast.

Felicity sat up.

'What's the bright idea, Terry?'

'I'm going to kiss you,' he said. 'It's no good screaming or making a fuss, because I'm going to do it just the same, and the fuss would bring the native population down on us too late, in any case.'

She sat quite still.

'It never occurred to me to make a fuss,' she said calmly, and the next moment she was crushed in his arms, his lips on hers, those firm, well-remembered lips which could make her forget everything in the world save that he held her.

When he set her free, she lay back with closed eyes.

'Well, it's over at last,' she said quietly.

'That how you feel about it?'

'That it was inevitable, yes. I've felt it over us like a thunderstorm that won't break, ever since that first day. Well, now it's broken.'

'And so—what?'

'And so—nothing my dear. Everything I said at first stands, even more firmly.'

'Janine would release me, Joy.'

'I know. That's why you can't ask her, Terry. She loves you in an idiotic, incredible way that would make her give you up and be miserable ever after, just because you asked her to. Besides—'

Her silence was eloquent, and he dropped his head in his hands.

'I know. Besides, there is all she has done for me, my work here for others—everything. Oh, I know, Joy. Release is out of the question.'

'Kiss me again, Terry.'

They held each other desperately, and then she freed herself.

'Now let's go back,' she said, and he untied the painter and paddled back the short distance in silence.

Janine was standing waiting for them, supreme contentment on her face.

'So you two have decided to make it up and be friends?' she asked as they came within earshot.

She linked a hand in an arm of each and walked between them back to the house. These two she loved – her husband and her – friend – how good it was to be with them here in the beauty of her home, so happy, so beloved.

Oh, Richard, thank you, my dear! You gave me Felicity, too.

She talked to them in her inconsequent, happy way, not noticing their silence, and inside the house she turned to Felicity again.

'And now you really will stay a day or two, won't you? Bennett can go up for your things tonight, or I can lend you what you need and you can go up either with Bennett or with Terry in the morning.'

Felicity tried to catch Terry's eye, but he deliberately looked away. If she stayed in the house, it should be through no machinations of his.

Whilst she hesitated, Janine pressed her.

'I would love to have you, Felicity, and you really don't have to go back tonight, do you?'

Felicity sighed and smiled and shrugged her shoulders.

'Well, on your own head be it,' she said, and Janine took her away to inspect their guest room, a lovely fragrant place of peace, overlooking the garden and perfumed with the thousand scents of a summer evening.

'I love your home, Janine,' said Felicity, looking round the fresh old-fashioned room with its polished mahogany and its jars of heavy-headed country roses. 'Here one could find—peace.'

'That's what I wanted this room to express,' said Janine slowly. She was extraordinarily at her ease with Felicity, and yet she still found it difficult to express the innermost thoughts of her heart, her vague dreams which of late had been less intangible and more attainable. 'You see, I was poor when your father married me, really poor, and everybody knew I was poor. The people in the house where I lived had enough to eat, and somewhere to sleep, of course, but they never had any real comfort or peace or pleasure. I used to dream that I had a place like this house, with the lovely country all round it, and money to spend on it, and that I could ask people to come here and stay, not as visitors exactly, but just to come and go as they liked, to have a real rest from worry and noise and anxiety. Sometimes people have to make up their minds about things, really serious things, and how can they do it with all the noise and bustle and anxiety about them? So I thought those people, too, would like to know about a place like this where they could perhaps see things more clearly and be able to decide what to do. 'I expect it all sounds rather stupid to you, but—well, I used to think those things, and now perhaps I shall be able to do them.'

Felicity put an arm about her suddenly.

'Janine, you're very sweet,' she said, and then moved away and began rather vigorously to brush her hair.

Perhaps vaguely at first she had toyed with the idea of taking Terry away from the girl he had married, the girl who could never possess him or be possessed by him as she could. There was something maddening in the knowledge that Janine, by her very gentleness and lack of suspicion, by her trustfulness and her essential goodness, was making that for ever impossible.

'I ought to try to do something for other people in return for all that's been given to me,' said Janine in her serious way. 'Not only material things, but – Terry, my husband.'

'You care for him an awful lot, don't you?' asked Felicity from the dressing-table.

'He's life itself to me,' said Janine, and then laughed a little at herself for her choice of words. 'That sounds silly, doesn't it? It's the sort of thing I say to myself, and it just slipped out. He really is my life, though. If anything happened to him, if I lost him, I—well, I don't think I could go on living.'

Felicity could have shaken her. With every hour she was making the barrier more impregnable, making her own position more unassailable.

'It's foolish to let anyone mean so much to you,' she said quietly.

Janine smiled. It was all very well for anyone like Felicity to talk, of course. *She* didn't know what it was to have a Terry.

'Well, that's the way I'm made, and I'm so happy loving Terry like this that I don't want to be any different. There's Bennett with the car. Will you go down and tell him where to go and what to bring?'

Chapter Fourteen

Janine looked up from her book, startled by the sound of crying. The walls at Four Ways were thin and the doors not always sound-proof, and the sounds came from the room which the maids used as a sitting-room.

Always tender towards grief, she put down her book and went to investigate, finding to her surprise that it was Hetty, the trim little parlour maid, who was usually so fresh and bright, Hetty who had a young man and was already gaily talking of marriage.

'Why, Hetty, whatever is the matter, my dear?' asked Janine in her gentle way, an arm about the girl's bowed shoulders.

Hetty looked up and tried to wipe away her tears with the wet ball of handkerchief which had already done considerable duty.

'On, madam, I'm sorry. I didn't want to disturb you, and you resting for a bit,' she said, gulping at her sobs.

'Never mind that. What's the trouble? You can tell me, you know, whatever it is,' for she had tried not quite successfully to check her suspicions about Hetty during the last few days.

'It's—it's Bob, madam,' said the girl, naming her young man. 'He's took—taken up with another girl, and he don't seem to want me anymore.'

'Oh, poor Hetty!' said Janine, her thoughts going at once to Terry and her own sufferings if she were to feel that he 'didn't want her anymore'.

'Poor Hetty. Perhaps you're only imagining it, though. Why, I thought he'd spoken about marriage to you.'

'Yes, and so he did, madam, but—but that was before.'

Janine decided not to enquire too closely into the suggested period.

'Are you seeing him tonight?' she asked instead, for this was Hetty's night out, and Bob usually came down on his motorcycle to see her and to take her out on the pillion.

'I dunno, madam. I—I thought perhaps, if you didn't mind, I'd go up and see him instead.'

'Perhaps that would be a good idea,' said Janine sympathetically, surmising that Hetty had good grounds for supposing that he would not come to her, and aware that, in like circumstances, she would certainly fly to Terry. 'Make yourself look specially nice, and you'll see everything will be alright. Would you like me to lend you something? We're just the same build and the same colouring. Come to my room and let me fix you up. There's nothing like new clothes to make you feel you can face things,' and chattering inconsequently to put the girl at her ease, she led the way to her room and opened her wardrobe, running her hands along the array of frocks and coats.

'What about this green linen, Hetty? I don't really want it any more. I've got such a lot of clothes, and you may as well keep it. There's a little muslin blouse that goes with it somewhere,' rummaging in a drawer, 'and you'll probably want the slip, because the blouse is so thin. Here, take the whole set. It all goes together,' and she pushed into the girl's hands a set of silk lingerie and a thin, embroidered muslin blouse.

'Oh, madam, I couldn't take all this!' protested Hetty, but Janine, flushed with the joy of giving, added a pair of silk stockings and some suede shoes. 'See if you can wear those shoes. They're not quite comfortable on me, anyway, but your feet may be a bit smaller.'

Hetty tried them on and was delighted with the result, drying her eyes and slipping away to her room with grateful thanks to Janine for both her sympathy and her practical help.

Janine smiled and returned to her book. It was so easy to help people when you had so much, and, blessed as she was in her beloved Terry, how could she ever do enough for others less blessed? She hoped Hetty would find Bob still faithful, and come back smiling on the back of the motorcycle at half past ten.

A thought struck her, and she went up to Hetty's room to tell her she could have an extension to eleven that night.

'Then Bob will be able to come all the way with you and see you safely in,' she said.

She paused on the landing to look towards the river, where for an instant a flash of white showed against the willows. That would be Felicity. She loved taking the crazy little boat as far as it would go down the stream, and had spent hours during her three days at Four Ways in that manner.

As she watched, the boat came out of the shadow of the trees towards the landing-stage, and she saw that Felicity was not alone. Terry was with her.

Janine smiled. She was glad to see him taking an hour off for once, and it was nice of him to find out Felicity and go on the water with her. She would have gone herself, but she had had a headache all day, and Terry had advised her to lie down in the cool with a book, and she had gone to sleep.

She put on a shady hat and strolled down through the orchard to meet them. They were laughing and joking together, and Janine thought how lovely it was to see them like that, for she was sure that Terry did not like Felicity, though he really was a dear and tried not to show it.

'Coo-ee! Terr-y,' she called, and they started a little and then came on towards her.

'I thought you were asleep, dear,' said her husband. 'I looked in before I went to find Felicity, and you were well away then.'

'Well, I'm awake enough now,' she laughed, and linked a hand in his arm.

'Headache gone?'

'Mm. I expect it was the heat.'

'Janine, I'm going back tomorrow,' said Felicity suddenly.

'Oh no, Felicity! Must you? We've loved having you, haven't we, Terry? Stay till after the week-end, anyway, and help me out with the people who are coming for bridge and supper on Sunday night.'

'Dear, I must go,' said Felicity, in that definite voice of hers. 'Really I must.'

Only in retrospect did Janine realise the strain that would surely have been apparent to anyone less dense and self-complacent than she. The strain was apparent in Terry, too, but here again she failed to realise it until it was too late.

'But I'm simply *counting* on you, Felicity. Terry, make her stay!'

'I'm afraid neither I nor anyone else could *make* Felicity do anything she didn't want to,' said Terry grimly.

Janine laughed a little at that and twined her arm more closely round his.

'Well, sometimes I wish that could be said of me! The trouble with me, as you tell me yourself sometimes, is that simply anybody can make me do what I don't want to do just by toiling me to do it!'

'You're wise, my child,' said Felicity. 'You stick to feminine helplessness. It's your long suit, and it wins every time, believe me! I always was short-suited in it!'

'Anyway, won't you please stay over the weekend, Felicity?'

'No, dear. Not for you or—or anybody. I'm going in now to change. I feel grubby and messy,' though she looked as immaculate as ever in her tailored white silk.

The few days in the country had added to her sunburn, and she looked golden and lovely as she stood there for a moment before entering the house. There was always a peculiar radiance about her, something sparkling as if from a secret source of light. She seemed so vital, the sort of person no one could possibly ignore or overlook. Beside her, Janine felt insignificant and colourless.

'Stay out here for a few moments, Terry,' she begged him softly. 'It's so lovely at this time of the evening – so still and peaceful and happy.'

'You are happy, aren't you, Janine?' he asked her suddenly. She looked up at him in surprise.

'Terry, what a funny question! Of course I am. Aren't you?'

'We're talking of you, my sweet. Don't wander off the subject. Analyse your happiness. Can you?'

'I don't know what you mean. Tell me.'

'Well, what constitutes your happiness exactly? Is it all this?' with a wave of his hand to include the house, the garden, the orchard about them and the stream below them. 'Or is it our work, being able to help people? Or is it—just us, Janine, you and I?'

'Yes, that more than anything, Terry. Us. You. Our love. All the rest makes it more wonderful and complete, of course, but the real thing is you and I, isn't it? All these other things don't really matter the way that does. I could be happy with you if we were poor and lived in an attic and never had any fun.'

'But you couldn't be happy here, with everything else that makes up our life, if I were not here? Is that what you mean?'

She stared at him.

'Terry, what weird things you say! You—you don't want to move up to town or anything do you! You wouldn't rather live somewhere else? Is that what you're trying to say?' she asked in a puzzled voice.

'No, dear, only—I wondered if—if all these things could constitute happiness for you if—if anything should happen to me.' She clung to him now, genuinely frightened.

'Darling, what is it? What are you trying to tell me? You're not ill or anything? There isn't anything the matter? Darling, tell me! You've got to tell me! I'm—terrified!'

He put his arm about her and held her closely to him, looking out over her head into a blank and empty future.

That afternoon he and Felicity had talked openly and without reserve or pretence or rancour. She had said that she must go, that it must end, that they must never see each other again. He had offered to speak to Janine, to sound her and see whether she had any suspicion, whether her adoration for him was really what they both supposed, or whether it was more a mere part of the life he had created for her at Merrow and could be dissociated from it without destroying the fabric of her happiness forever.

He had his answer. He could never leave her. Even if he did not owe her everything that made life a good thing to him, he could not leave her. She held him by her very helplessness, her gentle dependence upon him, her trust which almost maddened him by its completeness.

'There's nothing to be frightened about, Janine dear,' he said at last. 'I was—talking through my hat.'

She turned in his embrace and looked up at him.

'Oh, Terry, are you sure? You're not keeping something from me, are you?'

'No, dear. Nothing. Everything is—alright.'

She sighed with relief and snuggled down again.

'How you frightened me! You know, sometimes I *do* feel afraid, for no real reason except that everything is so marvellous and beautiful that I feel it can't last. Do you think like that sometimes?'

'I suppose all of us feel, in this world of change, that nothing can last for long, and the pessimistic vein in us takes it for granted that it is the best things that will vanish first.'

She was silent for a little while as they made their way very slowly through the orchard, the laden boughs almost touching their heads at times and forming a fragrant canopy above them.

When she spoke again, it was obvious her mind had not travelled far in those moments.

'You say there's nothing the matter, Terry, but I feel right inside me that—that something is troubling you. You haven't been yourself lately, the last week or two, anyway. You seem—moody and quiet. Darling, we aren't going to have any secrets from each other, are we? If something's worrying you, you'll let me share it?' Her persistence irritated him, and he frowned and let his arm relax a little.

'Dear, I've already *told* you there's nothing. Can't you accept that?'

'Well, I suppose I shall have to,' she said, with a little sigh that showed she was unconvinced. 'You see, when anybody is as much in love as I am, there's a sort of sixth sense created, and it's that sixth sense which keeps telling me you are worried and not quite as happy as you were. Terry, it isn't money, is it?'

'Good Lord, darling, no!'

'I've never been quite satisfied about—about that marriage settlement. It was all Mr. Tanner's doing, you know, I wanted just to hand everything over to you, but he wouldn't let me—no, please let me finish, dear! He insisted that it should be done his way, and I had to agree in the end, he was so determined about it. Anyway, I've made it alright if anything should happen to me, because I've left everything to you except five thousand pounds which Richard asked me to keep in reserve in case Felicity was ever in need. I have left that as a trust for her, but all the rest goes to you.'

'Janine, I do wish you wouldn't talk about it any more,' said her husband in distress. 'Oh, is that you, Gough? Do you want me?' as they became aware of the butler's portly figure dodging about amongst the overhanging branches.

'No, sir. I wanted to speak to Madam,' said the man, in his dignified way. 'It is about the car, madam, for Miss Felicity. Bennett says it wants a new ballrace and it would not be safe to take it up to town tonight, but he can get it done by the morning.'

'Surely she doesn't want to go back tonight?' asked Janine in surprise.

'That's what she says, madam.'

'I'll come in, Gough. Terry, come and persuade her to stay till the morning, there's a dear.'

Felicity was persuaded with some difficulty to stay till the morning, and then only because Terry flatly refused to take her in the two-seater.

Janine went to interview Mrs. Gough, and Felicity and Terry were left alone.

'Terry, why won't you let me go tonight?' she asked, with a note of desperation in her voice. 'Don't you realise that I'm at the end of my tether?'

'So am I,' he told her in a curious, flat voice.

'Then—'

'Oh, let's not flog the question any more,' he said wearily. 'I suppose I was a fool not to let you go, but—don't you see what it would have meant if I agreed to take you back to town tonight? I—couldn't have left you, Felicity. I should have done something mad. To have you alone with me like that for hours of the night —no,' and he turned on his heel and left her.

Dinner that night was a strained affair, though all three of them talked incessantly, gaily, Janine the quietest, though she, too, seemed to feel the need to keep up the tension.

After the table was cleared Felicity rolled up the rugs and pushed back the chairs.

'Find a dance band, Terry,' she bade him, and they danced.

Young Jack Conrad, the son of the works manager, heard the music in passing and came in at the hospitably open door to make up the four. He was very youthfully in love with Felicity, and she flirted with him outrageously, leaving Janine to her husband most of the evening.

'Hadn't you better dance with Felicity, just once?' she asked, as the evening wore into night and still he had not been near their guest. 'She'll think it's odd.'

'I'd rather dance with you,' he told her with set teeth, and she laughed, but there was still that note of strain in her laughter and she shivered a little.

'Are you cold, Janine?' he asked her.

'No. It's—oh, someone walking over my grave. I do that such a lot that I begin to think I shall end my days by falling down a city manhole. That's the only place where so many people are likely to walk!'

But when the dance was over and another starting, he walked deliberately across to Felicity and took her in his arms.

'Just once,' he said softly so that the others could not hear.

They were playing a medley of old tunes, reviving memories probably in many other couples than the one dancing in Janine's sitting-room, and, though neither spoke, each knew that the words, silly words but potent with meaning for such as they, echoed in their minds.

Save the last dance for me, sweetheart,
Just the last dance before we part …

In the gloaming by the fireside,
With you I'd be content;
In the gloaming by the fireside
Every hour would be well spent.
We'd see our hopes and dreams, dear,
Like pictures in the fire …

Felicity stopped, her face pale and strained, her eyes heavy with the tears they never shed.

'I can't go on, Terry,' she said, and broke away from him and ran up the stairs.

Janine watched her go with a little puzzled frown.

'What's the matter with her today, Terry? She seems in some sort of trouble, but when I asked her, she only laughed in that queer, defiant sort of way of hers, as if nothing ever really mattered to her at all.'

'I should leave her alone, dear,' he said. 'Are you off, Jack?'

The boy had shuffled awkwardly towards the door, aware that there was some domestic strain and anxious to be out of it.

'Mother'll wonder where I am,' he said, with a laugh. 'I only came out to post a letter, but I heard the music and saw you dancing.'

'That's quite right … Drop in any time. Jack. You know that, don't you?' said Terry heartily.

'Won't you have something before you go?' asked Janine, and went towards the sideboard.

The boy refused, and slipped away, but Terry followed his wife.

'I'd like something, Jan,' he said, and she was surprised to see him pour himself out a whisky and drink it off neat, an amazing thing for him to do.

Wisely, she made no remark but went with him on his usual rather perfunctory rounds of the house, shutting windows and locking doors, and then they went up to their room.

'Do you think I had better go and see if Felicity wants anything?' asked Janine doubtfully, looking towards their guest's door at the opposite end of the corridor.

'I shouldn't. Girls get queer ideas sometimes, and she may have wanted to get back to town very particularly tonight,' said Terry, rather awkwardly.

They began to undress, and Janine, in passing him, laid her cheek for an instant against his arm in a little intimate caress. Unreasonably, and with a little sense of shock, Terry found himself resenting her touch, and for a moment he stood quite still and tense, his lower lip between his teeth, his hands clenched.

'I—I shall have to go downstairs for a few minutes,' he said jerkily. 'I've forgotten some notes I promised I would let Conrad have in the morning. You go to sleep, dear. I—may be some time.'

Janine said nothing. A month ago, a fortnight ago even, he would have responded eagerly and warmly to that little gesture of hers. Tonight she sensed rather than saw his withdrawal from her. She could not understand him, and she was hurt, but she went on steadily with her undressing and got into bed, closing her eyes and trying not to let the sense of hurt go beyond her control.

He was tired, she reflected. He must have a lot to worry and exercise his mind, taking care of her affairs and making their schemes work out according to plan. He had had a busy day – no, that was not quite true, of course, because he had found time to take Felicity out in the boat.

Felicity.

That was the first hint of the coming trouble, but at the moment she closed her mind to it and refused to recognise it or to give it entry,

Terry was tired. Felicity had some secret trouble. That was all.

She resolutely composed herself to sleep.

She did not know how much later it was that she suddenly remembered that they had locked up and Hetty was not in. She felt a little worried over the girl, and hoped she would not be very late, meantime she must go down and unlock the back door.

And downstairs Terry, a silk dressing-gown over his pyjamas, had tramped from end to end of the lounge and then, feeling stifled and shut in, cautiously opened one of the French windows and went out into the garden. The night was a night of stars, full of enchantment, and somewhere quite near a nightingale was singing.

He stood at the corner of the house, drinking in the unearthly beauty of scent and sound and silence, and gradually he became aware that he was no longer alone.

'You?' he asked in a soft whisper.

She nodded, and came close to him.

'I smelt your cigarette and then leaned out and saw you here. You don't mind, Terry?'

He put out a hand and took hers and held it closely.

'We ought not to, Joy, but – we're only human.'

As if by tacit consent, they wandered away from the house and into the orchard, silent and dew-wet.

'Will you be cold, darling?' he asked, looking at her feet in fragile satin mules, and the edges of her pyjamas soaked already.

She pulled her mandarin coat about her and laughed softly, a note of derision in her laughter.

'Does anything like that matter just now?' she asked. 'Love me, Terry. Just for an hour, love me.'

He held her closely, kissing her hair, her lips, her throat, the white softness of her breast between the satin folds of her coat.

'This is madness, Joy,' he told her.

'Oh, Terry, why—why—why couldn't you have waited?' she asked, all her veneer of cool disdain gone, her defences down, her modernity flung aside and only the essential, primitive woman in her remaining, a woman robbed of her mate.

'Darling, I never meant to do anything else, I never meant or wanted to marry Janine,' he told her desperately, the truth bursting out at last.

'Then—why, Terry?' she asked him tragically.

'It was all through a moment of utter madness. We went out together. I had met her in Madeira and we had a day together when she missed the boat and was stranded. Afterwards she wrote to me to come and see her, and I thought it was to help me to get a job. I didn't know about Harrow being dead. Then—well, as I say, I took her out, and—well, men are rotters, Joy, in lots of ways. She seemed even more than willing, and a man takes what the gods throw in his lap, as a rule.'

'You mean – they threw Janine into your lap? *Janine?*'

'Yes. It's hard to believe, I know. Sometimes I can't realise myself that it actually happened. The kid was in love with me, and I—well, I thought she was a widow and missing her husband, and—well, that was all there was to it. I don't feel exactly a hero telling you all this, Joy, but I've felt that I wanted you to know that—that I did mean to wait for you, that I've never cared for her in that way.'

'What I don't understand is why you married her, Terry. If she was that sort—'

'Darling, she wasn't. I think she was crazy about me at the time, though it sounds a rotten thing to say.'

'Never mind. Let's be honest at least, and call things by their right names, it isn't hard for *me* to believe that she was crazy about you, Terry,' with a wry smile. 'Still I can't see why you married her. I know it can't have been just because of her money, or you wouldn't have been so obstinate about marrying me.'

'Thank you, Joy. I'm thankful to know that you really do believe that of me. It wasn't just the money, though I admit it did make a difference. I'll be honest. I was out of work and pretty hopeless. I'd lost you and never expected to see you again. I didn't care a damn about anybody on earth except you, and—well, I realised that she expected me to marry her.'

'But why on earth should she? After all, it wasn't like seducing a young girl.'

'That's just what it was, really. She—she was inexperienced, Joy. Your father had been ill all the time, you see.'

She was silent, clinging to him, her head against his shoulder, their faces turned to the peaceful, starlit sky.

'Poor Terry,' she said at last, 'and poor Joy. And, I think, poor Janine. To hold you and yet never actually to have you. That's what it is for her, isn't it? You're mine, Terry, really, aren't you?'

'To the end of everything, my dear.'

Suddenly she turned in his arms.

Terry, my dearest, give me this one night. Take one night for yourself. Afterwards—nothing. You can't leave her. I can see that as well as you, and I think we're both too decent to bolt and mess her life up like that. After all , you are married to her, and she isn't the sort to outlive a divorce. We won't go back to the house. It wouldn't be—decent. Let's take the boat. There are cushions and a rug in the hut.'

Neither of them saw the glimmer of white amongst the trees, and Janine's feet in dressing-slippers had made no sound. She herself did not know how long she had stood there, attracted at first by the glimpse of them amongst the trees and considering it her duty to prevent any further foolishness on the part of Hetty and her Bob. She had no doubt of the identity of the pair until she was close to them. Then, her hand going instinctively to her lips, her breath catching in a little sob of amazement, she recognised Felicity and Terry.

It may have been hours; it may have been seconds. She lost all sense of time. She became nothing but ears to hear, a mind to make the scene an indelible memory, a heart to suffer as she had never imagined anything could suffer and still live.

Softly, charged with passion and the bitterness of renunciation, their voices had come to her. They might have heard her difficult breathing had they been less absorbed in each other. She realised subconsciously that they had only to turn to become aware of her, but they did not turn. Led by Felicity, half unwillingly, half the helpless victim of his own passion, Terry moved away through the trees, his arm a dark line across her silk wrap, his head pressed against hers.

Janine watched them go, her eyes dry and burning, her throat parched, something very cold and terrible gripping her being. Then she turned and fled, back to the house, back to her locked room, back to the bed which she could never share with Terry again.

Strangely, she did not cry, though she was of the type to find relief in tears. This had gone too deeply for relief. Terry had gone from her. Even now he was with Felicity, lying in her arms, whispering to her all those dear things that had been hers, Janine's, but that would be hers no more.

She tortured herself by picturing them in the comfortable old tub, hers that Terry had painted for her.

'I know you can afford to buy something very posh, darling,' he had told her. 'Let me furbish this one up for you instead, will you? I shall feel I've done something for you myself, provided at least some little thing for your pleasure.'

And so she had loved the old boat, made gay cushions for it, bought a striped Indian blanket for it, and had cuddled up beneath the warmth of the rug in Terry's arms many a time.

Now Felicity was lying in his arms beneath the rug. Suddenly a white flame of anger shot through her. How dare she!

'There are cushions and a rug in the hut,' she had said – and Terry had gone with her to desecrate them!

The flame died again, leaving her utterly cold.

There were other things to remember, more important things than a few cushions and a rug.

'Joy' he had called her, and she had said 'my dearest' to him. Terry was Felicity's dearest, and she his joy.

Out of the jumble of misery and horror came the story at last. They had loved each other before, been lovers in actual fact before, probably. If she, Janine, had not come between them and married Terry, those two would by now be husband and wife, not skulking down to a boat on the stream at midnight in order to indulge in the pleasures of love-making.

She went over all the events that led up to her marriage, seeing clearly now that Terry had never thought of marriage, had never wanted it, had been forced into it by her stupid ignorance of life and of the sort of girls who made up his world. He had looked on her as merely the amusement of an hour. She had been 'more than willing'.

The memory seared her, made her writhe on the bed in an agony of shame. She remembered her exaltation that night, the eager passion that had swept her, not because she desired physical satisfaction but because she loved him with everything that was within her, and he had asked what she could give. How gloriously she had given! She had seen that act as the crown of life, believing that he shared it with her and saw it as she did. Wrong it might have been according to the standard of accepted conventions, but that night they had seemed above and beyond mere convention.

And he had seen her simply as 'more than willing'.

And the next day when he had come to her (very late, she now remembered), he had come with a feeling of slight shame, come because according to his code he had to put in an appearance, seeing that she was not merely a paid prostitute. He had come to find her all blushing and coy and bride-like, prepared for a marriage, which, in the end, he had been unable to avoid!

'She expected me to marry her.'

She ceased to writhe in agony. Even her hands relaxed their grip on the corner of the pillow. She lay very still, and in that hour, a new Janine was born – conceived in shame and grief and despair in those moments in the orchard, and struggling to life with the anguish of childbirth. She would never be the same happy, carefree, trustful girl again. She was a woman with her heritage of pain.

She rose at last. She could not endure that they should come back into the house, her house, whilst she was still there. She had no plan. She only knew that she must get away before they returned. Not yet had she formed the definite intention of leaving Terry. That probably in the end, for how could she stay with him and even pretend to be his wife when he and Felicity …

Oh, God! Terry and Felicity!

Without thinking what she was doing, she dressed, and then began automatically to tidy her dressing-table, lengthening out the last moments. The dark always made her nervous, and even now she feared it subconsciously, though it was absurd to be afraid of anything any more. What else could possibly happen to her?

Her rings lay on the dressing-table, and some bracelets she had been showing to Felicity and had not put away. Mechanically she pushed them into her bag and did not even know she had done so.

An owl hooted and the sound reminded her that she must hurry—hurry. Down the stairs like a ghost she went, out at the still open French window (thank God they had not come back yet!), and through the dark, scented garden she had loved.

Like a sleepwalker, sure-footed, noiseless, almost as if she floated on air, she found the road, its roughness not even felt through the thin shoes she wore.

Somewhere back there, they were coming across the orchard to go into the house again. She must hurry – hurry.

Chapter Fifteen

From the window of his office, a little makeshift place he had chosen because from it he could overlook the steel giant which was rising on the hilltop, Terry watched the coming of the dawn.

For the first time since the foundations had been dug, he looked at it without seeing it, without an inward vision of the great white building which was to see so many of his dreams fulfilled. He had even entered the office without glancing at the model of it which stood on a table opposite the door, and which he usually touched with loving fingers before going to his desk.

He was unconscious of his extraordinary garb even. He was still in dressing-gown and slippers, and in them he had come through the sleeping village, oblivious of everything save of his own pain and of the utter impossibility of re-entering just then the house which he shared with Janine, the house which actually was Janine's, the house which now, in the aftermath of surfeited passion, he felt he had defiled.

He sat with his head in his hands, a prey to the remorse of an idealist who had dragged his own ideals in the mud and had to take them up, wipe them, patch them up and turn them to the world again with such cunning that no one but he should ever know of the cracks and the mended pieces.

He and Felicity had said goodbye. He must never see her again. She had agreed to that, though her own heart was torn and bleeding, though she clung to him with her hands and her lips and arms which held him with a passion he had never dreamed of. How mad, how utterly mad, they had been to forge this unbreakable link between them, knowing all the time that they must part.

Janine, in her weakness, her dependence, her so obvious worship of him, held him as a stronger woman could never have done.

'You owe her everything and without you she would die. She's that sort. Oh, I know, Terry, I know!' Felicity had said to him, and she was only echoing his own thoughts.

'I can't lose you, Joy, not now!' he had said. 'You're mine. I'm going to keep you.'

She had held to him closely, but in the end he had known, as actually he had known in the beginning. He would not leave Janine, his ideals, his dreams, the work he had made the centre of his life.

And so, at last, Felicity had gone from him, stumbling, with eyes that could not see, with hands that pushed him away.

'Let me go, darling. Just—stay there a minute so that I can—go,' and she had gone from him, and then he had turned and come here so that he might be alone, so that the sight of all this that meant so much to him could give him strength and courage and decency.

He had no illusions about himself. He was no hero renouncing love for duty. Here actually lay his love. He was of the type to give the whole of his being to the passions of love whilst the moment held him, but his real and enduring devotion was to the work which Janine had made possible for him. He realised that even in the midst of his anguished parting from Felicity, and the knowledge made him the more unworthy in his own estimation. He had brought the woman he adored to sorrow, was living a lie in order to keep happy the woman who adored him, and yet he was not even a great lover. This grief would pass, its present shaft of pain would lose its power. His work would remain. That, and that only, could have the power utterly to devastate his life. He could not give it up.

Oh yes, he saw himself with no self-deceptive eye, in no heroic light, for his renunciation of Felicity and his cleaving to Janine. He was determined, however, honestly to keep the letter of his word to his wife, and as much of the spirit of it as lay within his power. Bitterly he regretted the past hour with Felicity, for whilst he had not been her lover in actual fact, there was nothing but the sentimental tie of the past to hold them.

She had given herself knowing that he meant it to be the end, but he could not excuse himself on those grounds.

He thrust regret from him and forced himself to look into the future, a future for Janine and him in which Felicity, his love, would have no part. Janine wanted a child. He had known that for some months, but he had hedged and procrastinated, unwilling to see her as the mother of the child whom for so long he had visioned as Felicity's. Well, she should have her child. That, at least, he could give her, and presently this turmoil and grief would be forgotten.

Deliberately he conjured up a vision of his wife, of her sweetness, her gentleness, her yielding tenderness in all her dealings with him, the heady delights of making love to her, and, towards morning, with the coming of the dawn, he rose from his desk and went back through the silent street and into the house.

Everything was as it had been. There was nothing to bear witness to the agony and pain of that night for the three who had seen the dawn come. Terry crept up the stairs and past the closed door of Janine's room and into the little room next to it, a room he used sometimes when he was very late and feared to disturb her. Flinging himself on the bed, he slept from sheer nervous exhaustion, waking unrefreshed, but firm in his determination to make what amends he could to Janine.

She was not down, and he breakfasted alone, thankful not to have to see Felicity.

'Your mistress not down?' he asked the maid who waited on him.

'I understand she has gone for a walk, sir. Mrs. Gough says her room is empty.'

He went on with his breakfast unperturbed. It was a habit of Janine's to get up and go out early and he felt relieved by her decision to do so on this particular morning.

Gough came to him for orders before he went, and he resented, without being able to explain, the man's growing antipathy towards him. He did not realise that, however well satisfied Janine herself might be, his own rather impersonal and careless attitude towards her was remarked and criticised by the Goughs, who were devoted to their mistress. Had he shown towards his wife the slavish adoration and devotion they felt she merited, they would not have resented his presence. As it was, they felt that he had married her for their late master's money and that alone, and no amount of praise from the village for his conduct towards the tenants nor his schemes for providing work made any difference to their private feelings against him.

'It's easy to be generous with other people's money,' was the burden of their criticism of him, and though they paid him necessary respect and gave him such service as seemed required of them by Janine, it was to her they gave their affection and allegiance.

During the last day or two they had felt they had cause for a further grievance against him, and he would have been surprised had he known how his least little action had been watched and interpreted since the coming of Felicity.

Mrs, Gough came to meet her husband when the front door had closed on Forder.

'I wish the mistress'd come in,' she said anxiously. 'Seems to me she's gone out on that wet grass with only her evening shoes on. She'll catch her death, and her used to London streets.'

'And a fat lot he'd care if she did,' grunted Gough, with a nod towards the front door. 'Shall I go and see if I can see her?'

"I shouldn't. She hates to be fussed over. Besides. Miss Felicity's going this morning, so she's sure to come in soon.'

But she had not returned by the time the guest was ready, and Felicity felt relieved that she had not to see Terry's wife again.

'Tell Mrs. Forder I am so sorry not to be able to wait,' she told Gough. 'I simply must get back before lunch. She'll understand.'

Felicity herself was in a state of uncertainty about Terry now that the daylight had brought some measure of sanity to her. She knew that he loved her and desired her, and they were drawn together by the events of the night even more than by the past years. She was ultra-modern in her regard of such matters. To her, her body was her own to do with as she liked, and she shared the views of most of her set in thinking a quite unnecessary fuss and value was laid on a merely natural function. By no possibility could she have concluded, as once Janine had done, that physical union must end in legal union. She realised how almost impossible it was for Terry to break with Janine, but she could quite calmly contemplate a future of some years, at least, with herself as Terry's mistress.

So she went from Janine's house tolerably content with life, and serenely unaware of the completeness of Terry's renunciation of her. By the time she met Janine again she would have been able to adjust her mind to the new conditions and act accordingly. Janine must not be, and need not be, disturbed.

But by lunchtime Janine had not returned, and as the afternoon wore on and Gough had telephoned once or twice to the office without begin able to speak to Forder, it was decided that he should go there personally and demand to see him. He had sent a message during the morning that he would not be home for lunch and did not wish to be disturbed for anything during the day, but the whole of the Four Ways staff were now determined that he must be disturbed.

After being kept waiting for some time, and becoming, in consequence, the more incensed against Janine's husband, he was admitted to Forder's room.

Forder looked up in some surprise, for no name had been given him.

'Oh, it's you, Gough! Anything the matter?' he asked.

'It's the mistress, sir. She's not been home yet, and we're getting anxious in case something's happened to her.'

'Not been home? Not since she went out before breakfast?' he asked, startled.

'No, sir. We thought you ought to know.'

'But of course! You ought to have told me earlier,' jumping up and getting his hat.

'They told me on the telephone you were too busy to be disturbed, sir,' said Gough resentfully.

'Yes, but—Good Lord! I'm leaving now, Miss Dean. I may not get back. Better leave the letters for signature at Four Ways on your way home. Come on, Gough. Let's get back to the house.'

Questioned, the servants could give no information.

'Can you be quite sure what she wore, Mrs. Gough?' he asked, before telephoning the police.

'Well, not quite, sir. Hetty usually looked after her things.'

'And where's Hetty?'

Mrs. Gough pursed her lips.

'Not come back since last night,' she said.

'You don't suppose she's with Mrs. Forder?' he asked, worried.

'Oh no, sir. She never came in at all last night. Not but what we're surprised. She was always about with that Bob, and saying she wouldn't come back and leave him with some other girl again. Took her luggage, she did. I shouldn't bother about her any more, sir, if I were you. She never meant to come back when she went off yesterday. I should say the mistress wore her blue and white dress and her navy coat. I can't find them, anyway. But she must have gone without a hat and in her thin shoes.'

A description was given to the police, and every hospital in the neighbourhood was rung up without satisfaction.

At last he rang up Felicity and told her what had happened, hoping against hope that Janine, coming in and finding that her guest had gone in her absence, had gone after her to make her apologies. It was a fantastic idea, but all the sensible ones had been exhausted.

But Felicity was as much in the dark as he, though she accentuated the thought that had been nagging at his own mind all the evening.

'Terry, you don't think she—knows?'

'My dear, impossible. How could she?'

'No, I suppose she couldn't. Can I do anything?'

'I can't think of anything I can do myself.'

'Poor Terry.' Her voice came softly to him. 'Poor sweet. You're worried, aren't you? Guilty conscience?'

'Not altogether, though that as well, of course. I simply can't imagine what can have happened other than an accident, in which case surely I should have been told by now? She always carried cards in her handbag, and she seems to have had that with her.'

'Would you like me to come down, Terry?'

'No, darling—no. Better not.'

'I will, like a shot, if I can do anything. After all, she's my stepmother, which would provide sufficient excuse.'

'Better not, Joy. Goodbye, my dear. I must think of something else,' and he hung up the receiver without even waiting for her goodbye.

Gough was hovering near, a curious expression on his face. If he had heard that conversation, which he probably had done, he had also heard the 'darling' which had slipped out. Oh well, what did it matter? What did anything matter but the fact that Janine was lost?

He tortured himself with pictures of her lying helpless, injured, left at the roadside to die by some callous motorist. One read of these things in the papers, but it was ghastly to think such a thing might happen to Janine, so soft and helpless and defenceless.

'Any reply from the police at Little Lamber, Gough?' he asked, as the man hung about in the hall .

'No, sir.'

'What do you yourself think has happened, Gough? I'm worried stiff.'

'I'm sure I couldn't say, sir. All I know is nobody about *here* would want to do her an injury.'

'Do her an injury? Great Scott, what on earth – you surely don't imagine, Gough, that there's any foul play?' – for in spite of the man's words, his face expressed precisely that.

'Well, sir, I don't say nothing about that. All I say is that where there's money there's funny dealings,' and he turned away and went to the kitchen, leaving Terry dumbfounded.

Who on earth would want to do Janine an injury for the sake of her money? Who would benefit by it? Absolutely no one on earth but – himself and Felicity!

If Janine really had disappeared, and people began to talk foolishly, as suggested already by Gough, very unpleasant things might be said about him. Him rather than Felicity, of course, because she was financially in a position to be more or less indifferent to the five thousand pounds which Janine had mentioned, and of which she was quite possibly not even aware.

He tore up to town, was received courteously but without enthusiasm by an extremely polite gentleman at Scotland Yard, and was promised such help as might be needed, though he left with the impotent feeling that he had not been taken seriously. How could he possibly impress a man like that with the image of Janine and the extraordinary improbability that she had gone away on her own initiative, either alone or, as was tacitly suggested, with another man?

Through the next day, and the next, nothing happened, though Terry appealed through the papers, had a message broadcast, and felt at last that the police were taking a reasonably serious view of the case.

And on the Monday, three days after Janine had so mysteriously vanished, Jack Conrad came rushing into the office, pushed up the wooden barrier without ceremony, and flung himself into the middle of a business conference over which Terry, white-faced and at high nervous tension, was struggling to preside.

'Mr. Forder, you'd better come,' he said breathlessly and without apology.

Terry rose to his feet.

'My wife?' he asked, white-lipped.

'They've found—someone.' said the boy shakily, and the other men in the room gave way with respectful sympathy so that Terry could go past them and out of the building.

'Where?' he asked briefly as they went.

'Down by the stream. They opened the dam this morning,' panted the boy.

'Is she ...?'

'Yes.'

With long strides, his face chalk white and his eyes mere slits, Terry reached the spot where, as soon as they were clear of the works, he could see a little knot of men. Just above that spot was the only deep part of the stream, and legend had already woven many stories about that strange, deep pool above which, and on either side of which, the placid, gentle little stream flowed. It was probably a spring, for even at times of drought the level of the stream did not vary greatly, though a dam protected the millpond half a mile above.

As Terry approached, the men gathered at the edge of the stream fell back to make a pathway for him, but Besley, the village constable, checked him with a warning hand.

'Take it easy, Mr. Forder, sir,' he said, holding him back from that which lay, a draggled, ghastly little heap, between him and the water's edge.

He cast one look at it, recognised the dress as Janine's, caught sight of the short, wet wisps of brown hair, and then someone came hurrying up with a cloth, which was thrown hastily over the pathetic little heap.

Sick and faint, Terry stood there, incapable of movement, vaguely aware of the sympathetic glances with which he was surrounded.

That – Janine! His gentle, sweet, tender Janine!

'God!'

The word burst from him like a sob, and some woman came from the back of the little knot of men and put a motherly arm around his shoulders.

'Come away, Mr. Forder,' she said gently, and he was conscious that he was being led away, leaving that covered bundle at the water's edge.

'I—can't—leave her!' he gasped, but someone took his other arm and they got him away, took him back to his house, back to the lounge which spoke of her in every nook and corner.

Besley followed, sympathetic but important.

'I shall have to ask you a few questions, I am afraid. Mr. Forder. Dr. Arkwright is in charge down there now, but I've got to make my report.'

'Make it—as short as you can, Besley,' said Forder, and he answered the formal questions, which were concerned with Janine's name and age, mechanically.

'You've had all that,' he said at last, wearily. 'Can't you leave me alone now?'

And, after a time, they left him with the doctor, who had finished for the time being his share of the business and left it to others to carry on.

The Arkwrights were the closest friends that the Forders had made in the village so far, and though both the doctor and his wife were older than Terry and Janine, their hearts and their sympathies had kept young. The older man had approached this affair with sincere sorrow and regret.

'Sorry, old man, terribly,' he said in his rather gruff way, when he and Forder were alone.

Terry looked up.

'I suppose there's no—use asking …?'

'Fraid not the slightest. I put death at two days ago, at the latest, as far as the first cursory examination goes.'

'Can I see her now?' asked Terry. 'I'm—quite able.'

Arkwright shook his head.

'I shouldn't just yet, Forder. She's—well—it's a ghastly sight. Sorry, old man, but you've got to know. You'll have to see her for identification, of course, but I should leave it for an hour or two,' and he went across to the table, poured out a stiff whisky, added only a spot of soda, and brought it back to him.

Terry shook his head.

'I'm alright. That would only—muddle me.'

The doctor insisted.

'They may come any minute to ask you to go, though I advised them to let you alone for an hour or two. You'll want—all the courage you can get.'

'You mean …?'

He shrank from the actual question, just as mind and body recoiled from the thought.

'She's been in the water two days, Terry, and—well—rats, you know—'

Terry shuddered and felt sick, but took a gulp of the whisky and sat down again, catching at the arms of his chair and gripping them until his knuckles showed white.

'It's—too horrible,' he said. 'She was—afraid of—mice even.'

The kindly doctor stayed with him until late in the evening, Besley and the police doctor came to ask him to go with them for formal identification, explaining that it made the procedure for the inquest more simple.

'Inquest? Oh—of course,' he muttered, and went shrinkingly with them.

He steeled himself to look, but saw at once that there could be actually no evidence save that of his mind that this thing had been Janine. There was the vague impression of her face, the soft brown hair which now was drying and curling in little tendrils about the head; there was her body, scarcely touched, and they showed him the clothes she had worn, the scraps of embroidered silk, the frock and coat.

Yes. They belonged to his wife. Yes, he thought it was his wife. No, there was nothing he wanted to ask, nothing more he wanted to say.

He went back to the nightmare of realisation, and through the ghastly night that followed he was aware of kindly figures about him: of the doctor's rotund little form; of Mrs. Arkwright's homely face and ministering hands; of poor Mrs. Gough, unfamiliar with her tear-reddened face; of the Cook and little Annie doing what they could for him until they faded away, one by one, and left him alone with the doctor.

'You go home now, Arkwright,' he said wearily, for the tenth time. 'I shall be alright.'

But the doctor spent the rest of the night curled up on one of the high-backed settees, whilst Terry snatched a few odd minutes' sleep stretched uncomfortably in his armchair, starting up now and then with the realisation of the tragedy which had stalked info his life the day that was at long last passing.

The inquest, a lively topic of conversation and speculation, seemed to Terry, stretched on the rack of his own remorse, unnecessarily delayed, but when it came, it brought down on him an avalanche such as in his wildest dreams he had not suspected.

The medical evidence, given gravely by the police doctor and with obvious reluctance and regret by Arkwright, revealed the amazing fact that the woman whom Terence Forder had identified as his wife was pregnant; it also revealed the even more amazing fact that death had been caused by a blow on the back of the head, given by some sharp instrument, possibly a stone, or a tool of some sort.

An open verdict was returned, to the incredulous amazement of the villagers and the workpeople, who had concluded that the tragedy was the result of an accident and that the girl had caught her foot and overbalanced, as one could quite well do in negotiating the bends and the overhanging branches of the little stream, which Janine was known frequently to do.

It was after that that excitement ran high, all sorts of rumours flew about, every manner of suggestion put forward. No one knew exactly where the most sinister of them originated, but before many days had passed people were looking askance at Terry Forder, and when Felicity came down for the funeral, when at length it was sanctioned, she had the uncomfortable knowledge that, for some reason, she came in for a share of the black looks with which Terry was favoured.

They walked back from the graveside together, for there was to be no feasting afterwards, and not even the clergymen had been bidden to the house. Terry's heart had turned sick at the thought of the conventional gathering of mourners, eating and drinking in the room that had been Janine's pride and delight, and an act which in other circumstances might have been understood was now construed into a confession that there was more in this than had so far appeared.

Many eyes followed the two as they left the little graveyard which surrounded the church and walked the few yards to Four Ways.

'How do you think he feels now?' asked one cautiously.

'Fancy her having the nerve to come, and to go back to the house with him!'

'You'd have thought they'd have waited till she was cold in her grave, poor thing.'

'Well – maybe she isn't going to be let to be cold there just yet,' said another darkly.

'Platinum blonde, I suppose they call her. Well, she got herself up strong for the funeral alright. I never did like that colour hair, and on the pictures they're always vamps.'

'Well, it's none of my business, but you mark my words – there's a lot as'll be said before Miller Neal lets up his dam again.'

'*And* a lot as'll be done. Funny thing 'e did 'appen to let up the dam just now. Anybody as belonged hereabouts would 'a' known this is the time o' year the millpond gets too full.'

'Anybody as belonged hereabouts – you're right, Muster Burke.'

'Decided onlucky fur the one as didn't know the dam mighter bin let up, eh?'

'Yus, decided onlucky. If it 'ad 'ave bin any other time o' year the poor lady might 'ave laid in the 'ole for months, and p'rhaps never bin thrown up at all. Very, *very* onlucky for someone.'

'I bet if it 'ad 'a' bin you or me, George, as wanted to dot the missus one and 'eave 'er overboard, we'd 'a' waited till Miller Neal 'ad finished lettin' up the dam, wouldn't we?'

'Net 'arf we wouldn't, old son.'

'Well, wot about the "Pig and Whistle", anyone?'

They all knew what about the 'Pig and Whistle', apparently, and by the time Felicity and Terry had gone into Four Ways and shut the door the churchyard and lane were empty.

Felicity poured Terry out a drink and stood by him whilst he swallowed it.

'Take a grip on yourself, old man,' she said quietly.

'Thanks. You're a pal, Joy.'

They sat on either side of the shining copper fire-dogs and thought of Janine. It seemed impossible, even after the horrors which had culminated in today's ceremony, that she had gone. Every corner of the house breathed of her. She had made it so definitely her own. The Hampstead house had been Richard Harrow's, and she had never attempted to rid it of its solemn grandeur and gloom. But Four Ways was her own, chosen by her and by Terry, furnished in love and happiness and glad anticipation. It reflected her simple, unassuming sweetness. It had caught the fragrance of her mind. It was old-fashioned and dignified, but its windows and doors were ever wide open to the sun and the wind and the perfume of flowers.

'I can't believe it, even yet,' said Terry heavily.

'Terry, did you know—about the baby?'

'No. And even now it simply staggers me. I asked Arkwright privately, but he said there was no possibility of mistake. It must have happened two months ago. She must have known, and yet she didn't tell me. That's what I can't understand. Why didn't she tell me?'

'Terry, you don't think there could have been—anybody else?'

'Good Lord, no! Not for Janine. She—well, she really did almost worship me, Joy.'

'I know, dear,' and they were silent again.

When next she spoke it was with an effort, and as if she apologised for her words even whilst she spoke them.

'Terry, you—have you—noticed anything? Anything queer about the people down here, the villagers, and some of your workpeople?'

He lifted startled eyes and she saw at once that she had made no mistake.

'Yes. Have you?' he asked.

She nodded.

'It's—pretty ghastly, isn't it? You can't go on living amongst them, can you? Village people can be so awful. You read about them in the papers. I suppose so little happens to them that they have to make the most of things like this, no matter at whose expense.'

'I can't go away, Joy. I can't give up my work. Besides it was Janine's, I did it for her as much as for myself. It was a sort of dream of both of us, and it's only just beginning to be something big. I couldn't give it up now, or leave it to others who wouldn't perhaps see what we want to do. We're making a success of it. I couldn't give it up. Why should I? It isn't my fault that—Janine is dead.'

'I shall always wonder if it isn't really—our faults, Terry,' she said quietly.

'Joy! Don't!'

'Are you sure she didn't know, Terry? I've got the sort of feeling that she did, and that she is the kind of person who might have deliberately chosen—that way out.'

'They say definitely it could not have been suicide,' said Terry in a low voice, gripping his hands together between his knees, his face white and strained and unnatural.

'Not intentionally, but carelessly, perhaps. She could have fallen when she was rounding that bend by the water-lilies, hanging on to that big branch, you know. I've nearly fallen there myself, and if she slipped backwards or tried to save herself as she fell, she could have caught the back of her head on the stump of a branch. Not if she were careful – but she might not have been careful.'

'Don't go over it all again, Joy. I've thought and thought until I've worried myself sick with thought of how it could have happened, and

I simply can't think about it any more. It's the future we've got to face and not the past. That's over and done with.'

'We hope,' said Felicity quietly.

'What do you mean by that?'

'My dear, we've got to face things. You know as well as I do what these ghastly village people think, or are trying to think. They hope to bring themselves to the belief that—that you and I are more closely concerned with Janine's death than we admit.'

'Joy!'

'I know it's occurred to you already, my dear, or I wouldn't give you something else to worry about. Since it really has occurred to you, why not talk it out with me and try to lay the ghost, if we can? The doctors vary a little in their opinion as to whether she met her death on that Thursday night or on the next night, but they are inclined to the belief that it was some time during the Thursday night. Now we were with Janine until – what time? Ten? Eleven?'

'Just before eleven, I should say, but young Conrad will probably know that, as she went up directly after he had gone and I went with her.'

'And then?'

'I—I felt worried and restless, so I came down and into the garden.'

'Yes. All that part. What time was it when we went in, do you suppose? Two o'clock? It must have been very late.'

'It was about a quarter past two. I didn't come back into the house when you did. I went to the office and worked till dawn and then came in and went to bed in the other room so as not to disturb her.'

'Did anyone see you?'

'I don't know. I hope they didn't. I was in pyjamas and dressing gown all the time. I took the cut through the orchard and over Burke's yard so as not to go out into the road, but I came back by the road. Why do you ask that?'

'Well—Mrs. Gough knew I was not in my room. When I got back I found a note on the dressing-table to say that Bennett had finished the car and could be ready any time I liked in the morning. She must have been in, found me missing, and written the note. I don't know what time it was, of course, but I am wondering if they knew you were out as well.'

'I can't see that it makes any difference,' said Terry with a frown.

'My dear, I hate to be saying all this, but I am afraid that soon they will be looking for—a motive. If they find out about you and me, it will be thought that—we wanted Janine out of the way, don't you see?'

'But, good heavens, Joy, I—it's—it's unthinkable! They couldn't possibly fasten a thing like that on me! They've no justification, no evidence, no possible reason!'

'You never know how things look to others, my dear, and the sooner we face that the better. To begin with, everyone in the village seems to know that she left every penny of her money between us two, except for a thousand to that orphanage place where she was brought up. If they know, or suspect, that we love each other –well, isn't the inference obvious to people who can believe any atrocity? After all, such things have been known.'

'But even if they thought it, they could never prove it. How could they when I didn't do it? You can't prove something that isn't true,' he protested, his brain still refusing to accept that ghastly possibility of such a charge.

'I don't know. That's what the law is always trying to do – to prove things which are denied and made to seem untrue. I hate to worry you further, Terry darling, but—there's another thing I have found out.'

'What's that? Better let me have the lot, Joy.'

'They've found the weapon which they think was used – a spanner. Jack Conrad told me this morning.'

'Well, that's nothing to do with me, anyway.'

'Isn't it, Terry? It belongs to the Bentley, and, according to Bennett, you borrowed it from him on that afternoon whilst he was repairing the car, and you didn't bring it back. Did you borrow it?'

'Yes. Yes, that's right, I did. I was going to tighten a nut on the motor mower, and then – let me think – I saw you getting into the boat, and I must have put the spanner down somewhere.'

'Can't you possibly remember where? You didn't throw it into the water by any chance?'

'Good Lord, no! Why should I? I must have just dropped it down somewhere, probably on that bench by the hut, when I got into the boat with you. Where did they find it?'

'In the water. They dragged the bed of the stream this morning. Jack was down there when they did it, and he heard Bennett say it was one he had lost and that you had borrowed it from him.' Terry ran his finger through his hair in a weary fashion. 'They seem as if they all want to rope me in, don't they? What on earth for? What have I ever done to them? Why should they try to turn every innocent little happening into evidence of guilt?'

'Human nature, for one thing, my dear. For another, it seems fairly certain that Janine was killed by someone, and she seems to have made herself very much liked in the village. Jack says she was always thinking of little kindnesses to do, and everybody feels incensed about her death and determined to bring someone to justice for it.'

'But why *me*? What have I done to any of them? Haven't I done my best, too?' demanded Terry with justification.

'Yes, but I dare say there's a feeling that you were—well, working under her instructions and feathering your own nest at the same time. You know the kind of feeling there is when the wife has the money. It's beastly to say these things to you, Terry, and like kicking you when you're down, but it's best to be honest, isn't it? You know that I'm utterly and entirely on your side, don't you?'

'Bless you, Joy. Dear, you do believe in me, don't you? *You* know I couldn't have done this horrible thing, don't you?'

'Of course I do, Terry. The thing is to make other people as sure and it's no earthly use being ostriches about it and burying our heads in the sand. We've got to watch everything that goes on, and one of the troubles is that I can't possibly stay down here with you. I shall have to go back to town tonight. You see that, don't you? I'm taking a flat, though, and shall get a maid and always be available to you, wherever I am.'

'Joy, you love me—and trust me?'

'Absolutely and utterly, to the end of the world, Terry.'

For a moment they clung together, children afraid of the dark. Then she released herself gently.

'Now I must go, darling. Don't come even to the door.'

Chapter Sixteen

In the corner of a lumbered room, on a crazy bed furnished with rough, spotlessly clean sheets, Janine lay motionless, her face white as death between the bandages, her thin hands almost transparent against the grey army blanket which covered the sheets.

In front of the fire, hunched in a sagging armchair, sat another woman, rocking herself to and fro, her strange, light eyes fixed on the woman in the bed, her lips moving soundlessly. Once or twice she rose, went to bend over the sick woman and to touch with surprisingly firm fingers the flaccid wrist. Then she returned to her chair with a satisfied nod.

The door opened quietly, and a man came in. He was spruce and well dressed, and he carried a good leather suitcase in one hand. Over the other arm hung a travelling rug.

'Anything doing, Marie?' he asked in a whisper.

'Still living. Still living. I told you these hands were as good as ever they were!' replied the woman, her voice and speech cultured and yet possessing a strange vagueness which matched the look in her eyes.

'Well, I'm off now. You've done well, old girl. You don't think there's any danger of her rubbing out now?'

But the woman did not answer, did not even appear to hear. She was bending over her patient, watching and listening, and nodding in a way that satisfied her and apparently had to satisfy him too.

He took out his wallet and counted a bundle of notes, laying them on the table and weighting them down with a feeding-cup.

'You'll have to do the best you can when she's conscious, Marie,' he said. 'There's enough money to see you through till I come back, anyway. I've left you fifty.'

'Better make it seventy-five,' said the woman, looking up.

He laughed harshly.

'Still sane enough to know the value of money, aren't you, you old bitch? Well, here's another fifteen, and that's the lot. You get her out of here before she can make trouble. Understand?'

'Oh, I understand alright—alright,' said the woman, and he turned and left her, closing the door cautiously behind him.

The woman called Marie counted the notes, stowed them carefully away in a tin, which she replaced in the cupboard, and went back to her patient.

Janine stirred and opened her eyes, but there was no light of reason in them.

'Don't wake yet, my darling,' crooned the woman to her, and in her voice was the note of the eternal mother which dwells in the most surprising places. 'Sleep again. Sleep for Marie,' and the eyelids closed slowly over the dark eyes, and she slept again.

Towards evening she stirred once more, and the woman went to her softly, raised her head and gave her food which she had prepared in the feeding-cup, trickling it slowly between the bloodless lips, whispering endearments the while. Then came the order to sleep again, and soon there was no movement in the room but the quiet breathing of Janine and the sibilant whispers of Marie.

When it was dark, she stole out on some errand, pausing only to brush and comb her wispy dark hair and to add powder, rouge and lipstick to her ravaged face. Her dress was neat and clean, but of a bygone fashion, and when she walked it was with the mincing step of a generation past rather than with the swinging stride of today.

When she came back, some hours later, her first thought was of her patient, and she was satisfied that Janine had neither waked nor stirred in the interval. Without undressing, she flung herself down on an old mattress in the opposite corner and was soon noisily asleep.

And with the morning Janine stirred to her first real consciousness for three weeks, though she was aware that she had dimly seen this room before, that it had figured in her dreams, and that someone whom she could hear but could not see had cared for her.

'Hetty,' she said uncertainly, not knowing why she spoke the name, nor why it should have come first into her mind, save that it was Hetty whom she saw first in the mornings at ... Where was it she lived? Never mind. She would remember later.

She slept again, and again when she woke that same name came to her consciousness so that she murmured it aloud.

'Hetty.'

The woman in the corner stirred and sat up, and instantly became aware of her patient. She jumped up with surprising agility, for she was a heavy woman, and crossed the room to where Janine lay with open eyes.

'So you are awake, my darling?' she asked in that crooning voice, and the fingers which went at once to the wasted wrist were firm and gentle.

'Where am I?' asked Janine in an uncertain voice, as if she had lost the art of speech for a long time.

'With old Marie, who is looking after you, my lamb,' came the soothing answer. 'First breakfast. Then we talk, if you like. You will watch Marie with the good things for you?'

Idly Janine let her eyes follow the movements of the uncomely body without being able to appreciate the scrupulous cleanliness with which the operations were being carried out. The feeding-cup, already clean and protected by a piece of linen, was scalded, and then the food, heated in a covered vessel, was strained into it through a piece of scalded muslin, and finally three drops of some amber liquid were added from a tiny bottle.

Too tired to resist, Janine let herself be fed, but this time she did not drop off to sleep immediately, as she had done every day for the past three weeks, since she had been carried up to this room from a car in the street, unconscious, bleeding, all but dead, and left to the crooning care of old Marie.

Instead she managed to raise herself a little in the bed, wincing as she rested her weight for an instant on her right arm, but finding it possible to rest it on her left instead.

'Where am I?' she asked again. 'How did I get here?'

'All in good time. All in good time,' promised Marie with a smile, as if at a favourite child. 'Hetty. That is your name, isn't it?'

Janine could not remember. That was odd. She tried, but nothing came. Yet Hetty had a familiar sound, and, after a moment of straining towards a memory which would not come, she nodded uncertainly.

'Yes. I think so. You see, I can't remember,' and she passed a hand over her head, pausing in surprise as she felt the bandages. 'Have I been hurt?' she asked.

'I should think you have! Run over in the street, and brought in here to me almost dead! It was lucky for you that they brought you to me. No one else would have saved you, no one in the whole wide world! You see these hands?' and, with a chuckle, she spread on the grey blanket her fine, long-fingered, beautifully-kept hands, white and strong. 'With these hands, the cleverest hands in the world, I brought you back to life. Whether I could give it all back to you remains to be seen. I wonder! And the pity of it is that I can never boast about it, or tell the world.'

'Why not?' asked Janine dreamily, only partially conscious of what the woman was saying.

Marie gave a grunt of contempt.

'Off' the register, my lamb! Me, Marie Hawk, the finest surgeon that ever held a scalpel! Off the register because of some fool woman who hadn't the courage of a louse! Because of one congenital idiot who offered me enough to equip a new operating theatre, the world has lost the finest surgeon it ever had! Me, Marie Hawk! But they saved you, my little darling, these two hands, in spite of all their medical councils! In spite of all the bigwigs who wouldn't do a tracheotomy to save their lives! Let any of them have tried to do what I did to you, my pet, and you'd be cold in your grave by now.'

But Janine was asleep again, and Marie settled her back on the pillow with tender hands, murmuring over her as a mother over her sleeping child, touching the tendrils of hair which showed, fine as silk, beneath the bandages.

'I had to cut off your hair, little one,' she murmured, 'but it will grow again. Marie will see that it grows again. Marie will brush and comb it. You'll see! You'll see! Marie's hands can do anything in the world. You'll see!'

And as the days passed dreamily by, each one bringing with it some new memory, Janine felt that life must always have held this queer creature, this woman with the magnificent brain no longer entirely within her control, with the hands that were those of a surgeon and those of a mother too.

Remembrance came back slowly, and yet too quickly for peace and happiness.

Marie called her 'Hetty', but she knew that that was not her name. She knew now that she was Janine – first Richard's Janine, though that memory was vague and cloudy and somehow not quite right; then she was Terry's Janine, and here memory began to work more quickly, bringing him back to her with a sense of longing and ecstasy mingled with a pain which at first she could not understand. Pain and unhappiness when life held Terry and their love?

Gradually came back the memory of Felicity. Felicity? No, Joy he had called her.

Joy.

But with the memory of Joy came increasingly the memory of pain, and at last she had the pattern complete, and for hours after the last piece had been fitted in she lay with her eyes closed so that Marie thought she slept.

Intolerably mingled with her pain was the knowledge that she had left Terry, had herself taken the irrevocable step to part them. Why had she done that? How could she have been such an incredible fool as to go away and leave him to Felicity without even a struggle? She must have been mad. Indeed, she was mad, or she would have made some attempt to step out of the way when, with a blinding flash of headlamps and a deafening roar, the great car seemed to leap at her and devour her.

'Who brought me here, Marie?' she asked suddenly, and the woman bending over a pot on the fire started.

'I thought you were asleep, my lamb,' she said.

'Who did bring me here?' persisted Janine.

'I can't tell you, dearie. Some man carried you in here and said, "Here's a patient for you, Marie," and just left you. They all know me and what I can do. These hands have done more marvels than the world will ever know. And they threw me out and disowned me! Me, Marie Hawk! They'll rue the day. Some day someone very great and important will be ill – the Prince himself possibly, God bless him! That'll be the time when one of them will remember Marie Hawk. Marie Hawk, they'll say! That was the wonderful woman surgeon who was taken off the register for an operation on some silly woman who didn't even die. Now if we could only find her, his life could be saved. But they won't find us, my dearie. Who'd think of looking for the great Marie Hawk in *this* dug-out!' with a gesture of distaste towards the lumber-filled attic with its crazy furniture and utter lack of refinement and comfort.

Janine did not ask her question again. She had already learned that once the unbalanced brain started on that train of thought, nothing could make it deviate into other paths. She let her own mind wander, dimly aware of the accompaniment of Marie's voice reciting tales of former triumphs, giving detailed and highly technical accounts of operations she had performed, and mentioning names which must, at one time, have been household words with her but whose owners would now most assuredly decline her acquaintance.

Poor, tragic Marie Hawk.

Yet throughout all the weeks and months of Janine's stay in that London attic the woman was meticulously loyal to the man who had paid her to keep his secret.

She was honest about it with Janine.

'Look, dearie. He ran you down, but he couldn't afford to be open about it. I know him well. I've known him for years. I took a bullet out of his spine, and through me he's as straight and strong today as ever he was. With these hands.'

'Yes, go on. Tell me about him running me down,' said Janine quickly, foreseeing the result of leaving the conversation to run its own course.

'Oh yes. Well, I can tell you something about it, but not all. He'd been doing something he shouldn't have done, and there was too much involved for him to risk it being known that he was on that road at all. He had to stop. He didn't know how badly you were injured and whether you'd seen the car or his number or anything. When he got out he thought he'd killed you, and he daren't leave you there, so he picked you up and brought you here to me.'

'Where is he now?'

Marie shrugged her shoulders.

'I don't know. No one ever does know. They come and go. I may never see him again – not until he gets another bullet in his spine! That'd bring him back from the ends of the earth sure enough! He knows that no one living could have done what I did for him. These hands—the hands of Marie Hawk ... and this time Janine let her ramble on, realising that it was useless to try to get more out of her if she were determined not to speak.

Besides what did it matter? Marie had assured her that she was going to get well, perfectly and entirely well, and she believed her implicitly. In that case, what did it matter who had run her down on that night of despair? It would have been better had he killed her, or left her there to die. What good was she to anyone? What good was she to herself?

'Haven't they missed me, Marie?' she asked later.

The question had hovered on her lips so many times, but she had never brought herself to ask it. Supposing they hadn't? Supposing Terry and Felicity had just accepted her disappearance and done nothing about it?

But Marie did not know. Janine had never revealed her name, and Marie had never asked it, content to call her 'Hetty' when she did not use one of the dozen endearments which came so easily to her lips.

'Wasn't there anything in the papers?' she persisted. 'How long have I been here? When did it happen?'

But again Marie did not know. She had no sense of time or the passage of the days. Every day was the same to her. The day began when she woke and ended when she was too tired any longer to walk about.

'There must have been something said about it, Marie,' urged Janine, but Marie only shook her head.

'What's the good of papers?' she asked. 'Nothing but trouble for someone, day after day. The last time I read the papers was when they had so much to say about Marie Hawk and that fool of a woman and the Medical Council. Medical Council! Pah! Lot of dithering old idiots muttering in their beards, muttering about me—Marie Hawk! Marie Hawk, the finest surgeon that ever walked a hospital ward!' and she was off again along the road to which all other roads led, and Janine lay back with her thoughts – bitter thoughts, sad thoughts, longing thoughts.

If she could just see Terry again! Just know he was well and happy. No, not that. She would hate him to be happy when he did not even know where she was. What could she do about it, though? Her pride would not let her send for him, send any message even, until she knew for certain that he wanted to know where she was.

Persuaded day after day by Marie to stay there, to eat the nourishing things which she brought in and prepared for her, to take at regular intervals the medicines and potions she mixed at the sink in the corner, Janine found health and strength returning, and by the sixth week she was able to stand and even to move about the room, clinging to Marie's arm or to one or other of the rickety pieces of furniture.

The bandages were taken carefully from her head every few days, and at last they were left off altogether and the hair allowed to grow where the skin had been shaved. Marie gloated over that red, exquisitely tender patch. It was the best and most delicate operation she had ever performed, she said, and her one grievance was that she could not give to the world the skill which had saved Janine's life.

The right arm and thigh had been injured, too, but these were now ready for massage, and Marie revealed her knowledge of that branch of her profession as well, massaging skilfully and with a complete understanding of her patient's strength and need.

'Marie, I simply must know now what is happening at—home,' she said at last in desperation. 'I am almost well now, and I can't go on living here indefinitely.'

'Don't I look after you, Hetty? Make you comfortable?' demanded Marie, hurt.

'Oh, Marie, yes! You do everything. But—don't yon see how I feel about it? I must know what has happened, whether they—they are looking for me, anxious about me.'

Marie sighed.

'Oh, well, if you must, you must,' she grumbled. 'I'll see what I can do about it.'

'Can't you get me a newspaper? Or can't I go out and get one, or—or telephone or something?'

'No, you can't,' almost snapped Marie, and she darted to the door and stood with her back to it, looking like a wild animal with its nest threatened. Then, with a change and a softening of her whole face, 'You stay here with Marie, my lamb. Marie will get you all you want. There's nothing in the world you can't have if you want it, if only you'll stay here with Marie, who loves you.'

Janine sighed. She was touched by the woman's utter devotion. No one had ever worshipped her like this before, but it was so fierce and possessive that it frightened her. She must get away somehow, somewhere, but she did not know where to go or what to do. Dare she go back to Merrow? Or to the house at Hampstead and find Mrs. Gough? But she did not know how to get out of this room in which she was virtually a prisoner. Marie scarcely left her, and whenever she did, even to slip downstairs for a few minutes, she locked the door on the outside and took the key with her.

'Well, try and get me a newspaper first,' she said, and sat down on the bed again feeling helpless and in despair.

Marie was rummaging amongst a pile of oddments in a corner.

'I remember now. Max brought some things for me to take care of for him. They were wrapped up in newspapers. Perhaps they would tell you something. Here they are,' and she pulled out a parcel, took the paper from it, wrapped it up again carelessly in a piece of brown paper, and brought the newspaper to Janine.

It bore a date some five weeks previously, though she had no clear idea of how much time had passed, and there, on the front page, was her own photograph and beneath it she read – incredibly:

'Mrs. Janine Forder, the dead woman'.

The dead woman. Mrs. Janine Forder. That was herself. The dead woman.

Carefully, so that she could take it all in, she read the column devoted to the subject of the scarcely recognisable photograph.

It was the one giving the account of the adjourned inquest, speaking of the finding of the body and of its subsequent identification by 'the husband, Terence Forder'. There was a reference to 'Miss Felicity Harrow, the daughter of Mrs. Forder's first husband', and there was the carefully veiled but unmistakable suggestion that death had not been accidental.

Janine sat with the paper in her hands, staring straight in front of her, trying to realise the incredible truth. Someone, some woman, had been found dead in the stream that ran through the orchard of Four Ways, and that woman had been identified by Terry, her own husband, as herself! Terry had said that some other woman was she, Janine! Some dead woman!

'Oh, Terry, Terry! Were you so anxious to be rid of me! So glad to believe me dead! Oh, Terry! My beloved!'

She dropped the paper and buried her head on the pillow, the sobs shaking her – desperate, hopeless sobs that seemed to tear her very body and soul.

Marie came across the room to her, raised her in her strong arms and held her against her breast, rocking and soothing her, crooning endearments to her. Her eyes had caught sight of the newspaper on the floor, and with the marvellous quickness of perception which alternated with periods of almost idiotic dullness, she pieced together something of the story from the bare headlines, which was all she could read at that distance.

'Never mind, my sweet, my darling. No man is worth it. No man in all the world is worth one tear from your eyes, one thought from your mind. There, there, my little bird, my pretty one, my lamb. You are safe with Marie. No one shall ever hurt you again or make you sad. Marie will make up for everything. Marie is worth all the men in the world. Don't cry any more, my pet.' Janine lifted her heavy head at last, her eyes swollen and almost sightless, her face patched and stained with her tears.

'He told them I was dead. They—they—perhaps they've buried me now!' she said hysterically. 'Read what it says, Marie! That's me – Janine! Me! They say I'm dead! Terry says so!'

Marie picked up the paper and read the column through, with various grunts and unintelligible exclamations, and then she threw it down again contemptuously.

'Pff! What does it matter? You're better rid of him,' she said, and then with the uncanny intuition of the not quite normally minded, 'Who is this Felicity Harrow? Is she the other woman in the ease?'

Janine shrank away, flinching.

'Don't, Marie!'

'H'm. I see she is. Well, you're well rid of them, both of them. What do they matter to you? Any children?'

'No,' said Janine in a low voice.

'Well, so much the better. You're free. Looks as if he's going to get away with your money, though.'

'How do you know I had any?' asked Janine suspiciously.

'Guessed it. Your clothes are expensive, for one thing; and here's another,' and she went across the room to the cupboard, brought something from it and put it into Janine's hands.

It was her handbag.

She gave a little cry of surprise and opened the gold clasp. Her roll of notes was inside, just as she remembered putting it there, and some loose silver and coppers in one of the divisions. Rolled up in a piece of paper were her rings, the two flexible bracelets of platinum and diamonds which she had picked up almost at random in her unconsidered flight. A flap-jack of silver and enamel, which Terry had given her, still held its film of powder, and the lipstick which she rarely used kept it company.

But there was nothing else. Her cards were gone, every scrap of paper such as accumulates in any woman's handbag, drapers' bills, letters – everything else had gone.

Her eyes asked the mute question, but Marie shook her head.

'No. I didn't touch a thing. That was how it was when Max handed it to me. He takes no chances.'

Janine fitted the rings on her fingers absently, and twisted the bracelets between them, her thoughts still on that incredible procedure at Four Ways. Whose body had they found? What poor woman had met the death which to her, Janine, would have been a merciful solution? Did she lie in a grave which would eventually bear the name of Janine Forder? Did Terry lay flowers on it? And Felicity?

The sobs of mingled despair and derision rose in her threat and choked her again, and Marie came back to hold her and pet her.

'Oh, Marie, what am I to do? What am I to do?' she asked when the storm had subsided again.

'What do you want to do, Hetty?'

'I'm not Hetty, really, you know,' said Janine.

'You are to me, and one name's as good as another when you don't care who calls you by it. Do you still want this man? Do you think he wants you? If so, why did you run away from him?'

'How do you know so much, Marie?' she asked in a low voice.

'I know most things, and what I don't know I can guess at. A woman isn't found miles from her home in the middle of the night, with twenty-five pounds and her jewels in her bag, unless she's running away from someone. Well, do you want to go back to him?'

'I don't—know,' said Janine, her eyes staring into space.

'Well, you make up your mind, my pet, and Marie will see that what you want you shall get. I'm going out now. I've got to see someone. You think about it and let me know when I come back,' and she picked up the shabby black bag without which she rarely went out, nodded briskly to Janine, and locked the door behind her, taking the key out of the lock with what Janine felt was intentional noise.

What did she want to do? What choice had she? She must either go back or stay away for ever, come to life or remain dead.

Every instinct urged her to go back. Everything within her ached for Terry, for his arms and his lips, for all his dear ways of love with her, for his laughing eyes and tender voice.

'My Jan.' She could hear him call her that now.

But she was no longer his Jan. She was nobody's Jan. She did not even exist. They had said she was dead. Terry had said so. Terry and Felicity.

What were they doing now? It could not be so very long since her accident, not more than a few weeks, anyway. They would not have done anything yet, he and Felicity.

Terry and Felicity.

How were they feeling now? Were they looking forward already to being together? To being married? There was no reason now why they should not marry. They would have all the money, too. Felicity's money, and hers, Janine's, left to her by Richard, who had loved her.

How troubled and upset Richard would have been by all this! Richard would never have wanted her dead, would never have wanted anybody else. She had been right in her first attitude towards Felicity. It had been a premonition. She ought to have regarded it as such and not have admitted her to her friendship and her home. Terry would have forgotten her. Already he was beginning to forget her when she returned to wreck their home.

She pictured her return, if she decided to go back. How would he take it? Would he welcome her, or – would he really in his heart be sorry? That she could not bear. To live with him where they had been so happy, and to know that all the time he was resenting her very existence, longing for Felicity, mentally putting her in Janine's place.

No, not that. Rather death, real death, than that.

Marie came back, giving her a keen glance before throwing down in its corner the mysterious black bag and herself into the lop-sided chair.

'Oh, but I'm tired!' she admitted for once. 'Fools of women!'

'Marie, what do you do when you go out like this?' Janine asked her suddenly.

Marie Hawk looked at her with her strange eyes narrowing.

'I wonder if you're interested, or merely curious?' she asked, and Janine saw to her relief that she was at her best, sane and collected. At such times Marie Hawk revealed herself as she had once been – keen, clever woman of the world and mistress of herself and her fate. Beside her at such times, Janine felt a mere ignorant and inexperienced child.

'Interested, Marie,' she said.

The older woman gave her a searching glance.

'I wish you were, Hetty,' she said, for she persisted in using the name by which she had first known her charge. 'I could use you and make you of use to others.'

Janine leant forward.

'Tell me how, Marie.'

'I'm going to trust you, because I feel I can. I am doing something outside the law, something for which I could get a long term of imprisonment if they didn't shut me up in a madhouse instead. I'm running a sort of private hospital where I give back life and health and hope to poor fools who haven't troubled about any of these things for themselves. I'm breaking the law in so doing, because, you see, I'm not a doctor!' – with that note of bitterness in her voice which Janine had come to recognise.

'I don't ask any questions,' Marie went on. 'I just do my job. I bring their children into the world for them, and nice messes they are too, sometimes. I see the children out of it for them as often as not, too – children born piecemeal, rotten, deformed, blind, horrible. You can't visualise the sort of things I see, Hetty. I do other things, too. I operate on poor things on whom the hospitals refuse to operate. I know I can do what they daren't try to do and couldn't if they tried. I operate on others who have been waiting and waiting for a bed in a hospital – waiting because they're poor and because the people who've got twenty or thirty pounds can get the beds first. Oh, I know what I'm talking about. Well, that's what I do – that amongst other things in which you wouldn't be interested.'

Janine was silent, trying to adjust her mind to this new conception of Marie Hawk. What a risk to take! What a sublime and awful risk!

'Well?' asked Marie. 'Interested? Or frightened?'

'Interested. Very.'

'Enough to help?'

Janine looked startled.

'How?' she asked.

'I want a nurse, another one, someone I can absolutely trust. I've got two, but they aren't enough. I can't pay you much. I often don't get paid myself. I have to make the money where I can, and you'd be surprised if you knew how much rich women will pay when their precious reputations are at stake. I take the money from them and spend it in my hospital – that's what I call it, though of course it's no more like a hospital than this room is like your drawing-room.'

Janine caught her breath. The words conjured up the sitting-room at Four Ways, long and low-ceiled and many-windowed, fragrant with the scent of flowers in summer and with burning pine logs in winter.

Marie rose from her chair and came across to her, laying a hand on her shoulder and looking down steadfastly into her eyes.

'If you are going back, you must go now, Hetty. If you're not going, will you come in with me? Will you take the risk? You don't know yet all the risks you'll be taking, but I shall tell you every unsavoury detail before you commit yourself. Only first I want to know whether you are going or staying.'

'I'm—staying,' said Janine, drawing a deep breath that was almost a sob.

'Good girl. But mind – no regrets.'

'No regrets,' said Janine bravely.

'Alright. Tomorrow we start, though I do most of my work at night. Tonight I've told them I'm not going. I knew I should be wanted here. I didn't think you'd go back to that—oh, alright, alright! I won't call him what I think he is. Come here. You've got to know things that'll put years on you if you're going to help me, but it won't hurt you in the long run. Please heaven I shall keep my senses long enough to tell you what you'll have to know.'

Chapter Seventeen

Terry Forder came in from his office, hung up his dripping mackintosh and flung himself down in the chair before the fire.

Since early morning he had been at work, and it had not been pleasant work. For a time the business which he had been organising and which would eventually move into the building now nearing completion had been almost at a standstill. Everything had been held up after Janine's disappearance and presumed death, and even now the work was proceeding slowly and uncertainly, no one feeling able to think far ahead. There was the matter of establishing probate first of all, and none knew more surely than Terry himself why the lawyers were so tardy, why so many legal quibbles arose, over the transference of the estate to Janine Forder's husband.

Doggedly he insisted that as much of the work as possible should go on, both for his own sake and in order that the men who depended on him for a living should not suffer. Yet he felt that every hand was against him. Some of the villagers passed him by in the street with the curtest and most grudging of nods; others adroitly avoided him by slipping down side turnings or into the 'Pig and Whistle'. In former days he had gone into the 'Pig and Whistle' himself, chatting with the villagers, getting to know them on their own ground. Now he kept away, knowing the sort of looks he would have to face.

He dare not resent an attitude which in any other circumstances he would have felt to be bitterly unjust, for he was conscious day and night of his own guilt towards Janine – not the kind of guilt these people sought to fasten on him, but that secret guilt of his unfaithfulness to her. He would have given worlds to know what had been her thoughts and what her knowledge on that last night, going over and over in his mind the hours he had spent with Felicity, in the orchard and in the boat-house. He could see no possibility of her having seen or known, and yet why else should she have taken her life? – for he could not convince himself that she had not done so, in spite of all the evidence and suggestions to the contrary.

And she was carrying his child! Knowing that, hiding it from him for some extraordinary reason, she had chosen death rather than life.

Why? Why?

His mind, released from the immediate demands of his work, flew back ceaselessly to his problem, just as his body came unerringly home to that place which Janine had made so perfect for him, that home which without her was a mere empty shell, kept by the servants in meticulous order, but only a shell.

He missed her intolerably, realising with wonder and a new sense of shame how much his personal happiness and comfort had been due to her thoughtfulness. He missed her ready sympathy. She had always had an open ear for his troubles, and he reflected how often he must have puzzled and possibly bored her by his long discourse on matters which were exercising his mind. Yet she had never appeared anything but deeply interested and eager to hear more.

Then her laughter. She had had the blessed gift of being able to find laughter in little things. She had brought lightness and relief to the dullest discourse by that happy knack of hers of seeing the funny side of things. There was no laughter in the house now, and certainly no funny side of things.

Janine. Oh, God, he wanted her! Just to see her again, to hold her in his arms for one minute, to tell her of all she meant to him, of the sweetness and the tenderness which he had never valued until it was lost to him.

He roused himself to find Mrs. Pringle at his side, reproach on her face.

'Oh, sir, you've not touched your dinner, and the halibut done in butter the way you like, and the potatoes just to a turn.'

He drew his chair to the table. He would never have had his meals at all if he had to get up and go to another room for them, so

Mrs. Pringle had taken to bringing them to him wherever he happened to be.

'Sorry Mrs. Pringle. I'm a little tired,' he said, with a smile which softened his lips momentarily but which did not reach his eyes.

'You don't eat enough, sir, if I may make so bold.'

'Think I'm fading away?'

'That you are sir, and so thin and white. Why don't you take a holiday, Mr. Forder, sir? Go right away from all this and try and forget it, if you'll excuse me taking the liberty.'

'What good do you think I should get from going away?' he asked bitterly. 'I should only be taking my troubles with me.'

'Oh, well, sir, you know best, but—if I may say so, sir, the mistress'd worry terribly if she saw you like this.'

'You may *not* say so, Mrs. Pringle,' said Forder, and he said it so fiercely and turned on her with such venom that she flushed up and withdrew hastily.

'It's a shame, that's what it is,' she confided to Bagg, the gardener, who had called in for his usual glass of stout with the cook. 'The way they 'ound 'im down is somethink crool, and if the mistress were alive today, God rest 'er sweet soul, she'd be the first to give that Gough and Bennett the sack for the way they're after 'im. 'Ell-'ounds, that's what they are, the pair of 'em. Gough with 'is tale of seeing the master and Miss 'Arrow up the orchard in the night with nothink but their night-things on, and Bennett with 'is spanner.'

'Still, Mrs. Pringle, there's queer things about it, as you must say yourself. Gough ain't the only one as saw the master in 'is dressing-gown and slippers. Mrs. Burke says she 'eard noises in the night and peeks outer the window and who does she see but the master in 'is dressing-gown, 'oppin over their stile 'andylike and going to the works. In the middle of the night, mark you!' Mrs. Pringle paused in the very act of twisting the stopper of a second bottle and looked across at him.

'Now look 'ere, Mr. Bagg. You and me's bin good friends since I bin down 'ere, but you and me'll part if I 'ear another word as you're takin' up with them as says the master done Mrs. Forder in, an you can take it or leave it.'

Mr. Bagg decided to take it, if 'it' included the nightly Guinness, and as he was understood to apologise handsomely to Mrs. Pringle, the matter was allowed to drop.

But over his solitary meal Terry was as well aware of the conversation as if he had been present at it. He often wondered bitterly what Merrow had talked about before the death of Janine, for certainly it seemed to have talked of nothing else since.

The inquest had been adjourned again and yet again, but finally a verdict had been recorded that Janine Forder met her death as the result of a blow on the back of the head, administered by some person or persons unknown, it having been established at length that death had occurred before immersion in the water.

Thereafter Terence Forder had been a marked man, and he was amazed at the lengths to which the villagers, who surely owed him no grudge, but rather the reverse, were prepared to go to provide themselves with ghoulish enjoyment. A police watch was kept on him discreetly, but there was no need for official action, there being no lack of private watchers. Wherever he went, eyes followed him and ears listened to him. Even in the ordinary process of business he felt that he was under suspicion, every word he uttered pregnant with double meaning to someone or other. He worked feverishly, spending himself in the service of those schemes which he and Janine had evolved, but he knew that some power had gone from both him and the work that had promised such success. Orders which he had confidently anticipated did not mature, and though the reasons seemed adequate in every case, he felt that actually there was personal animosity and distrust behind them.

And in the fragments of home life which he allowed himself, late evenings, early mornings, a few hours at weekends, he found himself missing Janine intolerably. He and Felicity corresponded, though he was certain that his letters were opened and scrutinised before they reached him, and she had the same belief with regard to his letters. Now and then they met in town, but never at her flat, and never in private, nor did she ever venture to visit him at Merrow. But he remained unsatisfied.

He had seen her only that day. Some business matter had taken him to London, and he had telephoned her and met her for lunch.

She was concerned at his haggard looks.

'Terry, you'll be ill if you don't do something about it,' she said as they took their seats in the crowded restaurant where they felt more isolated and private than in a quiet corner whose screen of palms might conceal anything or anyone.

'Oh, does it matter?' he asked wearily.

'To me, yes,' she said. Then, as his face did not soften or light up as once it would have done, Terry, is there something else? Something I don't know about?'

'No, my dear—at least—'

'Yes?'

'It is being said that Gough is telling a tale about having seen us in the orchard that night, and that I was heard to say that I only married Janine for her money, and that if only I could get free and keep the money, everything would be alright for us.'

'But, Terry, it isn't true!'

'I know. Probably the man wouldn't go so far as to swear under oath that he had heard those very words, but you know how time can alter one's memory of things said, and I really don't know what was said myself, do you? I know I did say all sorts of things that might be construed quite differently, and anyway, the story is so rife in the village now that probably a dozen of them are by now prepared to swear that they've heard me say something of the kind.'

'Terry, it's *criminal* of them!'

'I know. Oh, hell! I'm sick of life and everything in it. I almost wish they'd arrest me and get it over. I could put up a fight then, but no one can fight an intangible enemy who prods at you in the dark with poisoned pins and won't let himself be seen. I can't even tackle Gough, for he would at once deny it.'

'Do you think I could do anything if I went to see him? He used to be fond of me at one time, and I think Mrs. Gough still is.'

Terry shook his head.

'Better keep out of it, my dear. Anything you tried to do would only be turned against me later. No. Leave me to fight my battle alone.'

'But if you—lose, Terry?'

'Well, what would it matter?' he asked bitterly.

A shadow crossed her face. Surely, slowly she was losing him. She had never been quite certain of him, but she believed that if Janine had lived, after that night she could have held him. Janine's tragic death, coming right on top of an episode which she knew he regretted, had raised between them a barrier which might never be overcome.

She leaned across the table to him.

'Terry, don't I matter to you any more?' she asked.

'You know you do, Joy, only—'

Yes, dear? Only?'

'What's the use?' he burst out. 'I've nothing to offer you, not even the honour of my name. I can't take all this money of *hers*. I'm only keeping on at Merrow to finish what we began together, and when the new factory is finished, and everything running smoothly, I shall turn it into a company with the employees as the shareholders, a sort of co-operative concern with part of the profits as dividends and part going back into the concern for development. Then I shall clear out and take with me precisely what I brought – which is nothing.'

'You wouldn't even take me, Terry?' she asked him softly, though she knew, had known ever since the moment of their meeting that morning, that she had lost him.

'Joy, dear, don't you understand? How could I? I've nothing to offer you. I've less than a name now. I'm a marked man. If I'm not arrested and tried for murder and hanged, I shall still bear a name that stinks. Don't you understand, Joy?'

'Yes, my dear. I think I understand—quite a lot,' she said quietly.

'I know it's pretty foul of me, after—that night'; but she stopped him with a smile and a little tapping of her fingers on his arm.

'Rubbish, Terry, I belong to this generation, not the last. You don't have to make an honest woman of me, you know. I wanted that night as much as you – more, probably – and you don't owe me a thing on account of it. Also, as you probably know, I didn't sacrifice a maiden's virtue for you.'

He nodded. He had known that, too, but it had not mattered. Standards had changed, and he was of this generation as well as she.

'You'll—forget me, won't you, Joy?' he asked her.

'Oh, probably. Eternal fidelity to – well, to anything – is rather played out now, isn't it?'

He winced.

'Don't. That hurts,' he said in a low voice.

The waiter came to change their plates, and they made a pretence of finishing their meal, true to their code, which forbids any sort of public revelation of private emotions. Finish the dance though the feet are sore and blistered and the floor of red-hot cinders.

And afterwards they had said goodbye, eyes not meeting eyes, hands scarcely touching.

'Well—goodbye, Joy.'

'So long, my lamb.'

Sitting over his lonely meal that evening, he wondered if he would ever see her again. It was curious to wonder that. So many times he had told himself she was lost to him, and yet at the back of his mind he had not believed it. He had been so sure that if ever they did really part, he would feel that some vital part of him had been torn away, leaving him incomplete.

And yet what was it he really did feel? Regret, yes. Loss, yes. But irreparable, aching loss? Was he indeed capable of feeling anything deeply again? Could a thing that was already numbed and deadened feel anything at all?

He said it over to himself. Joy was gone. If they ever met again it would be as strangers, or, at the most, friends. He would never hold her in his arms again, never kiss her lips, her fragrant hair, her throat where the little pulse leaped beneath his lips.

There was no exquisite, searing pain at the thought. That was it, of course. He would never feel anything again. That was one faint blessing vouchsafed him against the curse of life in general.

He remembered that he had promised Bagg he would look up the original plan on which the layout of the garden had been started, and he went to the cupboard in the corner of the room where he thought it was likely to be. He turned over the oddments on a shelf, and a rag doll fell out, a shapeless, hideously ugly thing dressed in absurd clothes of red and green.

Fiercely he stuffed the doll back and shut the cupboard door on it and went back to his chair, his elbows on his knees, his face on his hands. He had decided he would never feel again – and that ridiculous rag doll had given the lie to it a moment later.

He remembered the coming of the doll. There had been a fair in the village that night he and Janine first came to Merrow, the night she had ever afterwards referred to as 'our first night at home'. They had been married a little over a month, but neither their rather hysterical honeymoon nor the fortnight in state at Hampstead had come up to the sheer delight and happiness of that first night in their own home. He had taken her to the fair, laughing at her childish enjoyment of it and admitting afterwards that he had enjoyed it almost as much and quite as childishly. They had ridden on the unbelievable animals of the roundabout, swung perilously aloft on the swing-chairs, goaded each other higher and higher in the aero-boats, and then, seeking rather less strenuous pleasures, they had gone the round of the booths and shooting ranges and all they had won was the rag doll!

Janine had carried it home with a large piece of white paper wrapped about it like a shawl, and in the semi-darkness it had looked like a baby cradled in her arms.

'Darling, how we shall scandalise the villagers!' she had whispered rapturously. 'They know we've only been married a month, and here I am with a baby already!'

'Yes, and a black one at that!' he had retorted, and, laughing idiotically, they had stumbled their unfamiliar way home and Janine had insisted that 'the ill-begotten child' should sleep in their bedroom.

Clearly every incident of that evening came back to his mind and with it came Janine – gentle, childish, fiercely loving, tenderly considerate of him, child and woman, friend and wife and adorable lover.

Janine!

He looked up, feeling that he must have cried her name aloud. But the cat curled up on the settee, the rather disreputable mother cat who had crawled by instinct to Janine, terrified and with her time very near, had been housed and loved and sheltered ever since – the cat had not stirred, and Bruce, the scotty on the rug, still slept and dreamed dreams of glorious fights on his native heath.

If I durst—but I durstn't!' Janine used to say with a laugh, prodding his heaving sides with her toe until, with a grunt, he would relax into more peaceful slumber and forget the unnumbered foe.

Janine – always Janine.

Until that ridiculous doll had fallen at his feet like that he had not been aware of missing her so acutely. Yet now he realised that he had never entered the house without looking round for her, never left it without that instinctive backward glance to one particular window, never passed the door of their room without his feet pausing as if he expected to hear her move within.

He had never entered the room since that night.

Janine.

And in a room in an old house in a forgotten, dusty corner of a London slum area, Janine paused in her work, straightened her aching back and looked up, her eyes wide and startled, her very heart listening—listening.

Janine!

Someone had called her.

She listened still, but now the voice was nearer – was the voice of a girl, thin, fretful, and it called 'Hetty!'

She bent over the bed again, lifted the sodden ice-pack and replaced it by another, dropping the used one into a pail at the side of the bed. In a minute she must go along to the refrigerator and see that the ice-boxes had been filled again. Curtis would want them when he came to relieve her at eleven.

She glanced at her watch, a plain, workmanlike affair in silver, with a leather strap. Thank heaven it was ten to eleven. She was dead tired, and even in the winter there seemed not a breath of air in this crowded corner of a squalid block of tenements. She thought longingly of the little flat she had taken, persuading Marie Hawk to come and live with her, though several times already she had had cause to question her wisdom in so doing.

Marie was a wanderer, a born bohemian, and she respected no rules except those of cleanliness. Day and night were the same to her, and even when she was wholly sane she was a difficult person to live with, untidy, unpunctual, with fancies for queer foods at unreasonable hours, exhibiting a total disregard for the convenience and comfort of others – always excepting Janine herself, whom she worshipped with a curious, hungry, possessive love.

The door opened and Curtis came in, a smile on his face and a light in his eyes as he saw Janine.

He was a man of some forty-odd, dark, thin, saturnine-looking, with an obvious mixture of races in his make-up. His skin was no darker than that of any average Englishman in the summer, and his lips were thin and his nostrils narrow, and sensitive. But he was betrayed in the shape of the cheekbone, the velvety darkness of his eyes, the coal-black hair, and above all by the tell-tale fingertips. Janine had been afraid of him at first, but then she had been afraid of so many things when she had begun work at this furtive little house. Now she felt she would never be afraid again. Certainly she would not be afraid of Curtis.

She welcomed him now with a smile, one hand pushing back the hair from her damp forehead with a weary gesture of which she was quite unconscious.

'Thank heaven you've come! I'm tired to death,' she said.

He glanced at her keenly without replying. Then he slipped away and she heard him talking to someone in the other room, a room which was both office and rest-room for the small staff.

'Get your hat,' he said, his voice slow and smooth and attractive. 'Shaw says she's not going for an hour, and will keep an eye on things. My car's outside. We'll get a breath of fresh air, yes?'

'Marie?' asked Janine uncertainly.

'Shaw will tell her. Anything you do is right, Hetty,' with another of his flashing smiles.

She put on her hat and her one coat, a warm grey one Marie had made her buy, gave a parting injunction to the girl in the office, and was soon lying back in the rakish sports car and realising how utterly tired she was.

Curtis did not speak to her until they were out of London and speeding along the Great North Road, and the world on either side dark and distant, nothing coming within their orbit save when some other car raced through the night with a blinding flash of headlights.

'Smoke, Hetty?'

'Please. Light it for me,' she said drowsily, and he pulled up by the side of the road, lit a cigarette for her and set it between her lips from his own.

'Why do you let me do that?' he asked her, leaning on one elbow and looking down at her.

She was incredibly changed, had there been anyone in this new life to realise it. She was older, thinner, graver, and yet more alive. There was knowledge in her eyes and a sureness of herself which gave her dignity and poise. Her eyes smiled up into his. 'I'm tired,' she said.

'That all?'

'No.'

'Then—what, Hetty?'

'I like you.'

'Again, is that all?'

She sighed and looked away from him, but there was no coquetry in her action. She was just pausing to think, and she could not think with his eyes burning her like that.

'I think so, Curtis.'

'I've got another name, you know.' She looked at him at that and smiled.

'Have you? I never thought of that. You're just Curtis to all of us, just as I am—Hetty?' with another smile.

'And actually I am no more Curtis than you are Hetty. May I tell you my real name?'

'Of course.'

'I am Paul Corani. At least, I *was* Paul Corani. That doesn't convey anything to you?'

She shook her head.

'No. Nothing. I am—Janine. Does that convey anything to you?'

'I know who you are. I have always known.'

She said nothing. It did not matter that he knew. That other life had gone so far away that she felt it could never touch her closely again.

'Janine, I am in love with you. Did you know?'

'I don't know. Perhaps—lately.'

'And you don't mind?'

She gave him a smile that was more sad than gay.

'There hasn't been so much in my life that I should mind,' she said.

'And you, Janine? What do you feel about it?'

She was silent, marshalling her ideas, and here again was evidence of the change in her. Gone forever was the impetuous, half-considered speech, the sentences that ended in nothing, the hesitation. She considered her thoughts and then spoke them.

'I don't think I feel anything, really. You see, there have been two men already in my life, Curtis. One of them loved me; the other I loved and—married.'

'Marriage! What is it to people who are earnest and intelligent? Do you believe it is necessary when people love?'

'Not when they love, perhaps, but—I've finished with it, anyway, so why discuss it?' with a smile.

'Good. Janine, will you come to me?'

She was neither startled nor shocked. No one could be shocked at anything in the world after living with Marie Hawk for six months.

She shook her head.

'It wouldn't work, my dear,' she said.

'Why not? I love you and I understand you. I shouldn't tie you down or expect impossibilities from you.'

He had not attempted to touch her, and she had no fear of him, even though she read passion and desire in his eyes. That was, had he known it, his greatest attraction for her. She could trust him utterly.

'I know. Thank you, Curtis,' she said quietly.

'Paul. I'd like you to call me that, in any case.'

'Paul. I couldn't come to you – not yet, anyway.'

He caught at the vague hope.

'Some day you might?'

'Yes. Someday I—might. Don't misunderstand me, my dear. I don't love you. I'm the sort to love only one man and to love him for ever, I think. That's why I say – not yet. You see, I must see him again, Terry, my husband. I must know, really *know*, that everything is finished forever with him.'

'There was another woman?'

She nodded.

'I can't blame him. I—well, I induced him to marry me, you see.'

He smiled, and she saw the dark gleam of his eyes in the glow of his cigarette.

'Oh, but I did! And he loved the other girl all the time. She's so lovely and fascinating and gay and—oh, everything in the world I'm not!' she finished, but there was a tranquil note in her voice, as if she had finished forever with repining and jealousy.

'I see. And how are you going to decide whether my turn has come or not?' he asked her.

She laughed a little and laid her hand on his.

'Oh, my dear, I do like you so much!' she said.

He lifted her hand to his lips. They burnt against her cool skin.

'For that much grace, the gods be praised. I'd better take you back now, or Marie'll get wild. She's been better lately, don't you think?'

'I don't know. She—she had rather a bad turn last week. I was alone with her, but it only lasted a few hours and in the morning she was alright.'

He frowned as he started up the car and turned it expertly.

I don't like your being with her, Janine. That's one reason why—'

'Why you burn to do rescue work?' she finished for him with a smile.

'You know the real reason. This living with Marie is only secondary. It worries me, though; I want to get you out of the thing altogether.'

'Well, you're in it yourself,' she reminded him.

He shrugged his shoulders.

'As a hobby in the first place; because of you later. *I'm* qualified, as I expect you know. I'm not likely to be able to practise in this country, though. I'm what is called a dago, I believe,' with another gleam of his white teeth.

'What nationality are you really, Paul?' she asked.

'Heaven knows. My father was an Italian and my mother is—the Duchess of Elsterham,' he said quietly.

Janine gasped, for he had quoted a very famous name indeed.

'Do you mean that?' she asked.

'To you, yes. To anyone else I should deny it. Oh, I'm not proud of it. Don't imagine that for a moment. I was an early indiscretion which I am sure she has long ago forgotten. She was merely Lady Leda Havering then, and my father was perfecting her knowledge of languages, and other things, preparatory to her anticipated marriage into diplomatic circles.-

'But—did anybody know?' asked Janine, still amazed.

'Her parents, of course. She wanted to marry my father. Imagine it! He was an Italian, but only accidentally. I understand his mother managed to get back to Italy before he was born, so as to bestow on him that distinction of birth, but—well, she had to hurry home from the Far East!'

Janine wondered if it were by design that he moved his hands on the steering-wheel so that she should see those tell-tale nails.

'You're terribly honest, aren't you?' she said softly.

'I must be with you, Janine. You see, even if you were free, I wouldn't marry you. It wouldn't be fair. You want children, and I could never give them to you – not white children.'

There was a long, fertile silence. She could not really picture herself living with him. He was so different from any other man she had known; to some extent he was repulsive. She shrank from the suggestion of colour about him. And yet he was so exquisite a gentleman, using the word in its true sense. For four months she had worked with him, been through horrible scenes and experiences with him, gone to the very dregs of filth with him – and he had never been anything but that, the most exquisite of gentlemen, shielding her, protecting her, caring for her.

He drove her back to the tiny flat which she shared with Marie, opened the door with the key she gave him and hesitated a moment.

It was after midnight, but she had done with mere conventions long enough ago.

'Come in and have coffee or something?' she suggested.

'Shaw'll hold the fort,' he said, following her into the living-room, a bare enough little place, but gay with cheap brightness, with a blue bowl full of yellow chrysanthemums and a cheery fire burning.

'Marie can't have gone long,' she said. 'Bless her, she's left me a flask of coffee and some biscuits. Light the gas, Paul, and draw the curtains, will you?'

He watched her as she laid a cloth with cups and saucers and plates and poured out the steaming coffee.

'I can never decide why you stay in that hole of Marie's,' he said as they sat down at the table.

'Can't you? I think somehow I've—found something I've always wanted. At least, I've found something that wants me. That's nearer the truth. I'm of use. I've found my vocation.'

'Nonsense. You're deluding yourself, my dear. You're not made for the filth and poverty and sin of life. You're made for—home and children and happiness and beauty.'

She shook her head, but she smiled across at him.

'No. I've tried to get those. I thought I had them—some of them, anyway. I've never had a child, but I had a beautiful home and every chance of happiness. It didn't work out, though. I—I made a muddle of marriage. I told you I started out wrongly. I thought if I grasped at what I wanted when I had the chance, it would make me happy. It didn't.'

'You can't pretend that the horrors you go through at that morgue of Marie's make you happy!' he protested.

'Well—in a way, they do. I am of use in the world. I've saved lives. I'm necessary. Don't you see what that means when I've always felt myself to be the round peg in the square hole? I thought I was cut out to be decorative, but I've found out that I'm meant to be merely useful, though it's taken hard knocks to teach me.'

He pushed his cup aside and stretched out his hands across the table to take hers. She left them in his, unresisting.

'Janine, come to me—now—tonight. You're necessary to me too.'

Her eyes were troubled and a little sad.

'My dear, I hate to refuse you. I do like you so much and I believe I could be happy with you, but—'

'But what? This husband of yours, do you mean?'

'Partly. I should have to *know* that he was happy with her and alright. But there's Marie. I couldn't leave her. And the work in Pilbram Street—'

'Listen to me, darling girl. That work is going to peter out, and that before long. Marie is getting to the end of her tether. The police are out after her, but they haven't been able to tie her down yet. She's clever and we are all loyal to her. But something will happen. She'll make one slip, and then—!' His gesture was expressive.

Janine looked troubled.

'I couldn't bear anything to happen to Marie. She's so—so fine somehow.'

'But mad, my dear. You've got to recognise that. Janine, come to me. Let me give you all the things you have missed.'

'You've said yourself you can't give me a child, Paul,' she said quietly, her steady eyes on him.

'Does that matter so much? Does it outweigh everything? If it does, you shall have even that. Oh, not mine, my dear. I wouldn't curse you with that. But there are ways known to doctors, I know them. I would let you have your child, Janine, a white child, without blemish or stain. Darling, I could give you happiness. I have plenty for us both, and out of this country I can work, and will work, so that there shall always be plenty.'

'I—don't think I shall ever be able to love anyone but Terry,' she said slowly.

'I'd risk that. Will you, Janine?'

But before she could answer there was a rush of feet up the stone staircase, the frenzied turning of a key in the lock, and Marie Hawk was with them, breathless, strange-eyed, commanding.

She took no notice of Curtis but addressed herself to Janine, who had risen, startled.

'Listen, Janine. It's trouble,' and the girl knew by the use of her own name that something had happened to stir the woman out of her course. 'It's Audrey Bannister. She's dead.'

She paused, panting for breath. She had run up three flights of steps.

'Dead?' echoed Janine, white-faced.

'Too great a risk, Marie,' said Curtis quietly.

'I know. I'm not a fool. She offered me two hundred pounds, and you know how we want a proper theatre. I could have got another hundred or two out of her afterwards.'

'I told you she'd gone too far,' said Curtis.

'I know. I know,' snapped Marie. 'Well, it was bound to come. You can't play with fire forever without getting burnt.'

'Anyone know?'

'Yes. The little fool sent her maid for me an hour ago. Of course I refused to go and told her to go for a doctor, but she spilled the thing, and Dan has warned me that Sir Herbert has informed the police. He can't save me, of course, but you've got to clear out, Janine. You too, Curtis.'

'They've got nothing on me, as you know, but Janine's got to be got clear,' he said curtly. 'Get your things on. Better not wait for luggage. Dan won't touch her, Marie?'

'No, not if they can get me,' she said grimly.

But Janine clung to her.

'Marie, I'm not going. I can't just run off and leave you the moment you are in trouble.'

Marie pushed her off.

'Don't be a fool! You can't do a thing for me. Anyway, they won't hang me. I'm mad! They'll just lock me up and keep me until I really am mad, and then what will anything matter? Oh, God!' breaking off and bolding her hands over her eyes whilst her unwieldy form staggered and swayed.

Curtis pushed her into a chair and caught Janine's pitiful, horrified eyes.

'Got anything handy?' he asked her, and she nodded and ran into the kitchen.

Marie tore her hands from her eyes and grasped his arm.

'Get her away, Curtis. Take her to that fool of a husband. Oh, I know you want her yourself, but she's not for you. Oh, hell! If only I can get five more minutes—five more minutes!' and she laid her head on the table and rocked from side to side.

Janine came back with something in a glass, and between them they forced it between Marie's lips, whilst she struggled in their hold.

'That'll bring me sleep! I don't want to sleep – not till I've got things settled. Listen, Janine. Go to your husband. Curtis will take you. He needs you. Understand? Terry needs you.'

Janine, white-faced, steady-eyed, shook her head.

'It is you who needs me, Marie. I'm not going. I'm nothing to Terry anymore.'

Then listen, you little fool. Your husband's likely to be arrested and tried for your murder. Now do you understand that he needs you?'

'You—you can't mean—that, Marie?' she gasped, looking from the distraught face to Curtis's and back again, bewildered and incredulous.

'I do. It's the truth. Now will you go? Oh, God, this pain in my head! This pain!' and a shudder ran through her, whilst into her eyes came a wild, hunted look that was infinitely pathetic to the two who knew what she feared.

Curtis put a protective arm about Janine.

'Come, dear. We can't do anything, you know.'

But she resisted him.

'I can't leave her, Paul,' she said in a shaken voice. 'She needs me.'

But it was clear that Marie Hawk needed no one just then. She lay huddled against the table, one arm flung out, her head resting on it, her lips muttering incoherently. She was oblivious of even their presence in the room, though Janine spoke to her.

There was a knock at the door, and Curtis thrust Janine into the kitchen and closed the door on her before going into the hall.

A policeman stood outside. It was Dan, their friend, who had already warned Marie to get Janine away.

'The young lady gone?' he asked in a quick whisper.

'Just going,' said Curtis,

'Hurry. Down the stairs and to the left, and don't come back, either of you.'

Curtis hurried back to Janine, who had returned to the living-room and was bending protectively over Marie's unresponsive form.

'Come, dear. That was Dan,' and he huddled her into her coat, gave her her hat, snatched up her bag from the table and rushed her out of the flat, not giving her time to resist any further.

A taxi took them to his flat, and when he had her safely inside the warmed and lighted hall he took her hands in his, speaking for the first time since they had left Marie.

'Dear, I didn't know where to take you, but you are quite safe here. It is too late to do anything tonight or to make any plans. Tomorrow you shall tell me what you want to do, and you shall do it – whatever it is, Janine. You trust me?'

'Utterly, Paul,' she said in a low voice. She was completely spent, and he knew it.

He tucked her up on the divan in his sitting-room, realising that she was too tired even to undress, and before he left her he mixed her up a drink which he insisted on her taking.

'It won't be sleep, but it will be forgetfulness for a few hours,' be told her, and when he tiptoed back into the room some ten minutes later he was satisfied that she slept.

Next day she refused to leave London until she had some sort of news about Marie, but it was not until the evening that Curtis was able to tell her that she had been taken by the police into hospital and that she was being cared for.

'And now—what, Janine?' he asked her.

It was a service flat, and he had had dinner sent up to them. They were making a pretence at eating it whilst they talked.

'Paul, did you hear what Marie said?' she asked very quietly. 'That they are going to accuse Terry—*Terry*—of murdering me? It would be funny if it weren't so—terrible.'

'I know, dear.'

'Do you think it's true?'

'Yes. I've made enquiries in that direction as well.'

'I've got to go, Paul. You see that, don't you?'

'Or write?'

She shook her head.

'No. I've got to go. I must see him,' she said.

'You care for him still, don't you?'

She nodded.

'Yes,' she said simply, but it was the death-knell to his hopes. He felt that no man in his senses could see her as she was now, gracious, gentle, steadfast, beautiful in her utter selflessness, could know she loved him – and not desire her.

'You want to know he is safe?'

'Yes.'

'And then—what?'

She lifted her head and looked at him steadily, and her eyes were misty with the shadow of tears—tears for Marie, tears at the thought of this dear friend's sadness, tears for Terry whom she loved.

'If he wants me, I must stay, Paul.'

'And—if not?'

'Then I'll come back to you,' she said simply.

'A promise, Janine?'

'A promise, Paul.'

Chapter Eighteen

Janine sat in her corner and watched the familiar landmarks growing dim in the darkness of the winter evening. So often she had watched for them in that six months of her happiness, for the passing of each one had meant so many miles nearer to Four Ways.

Tonight they meant as many miles nearer to—what?

She dare not think.

She turned to find Curtis watching her. He had meant to part from her at Charing Cross, but in the end she had looked so small and alone that he had jumped in beside her and been rewarded by her little smile of relief that was mingled with a sigh.

'I'm not going to hang on to you or worry you, Janine. I just want to be on hand—in case,' and she had slid a hand into his for a moment in gratitude.

The eyes she turned on him now were filled with that new look of understanding which they had worn since she knew that he loved her. She, who had suffered so much through love, was very tender to the love of others.

'Don't look at me like that,' he said. They were alone now in the carriage.

'Why not?'

'Because if you do, I might kiss you.'

She reflected on this and then: 'If you want to kiss me, you may, Paul.'

He made a wry face.

'Not when you invite me like that,' he said.

'I meant it, Paul – really,'

He shook his head.

'When I want to kiss a woman, she has to want it herself much more than that, my dear! No, Janine. Keep your kisses. I can wait.'

She frowned a little at that.

'You don't think—I shall stay with Terry?'

'My dear, I dare not let myself think anything at all. The train is slowing down. Is this it?'

'This is Forbury. We have to walk to Merrow from here.'

She left the train as in a dream, never even noticing the look of startled incredulity which the porter gave her when he took her ticket. Curtis had to pay for one, as he had not had time to buy one at Charing Cross, and she walked on into the road.

It seemed impossible that she had ever left it, impossible that she had not merely been to town for the day, shopping or to a matinee. Everything was so exactly the same. The old man at the corner of the station approach with his tray of evening papers just as he had always done. On the other side of the road two children swung on a gate, wrangling. A woman took in her final line of washing – the same woman, the same line of washing.

She walked on, dimly conscious that Curtis had joined her, but not including him in her thoughts. She felt the sense of homecoming. The bare branches of the trees, swaying in the wind, seemed to be bending down to touch her. Her feet caressed the rough stony road, harsh and familiar after the London pavements.

Curtis did not speak to her. Now and then, in the fugitive light of a passing car, he caught a glimpse of her face, rapt and peaceful. She was going home.

They reached Merrow, and she turned to him as if suddenly aware of him for the first time.

'This is—Merrow, Paul,' she said with a catch in her voice. 'We go along here,' and she led him through the straggling street, lit by the lights in the cottage windows.

And so they came to Four Ways.

Tree-guarded and alone, it stood back from the road, guarded by the gaunt arms of two giant oaks.

Janine paused and closed her eyes against the unbelievable sweetness of that moment. In December she could smell the roses of

June. Slowly she walked round the corner into the lane, where Terry had made a little gateway. From there she could see into the house—see Terry or—suddenly the thought pierced her like a barbed dart. Why had she not thought of that before? Felicity might be there! Felicity might be with Terry! Why not, since she, Janine, was dead?

Almost blinded with the pain, she pressed against the hedge, swaying a little, but when she opened her eyes the house was in darkness. Only from the back was a glow of light, and she shrank from being seen by the servants.

Curtis watched her unobtrusively, and stood in the shadow of a tree. If she wanted him, he was there. If not …

Voices came to them, and instinctively they drew more closely into the darkness. Janine recognised the voices. They were old Burke's, and Read's, the butcher.

'Wonder wot 'e reely done it for? Folks talked a lot about that blonde of 'is, but she never comes down, nor no one don't talk much about 'er.'

That was Burke, and Janine clenched her hands till the nails dug into the leather of her gloves.

'Dunno wot to think,' came Read's voice. 'Seems to me as 'e 'ad all 'e wanted without getting rid of 'er, seeing as it don't look as 'e wanted the girl. Wonder if 'e reely done it?'

'Oh, 'e done it alright, and I 'ope they 'ang 'im,' with an amazing venom in his voice. 'Nice lady Mrs. Forder was, always a friendly word, never no swank about 'er nor 'igh and mighty ways like that F'licity bitch.'

'Oh, they'll 'ang 'im alright when one or two round about 'ere's 'ad their say. 'E's fer the eight o'clock drop alright.'

Suddenly there came to them a strange sound, the inarticulate cry of rage of an animal with its mate in dire peril, and Janine flung herself out of the shadow, to confront them. In her grey coat, with her white face and her blazing eyes, she looked unlike anything human to their amazed and terrified vision. With a howl of fear they fled, but Janine had no knowledge of their going.

Straight to the house she went on winged feet, her hand finding the latch by instinct and familiarity. Through the hall she went and into the little room that had been their own sitting-room, hers and Terry's, their place of retreat where visitors never penetrated.

It was in darkness, but she found him there as she had known she would do.

He sat in the chair that had been hers, crouched over the dying embers of the fire, his head in his hands, his whole attitude one of weariness and desolation.

With that inarticulate cry on her lips again, she went to him and gathered his head to her breast, resting her own against it. Gone was every memory save that he was here alone and sad and in danger – her man.

'My darling,' she whispered. And again, 'My darling!'

His breath caught sharply and he sat quite still, afraid to move, knowing this thing a dream and not wanting to wake.

Her voice came to him again, and now he could feel the living, human warmth of her, feel her beautiful tenderness and compassion.

'Terry, it's Janine.'

A cry broke from him, a cry that was of fear and yet of unbelievable joy, and he turned in her arms to look at her, her face beautiful with its love, her eyes deep pools of tenderness.

'Janine!' he whispered. 'Janine!'

He tried to form words with lips that shook, from a throat that was dry and parched, but she pressed his head against her breast again.

'Don't say anything, Terry. Don't let us talk. It's enough just to be here with you.'

But in a few minutes he stirred again in her embrace.

'Is it really you, Janine?' he asked in a whisper.

'Don't you feel my arms, beloved? You are close against my heart.'

'After all the grief and the fear and the—pain. Oh, Janine, I can't believe in you yet, can't believe that you are real and alive, but—if you must go again, take me with you. I can't live any longer without you.'

He buried his face against her, believing in this incredible thing and yet not believing. Janine was dead and buried. They had taken her from the stream and laid her, after pain and grief and horror, in her grave. Yet he was here in her arms; she was warm and sweet against his heart, as she had always been.

'Stay with me, Janine!'

She laughed, and there was pure exultation in her laughter.

'You want me, Terry?'

'Forever, beloved.'

She caught her breath sharply and for an instant the world rocked about her. Then she bent her head to look deeply into his eyes.

'Terry, do you love me?' she asked in a breathless whisper.

'With all my heart and my soul and my life.'

For a moment there was silence in the room, and each could feel the beating of the other's heart. Then she spoke again, and in her voice were awe and a great peace, and she gazed out above his bent head with eyes that saw the glory of the heavens.

'Do you remember how we stood on the mountainside at Madeira and listened to the song of the birds?' she asked softly.

'I remember.'

'I tried to think of something then, but I couldn't find it. I've just found it. Listen, Terry. "Lo, the winter is past, the rain is over and gone; the flowers appear on the earth and the time of the singing of the birds is come".'

He lifted his head and listened. He took her hand and led her across to the window and flung it wide. Neither of them saw a man go quietly away into the night. They were conscious only of each other and of the flood of melody which poured across the garden from the woods beyond the throbbing, almost unbearable sweetness of the song of a nightingale.

They turned to each other, and their eyes were wet with tears.

'The time of the singing of the birds is come.'

Also by Netta Muskett

Give Back Yesterday

Helena Clurey has it all – a devoted husband, money and family. She is happy and secure, but her apparent contentment is about to be shattered by a voice from the past. Mistress she may have been, but that is not the way it is put to her: 'you were not my mistress - you were, and are, my wife.'

The Weir House

Philip wants to marry Eve. It is her way out - he is rich, not too old, and has been in love for years – but not a man she can accept. He has even secretly funded her lifestyle, such that it is. Eve feels trapped. Unlike her friend Marcia, who cheerfully accepts an 'ordinary' life without complaint, Eve has known better and wants better. A chance encounter then changesthings – Lewis Belamie pays her to act as his fiancée for a week. Adventure, ambition, and disappointment all follow after she journeys to Cornwall with him, where she eventually nearly dies after what appears to be a suicide attempt because of a marriage that has seemingly failed. However, the mysterious and mocking Felix really does love her. Just who is he; how does Eve end up with him; and what part does 'The Weir House' play in her life? Has Eve's restlessness and relentless search for stability ended?

ALSO BY NETTA MUSKETT

Through Many Waters

Jeff has got himself into a mess. It is, on the face of it, a classic scenario. He has a settled relationship with one woman, but loves another. What is he to do? It is now necessary to face reality, rather than continually making excuses to himself, but can he face the unpalatable truth? Then something beyond his influence intervenes and once again decisions have to be made. But in the end it is not Jeff that decides.

Misadventure

Olive Heriot and Hugh Manning had been in love for years, but marriage had been out of the question because of the intervention of Olive's mother. Now, at last, she was of age and due to gain her inheritance and be free to choose. A dinner party had been arranged at the Heriot's home, 'The Hermitage' and Hugh expects to be able to announce their engagement. Things start to change after a gruesomely realistic game entitled 'murder', which relies on someone drawing the Knave of Spades after cards are dealt. Tragedy strikes and other relationships are tested and consummated – but is this all real, or imagined?

Printed in Great Britain
by Amazon